# Hers Was The Sky

## by ReBecca Béguin

New Victoria Publishers Inc.

Published by New Victoria Publishers Inc., a feminist literary and cultural organization, PO Box 27 Norwich, Vermont 05055

Printed on recycled paper
Cover Art by Claudia McKay

Acknowledgements: With thanks to Holly Wolff for her support. Thanks to Beth Dingman initially for getting me off the ground about a vintage-flying book, then for her and Claudia Lamperti's guidance and criticism to make this book fly.

ISBN 0-934678-47-2

Library of Congress Cataloging-in-Publication Data
Beguin, ReBecca.
    Hers was the sky/ ReBecca Béguin
    p.   cm.
    ISBN 0-934678-47-2 : $ 8.95
    1. Women air  pilots--Fiction.     2. Lesbian--Fiction.     I. Title.
    PS3552. L374H47 1993
    813 ' . 54--dc20                                                    92-47053
                                                                            CIP

For Normajane

\* \* \*

Historical note: There was indeed a First National Women's Air Derby in August 1929 entered by many of the top fliers of the day, some famous then (like Louise Thaden, Ruth Nichols, Pancho Barnes) and yet, mostly unknown today. They flew well-known, new and also, untried airplanes. The models mentioned in this story, while used fictitiously, are based on real craft of the times. So also, the flight route which indeed, did chart new terrain for domestic air travel from west to east in the United States. Mishaps and mechanical problems are based on historical data, though again all towns, locations and events are used fictitiously in this story. All characters are fabrications and not portrayals of any real persons, living or dead. Their collective struggles and accomplishments as listed in the Derby Roster, however, are based on what women pilots dealt with at the time.

For historical data, see the Smithsonian Institution publication:
Kathleen L. Brooks-Pazmany, *United States Women in Aviation 1919-1929*, 1983

Map of Air Route

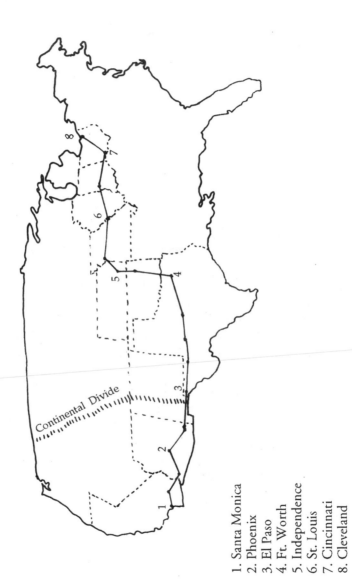

1. Santa Monica
2. Phoenix
3. El Paso
4. Ft. Worth
5. Independence
6. St. Louis
7. Cincinnati
8. Cleveland

Continental Divide

# Derby Contestants:

Roster in aphabetical order, courtesy Eleanor Wilson

*Aircraft classifications—Lightweight: CW, Heavyweight: DW(over 1500 lbs.)*

1. Marsha Banfill, 23. Commercial pilot representing Morton's traveling Apparel for Modern Women.
   AIPLANE: green, red, gold Spartan.
   Registration: C-99-8       Weight class: DW
   Accomplishments: 190 solo hours.

2. Madelyn Burnett-Eades, 25. Australian pilot, flight instructor.
   AIRPLANE: blue-grey and white Eaglerock Bullett
   Reg: C-708-8       Class: CW
   Accomplishments: Flew as navigator across Australia, Perth to Sidney.

3. Pamela Christy, 24. Actress and movie stunt flier.
   AIRPLANE: red Bellanca CH
   Reg: C-106-8       Class: DW
   Accomplishments: 300 solo hours. Attempted Atlantic crossing; rescued.

4. Louise Gibeau, 27. Canadian stunt flier.
   AIRPLANE: tan and green de Havilland Gypsy Moth
   Reg: NC-425-8       Class: CW
   Accomplishments: Expert in precision aerial maneuvers.

5. Ruth 'Stevie' Lamb, 24. manager of aircraft service and repair company.
   AIRPLANE: gold and black Golden Eagle Chief
   Reg: C-56-C       Class: CW
   Accomplishments: Mechanical engineer, first in automotive, later in aircraft.

6. Alexis Laraway, 25. Mail carrier in Alaska.
   AIRPLANE: white and red Travel *Arctic*
   Reg: NC-0505-8       Class: DW
   Accomplishments: 180 solo hours in Alaska.

7. Hannah Meyer, 28. New York socialite.
   AIRPLANE: green and gold Travel Air
   Reg: NC-0401-8       Class: DW
   Accomplishments: first woman to own controversial Beech Whirlwind; fundraiser and lobbyist for women's flying events.

8. Sarah Morris-Newton, 21. Part of a husband and wife commercial team.
AIRPLANE: blue and white Waco taperwing
Reg: NC-073-8          Class: DW
Accomplishments: Relief and rescue missions in U.S. Trained in time to gain the 120 solo hours to enter this race.

9. Hazel Preston, 26. Sales representative, Beech Aircraft, West Coast.
AIRPLANE: blue and gold Travel *Zephyr*
Reg: NC-0415-8          Class: DW
Accomplishments: First woman pilot to hold three records simutaneously—altitude, 16,700 feet; speed, 156 mph; endurance, 22 hours, 52 mins. solo non-stop flying.

10. Jo (Josephine) Russell, 29. Flight instructor. Independent sales representative.
AIRPLANE: white and brown Rearwyn
Reg: C-1103-8          Class: DW
Accomplishments: 336 solo hours. Advocate of pilot safety, including parachute jump training.

11. Nancy Saunders, 27. Business manager secretarial company. Avid sportswoman. Parachute jump instructor.
AIRPLANE: brown and blue American Eagle Wright.
Reg: C-395-8          Class: CW
Accomplishments: Advocate of women in commercial airline business. Highest number of parachute jumps of any constestant: 10.

12. Maxie (Maxine) Schulz, 27. Rancher. Independent sales representative.
AIRPLANE: black and silver Curtiss-Robin 'Miss Mary Mack'
Reg: C-010-8          Class: DW
Accomplishments: 175 solo hours; pursuing a career in aerial surveying.

13. Lila Wilczynski, 23. Part of a husband and wife team, commercial fliers.
AIRPLANE: green and white Monocoupe.
Reg: C-441-8          Class: CW
Flew flood relief along the Ohio River solo and with her husband during the flood of 1927. Popular speaker and advocate of women pilots, in part due to her petite build of 4ft 9 inches.

14. Eleanor Wilson, 27. Sales Representative, Lockheed Company. Journalist with focus on flying events nationally.
AIRPLANE: maroon Lockheed Vega
Reg: NC-353-8          Class: DW
Accomplishments: 225 solo hours. Advocate of women commercial pilots; fundraiser for meets. In training for atlantic crossing, scheduled for

# 1.

## Santa Monica Airfield, California, August 1929

Hazel Preston, dressed in a grease-stained shirt, baggy riding pants and boots laced up tight at the calf, strode briskly across the airfield. With a sweeping glance she took in the row of silent airplanes—how their highly polished surfaces glinted in the early morning sunlight, how the breeze off the Pacific teased their rudders.

But Jo Russell's brown and white Rearwyn, was gone. Its place in the neat row of planes looked to Hazel like the gap of a missing tooth in a perfect set of teeth, while its shape was still outlined by the dew against a dry patch of earth. Slapping her thigh with a folded road map in agitation, she paced along the twenty feet from absent wing-tip to wing-tip, and stared at the lines the tires had left down the length of the field. "Damn." She swore under her breath, brushing her fingers through her short, dark hair. Jo had specifically said to meet at seven o'clock to go over flight routes. It was after seven; why was Jo doing a flight test at this hour unless it was an avoidance tactic?

"Hello there," a melodious voice greeted her. "You look more like a disgruntled rider unseated by her horse than the top woman flier in the country!"

Hazel turned sharply to find someone setting up a tripod and camera directly in front of Hazel's very own Beech Travel Air, her Zephyr bi-plane. A woman photographer of all things, slim, hair bobbed, wearing a fashionable bowl of a hat (the kind that Hazel usually made fun of—but somehow on this woman it looked terrific), and a low-waisted cotton dress.

The woman was walking toward her, hand outstretched. "Hazel Preston, yes?"

All Hazel managed as a response was, "What...?" But she shook the hand, remarking inwardly on the woman's slightly slanted green eyes, etched with fine crinkles as she smiled—also the round cheeks, and the definite dimple in the chin. Then tersely, as if by rote, Hazel managed to say, "I've set some records, that's all. And others are determined to break them."

"Of course!—isn't that the statement you make to the press? My name is Vera Davis. I'm a photographer—"

"Well, I don't usually—" Hazel began gruffly.

1

"Yes, I know you don't. But I'm here for Eleanor Wilson; she needs a photograph to go with the article she has to write on you. She warned me quite frankly of your disdain for picture-taking." Vera Davis looked down to study her light meter. "Why? Why are you camera-shy, Miss Preston?"

Awkwardly, Hazel rubbed the knobby bridge of her nose between thumb and forefinger, shrugging. "Self-conscious about my nose, I guess. I had a bit of a run-in with some machinery once."

"Ah, but I've looked at most the photographs of you, see—those I could find—and the solution is obvious. No profiles for you—certainly no three-quarter views. Hazel; May I call you Hazel? Or do you go by 'H.P.?'—that's for 'Horse Power,' isn't it?" Vera Davis walked back to her camera, adjusting it as she spoke. "So, you are shy about your broken nose—an accident that didn't even happen when you were flying, but goes back to your farm girl days—am I right...?"

Hazel turned away, irritated by the presumption of this woman, her intrusion, yet was startled that this stranger knew so much. It reminded her all too clearly that much was written and said about her nowadays. The price of fame, she thought, scowling to herself.

Vera, adjusting the camera, seemed to take Hazel's silence in stride, and continued talking as if there had been no pause, "...but I feel that a direct shot, yes, with you looking straight into the camera would be entirely flattering. That's all I'll do. After all, it's my responsibility to make you look good."

"Oh well, if it's for Eleanor, I suppose..." Hazel made no movement toward the line of the camera. "... but only Eleanor calls me 'H.P.'"

"Ah, then I apologize...Please," Vera Davis made a sweeping motion to invite Hazel, "right there—maybe with a hand leaning on your propeller at its rakish angle."

Hazel followed orders reluctantly.

"Yes, the light is perfect." Stooping, Vera peered into her view finder. "Upside down and lovely...She told me I should try to find you early, before you got caught up in all the details of the day. You must relax your shoulders. And that tight knot in your jaw. Look, I'm only here to advance your career, maybe you can help me advance mine too."

"I, oh—" Hazel tried to stand still, flustered. She had never been so accosted, not quite like this, even by the men photographers who constantly swooped in on her, and she felt clumsy, put off.

"By the way," Vera looked up suddenly, a smile accentuating her cheeks, "tell me, what's a 'rag'? When I was on my way out here, lugging all this equipment, I was taunted by two men in overalls. Mechanics, I assume. 'Oh, another rag,' they said and laughed. They were speculating whether this was my portable airplane and did I expect to get it off the ground?"

Hazel smiled slightly without realizing it. "Rag?—oh, that's ground crew

2

calling you that. We have to take what we can get with ground crew; it's the unpredictable element in this upcoming race. We can count on our own escort-crew for respect, but I'm afraid the airfields are full of a seedy lot who don't much admire women flying or demanding attention for their airplanes. 'Rag' is shop talk for anyone who doesn't know anything, so of course women, especially, are called that. It gets better. 'Rag' can also mean grease rag, privy rag, sop rag." Hazel flushed as she said the last one. "That refers to our monthly habit of—"

"Yes, I get the picture. I suppose things have changed in the last few years now that more and more women are flying—I never heard talk like that before. Now, how about you climb up onto the edge of your cockpit?"

"Wait! You've taken a picture of me?"

"Exactly." Vera Davis was already moving the tripod, squinting at the sun. It was then that Hazel noticed the cord and hand-held button. "That's it, swing up and then stop, yes, with one leg over."

"This isn't the side I mount from—"

"Stop. Yes, Like that. The light's from this side. I can flip the picture later, if you want. How do you feel about flying in an open cockpit as opposed to the trend now towards closed ones?"

"I prefer an open cockpit. It's part of the fun of flying—I feel the sky." Hazel perched, looking down at this person she couldn't quite figure out. On the one hand Hazel was fascinated, as if held in a spell; on the other hand, she was wary, as though she were being made a fool of.

"Yes, hold that pose, but look out at the ocean. Show me how you *feel* the sky. What about bad weather—do you like the sky then? Good, good. Focus on one of those beautiful eucalyptus trees. Now climb down, and how about pointing to that freshly painted Derby logo on your fuselage…yes."

Inwardly, Hazel fumed. Rot, this woman is making fun of me. I don't like it. Outwardly, Hazel complied, her hand touching the white circle of words against the blue of her Zephyr: *Unity for Service, National Air Exchange.* She grunted, "It's too utilitarian a motto for this experiment, but I refuse to admit that what we do is dangerous—that's off the record. To most reporters I say this event is to demonstrate that we women are ready to be career pilots."

Vera spoke hastily, breathlessly. "Which is why it's most important to document this race. You know, I'd hoped to photograph the contestants all along the way. Maybe for a magazine article, but I'd much rather a book. If only I had a way. I don't suppose you'd have room to take me aboard?"

"With me?" Again Hazel balked, offended by the presumption. "This is a one-seater! And anyway, it's against the rules."

Vera laughed then, her head tossed back. "No, no. I meant in one of the escort airplanes."

"Every seat is accounted for very carefully. The escort is made up of crew with mechanical experience. It's all very bare bones...."

"Of course. Eleanor has looked into it already. But I keep hoping. I think it should be recorded—what you are all about to undertake here—fourteen women commanding their very first, exclusively female event. Not to mention the fact that you are charting a totally new course, west to east. I for one, would like to document it, the whole way. It is my dream. If I could steal some airplane and come too!"

"You fly then?" Surprised and curious, Hazel approached the camera.

Vera grinned. "Yes, and I'm an experienced wing-walker too."

"Good God," Hazel said with some reverence. "Isn't that a bit out of date now?"

Vera was close enough to grasp Hazel's fore-arm. "Look at me. I'm a good ten years your senior. That's what mad young girls did then. We walked wings because we wanted to fly. But we didn't have the means or the machine! I took up with a young man who was trained as a pilot during the war. He took me along to all the barnstorming events. That's how we made a living. As part of the deal, he had to give me lessons. I have a hundred hours! I'm short only twenty hours to qualify for this event. But I don't have an airplane, nor have I been able to carry on with training, except sporadically. You understand, I don't have to explain. My young man was killed. I know you understand because it happened to your brother too."

Hazel winced at the painful reminder, and once again that Vera Davis knew details about her life. "But not when you were performing?"

"No. My act was to come next. He always did the aerial acrobatics first." Vera spoke without self-pity, and also without constraint. "That was over ten years ago. But it's you now, see; you and the other young women. And you're all young! You are one of the three oldest and aren't you only twenty-six? It's a matter of timing. We paved the way, but I can almost guarantee you that many of us who went out there to do head-stands on wings while in mid-air—of all madness!—really wanted to do *this*." Vera gestured towards the line of airplanes, then looked away. "But I have another trade now. My father was a photographer. I helped him, even when I was little. He taught me—showed me the ropes. Now that's what I do, and I do it well. I take pictures of airplanes, of pilots, of sky and cloud. I take pictures from mountain tops because I can't take them from the air—yet. Because that is what I love." Vera turned, starting to dismantle her camera. "Thanks. I think you'll be pleased with the pictures. I'll do my best."

Hazel didn't want to let the moment pass; she was shaken, moved by Vera's story, and distracted from her earlier annoyance. Come with me, let me take you on my wings, she wanted to say, embarrassed at the absurdity of her thought and her feelings, hardly aware of how quickly and efficiently this

4

woman had charmed her. "Wait—" she said with a hand outstretched. Then she was rescued by the distant drone of an airplane. It was Jo returning, curving in from the west over the ocean. Hazel shaded her eyes to watch.

"Who's coming in? A Rearwyn, yes? It must be Jo Russell then."

Hazel gave Vera a side-long glance. "You know us all then?"

The photographer did not look back, but tilted her head up to watch the landing. "Yes. I know all of you. What you fly, what your dreams and goals are." She gave a sharp nod. "That one—I know she helped you with your mid-air refueling when you soloed over Florida for twenty-two hours. And I know she wants to beat you in this derby. And that she has a hard-driving sponsor who expects nothing less from her." Then she added with a slight twist of sympathy on her full lips, "It can't be easy for you, Hazel Preston, to be in a competition with an intimate."

Inwardly, Hazel gasped. How does she know about us? *What* does she know about us? Was it Eleanor who told her? Or does she read between lines? Jo would simply die if she knew what this stranger intuited. Jo was so anxious about privacy—their privacy! Hazel found herself muttering, "No, it isn't. It won't be—"

"Here she comes, a smooth, sea-level landing. I'll see you again, I'm sure. We are scheduling a group portrait tomorrow before you all go. Until then...." Vera Davis began to walk off, heavy wooden tripod balanced on her right shoulder. The large camera was packed away in what looked like a picnic basket slung awkwardly from her left.

"Look, Vera! May I call you Vera—"

Vera turned, smiled over her shoulder.

"I will see what I can do...about taking you along. All right?"

"It would be magnificent. By the way, I am a regular 'grease rag'. I know how to change oil, refuel and do pre-flight checks."

The brown and white Rearwyn sputtered to a stop; Jo Russell swung it into position so ground crew would be able to push it backwards into the line-up when they came to work. Removing her helmet and goggles, and tossing her head so her blond locks fell free, she swung out of her cockpit as Hazel rushed forward to give her a hand down.

"I was here at seven!" Hazel began, waving the road map at Jo with her other hand, her prior annoyance resurfacing.

"I know, I know. I wasn't gone long, was I? It was my last chance; the rest of the day is going to be busy around here, and I'm going to get nervous...." One by one Jo pulled on the fingers of her leather gloves until they slipped off her hands; a gesture that always made Hazel weak-kneed with want.

Hazel enveloped her, forgiving all, a brush of a kiss to Jo's lips. Tensing, Jo pushed her away, hissing as she looked from side to side, "For God's sake, not here, Haze! The last thing I need is rumors in the ground-crew."

"I don't care," said Hazel grumpily, feeling suddenly smaller than her slightly-built companion. "I'm so happy we're together in this, that's all."

After all, how many long nights had they dreamed and schemed together, only to take off separately in the morning for different parts of the country, different work?—All to bring this event about. It thrilled Hazel that they could share the upcoming time together, their careers running in a rare tandem. Now she had the prospect of a whole string of nights with Jo right beside her.

"Where is ground crew anyway?" Jo surveyed the field, brushing wispy hair out of her face. "They should be here to get my airplane out of the way."

"I don't expect they'll do anything before eight. Look, shall we breakfast over maps?"

Jo turned away brusquely, inspecting the wing flaps of the Rearwyn. "Listen Haze, this is awkward for me but Taggart doesn't want me conferring with anyone else. He has my flight route all worked out for me."

At the mention of Jo's sponsor, Hazel stopped cold. "He what? But we agreed. We've discussed possible coordinates all along, at every meeting. This is information we all share."

Jo sighed. "Nowhere in the regulations does it state that we have to discuss our flight plan. Taggart pointed that out yesterday. There is nothing to say he can't ask me to follow a confidential plan."

"Confidential! Jo, I don't believe this. *We're the ones who made up the regulations!* There is nothing in the regulations because we always shared information. We have a spirit of cooperation here. It's called safety. Aren't you the big one for safety? Aren't you the person who insisted on parachutes and jump training? I don't understand this—"

"It's not my choice!" Jo shouted. "This is my sponsor's request. I'm beholden to him, aren't I? This is his goddamn airplane, isn't it?" She banged on the brown fuselage with a fist. "Not everyone can luxuriate in the kind of independence you're given by Beech Aircraft Company, sales representative that you are! In fact, you, and Eleanor with Lockheed, are really the only two who enjoy that sort of privilege. Some of us have to bow and scrape to get what we need. Some of us like Stevie and Maxie—oh not Maxie, she has money at her fingertips—but Nancy, Louise and Madelyn would know what I'm up against."

"Jo, darling...." Hazel whispered.

Jo leaned with her back on a wing, crossed her arms fiercely. "Don't 'darling' me right now. I'm serious. Don't you think I'd like to be Beech's 'golden girl?' Do you think I like having Taggart as a sponsor? Do you think it's easy working with him? Don't you think I know what people say about him? Yes, he's rather tactless and doesn't take the trouble to hide his disdain for women fliers. Yes, he makes jokes ridiculing us; yes, we are either rags or

6

Powder Puffs. So do a lot of people—including ground crew at every damn pit-stop. But, he's a maverick and so am I, really. And he is the only person who stepped forward to offer me an airplane to fly. Could I turn that down after months and months of searching and all the possibilities that evaporated? I do what I can. Anyway, he thinks road maps are almost worthless."

"Why?" Hazel looked down at the one she had been twisting in her hands.

"He is using railroad surveyor maps because the elevations are carefully outlined and most main lines run either east to west or north to south. Any track that goes through a mountain pass can always become a point of easy reference. There, I have already said too much. This is a competition after all, remember? Ask Gus to get one for your meetings—that's up to you. Cooperation is all very well, but I am also responsible for making a good showing with his airplane. Tag has taken a speculative risk with me in starting up his company. He has a lot riding on this race. Every dime has gone into making his start-up fleet. Two measly airplanes! He needs to show his investors what his prototype can do. If I do well, he has a business and I have a career with his company like you have with Beech. There is room for more than just one like you, you know. If I don't do exceptionally well, I prove we *are* Powder Puffs, plus I'm out of work. I have to make a very good showing, Haze, in fact, I have to beat you out, if I can. And don't think I'm not going to try. He has given me a plane that could just do that. Something of a match—!"

"Please, don't start *that* again," Hazel began, then tried to soften her tone, speaking carefully, "I worry about you trying to push against my Zephyr. I don't mean to scoff at the Rearwyn, but Taggart would have been more fair to you to keep it classified as CW—"

At Hazel's reference to the lightweight airplanes, an entirely different race category, Jo snorted so that the hair which had fallen back across her face, flew up. "You know perfectly well that the serious competition is *not* among the CW airplanes. Lightweight is just that, *lightweight!* He isn't interested in selling a sports airplane but a real commercial, working model that can ultimately carry passengers or cargo. We had to enter as DW, no question, with a more powerful engine that can sustain stronger winds, higher altitude, heavier weather—a workhorse. The fuselage and struts are alloy-reinforced to bear up under the stronger engine vibrations while keeping overall load to a minimum. It should match any Beech just fine. He believes in his design. He has to. I have to."

Hazel wanted to dismiss the tension between them—wanted to gently push Jo's hair away and kiss the challenge away from her eyes. Instead she said, "Trouble is, hon, how can I compete with you really? Lordy, we finally get to be together for a full week. Do you know how long I've been looking forward to this? Isn't the point for all of us to make a good showing? Can't we keep pace? I won't push."

"Everyone expects you to win, Haze. Beech does, the press does. Just how long will you keep your job if *you* lose. You'd damn well better push because I will." Jo moved abruptly aside, throwing her glove down on the ground. Or had it slipped from her pocket?

Hazel couldn't tell. She joked, "What!—are you throwing down the gauntlet?"

"Why yes, yes I am," said Jo, bursting with the musical laugh that had captivated Hazel since the very first time she'd heard it.

"Come on, not really. Don't let Taggart set you up against *me*."

Jo recoiled, her jaw clenched. "That's quite uncalled for, Haze. Or are you going to use his line too—that I can't think or act on my own? I'm tired of being referred to as the Queen of Safety Regulations. I'm as daring as any top-notch flier. I want my name in big print too. I'm going all out because, damn it, I want to!"

"Okay, okay, one thing though," said Hazel, bending down to pick up the glove, then stopping. "We leave this contest when we leave the airfield at night." Even as she spoke those words, her insides knotted up and she wondered suddenly how on earth she could count on them to hold true? Her earlier reverie of sweet nights together was evaporating.

"Yes," Jo answered too quickly. "On the condition that we do not discuss the details of our routes, navigation and cruising altitude. I will share as much as I can in the general meetings."

Hazel's heart sank; they had always been open with advice and tactics. To talk about their passion for flying in every detail was part and parcel of the passion they shared when they made love. Hazel remembered Jo saying, 'I want you in your airplane.' And how they had laughed in the fantasy of that—in midair? Upside down? Out on the wings? At full throttle and ten thousand feet? No, they would leave impossibility to Hollywood and the movies, to Pamela Christy, the actress aviator who posed for publicity on the wing of her (grounded) airplane in a bathing suit.

Hazel swept up the glove, scraping her knuckles against the earth. It lay, sweat-softened leather, across her open palm as her eyes locked with Jo's. "Okay then, my love. We're on." And with that, Hazel tossed the glove in the air, caught it, noticing it was the left one. Producing her own leather gloves, she handed Jo her left one.

"There he is. I have to go now." Without a second glance, Jo took the glove and walked off towards the Pilots' clubhouse, a low-slung bungalow beyond the runway. Emerging from the doorway, Taggart took a few steps and stood waiting, showing impatience with his nervous smoking.

Across the distance, Hazel assessed him in a brief, suspended moment before going her own way. Dressed neatly in new white overalls, he was a tall, slim man with chiselled features, his hair slicked back. The kind of man who

8

assumed he was attractive to women without making an effort in their direction. He did not call out a greeting or even look at Jo as she drew near. Hazel hated the way Jo's shoulders drooped, followed by an acquiescing tilt of the head when speaking to him. She could not shake her anxiety about him. By deliberately refusing to let Jo share information, he was driving a wedge into an otherwise cooperative venture, reminding her that yes, the 'real world' of racing was played out with much more secrecy and fierce competition. Men's racing!—Oh, she had grown up with it when she used to help out her brother, Dewey, back in the days when he raced automobiles. Why—she brooded as she sadly tucked her map in her back pocket—did she have to be so idealistic as to believe that women would be more open?

What galled her most was that Mr. R.Q. Taggart had never bothered to introduce himself, nor follow the usual and available channels of communication with the organizers of the Derby. Sure, he had filed his airplane on time as a competitor, but had not even put in an escort mechanic for Jo. A seat had automatically been reserved on escort for Jo's mechanic, but he had let the deadline pass without filling it. Why? Why didn't he at least have the courtesy to say he didn't want it? She didn't like it that he wouldn't deal with the organizers, that he didn't come to meetings, that he seemed to disdain, by his silence, any of the help Beech and Lockheed mechanics were providing, and most of all, that she didn't know anything about him except through Jo. Yes, that's what really bothered her. She was tempted to confront him right now, but that would only annoy Jo.

An engine sputtered, then went into a smooth idle. Hazel glanced down the row of planes to where Stevie stood next to the open cowling of her Golden Eagle Chief. A wiry woman with a lock of dark hair that dripped over her forehead, Stevie looked pale and agitated as she conferred with a Beech mechanic and her taller, rounder friend, Marsha.

"Is there still a problem?" asked Hazel, running up.

"Yeah, once the engine warms up and I'm at cruising speed, I start losing electrical power. Something didn't go right when I put in your Beech J-6," Stevie stared into the engine Hazel had confidently sold to her a month before. "It takes too strong a pull. I don't know—I have half a mind to put the Hobarth back in. Except it's too darn late for that."

Hazel stood with her feet apart, arms folded and hands under her armpits as she watched the mechanic test out the electrical system yet again. Marsha's lips were pursed and white because Stevie was at wit's end and the race wasn't even underway. Stevie prided herself on being a highly competent mechanic, having managed her father's garage since the age of sixteen before switching to airplanes. Serious problems going on until the last minute were like an insult to her. Hazel wanted to encourage her to keep a level head, "Look, you've re-wired everything to fit with the specifications. I'd keep after that."

9

Stevie's voice cracked with tension. "You keep saying so, but why can't we find it?"

"Marsha, get her out of here. Take her on a long walk. Go to the beach. I'll stay with the guys. It has to be staring us in the face and we're not seeing it. The J-6 was a fine choice. I stand behind what I sell. I'm not going to take off tomorrow until you can."

The color came back to Stevie's face. "You can't do that. The race is riding on you."

"That's why I intend to have you ready on time. Get going now."

Stevie relaxed a bit, leaning on Marsha's shoulder. She didn't say any more, but let herself be led away while Hazel turned towards the airplane and rolled up her sleeves. She meant every word she had said to Stevie, cursing under her breath in the hopes that she could meet her promise. With the Beech mechanic, she started to go over the entire electrical system. She forgot about time and the increasing heat of day as she concentrated, until she began to wonder whether it was all in Stevie's head—pre-flight jitters. Everything looked sound. Finally they determined the problem must be in the magnetos—some factory-made imbalance. Whatever it was, the problem only surfaced once the engine was hot and had run over some time. No short test run today would show them anything new. So, replace the magnetos, and hope that the first leg of the derby, a sixty-five mile hop to San Bernardino would be the successful test they needed.

It was then that Eleanor Wilson's voice broke through her concentration. "Thirsty, H.P.? Have some nice tepid lemon water." Grinning, a woman with short, sandy curls and wearing shapeless overalls, thrust a glass jug into Hazel's greasy hands. There was something flippant in those blue eyes, something resolute and serious to that mouth.

"Eleanor!" Hazel thumped her friend's back and took a long drink.

Eleanor held up a sandwich. "Here, try some of this cucumber sandwich. Very refreshing. Alexis is passing them out—she says she's going crazy over the abundance of fresh vegetables and fruit here in California—nothing like it up on her tundra routes."

Hazel took a bite willingly, then nodded towards the maroon Lockheed airplane at the end of the row, "I saw by your Vega that you were in. When?"

"Last night. Late. Listen, I have to wire my interview on you by five this afternoon. Can we meet after lunch?"

"Sure. By the way, your photographer has already been here."

"Vera? Good, good," Eleanor whipped a pencil from behind her ear and jotted down a time in her notebook. "Listen, we have a problem. Maxie dismissed her mechanic."

"Uh oh. What now?"

"Well, she says she will not tolerate anyone who calls her 'damn pair of grease-britches' to her face—"

"Hell with that; I do it all the time. It's not like her language is spotless. In fact I feel the reality of us keeping our language ladylike in this damn race is pretty poor. Prohibition is one thing, we all deal with that, but telling us we can't swear—!"

Eleanor looked at her coolly. "You aren't a *male* mechanic. It is a different matter."

"Ellie," Hazel protested. "Do you know how many mechanics I interviewed to find Sweeney for her? There's no one else to find at this point. He's the only one who really knows Curtiss-Robins."

"Gus does," Eleanor referred to Hazel's own stalwart Beech mechanic who had been with her in all her past events.

"He has enough to do organizing crews and trouble shooting for all Beech airplanes. Maybe I can get him to talk with Sweeney, get him back on somehow. I know Maxie isn't easy to work with, but hell, it's partly why we love her."

Eleanor shook her head. "Sweeney is not the problem. It was Maxie who fired him, saying his attitude was wrong, and that she wasn't going to have someone aboard who wasn't with her all the way. Swearing at her was the final straw, see. You don't tell Maxie that counting on her 'Miss Mary Mack' is as good as betting on a lame nag the day of a race."

"Aw, come on, that's how guys talk. She has to know that. He was probably just seeing if he could rile her—"

"No, no H.P., you could say she didn't like the way he was feeling it up, you understand? She said he messed up the tuning. Basically, he isn't really committed to our cause. She has already gone to Gladys Jenney about it."

"She went to Gladys without talking to you or me first?" Hazel fumed. "You don't start talking to National Air Exchange Officers before going through us. I could have settled it, told him to mind his manners."

"Look, you know Maxie, she's not going to put up with anything she doesn't have to, especially men. She can't stand him! Thinks he's uncouth and unclean. Anyway, she thought Gladys might be able to arrange a new crew member more easily at this point. Besides, I wasn't here at the time, and you were in conference. I don't blame her if she isn't comfortable. And it's true that we need totally dedicated—"

"He was clean and well-mannered enough when I interviewed him," Hazel fumed, leading Eleanor off the field, jug still in hand. "Hey, wait a minute! What about Vera Davis? Tell me, what do you know about her?"

"Vera? I met her on an airfield in Nevada. She approached me, wanted to take pictures, be my photographer. I saw it as a professional inquiry since I'm a reporter. Very insistent. She's quite the flatterer, hard-driving. Won't take no for an answer. What does she know about Curtiss-Robins though?"

"No, no—she doesn't. I mean she knows how to do basic mechanical checks, routine things. El, she used to be a wing-walker! The point is, she wants to come. She wants to document the race. I'm interested in that."

"You want her on as an official photographer?"

"Yeah..." Hazel was almost breathless with an excitement she hadn't anticipated. The idea of an exclusive photographic witness to the race played in her mind. "...Come on, it's right down your alley—promoting ourselves the way we women want to be seen. What better than a woman photographer to do it, along with your persistent articles, of course."

"Hmm." Eleanor seemed to be turning the thought over, not quite convinced. She started to say something, then stopped.

"I'm the one who won't take no for an answer!" Hazel said triumphantly, deliberately ignoring Eleanor's guarded look.

"Well, I'd say it were brilliant if I—"

"So, to hell with Sweeney then," said Hazel, arms up in optimism. "She can take over some of the routine responsibilities and free up Gus in case Maxie needs help on Miss Mack."

"Well then, I'll drink to that." Eleanor took the jug of lemonade. "Mostly because I'm thirsty. But what about her photographic equipment? She's not a woman who travels lightly."

Hazel's face fell. "How much does it all weigh, do you suppose? Maybe we can distribute her stuff among us. Not me because of all the tools I'm carrying. In fact, some people are looking for extra weight—Alexis, for instance. Why don't I leave it to you—discuss it with her and Gladys."

Eleanor grinned. "I'd be glad to."

Hazel scrutinized her friend. "Do I detect a particular interest? Why do I think her flattery got to you?" She was careful not to add, because it certainly got to me.

Eleanor shoved her. "Purely professional. We have collaborated on a few articles. Besides I'm in serious training—"

"Oh, right. What about after you've made it across the Atlantic?"

"I'm too one-track minded for affairs of the heart, so I'm told. I think it's you—"

Hazel cut her off sourly. "I have enough trouble with Jo, thank you. I'm afraid Taggart is much more of a sore point for me than Sweeney could ever be for Maxie. If there was any way I could fire him, I would. Frankly, I'm really worried."

Eleanor nodded. "Yes, I can see how you would be. He is almost impossible to interview; believe me, I've tried. He's very cut and dry; gave me a written piece on his airplane and his goals, said I could use that information. I've been asking various mechanics and organizers about him. Seems he was known to be on various circuits in the past, but doesn't fraternize. One of my mechanics thinks he must have been living in a hangar for a good many months making his prototypes because he hasn't been around for a year or two. The shop mechanics made snide remarks about how he must have had to lie low for awhile, implying debts, I assume."

"Ah well, he is definitely a problem between Jo and myself." Hazel's jaw tightened in renewed irritation. "I thought the race would bring us together, instead it seems we are further apart than ever. I think I should follow your example and immerse myself in my work. Besides she has social obligations this evening that I'm not invited to. There are certain places, situations she can't or won't take me, El, as if she might give something away about herself. She is afraid of talk about us, or maybe I'm too ungainly for her socialite circle, I don't know. Anyway, I wouldn't have anything fit to wear."

"True, can't very well go to a fancy restaurant like that, can you?" Eleanor clucked sympathetically. "I'll lend you a dress, if you like."

Hazel shrugged, eyeing Eleanor, similar in height and build, but so much more lovely, fluid in her movements. She felt clumsy by contrast. Even so, for a brief flicker of a moment, she imagined herself showing up at Jo's hotel in one of Eleanor's dresses. But no, the risk of Jo's passing look of scorn was too great; she didn't want to arrive as the unwanted guest.

"No thanks." Hazel jabbed the ground with the tip of her boot. "I'll catch up with her later in the evening after all the hoopla. I'll be busy here until dark anyway. I would gladly embrace her into my life, you see, but it isn't like that with her. I suppose her world is far more complex than I'm used to. And I'm so naive as to think she can fit into a simple one. We are equals only on the airfield or if we are alone—very carefully alone as though we were having a secret affair."

"Aren't you private anyway? Discreet?" Eleanor queried.

"Yes, but to me it is my life! I don't know how to be discreet. That's the trouble; I talk about her and us as though everyone knows and doesn't give a damn. And she is constantly guarded, scolding me. And now on top of every thing, she has this hard-nosed sponsor and what do I become?—nothing but competition!"

"I wish I could tell you not to worry." Eleanor handed the water jug back to Hazel. "I'm sure it's just nerves right now and once under way things will sort themselves out. If she needs to make a good impression for her sponsor, let her. She wants a career too, and God knows, it's hard work getting going and keeping going. She'll need you as time goes on. Besides Taggart isn't coming along. Thank your lucky stars he chose not to sign up as escort crew. We leave him and all the Hollywood fanfare right here on the coast with the orange groves. Once we're on our way, it will be on our own terms. She'll be as filthy, bone-weary and determined as the rest of us, H.P. You'll see."

*I have always been supportive crew for my husband in his races. This is the first time we have switched positions, but I see our career in total tandem. We fly rescue and relief missions together. I would like the right to fly in a race together. No race can be worse than some of the flood relief we've done.*

      Sarah Morris-Newton           —*from a Journalist's Notebook, E.W.*

## 2.

### Derby Day

Fog hugged the Pacific coast on the morning of the Derby, closing in the airfield and muffling preparations; crews and sponsors conferred with pilots over all the last details of the race before the two p.m. take-off.

As the last wisps of mist steamed off the runway, Eleanor began to gather all the contestants for the official group photograph. Vera was already setting up her camera at a distance which would allow her to get as many of the airplanes as possible for background. With a bit of lime she marked semi-circles where she wanted her subjects to stand. "Taller ones in the back," she said with a dismissive wave of her hand, letting them organize themselves while she looked through her lenses.

Hazel found herself placing her toes on the curve of the white line next to Eleanor who threw an affectionate arm over her shoulders. Grinning and still in dirty work-clothes, Maxie tucked in on her other side, smoking the end of one of her small cigars. She crunched it underfoot. Stevie took the front, and, of course, Jo who avoided eye contact with Hazel by sticking close to Alexis on the other end next to Pamela Christy. It was the first time Jo wore flight clothes for a photograph.

"Stop moping," Eleanor hissed in Hazel's ear. "Don't tell me you wanted Jo to stand in front of you so you could put your arms around her."

"One can dream." Hazel said, pouting. "We were supposed to have last night together after that dinner of hers with all those society friends here to see her off. Well, I got done here by dark, went to my hotel, waited and waited around. Nothing. I called her room. I even thought about going to find her. At midnight she telephones me—midnight!—saying her social obligations had delayed her, and she wanted just to stay in her own hotel and get some rest for today...."

"All right, everyone!" Vera clapped her hands. "I want winning smiles from everyone. Yes, now you have to hold them—"

"Frozen!" Maxie laughed, speaking through her teeth which clamped together, her lips wide. "Doesn't she know pilots don't smile; we're usually too frightened. We don't even grin up there."

14

All the pilots began to chuckle making comments through their teeth. "That's it. Relax." Came the command from Vera. "I need you even closer together."

All fourteen snuggled in, shoving and poking, a superficial camaraderie taking hold. Yes, thought Hazel, it's easier for Jo to drape herself around Alexis whom she hardly knows, than to acknowledge any acquaintance with me. Jo *has* changed since Florida.

"Are we done yet?" Stevie said glowering. Eleanor had pried Stevie away from her work on her plane, the Chief, and the grease on Stevie's left cheek gave the appearance of a side-burn. Her stained hands remained deep in her cover-all pockets.

When Vera declared she was done with many thank-yous, the group dispersed rapidly in different directions. Hazel glanced wistfully after a retreating Jo. Eleanor gave her a light tap on the back, and sprinted away to begin her next pre-race task—the press gathering to negotiate their vantage points for the race.

Only Maxie was still near Hazel. "Y'always did take Jo far too seriously. You run after her, you oblige her. I'm one for having fun, myself. Especially sex. Nothing should be so serious ya can't have some fun at it. But I don't know about you. Do you really like sex? I mean, do you really like to go to bed with women? I mean, and really go for it, all heart, total pleasure, breasts, ass, wide open thighs, wet dark interiors, rhythm, crescendo—ahh and all? Because I do."

"Max!—" Hazel sucked in her breath, then relaxed, not about to get caught off-guard this time by Maxie's habit of unabashed frankness.

"I sometimes regret I ever introduced you—"

"Don't say that," Hazel snapped, turning to face Maxie. "You did me a great favor."

"No, I'm not sure I did at all." Maxie shook her head. "You're too honest, too down to earth when it comes to your heart. Is that why you fly?—to get your feet off the ground? Is that why you love her? Does she think about you when you're not with her—the way you do about her? Why is it you make yourself so available to her while she always seems to avoid you? I think there are some kinds of risks that only you seem ready for..." she jabbed Hazel with a finger to the shoulder, "...emotional risks."

Hazel made a move to run across the field after Jo. A strong hand stayed her. "Preston, don't run after her, or you will never give her the chance to seek you out."

"If I don't, she won't seek *me* out. *That* much I do know, Max. We are at the point that she expects it of me."

"Well, one of these days, surprise her. Be gone."

"I can't." Gently, Hazel pulled Maxie's hand from her shoulder, kissed it, their eyes meeting—Maxie's deep and brown, friendly but sad. It was those eyes which made Jo say that Maxie and her dog looked alike. But Hazel saw more than soulfulness there—a twinkle of tease, a hint of wanting something.

"She'll never be easy." Max warned.

"Who of us are in this business?" Hazel strode toward Jo and the Rearwyn. But Jo had already gone off for a last conference with Taggart so Hazel busied herself with her own flight plans.

The general anticipation and tension grew as the morning hours passed—too quickly for some, much too slowly for others. When Hazel did find Jo coming out of the clubhouse, she was in a state of great agitation.

"Tag's not going to give me an accompanying mechanic, Haze! Too expensive. Can you believe it? He says I must rely on ground crew and he will send in people should I need help—the big stops anyway. And he waits until the last possible moment to tell me! Always promising, promising—and now....he would have said nothing about it, but I pressed him." She paused, about to hurry away again. Then she turned back. "Anyway, now there is a seat for that photographer, Vera."

"We already have her on board," Hazel answered quietly, "but there was only a vacancy because Sweeney got fired.

Jo's eyes blazed with bewilderment. "What?"

"Gus has been handling the details of escort. The sponsors' deadline was last week. If Taggart was going to put someone in, he would have had to settle it then."

"Last week! Why didn't I know about it till today? I don't understand why Tag didn't bother to tell me...but you, why didn't you tell me—?"

"Hey, don't blame me. You're the one who's not interested in communicating. And how in hell am I supposed to know he didn't talk to you—I mean, I knew about the deadline. That information was given out to sponsors right from the initial entry registrations. I didn't know that you weren't aware, or that Taggart hadn't ever told you he wasn't putting someone in. And as far as I know, he never even petitioned for a late addition. Until Maxie fired Sweeney there was no vacancy."

"Sweeney—?" Jo's mouth gaped for a moment only, because she was good at keeping her demeanor.

"What?"

Jo shook her head in some private vexation. "Nothing." She looked up at Hazel, her lower lip tight, perhaps to prevent it from trembling in rage, in frustration, in nervousness. "If Tag has decided to handle the job in his own way, I guess I have to go along with it. I just don't like surprises. Thank god you're so calm, Hazel. I like that about you. I get so...so pent up, and then you counter it—you're so...level-headed. I think it's because you're my simple farm girl."

Hazel frowned. What did being a farm girl have to do with it? Jo's kind of compliments never made sense to Hazel. Farm girl simplicity? Jo could never get enough of saying that—was it some counterpoint to own her 'citified ways.' But the melting eyes, yes, Hazel understood that look. Wanted it.

In a moment the look was gone too. Jo straightened the collar of Hazel's shirt, a brief motion, an afterthought. "It's almost time, isn't it? I have to go get ready, and pray that Taggart's opinion is correct—that I'm not going to have any trouble. I suppose we shall meet again in San Bernardino?"

"Yes." Hazel did not respond to the jesting tone of this last sentence. Walking part way with Jo, both fell into silence. Then as she turned to her own airplane, she thought, I do love her.

*Take off: Santa Monica to San Bernardino*

Fifteen minutes seemed like an eternity; the pilots paced about in separate frenzies. Hazel kept her nerves under control by inspecting everyone else, taking in details she wanted to remember. Vera Davis, along with a host of other photographers, stood with portable camera in hand at the edge of the runway. She would fly in one of the four seaters with rear escort. And in readiness, she wore coveralls, well-tailored ones at that, with pleats at the waist, cutting pleasant lines from her round hips. Stevie never looked like that, nor Eleanor for that matter, in their bulkies. Ah well, the speeches were over, the flags, red, white, and true blue like the sky, fluttered in the breeze, keeping tandem with the windsocks.

Everyone had drawn their positions for take-off from Gladys Jenney's wide-brimmed hat. They would draw anew at the start of each lap, keeping to an arbitrary but fair order each day.

How many times had Hazel scanned the skies for information she already knew? She fumed to herself while Beech mechanics stood about and chewed their tobacco. She checked her watch again. Five minutes to go, five minutes to go. She couldn't stand it. Weeks of preparation seemed distilled into these few eternal moments. Looking over the field at the waiting planes, she wondered at their well-oiled and finely-tuned silence. Had these airplanes ever looked so bright, so adorned, like well-scrubbed children in Sunday clothes?—never to be seen so clean again. Even in her impatience, she could find a flicker of simple appreciation and pride. Perhaps what stood out the most were the stark, white identification numbers on all the wings, each sporting an extra '8' for the eight laps they would fly. A number which would endure—forever identifying them as part of a race that would surely set a precedent.

With a sweeping glance she appraised her fellow pilots, spied Jo standing face into the wind, hands clasped behind her back. That self-possessed stance

17

could only mean one thing—Jo was nervous. Only Pamela, the movie star, seemed genuinely bored, camped out in front of her red Bellanca sports plane on a folding canvas chair. Dressed in a white silk flight-suit, helmet and goggles on her lap, she smoked a cigarette while exchanging pleasantries with her crew. Well, she was used to waiting around between movie takes, that one. And she was in the first half of the draw! Looking glamorous under any circumstance was part of her training.

Hazel checked her watch again. One more minute. In the spectator stands, sponsors and representatives from various airplane companies stood to witness the start of the race. Odd, but she didn't see Taggart there. Wasn't he going to watch Jo take off? Gone already? Hazel took it as a good sign.

Next to the matronly Gladys Jenney, elegantly dressed in summery rose, Hazel did notice a most dignified, dapper, and portly old Mr. Maximillian Schulz—the extremely wealthy grandfather whom Maxie wanted no part of if she could help it. Well, in this case, she couldn't quite help it because he was avid about flying in his own right. Maxie always claimed she came into her love for flight quite independently, and that he only saw airplanes as a more fanciful, sporting way of speculating with his wealth than with the more down-to-earth automobile. Maxie had protested vehemently about his appointment to the Board of Sponsors, but Eleanor had procured him quite separately at an air show, and in all innocence to Maxie's feelings. Besides, he had also underwritten a general fuel assistance fund which even Maxie couldn't argue with because it benefitted all the fliers, very much making the race possible.

There was Maxie now, staunch and sturdy, dressed up in black and silver to match her Curtiss-Robin, 'Miss Mary Mack.' Typically, she held a book— she was a voracious reader of the modern novel—and already had her helmet and gloves on as she talked to Alexis Laraway, an old friend she had enticed down from Alaska mail-runs for the race.

Two o'clock. The radio signal from their final destination in Cleveland blasted through to loud shouting and applause all over the field. Photographers bustled for their last pictures. Through a megaphone Gladys Jenney announced, "Ladies, start your engines!" A race official waved the white starter's flag. The Derby was underway.

Deafened by the roar of pistons Hazel felt sweaty, not so much from the heat as the anticipation. Pulling on her own helmet, she watched as Louise Gibeau, the Canadian stunt pilot, made ready to lead off in her De Havilland tan Gypsy Moth, to be followed by Madelyn Burnett-Eades, the Australian, in her grey and white Eaglerock Bullett, both of them flying light planes. They were rolling forward while Marsha Banfield waited in third position, her red and green Spartan firing up. Hazel's jaw clenched—even though Marsha and Stevie were flying in separate weight categories, with Marsha in the DW or heavy airplane category, they were going to keep pace with each other. Competition didn't seem to be getting the better of their relationship.

Catching sight of Nancy Saunders, she frowned. The airplane Nancy had ordered as an independent, self-sponsored entry, had not yet arrived in spite of all the last minute efforts and assurances from the manufacturer, but she still hoped to catch up in the first leg of the race.

"Contact!" Pamela Christy fired up next.

Hazel turned and climbed up on the lower port wing of her airplane, hands tucked up under her arms. Gus, her right hand man with his balding head and weathered but youthful face, leaned against the fuselage, ready to give her taxiing directions.

Nearby, all the Beech mechanics, dressed in newly starched company over-alls to see the pilots off, made comments as they spat their tobacco. "Christ, did you see that? Pretty rocky take-off."

"Nah, she's all right. Wind took her a bit."

"Hazel, it's beginning to blow a bit—you take note of that...northeast." It was Gus calling up to her; she nodded. Her life depended on him; she trusted him implicitly. He, like her brothers, had always accepted her for who she was, counseled her as an equal. In secret he had painted the crew cheer on her wing, *Press on, Preston*, in gold letters so she could see it when she was in her seat.

Still ahead of her were Sarah Morris-Newton (bound to be a challenge for lead position), Jo Russell, Stevie Lamb, Hannah Meyer and Alexis Laraway.

The butterflies in her stomach were more for Stevie than herself. Would Stevie's airplane bear the engine switch? And what about Alexis as a contender? Hazel didn't know what to expect from Alexis who was flying a Beech Travel Air too, but which featured a closed cockpit. They each had a Wright J-5 engine, but Alexis held the advantage of less wear and tear on her craft, carefully tuned with the help of her brother, Alan.

That was what it finally came down to then—who had the better team, the most precision?

It was time for Hazel to climb aboard, fit her earplugs in place, pull the goggles down off the brow of her helmet, go over her cockpit checks one final time. Then she pulled on the straps of her parachute pack, securing its buckles before adjusting her seat strap. She read the gauges in an arc on the panel before her including the compass that jutted out. in the center. Settling into her cramped quarters, her feet resting on the rudder bar, she nodded, 'thumbs up.' The airfield's ground crew pulled away the brake blocks, signalling instructions for take-off. Flicking on the electricity switch, she pressed the self-starter, easing the throttle. The variable pitch, Hele-Shaw propeller sputtered into action, picking up speed until it became a blur.

Standing by, Gus directed her to roll. Her goggles cut visibility so she was only able to see him out the corner of her eye. She could not see anything directly in front of her due to the large engine casing, and had to rely on him to indicate that Alexis was out of the way.

In minutes she was under way too, oblivious to her screaming engine though its vibration shook her to the bone, as she concentrated with her hands on the throttle and stick. She left Maxie Schulz, Eleanor Wilson, both with heavy aircraft, and Lila Wilzcynski to follow.

Ascending to full power, tail-elevators at half position, flaps neutral, she eyed her notes and map taped on the instrument panel. Like the other contestants she was to maintain at least ten thousand feet, weather permitting. Anyone running into trouble was to fly lower and to the nearest airfield so that spotting the craft would be easier for pilots above. Escort-crew airplanes would then follow disabled contestants and assist in repairs.

After reaching her ceiling of thirteen thousand feet, she need only keep track of time and Jo. Her left hand felt the tightness of Jo's glove.

She expected Stevie's plane to appear below, but it was the green and silver of Hannah Mayer's Travel Air that she saw. Yes, she could make out the numbers across the upper wings, NC-0401-8. She was worried. She hoped it was just some minor engine adjustments that put Hannah there; couldn't it wait until San Benardino?

As she monitored her own course due east, Hazel thought about how hard Hannah had worked to raise funds for the race, and that while she flew a plane competitively matching Hazel's own for this year's Derby, Hannah's real pride and joy was in a hangar on the east coast. As an owner of the new Beech Whirlwind, still registered with the Federal Aviation Board as an experimental 'X' as opposed to a regular class 'C,' Hannah had invited Hazel to test it in September, this after Hazel had petitioned Beech for the right and been sidestepped time and again on the company-owned models. It all boiled to men getting the early chances on this prized possession while women were not, and Hazel the top Beech woman test pilot at that! "Never you mind," Hannah had said to her, "They can't stop you from testing mine. We'll sponsor our own independent test just as we have sponsored our own independent race."

"But you should do the test yourself," Hazel had protested.

"No," Hannah had said, "You've got the hours and experience behind you, and the name. If you put it through its ropes, it's bound to get the new rating and approval for competition. I don't have enough experience, but I will by next year! We have to keep up with the technology."

Indeed. For one thing, the Whirlwind boasted an electrically manipulated rudder instead of the direct foot-control Hazel was used to, and she was suspicious of this feature until she could witness its reliability for herself . Moreover, that bird could soar at upwards of 170 mph, and here she was, the holder of the women's speed record at a mere 156, expecting few to top the 140 range on any of the upcoming laps.

Hannah was no longer in sight. Trying to keep to her task, Hazel clawed her way across the sky at 135 mph. Then hastily, she consulted her navigational chart, easing her craft by degrees to compensate for the wind, wondering if Sarah Morris-Newton could keep a similar pace because she had a J-5 engine too, in her Waco Taperwing. No experience compared with Hazel, but she was smart; her husband, Sam, had taught her well and she had a knack. Her test times were very close to Hazel's. In fact she was more of a threat than Jo, if numbers meant anything.

But she hadn't exchanged gloves with Sarah; she didn't feel any sense of competition from that direction—yet. Only time would tell.

Re-reading her compass, monitoring the altimeter and pressure gauges, Hazel began to feel confident. They were in the air, and it seemed like they were going to make a fine show of it. Perhaps Stevie would hold on. Below her the heat of the land billowed and shimmered in waves across the desert. She seemed to float along with it, pushed by a tail wind. And yet the flow of air was deceitful, trying to blow her north a bit.

Reducing speed for gliding approach, easing the flaps down and the elevators into neutral, Hazel descended into her final flare-out. She pushed the elevators up as she put herself down into the thick dust and heat of the San Bernardino airstrip with barely enough distance to avoid ground-looping—the kind of half pivot which put a great strain on landing gear. She exhaled in relief as she came to a stop. Then she began to worry about the others. If anyone misjudged the runway length and put down a bit too late in the dust cloud, they'd be in trouble with their landing gear.

She watched for the signalman with green 'all-clear' flag to wave her forward and waited for the ground crews to help push her to the side of the field. This first hop had been nothing. A test run. An afternoon joy-ride. A chance to get rid of the jitters.

Stevie came in next, then Jo. It looked as though everyone had arrived in order except for Hannah. Hazel, still up in her cockpit, wiped her goggles clean and stretched to relieve her body of the engine's echo. She turned to watch Maxie begin her descent, then hopped out for conferences, refreshment and of course, to look for Jo.

It was Alexis Hazel met first as she made her way down the row of tidy airplanes. Alexis—her fire-red hair seemed to reflect the sun like a highly polished helmet of brass. Why wasn't she some sort of matinee idol? She was more striking than Pamela, had the presence of some warrior goddess of time before time who had been given command of the air currents on her own feathered, living wings. She sat crouched on the fuselage of her white Travel

21

Arctic, talking jovially to her brother, Alan below. Al and Al, as they were often called, had a closeness that came only with hours of flying, of relying totally on each other. It was easy to tell that Alan thought the world of his younger sister. But he was tough on her, grilling her about the flight, running through checks while dust devils swirled about and between the planes.

Hazel stopped to chat, helmet, goggles and gloves hanging from her hand as she idly whacked her thigh with them. "So, how are things then?"

Alexis laughed carelessly. "Al is worried as always. I'm feeling a vibration—seems like it's coming from the exhaust manifold but that might just be magnifying the sound. Nothing is skipping." She slapped the fuselage. "She's a Snow Goose, not used to such heat. We usually have her conditioned for the tundra. That's what I think it is. Or a loose clamp. What about the resister valve, Al? I'm going to let him check. Here, would you help me with this?" She lifted something out of the cockpit and began to hand down a box. "Careful, this is Vera's big camera."

Hazel dropped her helmet as she maneuvered to take the box carefully. "Heavy enough."

"It fits tidily behind my seat. Al says I can use the extra weight." She winked. She didn't wait for Hazel to accompany her, understanding that Al wanted Hazel's opinion. "I'll bring you water, Al." She turned to go, Vera's camera clumsily under her arm.

"Water, yes please," Al replied absently, wiping his freckled brow with the back of his hand. "I'll go through all the valves again, Alli. Doesn't make sense though." He cocked his head to the left slightly. "Oh, I dunno—never does make sense till you find it. Do you have a minute, Hazel?"

"I haven't known Travel Airs to have exhaust problems, more problem on the carburetor end. Carbon build up is often...."

"Actually," said Al quickly, his voice lowered as he ducked into the shade of the double wings. He stood there a moment, not saying anything, just fiddling in his shirt pocket until he had a toothpick which he stuck between his front teeth. It was a gesture Hazel knew well. Her brother had done that too, because he couldn't smoke around engines. "There's something else I wanted to talk to you about. Not something I wanted Alli to hear. She has been a bit tense as it is. It's more of a crew problem. You being one of the organizers...." There was a long pause while his toothpick moved up and down between his lips as he rubbed the back of his neck. "Sweeney was here when I got in, you see—"

"Sweeney? Well, he's a free man, but he isn't with us. I don't expect him to hang around every stop." Hazel paused, frowning, "Do you?"

Al began to unpack his tool case, putting the tools carefully on the wing. Hazel moved into the shade with him, tucking her helmet under her arm.

His lips tightened into a thin line. "Sweeney came to me I guess because

22

I'm an independent sponsor and still tied into Beech because of Alli's plane. He wanted me to put in a good word for him, get him back on. I listened. At first he sounded real contrite. Yes, he'd been rude but he wasn't real used to working with 'dames.' Said he had some commitments and needed to get east."

"There are plenty of other ways to get east," said Hazel impatiently.

Al put up a finger to emphasize his point. "My point to him exactly, but he is persistent. He said I was the only one who could help him; everyone else was a company man—that line. Sam certainly isn't. But no way he'd go to Sam—ex-military man that he is."

"He had no business dealing with Maxie the way he did, if this lift meant so much to him."

"In any case, his tone began to change. He got really persistent. I said, look, you know, I'm not an organizer—that it was strictly out of my hands. Then he started cussing, spitting his tobacco, all that. The politeness changed to anger, and he actually started threatening me! I asked him what the heck was eating him? That he should see you. As he walked away he said something about Beech going to 'get it' if he didn't get back on."

Hazel frowned suddenly worried. "He isn't going to come talk to me about it, Al. Yes, I know he has a grudge at this point, but I won't help him solve his problems."

"There's something else. Have you heard anything about betting?"

"Betting. It's illegal on this circuit like everything else."

"Yesterday, one of the ground crew mistook me." Al smiled slightly. "I hadn't shaved and was pretty grubby. Anyway, he approached me, asking jovially if I knew where 'Fido' was, because he wanted to place his bet. I said I didn't know, but playing along with him, I said I wanted to bet to, but didn't have the low-down."

Hazel shrugged. "I certainly expect ground crews on the airfields to place a sporting bet or two."

"Uh-uh, this is more serious, I think. Somebody has organized it. 'Fido' is only a carrier."

"Hm. So what are you suggesting—that Sweeney is involved?"

Al nodded, wiping a wrench with a rag. "Well, I'm wondering. I want to keep an eye on what's going on. Gus would let you know if something was brewing."

"He would if he knew, but you know him. He lives clean, and part of that means he really doesn't fraternize with ground crews anywhere more than he has to. He isn't going to be around them except over an airplane. That goes for you too. Obviously you're going to have to shave less often!"

"You have a point...Hazel, you remember the Robertson case, don't you?" Al's red eyebrows knit together as he pulled on the toothpick.

Hazel forgot about her thirst. "Yeah, the guy who was tampering so he could win the 1927 Cross-Run." Then added with a rueful shrug, "But he was after the purse which was about five times higher than what we're after."

"True." Al removed the toothpick pointing it at her. "But after the case was settled, don't you remember reading that there was evidence pointing out that, through his own crew, he had placed bets on himself at every stop, stakes that were considerably higher than purse money?"

"Ah, that's right...." Hazel chewed her lower lip in thought. "Eleanor wrote an editorial on it too. Nothing conclusive."

They both turned at that point to watch an airplane come in. Hazel shaded her eyes. "That should be Eleanor right now. But looks like Lila."

Al grunted in agreement. "Yeah, well you know what that's called, don't you—what he did? It's called dog-fighting."

"Dog-fighting? Yes, I've heard about that. Dewey—my brother—talked about it being done in car racing too, though it wasn't called that." Hazel gave a worried sideward glance. "You can't be serious about that on our circuit?"

"I honestly don't know. I just worry. Sweeney was real peculiar. It's the whole thing of him pressuring me. Why does he want to travel with us so badly just to get east?"

"But Al," said Hazel in disbelief, "we're not made up of crews like that. The pilots have to be part of it, paid off by the Big Guns and all to keep certain finishes predictable."

"I know, I know. I don't want to look for anything that isn't there, but..." He snapped the toothpick in half with two fingers. "I just want to poke around a bit more."

Hazel slapped him on the shoulder. "Alan, you are so protective! But sure, go place a friendly bet if you can. Let me know who the crews are rooting for!"

He nudged her gently with his fist as he looked over his shoulder. "Here comes Alli. I'll let you know if I come up with anything."

Hazel nodded and said, grinning, as Alexis walked up, "Here's your water-bearer."

"So, have you two solved the problem yet?" Alli looked hopeful.

Alan shook his head between gulps of water. "Don't worry about it. Go mingle with the curious." He gave Hazel the jug. Then the two women retreated, leaving him to tinker.

"Anyone have trouble landing?" Hazel asked as they made their way to the refreshment tent set up by the National Air Exchange.

"Marsha had to ground-loop and one of the undercarriage struts needs to be replaced."

So the landings had gone relatively well then, a good sign, and the late

24

afternoon belonged to them. It was time to exchange information, prepare for the next lap. Hazel wanted to find out what news had come through on Hannah, and what was up with Eleanor. How was Stevie's engine behaving?

"A word to the wise," whispered Alli as they neared the crowds, "some of the reporters are real sharks. I must attract them. They can't ever believe we know anything, especially mechanical."

Indeed, the local newspapers and hosts were ready with questions and cameras. Hazel took it in stride as best she could for someone impatient with crowds, accepting a glass of punch amiably from the society ladies amid their predictable inquiries. "What made you decide to become a pilot, Miss Preston?"

What should she say today? I ran away from a boring marriage? I was jilted by my one true love—how else to mend a broken heart? Nah, that was right out of one of Pamela's movies. Should she talk about her girlhood dream when she used to drive a tractor over the seemingly endless field, imagining that somehow, if she could open the throttle wide enough she would suddenly leave the ground far below? No, that was too personal. Dull truth then? "I wanted to race automobiles like my brother, but I got a job in a company selling specialty fuels which involved aircraft, and well, one thing led to another...."

How downright disappointed they always looked, her mystique—not that she felt she had any—instantly flattened.

Meanwhile she kept close scrutiny of the skies, waiting for all the birds to come home to roost. When Vera came in, she would ask her to take some pictures around the airfield, get her to talk to airfield crews, see what reactions they had to the race. She worried about whether Nancy Saunders had gotten her Eagle yet.

As she began to move through the crowd to find Jo, she came across Vera's camera on a table. Someone else had brought her tripod. Without second thought, Hazel flipped the brass latches and lifted the lid. From under green velvet lining, a large lens glared up at her. Vera's third eye. She let the lid dropped softly back into place. She had been too personal, somehow too intimate. Or was it as though the camera took her in like some living thing staring at her, seeing all?

"Hey there. That's personal property of Miss Davis." A man gestured her way, jabbing the air with his cigarette. On his arm he wore an official Derby arm band. Alli must have appointed him guardian.

Hazel looked up the way one does when secure in a role. "Yes, I'm quite aware of that. I wanted to see if it had come along intact. It has. I am Hazel Preston, one of the organizers."

He grunted, half apology, half in retraction.

It was then she noticed Jo hemmed in by a reporter. She eased her way to

25

take in the conversation. He was needling Jo in a flat tone, even as he sweltered in his shabby suit. "You don't really mean that all these women actually jumped out of airplanes."

Jo brushed her hair back with her fingers as if to keep her composure. "Absolutely! We all practiced jumping from progressively higher places, until we could land well from a height of twelve feet. Everyone had to successfully execute an actual parachute jump."

Pen to his lips, perhaps he actually was in awe. "Fascinating...but even with that preparation, this can't be compared, surely. The sponsors obviously have to go easy on you gals with these short hops from place to place. Isn't it true that you ladies can't take more than that at a time?"

Ah, she is keeping awfully cool, thought Hazel as Jo spoke slowly, icily. "That's not the point. You can set up a race any way you want. We're not trying to set endurance records here. We're creating a uniform measure of our times against each other. In fact, men's derbies are set up much the same. The big difference is that we're doing it from west to east. Most races start in New York and stay east of the Continental Divide. In fact we are creating navigational maps in the process. Not only that, but confronting weather patterns that can be surprising if not downright dangerous. It's a very different thing to take off in the sandy heat at sea level than it is on a cool, misty morning at four thousand feet..... You know, you *fellas* (she said it with emphasis in response to his use of 'gals,') coming around with your inane questions really annoy me. Do your homework and ask intelligent questions!"

Hazel raised her eyebrows slightly. At least Jo had managed not to swear. Maybe he was hoping she would.

"Now listen here, honey," he snarled as he took notes, "temper temper. Are all you gals so hot-headed?"

Hazel saw the storm brewing behind Jo's eyes, as she said, "And don't you 'honey' me. We are under enough strain without this nonsense. Whether you want to take us seriously or not is besides the point. Do you really understand what we're dealing with? Mechanical failure, the durability of any particular model, weather, nerve. And don't think it isn't fiercely competitive, as tough as you'll find anywhere." Jo scowled openly. "You are like the people who think women fly only to prove how safe flying is. Well, it's far from safe, let me tell you. You try it sometime."

Oops. Why is she taking that tack? Hazel thought maybe it was time to interrupt. Don't go ruining months of publicity, Jo. That's all he needs, a pilot who declares the danger in all this. 'Queen of Safety', at that. Oh boy.

"What my friendly competitor means," said Hazel approaching, her head at a jaunty, careless angle, her arms folded, "is that we are in the process of proving how reliable airplane service is becoming. And we want to pave the way for women to be employed as pilots of commerce." She had hemmed him in from the other side, so that it was he who was cornered now. Jo shot her an appreciative, yet irate gaze.

At least we're on the same side for a moment, Hazel thought. The reporter turned his attention to Hazel, flipping the pages of his note pad. "And you are?" He seemed mildly aware that he was no longer looming but being squeezed. Hazel noticed how hot and uncomfortable he was.

"Hazel Preston. We all want to prove ourselves. In ten years we won't have to answer questions like this. Women will be part of the everyday flight routes as pilots and navigators, not a novelty."

"One last question then, Miss Preston," he pursued as Jo began to sidle away. Was that a slight wink she gave as she left Hazel to him? "Is it true—what Miss Russell has said? What is your sense of the mood and competition?"

She laughed it off. "I like to think of it as a cooperative endeavor. The purse is nothing compared to that in men's races but we are just as determined and we are aiming for higher 'stakes.'"

By the time the last escort-crew airplanes had come in, the dust had settled and the sun was low although the heat remained. Most of the pilots had finished up conferences and mechanical checks, and gone to settle in at the hotel they had booked. Hazel remained on the field, going to seek out Vera for reports on Hannah and Eleanor.

She wasn't surprised to find Vera at Maxie's 'office' which consisted of a canvas ground-cloth flung under one of Miss Mary Mack's wings.

Maxie was lying with a book open in front of her, but had turned away from her reading. "Roasted chickens over an open fire, is what I hear," Maxie said loudly to a worn-looking Vera. "I like to cook that way down on my ranch, but if I go to all the trouble, it's more likely to be a side of beef."

That hardly sounded like flirtation, but with Maxie one could not always be sure.

"How was your flight?" Hazel said, looking down into their shade longingly.

Vera motioned her to come and sit down. "Like being dough in a mixing bowl. But I didn't expect better."

"What happened with Eleanor and Hannah?"

"Hannah had trouble with the fuel line, or the fuel mix. She was off again shortly after Nancy's Eagle Wright was delivered. I helped do the checks on all the planes. Eleanor had her spark plugs changed. And then we all came along. I guess I'm supposed to pay attention to the Curtiss-Robin on pre-flight checks, so I thought I'd meet with Maxie."

Hazel took a seat, not wanting an explanation.

"That puts you in advance crew since I'm in the first half of the draw

27

tomorrow," said Maxie. "And from Colexico to Phoenix you'll navigate." She offered some maps for Vera's study.

"How much time will you have to do your photography?" Hazel asked.

"With my big camera? Not much. I'll have to stow it away with Alexis and Marsha before they set off. I'll have to rely on my trusty hand-held variety." Vera patted the camera slung from her shoulder in a leather case.

"I'm going to ask you to do something then—but first…Max, do you think there's any betting going on?"

Maxie let out one of her deep guffaws. "Ask me if there's any bootleg around."

"No, I mean serious betting. Bookies and all. On and off the circuit?"

Maxie leaned back on the ground cloth, her head almost hitting the fuselage, a skeptical look on her face. "On us? Nobody takes us serious enough for that! The Powder Puff circuit. Can those gals even fly? Who's gonna think we'd ever get far enough to put money on it?"

"I don't know. But maybe someone is taking it seriously enough."

Then Hazel turned to Vera who was intent on adjusting something on her camera. "I was wondering if you could take pictures of ground crew and airfield too, talk to crew, see what the prevailing sentiment is. You have an ideal role for this that I can't get—"

"Ha!" Maxie rolled her eyes. "You can bet no one's going to talk to ya. You're out of range. I, on the other hand, can always be looking round for a nip from some guy's flask."

"Max, Max, for shame." Hazel shook her head.

"Not that I'd drink any," Maxie hastened to add, but chuckled. "I'm being a good girl. But what's the fuss, kid?"

"I don't care about betting if folks want a reason to play around with their money. I just don't want any of our airplanes played around with or crews manipulated by betting. That's what I worry about. That they just don't start tinkering with the planes."

"You're not serious!" Vera rubbed at the lens of her camera with her sleeve, face flushed from the heat. "Would they? Surely not!"

"Depends. If I put all my money on someone and she was falling back, wouldn't I think of finding a chance to fix things? Horse racing is notorious for that."

Vera laughed, although her question seemed serious. "That's why you're suspicious? Because you think the petty betting between the guys on the circuit—"

"It's simple to mess with the fuel mix. Someone could put oil in the gas, just enough to make a difference. All it would take would be something to cause a delay beyond time allowance, so you accrue penalties—a flat tire, a weakened strut. Easy enough to do around unsuspecting people."

28

"Yes, impressionable ladies that we are. Sitting ducks." Maxie added.
Vera laughed carelessly and shrugged. "And small potatoes!"

"Yeah well, maybe so," sighed Hazel, feeling slightly foolish. "But male pilots don't just go around trusting everyone. Why should we?"

"Oh well, I'm certainly game if it would ease your mind," Vera cut in crisply. "You want me to take photographs, engage in conversation and listen to what idle bits of talk come up. I'm crew, after all, and the guys even get blankets and mattresses and warm water for bathing in the morning. I could sleep right in the hangars—"

Hazel laughed, relaxing just a bit. "No one's asking you to sleep in the hangar. I do believe there is room at the hotel."

"Cozy up to the boys but don't sleep with them?" Vera teased.

Hazel nodded. "Right. I think you of anyone could get a sense of each airfield, and what kind of reception we're getting."

Vera began to talk quickly, looking away as if in thought, "I might be able to glean a thing or two, wave my camera about. In my experience, folks like pictures taken. They always want to know if they can buy a print for the family back home. I could have a whole side-line—"

Maxie began to clean the grit out from under her fingernails with the point of a small screwdriver she had found in her shirt pocket. She said to Hazel, "What did you hear?"

"Al thought there might be something afoot. Someone asked about a bookie."

"Eh, you worry too much about everything, Hazel. You can't control it all."

"And I don't want to," Hazel countered too defensively. "I just don't want what we do to be threatened, interfered with. Any extra strain—"

"I don't see how betting would make any difference." Maxie sat up, almost comical in her appearance, her hair still plastered down from wearing a helmet. Hazel saw how hot and tired they looked, and thought she would let it go for now; at least Vera had agreed to check crew out. They *all* looked ridiculous with plastered-down hair. It was time to go freshen up.

Dressed in the cinnamon silk pajamas Jo had given her for the trip, Hazel lay on her narrow bed in a narrow room, bathed at last but restless. Surely Jo had retired to her room by now? The hotel hallway outside seemed quiet, everyone eager to rest up for the coming day. No, Jo was not going to come to her.

She didn't have a robe, always tending to be spare with her flight luggage, but the men were all housed downstairs, so what harm could there be roaming the hall? Barefoot, she slipped from her room, counting the doors down to Jo's, gave a soft tap, and was rewarded with a subdued grunt.

Unresponsive, even as Hazel entered, Jo sat in a chair next to a gas lamp. Swathed in slate-blue silk and a quilt, she was reading a newspaper article by Eleanor. She said, "I should get Ellie to preach women's equality to that pilot's wife who gave me such a hard time this evening, saying it was bad enough the men had to race."

"The long-suffering one who called me mannish? Yes, it's always harder to take an insult from a woman, more disappointing...."

"Face it, Preston. We're aberrations." Jo rustled the paper in annoyance.

"Yes, yes, but I forget." Hazel lay down on the bed. There was a long silence until she thumped the pillow to better support her head. "All I know is I didn't bargain on being in separate cockpits at night too."

"What did you expect? We're on the circuit now. This isn't Maxie's guest bungalow—adjoining bedrooms, private bath." Jo didn't look up from her paper.

"This is 1929, for godsake. This is the wild frontier, anything goes. Why do you think Maxie bought a ranch out here?"

"Darling..." Jo rarely used endearments. Hazel braced herself for the chastisement that would surely follow the long pause "...you know perfectly well that Maxie bought her thousand acres so she could carry on in private. Not only that, but she has a grandfather who dotes on her. Where did he get his big bucks from if it wasn't one speculation or another? He's no better than Taggart—just richer at this point, because he succeeded in railroading people. Someday Tag can pamper his grand-daughter, just like Grandaddy Schulz does, backing her in any new travel plan and fancy of hers. And most of the time it's in pursuit of a woman—"

"Not flying. Flying is from her heart," Hazel cut in.

It made Jo look up from the paper at last, just her eyes peering over the top. "It was because *I* was giving joyrides at Saratoga that she came to try it."

"Yes, yes," said Hazel wearily. "It wasn't simply the fact that you were a woman doing it, and she already had a fascination—!"

"—for women." Jo mumbled, eyes having disappeared again.

Hazel lay back on the bed. "Ah, you never stop."

"I hope not. Anyway, neither of us can afford such luxuries. It's all very well to hide out now and then, but the rest of the time we have to be on the world's terms. Besides, Maxie is probably settling very comfortably into her bed alone tonight."

Hazel scoffed. "Not by choice and only if she has found a nip of bootleg."

"Hm, yes. It is perhaps a bit too soon for her to have conquered the photographer." Jo put the paper down on her lap.

"What, Vera?" Hazel sat up with a start and then sank back, groaning. Why didn't she like the thought? Then cuttingly, "No, we are all as dedicated

30

as you are, totally focused and cold. Won't you even let down an inch? I was looking forward to our time alone together. You know, leave everything at the airfield. I was hoping for a little intimacy, a crack in the facade."

"Oh Haze, what do you want from me?" Jo rattled the paper. "I'm unwinding, all right? I'm reading this positively fascinating article on all of us." She sat back in her chair, one leg hitched up as she looked for her place again. "I mean, can you believe this? The whole article is really a vehicle for Pamela and her sponsor, that la-de-da film-producer. If I didn't know Eleanor, I'd have thought she had gotten paid off to do this. Pamela, Pamela. A bit about Eleanor herself and all the Atlantic business...."

"Well, that's *why* it includes Pamela. Eleanor has her eye on the Atlantic."

"Listen to this interview of Pamela: 'The cameras caught me smiling after my rescue but my heart was sinking with Miss Liberty. I'd like to say she just folded up and sank, after being faithfully buoyant until help arrived, but it wasn't nearly so pretty. In fact she cracked apart and exploded only minutes after I had been taken aboard ship. The port wing floated on the waves long after the rest was gone. It was dreadful, very hard to watch even from the safety of that freighter. I was in shock for some time....' Oh, she'll make a hell of a movie about it, won't she? If I didn't know better I'd think it was a publicity stunt. There's more: 'I will consider this race a success if everything goes hum-drum.' Can you believe that? I'd like to see Pamela go through one hum-drum day. She wouldn't know how. Oh, look, even you get mentioned—with all your accomplishments, why not you for the Atlantic? I quote: 'Because Eleanor wants to cross an ocean and I'm a confirmed—'"

"—landlubber from the mid-west." Forefingers waving like a conductor's, Hazel finished with her. "I don't say Land Amighty for nothing, you know."

"'Still favored to win the upcoming Women's Derby....'"

"Only because I have the faster plane," Hazel sang out halfheartedly.

Jo tossed the paper down with finality, leapt up to stand at the foot of the bed. "Won't they be fooled!"

Hazel held her arms out and open. "Come here—you know I'm not going to get into that."

More abrasively, "And won't you get fooled too."

"Yes, yes. You aren't in the spotlight any more for today, or haven't you noticed the closed door?"

Joe gave her a sideward glance. "I noticed. But this is my room. You can't stay here all night."

"I'll creep out on tip-toe, having stolen kisses from your lips, aberration that I am. And everyone else will hear me. Or shall I go to the washroom first and make sure to pull the toilet chain?"

"The goddam bed is too narrow, Haze. We have a serious day of flying ahead of us. I need sleep."

"You need your tensions eased."

Jo smiled down at her and then fell gently into her arms, silk slipping between them. All Hazel cared about was to have her lips on Jo's full, warm ones, their mouths opening to each other. This is what I fly all day for; please let me have this. Win if you want to, Jo. Urgently she began to unbutton Jo's shirt to find her firm breasts.

Abruptly, Jo pulled away, her body rigid. "I can't Hazel. I can't let myself go tonight."

"Come on, sweetheart. I will make the tension go away. Give." She pulled Jo gently back, but the kiss she got was evasive.

Jo sat up, buttoning her shirt, her back to Hazel. "Maybe it's because of the race just starting. I'm too worried. If I give in to you here…."

Hazel moved onto her side, aching between her legs and in her womb. "I just want you. Are you really so steeled? Come to me." In profile, she could see that Jo was biting her lower lip—no tears, Jo was too knotted up for tears. Too bottled up to let lovemaking soothe her. With fingertips Hazel rubbed her back.

Jo sighed. "It's too strange here. I feel uneasy. Can you understand that? Don't you ever feel that?"

"No." Hazel never did—fool that she was.

"I mean, there isn't even a lock on the door."

Hazel shifted and sat up on the opposite side of the bed, ruffled Jo's hair tenderly, kissed the back of her neck, then rose. "Do we have to be rivals even in the only privacy we have? Must it go so deep?" Already her hand was on the doorknob.

Without turning, Jo said, "If I let myself be pliable, vulnerable to you, I'm afraid I'll lose my nerve."

"I hoped for a miserly glimpse of you. Did I get it? Sleep well, Jo."

*Some people like to climb mountains; I like to fly—for the sport of it.*
*Nancy Saunders.*

*—from a Journalist's Notebook, E.W.*

## 3.

*San Bernardino to Yuma*

Hazel watched high mercurial clouds run in rivulets across the pre-dawn sky as she walked the quarter mile to the field. Most of the pilots were still breakfasting at the hotel, but she was edgy with anticipation and wanted to be on her way. She decided that the clouds she watched were moving at about ten thousand feet and would surely evaporate in the torch of the coming sun.

The bustle of the day had begun on the airfield, a camp coming alive. She accepted a mug of coffee from one of the ground crew. What were the men eating? Fresh bread with *real* butter, she hoped; she hated finding that they had put extra-fine lubrication gel on their bread, even if it did look like lard, though she was always game to apply a bit of the stuff on her cheeks against windburn. She began to pull the sheathing off her Zephyr. The dew-count was virtually nothing, a pattern of drops left in the dust.

Across the runway, she spied Vera, camera and tripod set up, holding a tin mug of steaming coffee, and talking to a small group of bleary-eyed crewmen. Well, well well, the photographer up and busy already? That would explain why Hazel hadn't seen her at breakfast, and that she wasn't in bed with the yet absent Maxie either. Hazel didn't quite want to admit to herself that she was pleased to find Maxie hadn't seduced Vera. Vera did not look her way, and Hazel was happy to let her be, going about her own pre-flight checks.

The sun was already hot and the clouds gone, all the pilots geared up for take-offs when Vera finally approached her, her cameras having been stowed away and her work on Maxie's Curtiss-Robin done. Hazel had had her own briefings by that time and held a paper listing the day's coordinates as she leaned with her free arm against the Zephyr's fuselage. "Hello Vera. Some last minute changes, I'm afraid. We're going to Yuma, not Colexico. A sandstorm has turned the runway into a dune. Yuma may not be much better." She swung up into her cockpit to tape the paper onto her control panel.

"I see." Vera shielded her eyes as she watched Hazel. "By the way, I had a busy time of it this morning picture-taking and sleuthing a bit. The ground

33

crew here is quite happy to pose for me, but it's a bit too much of a novelty for me to be a woman photographer, and they don't quite get it that I'm not in the race. This is a pity. Anyway, a photographer is supposed to be invisible, part of the scenery."

Hazel jumped down, her parachute in hand, beginning to strap it over her leather flight jacket. "You got something though?"

"Well, I was setting up a frame which included part of the maintenance hangar where they have a flight board—where things are written down that need to be done. I saw something written there, erased already, other things chalked over. An airplane came through yesterday just ahead of us. Departure time underlined—before we were to arrive here. All I could make out was this: NC-060. Refueling for Phoenix. Are any officials running ahead of us?"

"No, only advance escort fly ahead of us, leaving just before we do. We have no need. Arrangements are made with the National Air Exchange. Changes are made by telephone or telegram." Hazel adjusted her straps, grimaced at the discomfort. The airplane in question must have left after Al Laraway came in yesterday. And maybe that was how Sweeney had come to be in San Bernardino, and maybe how he had left. "No make on the plane?"

"No. If our flight route is an uncommon one, does it seem odd to you that an airplane unconnected to us should go to Phoenix too?"

Would Sweeney have gone on to Phoenix that way? It had to be a double-seater then. Whose? Hazel enjoyed Vera's alertness, the sparkle of intelligence in her eyes. "I don't know if I would have picked up on that, Vera, I must confess. I'll ask Al what he thinks. Did you ask anyone about it?"

"I didn't want to be direct, but I thought I might look at the flight board when we get to Phoenix. Also, I think the evening might be a better time to take pictures—a different mood, different sense of activity. It's more likely that ground-crew will have something to say after a complete day of flying."

"If bets are on," said Hazel putting her helmet on.

Vera turned away abruptly. "The draw is on. Here comes my crew. See you in Yuma."

Hazel said, "Yes, and I'm in the first half."

Vera gave her a nod and a wave over her shoulder before hastening to her own craft which had fired up.

Watching until the plane's departure, Hazel pulled on her gloves, yanked Jo's left one, working her fingers in, before swinging aboard for final cockpit checks. As she flicked on the electricity, she watched Stevie barreling down the runway at full throttle, mentally pulling up with her. The plane wobbled slightly as it lunged into the air until Stevie equalized and climbed.

The lead crew-planes always pinpointed wind torque, and made take-offs for the contestants more of a known variable. Even so, the first in the draw served as indicators. No one wanted the lead position too often. But then, being in the second half had its draw-backs too. More dust upon landing, higher airfield temperatures as the desert sun took over from the cold. All the while metal contracted or expanded, constantly changing the balance in engines, even check after check.

The local crew stood in quiet efficient poses beside her, ready to remove brake blocks. One man hopped up on her wing, yelled to her underneath the thunder of engines firing up close by. "Watch the wind coming up starboard southwest at 23 mph."

"Affirmative."

"Sand in the wind up to three thousand feet, then you're clear."

"Affirmative."

"Godspeed."

A lot of guys said that, but Alli said, 'Goodspeed' because she'd heard it up in Alaska, and it was catching on with the women.

Hazel's heart pounded in anticipation as she watched Jo's brown and white Rearwyn take to the air. Identified as C-1103-8, it didn't have any pet name or term of endearment. Jo was too practical for that. A machine was a machine, as if to prove she wasn't sentimental, not girlish.

Next in the draw was Maxie with Hannah Meyer, Madelyn Burnett-Eades and Louise Gibeau to follow. Then Sarah Morris-Newton. Today times would be set and make a difference.

Sarah. Hazel had the opportunity to chase her since she was next in line. Her first lap had been only a minute better than Sarah's but she knew it didn't mean much. And Jo had a slight advantage. Hazel had to slice away five minutes to keep at pace, not allow the gap to widen. Could she get in before Sarah? Landings wouldn't necessarily come in order any more. Altitude could make a difference—one could either catch or fight a wind.

The Zephyr rolled forward as crew pushed it into position while she kept an eye on the signalman. And then she had it—the run of the strip. Full throttle into the air. Press on, Preston. She cheered herself on as the wheels left the ground. She pulled on the stick with both hands and angled upwards. As her left hand tightened, she could feel the seams of Jo's glove strain. Gritting her teeth, she loosened her grip, afraid those threads might snap any moment, and threaten to unravel like her relationship with Jo.

The course to Yuma stretched southeast over the desert and the arid Coachella valley. Next, the route crossed the Sand Hill at angles. Yes, there was the railroad that she had pencilled it from the map Gus got for her. Yuma lay just beyond the Colorado River, and they would all have to slice across ten miles of Mexico. She could see the desert far below, washed out by the glare of the sunlight. A postage stamp view of it sliced away by the wings, unless the plane banked, and then all she could see was sky.

Hazel no longer had Sarah in view because she stuck to her own coordinates rather than tracking. Or had Sarah deliberately dodged her over the Coachella? True, Hazel had been paying much more attention to the way the land dropped away back there, below sea-level, than to keeping an eye on Sarah. It was her own fault.

After two hours she began her descent for Yuma, static whining faintly through her radio receiver while she waited for a homing signal. Down through the shifting layers of air and into the heat. There was no reason to think she hadn't done well on the two hour flight, but there was that gnawing question at the back of her mind. Wind speed measured at a gusting 26mph, coming at an angle to her preferred course. And she dreaded the sand she would find.

Then a faint, but steady beep sounded on the radio. When she had the airfield in view she could see the sand blowing south to north across the runway. Visibility was poor as she peered through her goggles, not wanting to be blinded at the crucial moment she had to land. This sand—it couldn't be good for the engine.

She made one wide circle above the airfield to make certain of clearance, banking to starboard as the ailerons moved into opposing angles. She took her time, fighting the gusts, watching for the signalman's yellow and black checker flag. One side of the meager runway was covered up with sand. She cut power to glide in, took on the runway left of the sand, so avoiding the creeping grit. Crew were obviously trying to shovel and sweep the sand clear between landings, but it was like trying to keep water back.

She taxied to a rolling stop, Beech crew with the red name across their backs were running up to assist. Eyeing the parked airplanes, already in the process of being sheathed—only three were in—she could immediately spot Jo's Rearwyn. Maxie and Hannah were in. Where was Stevie? Why hadn't Sarah landed yet? And what the hell was Jo's time? As Hazel disembarked, pulling out her earplugs, heaving off the cumbersome parachute, the next plane approached. An Eaglerock Bullett—Madelyn! That meant she had exceeded both Madelyn and Sarah, unless Sarah had been forced to land short of the leg.

Yeah, and Stevie…and what about Louise? True, their air speeds were not as close to the more powerful planes, but still…she worried. The conditions made her nervous.

And then she was swept up by the activities of Yuma's ground crew. "What's my time?" She asked Gus, trying not to sound too eager to hear, but went on stowing her gear.

He slapped her on the back. "Good. One hour and fifty-three minutes. You couldn't ask for better, considering the handicaps." His thumb pointed towards the wind and sand.

"Yeah, well?" She persisted because he damn well knew what she wanted.

36

"Miss Russell came in at one hour and fifty minutes."

"Shoot." Hazel tore off her gloves, slapped them against a wing. "You said I had the faster plane."

"Steady on, there. It's true. I think she's pushing it, and she'll have to pull back. Those plugs of hers are taking a beating. Course, I'm not one for saying anything, and it wouldn't be my place tellin' her, all due respect. If I were her sponsor, I wouldn't ask her to wear those plugs out. They're going to give out on any lap now. And again, and again. Till something bigger burns out."

"What does she have now, an eight minute margin?"

"We'll catch her yet."

"Nah, she's taking the wind better. The Rearwyn will catch the edge on it's design."

Gus screwed up his face as he looked up. "You lost your time on the circle, is all. The wind wasn't as bad when she came in. Died down a bit. Comes and goes."

At that they turned to watch Sarah's white and blue Waco Taperwing arrive, dodging the encroaching sand just has she had.

Marsha Banfill's Spartan was next, ground-looping at the end of the runway. Conditions were getting worse.

As she went over the engine's performance with Gus, she spotted Eleanor's maroon Vega approaching—and listing badly.

"All hands, all hands!"

Having barely helped sheathe engines against the dust, Vera and Maxie turned with exclamations at the next descending aircraft, and scrambled. Hazel was ahead of them, running towards the runway, crying, "She's going to hit, she's going to hit!"

The Vega was lifted clumsily at the last moment by a gust of wind and plopped down with a skid and then a bounce as the wheels caught in the sand which caused the plane to up-end and stick just like that, its snout buried in the most undignified manner. This happened so quickly and yet, for Hazel, ever so slowly.

"I hope she's not hurt," Vera panted, coming up behind Hazel. She pulled her smaller camera out of her shoulder bag. "Damn it's hard being a photographer and part of the action too."

"Be a photographer then! We have enough muscle. Go on, rag." Hazel slapped her on the shoulder.

The ground foreman shouted through a megaphone. "Clear the runway. Aircraft approaching. Clear the runway!"

People massed around the Vega like so many ants over a dead bug, the medic climbing up to the closed cockpit to check on Eleanor. "She's okay. Move it!"

And the crews all heaved and shoved to the orders from the megaphone, wrenching the plane out of the sand, then as fast as possible across the runway. Nose away from the wind.

Lila Wilczynski's green and white Monocoupe was circling. Race officials would only time her for one circle to compensate for her landing approach since it wasn't an error in her judgment.

It seemed like hours to Hazel, pushing the Vega across the strip, but it was done in minutes. She felt her own fear all the way up her spine like sparks shooting into the depths of her brain. God, and this is just the beginning. When the job was done. She asked Vera, "What did you get?"

Vera's face was flushed with excitement. "I managed to get a picture just before the propeller came free of the sand—and the tail up in the air."

The medics were at the cockpit, helping undo the hatch. Hazel went to stand by Jo who appeared from the other side of the Vega, forgetting about their rivalry as they waited for Eleanor who crawled out, waving and grinning her toothy smile at them all. Everyone cheered.

"I hope it's this easy when I reach Europe," she yelled amid laughter. "What are the damages?"

"Airfoil needs replacing," answered the local Lockheed mechanic, then ran off to the radio operator for a call through to Lockheed in California.

Eleanor would have to wait for a replacement propeller to be flown in— she hoped not more than half a day. If it bothered her, she didn't show it, but jumped down into the grasp of her friends. "I seem to be having my share of delays. Hope I get them all done at the beginning, spare me later. What's my time, I wonder?"

"Two hours, thirty-two."

"Plus penalties." She shook her head, hand up to stop any comparisons or condolences. "You two—don't tell me anything. I don't want to know. God, my head hurts. Where's Vera. Ah. Vera, come help me deal with reporters."

A medic said, "This way, Miss Wilson, the doc wants a look at you."

No way was her time competitive at this point since Eleanor was flying weighed down by extra fuel. While most pilots were flying with enough fuel for each lap, plus reserve, Eleanor was flying at a constant full in training for her future flight across the Atlantic. Later on, she'd lighten up, way up. But it caused Hazel to wonder aloud to Jo whether the weight had shifted upon landing, or made the plane more clumsy on the wind.

Jo's response was directed to Eleanor encouragingly. "Can you lighten up your tanks now, Elly? You've done a sea-level take-off fully loaded—isn't that proof enough?"

Eleanor's thoughts were her own as she left the two standing slightly apart, silence like a truce falling over them. Hazel wasn't about to say anything more, afraid she'd say something wrong. When the silence was about to become unbearable, they were distracted as Alexis arrived in her closed cockpit, Travel Arctic J-5.

Where was Stevie?

Stevie was down. Word came in on the radio and made the rounds. One of the rear escorts was assisting her so she could get to Yuma. No one knew what ailed Stevie's Eagle Chief.

Another escort was flying to Colexico where word had come that Louise Gibeau was forced to land. Her wing cables had snapped—how many, no one knew yet. Maybe they would find out by evening in Phoenix.

"Damn," Hazel muttered in the pilot's lounge, staring into her glass of water as though its transparency would reveal some picture. Clarity, at any rate. Had Stevie still had an electrical problem? Had she lost power? Or was it something else?

Jo sat across the table from her, eating a piece of melon with a fork. "Haze, don't fret yourself."

"I can't help it, it's the not knowing."

"Come on—you do let yourself get so bogged down. Look, I want to show you something. Tag got a promotional story to the Phoenix papers for tonight. This was delivered by air courier. I found it when I came in." She handed over an envelope containing press copy and photographs. "Not only do I get some coverage at last—it helps that I'm in the lead!"

Dutifully, Hazel looked through the file, genuinely pleased—anything to have Jo feel less ignored as a top contender—until she came to the photograph. What the hell in horse apples is this?—Stunned, she sat in silence. There was Jo, goggles on her forehead and that radiant, easy smile of hers. With his right arm draped over her shoulders languidly—no possessively— was R.Q. Taggart like a handsome, matinee idol (thick, wavy hair, neatly parted, a jaunty angle to his head,) but without humor in his smile, much less in the distinct creases about his eyes.

"You making a movie together?" Hazel asked glumly.

Jo laughed up and down her musical scale. "Whatever works, Haze."

"I didn't think you'd go that far."

"That far? I'm not having sex with him."

"Distortion. Reducing yourself to the level of Pamela—the very one you like to poke fun at. Hollywood through and through." Hazel tossed the file back on the table. "That protective arm there as he towers over you. How can you stand it."

Jo's lips tightened, almost a smirk. "I don't take it seriously, Haze. Come on. He's trying to sell his airplane."

"And you? Do you have to resort to this? Where's your integrity? I don't understand—"

"Because this is the world! Honestly, you are so 'down home.' Eleanor understands; she even has that photographer along, capitalizing on her crash landing." She shook the papers emphatically. "The public wants romantic fantasy. Glamor! It's harmless."

"Is it?" Hazel leaned on the table with her elbows, her glass of water empty. "And that photographer's name is Vera. Why don't you ever call her that? And she's not here just for Eleanor but to record everything about us."

Jo bristled. "Yes. It's never bothered you that I call Pamela 'that actress.'"

Hazel sighed, sat back in her chair, tilting. "I happen to respect Vera. That's the difference."

"It's because she flattered you with a photography session that might do you justice."

"I don't really know what's eating you, Jo, but it can't be me, or Vera for that matter."

"Don't be crude," Jo snapped, pushing her plate away.

Hazel flushed. "I didn't mean—"

"Of course you didn't—that's what is so irritating about you. Always on the level. Only I would think innuendo and double entendre."

"That was uncalled for. You hardly let me touch you as it is," Hazel snapped, her voice rising.

"Shh." Jo clamped a hand over her wrist. "We're not alone in here."

All too aware, Hazel glanced around at the comings and goings, took in the clink of cups and plates, the buzz of conversation. Leaning across the table, she spoke in a low voice "I don't care who your sponsor is or what you have to do to for publicity. You chose him, that's your business. You could have had Lila's Monocoupe. No, no, don't interrupt—*I know*—you wanted to have a heavier plane and join the *real* competition. Fine. Now we're at some different place together. Perhaps, if we can't be friendly we shouldn't seek each other out—only when really necessary. I can't take this, not with everything else I have to see to. I don't need you as an adversary, but you're angry at me even for trying to get you the Monocoupe. I never meant to insult you. I just wanted you to have a good race. Bottom line is this, I respect good flying. That's what we all respect. And it will continue to be what really counts, never mind the publicity. Never mind weight classifications. You have your margin of time over me. I respect it. You will do your damndest to widen it, and I shall do my damndest to reduce it."

Hazel was saved by Alexis who came up behind her and caught her chair. Head tilted back, Hazel looked into her face with its creamy skin rich with freckles, framed by a cascade of red ringlets. The dancing, green eyes held her gaze. "Alli! How is it going?"

"Nothing has turned up, but I still sense something. Rough. We've adjusted the valves. Compression checks out, but there's something with the exhaust—"

"You aren't burning oil, are you?"

40

"No, it's not that, more like something loose, a vibration."

"All the time?"

"No, only from a hundred and twenty up." It was Al coming up behind Alli. There was a furrow of real worry there between his eyebrows.

He tugged on Alli's sleeve. "We'll brief you later, Hazel. We don't have much time right now, and I want to run through some checks." He hesitated a moment, glanced around the room, not to find anyone, just impatient or nervous.

"I'll come by to see you unless I get wrapped up in other things, otherwise tonight." Hazel said, thinking, he must have found out more.

"Affirmative," He gave a sharp nod, ushering Alli along. "We're in the first half, but I don't know if we'll be ready. Perhaps this evening would be best. Let's make a point of it...I have some questions."

Alexis squeezed Hazel's hand. "Listen, be a dear and encourage Marsha a bit. She doesn't look at all good—upset about Stevie's trouble, if I had to guess, though she isn't very forthcoming."

"I'll talk to her." Hazel watched as the two left. That closed cockpit sure left Alexis free of chapped cheeks.

Jo was finishing her melon. Hazel pushed herself up from the table. She started to stride out of the lounge, heard a chair scrape along the floor as Jo jumped up. "Haze!"

Hazel paused, but didn't turn.

"It's true—it is respect I want. That is what I want."

What a fool I am, Hazel thought angrily, stepping out into the blinding sunshine. She never did want my help. She resents everything I did to help her get in this race. And everything I did was out of passion! Foolish to think she would be satisfied with the Monocoupe!—how could I have been so blind? Perhaps it isn't me she wants, but what I have.

Before her, the airplanes sat glinting in the raw sun. She could see the crews checking systems. To her right, great hangars loomed open; she could see the Travel Arctic in one of them, but instead of walking over there, she retreated to the rear of the clapboard building for a moment of solitude, and maybe find shelter from the grit and wind. Rounding the corner, she ran into Vera. Standing against the wall and in the scant shade which the gutter above provided, she was smoking. Startled by Hazel, she was hurriedly stuffing something into the camera case at her feet.

"Hey 'rag,' you startled me...." Vera spoke through lips that held a cigarette. She had removed the top of her coveralls so that the sleeves hung from her waist. Underneath she wore a cotton teddy, revealing well-tanned, shapely shoulders above the slight swell of her breasts. Grinning, she exhaled a plume of smoke. "You have found me in my moment of vice, but I'm due to take off in a few minutes."

41

Recovering from the tingling shock of the sight of Vera's bare shoulders, Hazel smiled sheepishly. "And I came to collect myself. We seem to need the same spot." She noticed the map hanging from Vera's hand. "You're navigating the next lap?"

"Monitoring the coordinates, yes. Not really flying, is it?"

Hazel stood next to her, leaning back too, and looking at all the old airplane parts in the back field and the wide desert beyond. She didn't have anything to say to Vera, and yet wanted to. Why so uncomfortable when the silence itself was easy? Vera asked nothing of her and presently stumped out the cigarette underfoot, slipping into her top again. Hazel saw how her flight suit already had grease and sweat stains. "Time to wash your suit, Vera, or you will really look ragged."

Two inches away from her, and hoisting camera strap onto shoulder, Vera's eyes were playful. "I wash the armpits at night. I plan to let it get greasier, and use it for rags when the race is done."

"Not preserve it?—for a museum?"

"I'll have to answer that in Phoenix. I must be off." Vera waved as she rounded the corner and disappeared. Was that a kiss she blew?

Hazel followed, having no desire to be alone any longer.

The Lockheed, two-prop transport waited in position at the end of the runway. Referred to as the C-175 because of its registration, its crew prepared to embark. They clustered near the wings, putting on their gear. Hazel made her way towards her own airplane as she watched Vera climb in; watched take-off as she began her own pre-flight checks with Gus. As the four-seater transport left Yuma, the sand was still blowing, the sandbar still covering part of the runway. Only two escort-planes were in the lead, three stayed back to assist, and one had mechanical problems of its own.

Brake blocks were being removed from Jo's Rearwyn as she climbed in, waving some last minute instruction or question. Before long she was firing up, leading the draw since Stevie hadn't caught up yet. Next in line was Maxie.

*Yuma to Phoenix*

Hazel took off with Marsha Banfill and Pamela Christy in position to follow. Eleanor would have to wait it out in Yuma for a while until her propeller came in. Lila, Nancy and Alexis all hoped to be in the air within half an hour. Lila's Monocoupe had rudder problems, Nancy's Eagle needed fine-tuning now that she was underway and getting used to its idiosyncrasies. Al and Al were just cleaning up after replacing valves. Why her own bird flew so well, Hazel couldn't fathom, but she and her team had not come across any kinks.

She wasn't the only one. Jo's Rearwyn was doing well. Pamela's Bellanca too, and Pamela's time was steady although she was over two hours on the last leg due to the winds.

Hazel hoped time was on her side—time and the sky. She was running ahead of the wind as though she had sails and was crossing a sea, smooth as glass. Any turbulence was well below her plane for the moment. This was desert flying—no clouds at ten thousand, only the thick mirage of the land itself evaporating. Sometimes there was no haze at all, only the stark, arid ground far below. She felt as though she could reach out with her hand and draw a picture in the earth which was as clean as slate. Only the Gila River could cut through it. She was so high she couldn't even hope to find her shadow as it slid across the ground over every bump and cleft like a lizard, silent and quick. She understood that she was ready for the long haul, finding her pace. After Phoenix when the laps were longer, she had confidence she could cut her time.

Fatigue had begun to creep over her from the roar and vibration when she sighted Woosley Peak, an encouraging beacon on her flight path, some six thousand feet below her. She was coming into Phoenix where Gus had warned her that the Derby would cause almost as much of a frenzy as a rodeo. Be ready for cowboys and horses, crowds and parades. No rest. Only Eleanor could up-end her plane, and get out with a smile, looking refreshed. She thought of Pamela, smiling on that freighter while her airplane sank. How did they do it? A smile and a wave, even when the chips were down. That, thought Hazel, made a hero. She would do it too, even if it killed her. All of them would.

When she landed, she discovered Jo was already wowing the crowd, her name and picture fresh from the papers. Coming in first, she had taken the role of winner as if determined to make her name a household word. Taggart had timed this right. Hannah, Madelyn and Sarah were also doing their part, but where was Maxie? Of all people, Max liked a good rodeo.

Hazel had to laugh when race officials offered to trade horse and cowboy hat for her airplane and goggles. Vera, camera in hand, coaxed her laughter further, and snapped pictures. Then, like the other pilots who had come in ahead of her, she too, rode along the edge of cheering crowds. The rodeo marshall who led her western mount, laughed at her English-style jodhpurs while he rode in his chaps. Of course, she thought, it would make more sense to wear leather chaps for flying, ah, but they would be too stiff. What could she do but grin and wave, wondering what had so quickly become of her wings?

Well after all the hoopla, Hazel glanced over the row of planes again, but there was no way to conjure up Maxie's. The first part of the draw was in. No Maxie. And except for Marsha who was due soon, the others would be late and the crowds gone.

Vera was already helping clean the airplanes and sheathe the engines until evening maintenance and refueling. Hazel walked over to where she was working and flopped down on the withered grass nearby, wiping her forehead with her sleeve as she offered up a canteen. "Want some water?"

Vera joined her, sagging. "I want a pool of it. Listen, word has come in and ground crew is abuzz with it. The Canadian stunt pilot, Louise Gibeau, has put in a formal complaint that someone may have put acid on her wing cables. Those are the ones that snapped. She is going to send them in for closer inspection. And all her cables will be replaced tonight. Is that what you were talking about?"

Hazel sat up in thought. "Acid? Cables can snap. Her sponsors gave her an old airplane, you know, an old de Havilland, because her own airplane wasn't registered in the United States. She was very sore about it because she had no time to petition. It was a last minute thing. She is used to better flying equipment. She's a friend of Maxie's and I've only chatted with her a few times. Very high-strung. Has a chip on her shoulder. But who of us doesn't in this business? Normally, I would think she's just sore, and the investigation would prove it out. I hope that's the case. But yes, if there is betting going on, something like that could happen. I wouldn't expect it so soon because times have to be established, and frankly, she isn't in the running."

"But what if it isn't betting? What if it's a person or people that want this race to be a failure?"

Hazel sat up, aghast. Finally she said, "You mean because they want to show that women shouldn't be racing? Sure we've always had people like that, but as far as I know not such a direct, personal attack. It's more on a company board-room level—not funding us, not sponsoring us. Eleanor and I run into that all the time. And Hannah—though she tends to go to wealthy people who like novelty and adventure. Then there are always newspapers not giving good enough coverage. Airfields not giving us the time or space. But after all, the National Air Exchange is most supportive. We've put together a race circuit where there wasn't one, because that's the only way we could do it. Why would anyone get so nasty if money isn't involved?"

"A personal vendetta?" Vera suggested, capping the canteen.

"Louise? Everyone loves her. She's Canada's glory. Her government even made a protest over her airplane not being accepted. No, it doesn't make much sense to me." Hazel stood up to shake loose her emotions. The idea of a personal attack unnerved her but she didn't want Vera to see that, and besides, an airplane approached. Was it a Curtiss-Robin?

No, it was Marsha Banfill's Spartan. She felt Vera coming to stand next to her as they watched Marsha land.

"Something's not right," said Hazel in response to the bump and skid. She waited until the plane came to a stop, then grabbed the canteen from Vera, eyes fixed on Marsha who was trying to climb out of her cockpit. Crew rushed up. Hazel was the first to put her foot on the wing, jumping up to support Marsha who was doubled over. Gus came up from the other side to help her.

"Here, have some water." Hazel brought the canteen to Marsha's lips.

Pale and trembling, Marsha gasped between gulps, "I didn't...think I'd make it."

"Get her to cover," a medic said, taking over from Hazel, as they helped Marsha down off the wing.

When Hazel turned back to Vera, she found her replacing the lens cap on her camera and winding the film. "Don't miss much, do you, rag?"

"Not if I can help it. Pilot fatigue?"

"Yes. Maybe dehydration. Lucky she wasn't in the first part of the draw and expected to get up on a horse."

Vera smiled. "You mean like Jo?"

Hazel didn't say anything, just stuck her hands under her arms, ever watching the crews about the planes, and the empty sky.

"I got a few good snapshots of Jo, by the way, not real portrait, newspaper type."

"She'll be pleased. She has been feeling slighted, ignored."

"And wants to have a presence? So I see by her time. Relax the muscle in your jaw, Hazel. I know it's not easy. She's afraid."

Hazel looked into the brown eyes squinting against the bright sun. "Afraid? We all are."

"No, I mean that she's afraid of you, what you are, what you've achieved. You're someone to be measured by. You see being out on the edge as natural. Farm girl from Kansas becomes top flier—just because your father sold tractors and your brother became a car-racer? Paved the way for you? You were expected to have become a farmer's wife not a fuel specialist. You have to see that considering her society background and the expectations and entitlements that she has given up, she's sticking her neck out to be a pilot at all."

Hazel shifted uncomfortably. "The way I see it, she's had all the opportunities. She has had access to money, private schools, a fancy women's college.... It's a principle now for her to refuse any help."

"Hand-outs too often have strings attached."

"Yeah. But she went into flying with her family's approval. She's gone step by step just like me. She did in-air re-fuelling for me when I soloed over Florida. No woman had done that before. But she sees it as helping me, not a feat she can claim as her own." Hazel's tone grew bitter. "Now I am something to push away because the help I offered wasn't good enough. And look what she has gotten for it, a sponsor she can bang her head against, and an airplane that will probably fail her though she believes it's absolutely tops."

"Isn't it simply an untried model?" They had walked by now to the shade

45

of Hazel's Zephyr, and were sitting under the port wings.

"Of course it's an untried model. All I know is that Wright-J engines are the most reliable to date—and she doesn't have one."

"You don't think she can keep her lead—do you?" Vera asked, tucking her camera away.

Hazel shrugged. "I could set a pace tomorrow that she could not keep up with." She felt Vera's close scrutiny. "Does that sound arrogant to you, Vera?"

"It would if I didn't think you know your stuff. But if you know it, she must know you can beat her easily."

"You're the one who said she sticks her neck out." Hazel lay back on the ground, a gesture of disgust.

Vera sat, looked about from the shelter of the wing. "Hm, It's almost comfortable under here. Throw a tarpaulin over the wing and you could even have a tent. Back to what we were talking about before, I have something else I'm stewing about in light of Louise's weak struts. Hazel, you don't think someone on the crew traveling with the Derby would tamper, do you?"

"Oh God." Hazel answered quietly. "I trust them implicitly. Gus is my guardian angel. He's the one man I can always talk to. He paves the way for me, for all of us. The leg work he has done to make this race work—lining up mechanics, making sure of spare parts! And Alan Laraway, Sam Morris-Newton. In fact, Alan is the one worried about betting, which reminds me, I have to catch him as soon as he comes in. No, no chance!—the guys that come with us are loyal or why would they bother?"

"I don't know," Vera began, "but I might just like to stay on the airfield at night anyway. Here. I mean, we all leave, and I know there is a certain amount of security with traveling crew camping out, but still...we have no security coming from the pilots. I'm your token woman on the crew and along only because I'm a photographer! I'd like to a keep closer watch. Crew needs to keep with the aircraft anyway. There are blankets. I could sleep under an airplane, this one with your consent. It would be like old times. I used to live that way in my barnstorming days."

Hazel looked at her in shock. "Yes, but you had a man with you then!"

"There are lights on and activity all night, radio bulletins coming in. I can handle myself! In the dark I'd just be another guy, besides I think I'd be more comfortable."

"You wouldn't get any rest. And I'd worry about you. I don't think it's necessary."

"Well, stay and protect me then!"

Hazel didn't have time to respond, nor wonder if Vera was serious or joking. Miss Mary Mack was coming in. Definitely the Curtiss-Robin!

Pilots lingered in the refreshment tent near the runway, informally conferring over maps. The sun slanted in the west, casting long shadows across the desert, shadows that seemed to race towards the women who were eager for relief from the heat. They lingered waiting for all the airplanes to be in so the next day's draw could be established. Vera paced back and forth between tent and runway, waiting for her big camera to come in, muttering something about how perfect the light was for shots. She left three women, seemingly at ease around a table, calling them "a particularly engaging tableau," and went to find Eleanor who had even caught up, landing shortly after Nancy and Lila. Stevie was off to see how Marsha was doing at the hotel.

Under the canopy Maxie was saying "...and so I come across railroad tracks and decide I'd better follow them," Maxie embellished her story with a flourish of her hand. "Well, what I find is a settlement, a bunch of adobe shacks, and I decide to land on a relatively clear section of the road. Ah, how the chickens squawked! What are they speaking when I climb out and ask for directions? Spanish! I'm *across the border* in Mexico. Can ya believe it? "

Hazel sat, listening attentively although she had heard the story tumble out when Max landed. This time around the story was for Jo's benefit. Leaning across the table, chin in hand, she reached for a fruit bowl, all the while watching the sky and the coming sunset. "How do you explain it, Max?"

"Don't ask," huffed Maxie playfully, but Hazel knew it was to cover her tension. "I meant to do it!—go to Mexico. Most direct course to Phoenix." And Maxie laughed in that deep rolling way of hers.

"Well, it's good you can take it so cheerfully." Jo slapped Maxie on the back, squinting into the western horizon. The light dazzled them suddenly as the sun began to sink, no longer giving them shade under the canopy, but casting long shadows instead. At this rate flares would have to be put out before long; airplanes were supposed to land before dark, even if not at the designated airfield.

Maxie continued as though reluctant to give up the trio's unspoken, but agreed upon watch for the last pilot to come in. "Cheerfully! Why, if I didn't do that, Jo dear, I'd be sunk. I mean, I only added about an *hour* to my timesheet."

"But tell me," insisted Hazel, peeling an orange with her small pocket knife. "Do you know where you made your mistake?"

"Why, you persistent little devil."

"Oh, you've called me worse," said Hazel pointing a finger as she passed orange sections to Jo.

"True. But remember you told me to watch my goddam language this trip."

"Then call me something in Spanish! I bet you know a few. Now tell me what went wrong."

"I guess I copied my coordinates out wrong. I remember looking at my compass and thinking things looked strange. Then when I went to check my map, it flew out of the cockpit!" Maxie slumped in her seat, her laugh gone. "But don't think I'll ever confess that to Eleanor if she decides to try and interview me about it."

"She wouldn't ask. But she'd want to know all about Mexico. We all put down in the wrong places sooner or later," Jo cut in softly, between bits of the orange. "It will be time for dinner soon. Should we go eat? Frankly, I'm starved. And tired."

"I hope we have beefsteak." Hazel scooped up the orange peelings into a neat pile as Hannah Meyer arrived to announce that dinner was soon to be served in the pilot's lounge.

"Chicken, I'm afraid," said Jo ruefully.

"But this is steer country!" Maxie hooted. "What the....?"

Hazel wagged a finger. "Now, now, maybe in Fort Worth where the airfield is right next to the stockyards."

"Maybe we should get our food and come eat here," Jo suggested just as the distant roar of a plane could be heard.

"About time she got in. I want to eat." But Maxie was smiling.

Jo concurred. "I want to get away from this dirt and have a bath."

The three walked out to the runway. It was a crew plane coming in—rear escort. It landed efficiently, Alan at the controls. Hatch up in a flash, he jumped out fast, haggard, distraught. The three pilots ran forward along with crew. Alan was clasping Gus by the shoulders. Was she in, was there any bulletin? With a few short commands, the C-175 was rolled out and refueled.

Gus pushed Hazel back. Absolutely not, she could not go. Be sensible. This was escort responsibility. Besides, it was in the rules: during the duration of the race, competing pilots were to keep to the schedule and request assistance from escort only, not other competitors. Within minutes the C-175 was underway with Gus piloting, Alan beside him, leaving a despondent cluster of women pilots on the airfield.

"Who the hell wants to eat?" Maxie spoke glumly. "Come on, let's help put the flares out.

No one wanted to leave the airfield. Vera's first night of surveillance was accompanied well into the evening by all the contestants, grubby and tired, still in their flight clothes.

A pilot was down. Speculation about what could have happened made the rounds in the gathering darkness while the radio kept mute. Keeping vigil on the field itself or else in the pilots' lounge, the women waited for word to come through. At least a word. One thing they knew—since rear escort had seen no sign of her, the pilot had crash-landed somewhere.

Gladys Jenney put a call through finally, urging them all to stay calm, to get some rest, and that the race itself was not to be delayed. Hazel didn't doubt for a minute that Eleanor had put a call through to Gladys first, requesting the firm but motherly advice.

A second and third crew plane took off into the night with race officials and a doctor.

Alexis was down.

*Stunt fliers are, like circus performers, not appreciated for training and commitment, but for spectacle. Defying death. Defying gravity. I wanted to participate in this Derby to be taken seriously.*

Louise Gibeau        *—from a Journalist's Notebook, E.W.*

# 4.

No thought of dinner was on Hazel's mind, no question of hunger; she only took one bite from the biscuit dipped in chicken gravy that Maxie brought out to her. The radio's silence unnerved her.

Leaving the other pilots to do the pacing, the vexed waiting somewhere else, she tried, instead, to maintain a focus, a preoccupation as she kept a ear open to the radio. Because she had misgivings about whom to trust on the local crew and because Gus was all too obviously absent on the search and rescue mission, she personally supervised the evening's re-fuelling.

She avoided both Sam Morris-Newton and Frank Wilczynski; though each were husbands and strictly personal crew to their respective wives, Sarah and Lila, they assumed a take-charge attitude that she thought was out of place—barking orders, demanding attention. She left them to take on CW airplanes and independent racers. That meant Jo could oversee her own airplane with them.

Lockheed's Phoenix man was there—Melvin. Instinctively, she allowed herself to rely on him. He reminded her of her father, not his large physique nor even his similar age, but a certain understated patience built into his solid frame. He was a man who knew perseverance, a lifetime of it. He was tired but would never give up, as if he had kept many such vigils. Her brother, Dewey, might have been like that one day if his life hadn't been cut short. His patience was something Hazel understood, perhaps was something she would acquire if she lasted.

Maneuvering the fuel barrels on dollies with ground crew, she took on the slow task of regulating the right mix of gasoline to oil, as crew pumped the liquid into each airplane.

Meanwhile, Maxie and Vera took to helping set out the barrel-flares down the length of the runway.

Someone had provided gas lamps under the refreshment tent where Eleanor sat writing out her news report between valiant efforts to placate and advise the other pilots, something she did well. She also kept going to to the hovering reporters, saying, "Anyone who needs to go rest, go rest. Come back if you want to, otherwise we'll let you know what has happened as soon as a bulletin comes in."

When the refueling was done, Jo left with Lila and Nancy to rest a while, but Hazel felt as though she had enough energy and stamina to walk to Cleveland, never mind fly. She went to keep vigil in the tent, staring out at the flares, sending Maxie, Eleanor and Vera off to rest too.

But Maxie lingered, puffing on a cigar. They did not talk.

The black horizon loomed against the last gold of the sky. Twinkling lights from outlying settlements and farms began to show in that darkness. Then the flares seemed brighter than anything else. After a long time Maxie said, "I'm going to find us some blankets. It's gonna get dang cold soon."

Hazel nodded. They weren't going to go anywhere.

She sat down in a chair and put her feet up on a table, pulling loose the laces of her boots. The men of the crew seemed subdued although lights burned everywhere. No obvious card games tonight, she observed. She could hear the metal roofing of the hangars contracting. It sounded like rain.

Her mind seemed alert, yet dream-like images of Gus and Al's search enveloped her. How could she have consented to stay behind? They should all be out looking. Damn the rules, the schedule and time! She imagined Alexis sending up flares. Perhaps it would be easier to find her in the dark if she made fires. That's what they had all learned in whatever unconventional training they may all have had. You set up markers if you had to land, unless you were too injured to help yourself.

The truth of it was, Hazel had never had to make a forced landing. She had scraped off a shed roof once. Broken a strut or two. She thought of Stevie who had landed in sand when a fire broke out in the fuselage locker. Faulty wiring? She landed and put out the fire with handfuls of sand, and waved at the circling crew plane. She had had enough power after some disconnections she made, to take off. No control panel, but who needed that if one still had a compass?

Still, Hazel had never even had a close shave. All she could do was imagine what it would be like. Not knowing was the hard part. At least if she herself were down she would know. What gnawed at her now was that it was happening to someone else and she couldn't do anything to help. Alexis, for godsake! Alexis who flew over miles and miles of tundra as a matter of habit. She had flown all the way down the coast from Alaska, sometimes well over ocean. Ridiculous that she should have to come down on such an easy run. Hazel paced again. Awake again.

Maxie came back with blankets, threw one around Hazel.

"Wanna smoke?" Maxie handed her a cigar.

"Yes." Hazel waited as Maxie lit it for her. She smoked it until she coughed, Maxie thumping her back and telling her to put her arms up.

"Don't inhale the goddamn thing, Preston. Just puff or I can't ever offer you another one."

Hazel laughed. "I'm fine."

"That's better." Maxie smiled back in the dim light. "I have a ground cover under Miss Mack. Want to come rest? I think I need to or my eyes won't focus on my coordinates tomorrow."

"I'll come when I can't stand up any more. I think I'll go over my map."

"You'll know where to find me if ya need me." Maxie squeezed Hazel's shoulder, her voice lowering, almost as if talking to herself. "If this turns out badly, you know I am going to feel awfully responsible for getting Alli to come down here for this filthy race, don't ya? How am I gonna live with it? How?"

At a loss for words, Hazel placed her own hand over Maxie's.

When Eleanor and Vera came back, they found Hazel hunkered down in a chair from the field house, stockinged feet up in another one. Head at an angle, her chin rested on her left shoulder. She jumped at the sound of their footsteps. The lamp on the table had gone out, but her map was still spread out, weighted down at the corners with stones.

"Oh dear," said Eleanor, holding a lit lamp, "I'm afraid we woke you."

"No, no," Hazel sat up groggily, moving her shoulders to get the kink out. "What time is it?"

"Midnight," said Vera. She was dressed in a woolen sweater, and baggy trousers. The wad over her arm was wet coveralls which she began to hang out over strategically placed chairs.

"Washed your armpits, eh?"

Vera laughed. "Yes. I did take in your remarks earlier today."

Hazel got out of her chair. "Here, let's see if we can get this lamp lit again."

Eleanor still wore her usual uniform but she looked less worn. "Lamp's out of fuel, I think. I can't say I minded getting all that grit off of me."

"Are the others resting?"

"It's the best thing to do."

"What about you two?"

"You know me, H.P., I sleep on the run. I had a good sleep while I waited for my prop to come in." Eleanor said.

Vera was looking out at the length of flares which burned with low, glowing coals. "How bright the stars are now, how close. They seem to outshine the flares."

Hazel pulled on her boots. "Someone was out there with Melvin dumping coal into them a couple of hours ago, but I suppose we could take a turn at it."

"Don't you want to take a turn and go freshen up?" Eleanor asked, scrutinizing her.

Hazel snorted. "What?—You think I look grubby? I'll get a bucket of water from crew."

"You'll feel a whole lot better if you do."

"Who said I wasn't feeling great?"

"Jo said she would wait up."

"She'll have to come here."

Vera changed the subject. "Where's Maxie?"

"She went to sleep under Miss Mack."

Eleanor laughed. "*Under?* Doesn't seem in character."

Hazel feigned a scowl. "Honestly." She shivered under her cloak of a blanket. It was true—she was sweaty and dirty and stiff, but she would change in the morning. If she didn't feel so lousy, the company of her friends would have seemed downright cheerful. They were all trying their best.

They made their way to one of the hangars in search of the coal bucket and shovel. At the hanger they checked for the latest news. There still was no bulletin. It wasn't good; it meant the search party was still looking.

Sparks flew up with each new load of coals in the braziers as the three made their way down the runway. They huddled for a while at the last one, warming up.

Alexis was down, dammit. Why no word yet? Hazel blew on her hands, then held them over the coal fire again, stretching her fingers. Her deep fatigue had changed into an explosive impatience. A fury. She wanted answers. Crew planes would have to go somewhere for refueling if they hadn't found her, and could put word out. That there was no news must mean they had landed in the desert somewhere to help her.

She began to think back to Al and Al's concerns over the Travel Arctic—how Alexis had been nervous. What had happened—mechanical failure? Pilot error? They had all had to face sand blowing. Was there something about the Arctic, about its design that had caused it to take in too much sand somehow? A nagging thought kept surfacing, in spite of her denial—was it possible that someone had tampered with the plane? Ever since Louise's complaint, and Al's report, Hazel had grown more and more anxious. She could feel it all the way through her like a poison, a stimulant.

She trudged back up the runway with the other two, stopping to check on Maxie who lay huddled in blankets and now was rolled up in her ground cloth too.

Eleanor bent down, leaning on one of Miss Mack's wings and whispered to the others, "Maxie's out for the count. Don't suppose she got hold of any bootleg, do you, H.P.?"

"Hey, not that she let me know about. She said she'd be good on this trip. I have to trust that. She could just be tired."

53

"She looks halfway comfortable," said Vera. "I think we should look to do the same. Can we use your wings, Hazel? I'm sure I can find a ground cover."

Hazel nodded. "That would be good. The Zephyr is closer to the hangar so we can hear the radio. I'll go get the lamps and some more oil."

She left them and went back to the clubhouse. To her amazement, Jo emerged from the lit doorway.

"Why didn't you come?" Jo asked softly, an edge to her voice. "I thought maybe something had happened. Anything yet?"

"No." Hazel was about to brush past her, when Jo caught her, enveloped her. Returning the embrace, Hazel slumped against her, burying her face into Jo's shoulder. What respite. The warmth sent shivers down her back.

"You said we should seek each other out only when it was really necessary," Jo whispered.

"I didn't think it would be necessary, did I? It's only the second lap, for godsake."

"She must be all right. Don't you think she's all right?"

"Who dreamed up this harebrained scheme anyway?" Hazel rubbed her cheek against Jo's.

"We did."

Hazel croaked, "I'll never forgive myself."

"Yes, but we knew the risks. This has never been a frivolous adventure."

"Weren't you the one who told the reporter it was dangerous?"

"I was thinking, Haze…just south of the Gila Mountains, the air was choppy at twelve thousand. I had to go higher, higher than I wanted to. If it wasn't something mechanical, that's the one place she could have run into trouble. It was like waves slamming into the mountains. Maybe she was caught in a downdraft."

"I didn't feel it. If there was a problem with the plane, I just hope she jumped. There must be some complication for us not to have word yet.

"You know we have to go on, don't you? No matter what."

Hazel pulled back, their arms still entwined. Looking into Jo's face, she could see her own pain reflected in the furrows across the brow, the distinct lines around the eyes. She replied evenly, "Against all odds, yes. Hasn't it been that way all along?"

"Alexis would want us to go on, wouldn't she? We all demand that of each other. You know I'd insist you all carry on, even if something happened to me. Don't you?"

"Affirmative. You had better understand that from me too."

"It isn't going to be good, is it, Haze? I can feel it. We all feel it."

Hazel held her hands. "Yes, we feel it. You should go get some rest. Is the hotel comfortable?"

"Fretted over a bit too much by the proprietor—he isn't used to a house full of dames. It's obviously set up for men from the railroad, and the mail pilots, but he set aside one wing for us. It's a curtained-off bunk room. The Newtons and Wilczynskis get real rooms. But it does have a bathtub. And it's close—just across the tracks, about a hundred yards off. We'll hear if an airplane comes in. I'll go back. Sop-rag time. My head hurts. I feel so heavy I don't know how I'll get off the ground tomorrow. You're staying?"

"Yes."

*I have done all kinds of air shows and tours before this, and I've never run into so many problems and frustrations as in this race, of all the confounded times.*
Stevie Lamb                                                  *—from a Journalist's Notebook E. W.*

# 5.

*Phoenix to Douglas*

Alexis! Hazel woke up with a start. Smelling of stale sweat, she sat up, barely avoiding a bump to her head from the low wing above her.

With the first light at around five in the morning, mechanics began to move around. The clink of buckets, the sound of sloshing water reminded her all too clearly of where she was. Dully, she saw that the flares were all out. The sky had a slate-grey mood to it.

The promise of hot water alone seemed to ease the ache in her back. Did she smell coffee? She wanted it strong, bitter and black with a lump of sugar to take the edge off.

Her stomach growled. If she were lucky, maybe she could get a bowl of oatmeal. The hotel was supposed to send a big pot of it over, but when?

Before the race she had dreamed of waking up with Jo's naked warmth against her. How easy it would be to linger. Another day at the races? Oh, but we really, really must get up now, dear. Not yet, not yet. I want you closer, longer. It isn't breakfast I want, but my hand coursing....

Damn. Hazel cast off her blanket and pushed herself to her feet, using the wing for support. She had slept on the ground, been aware, off and on, of the cold, of the ground being hard, of her hip bones digging—only to wake up ravenous for Jo. Why such punishment? Her mind was cloudy from nightmares. Alexis! The wind blowing Alexis over the Gila Mountains in her parachute. And Hazel running to the edge of the runway to try and catch her. Hazel remembered Jo saying: "You know we must go on without her." Hazel knew now that there was a part of her that would not go to sleep at all for the rest of the race. Nerve had to take over.

"I've brought you some water," A gentle voice called out to her. Vera arrived with a steaming bucket. "If we put some blankets up, you can have your own private bathroom. How's that?"

Hazel grinned through puffy eyes. "I thought you were still under there asleep." She glanced back under to see if Eleanor was there. Hadn't she kept halfway warm by bracing against El's back? "Hasn't a bulletin come through yet?"

"Only that the National Air Exchange has called on more pilot volunteers. They're concentrating on the mountains." Vera was bustling about, throwing blankets over the wing, but they kept slipping. "How about I just hold one up here for you?"

Hazel watched her out of both amusement and gratitude. "Why are you doing this?"

"Don't you have some flying to do today?"

Stripping down to her underclothes, Hazel looked into the steaming bucket. "Lordy, it even has a clean rag in it. Not your coveralls all torn up yet?"

"Not a chance—"

A pair of round brown eyes came to peer over the blanket, a husky voice said, "Looks inviting—may I join you?"

"Sure Max."

Amid the banter, a rumpled Eleanor sat up grumbling, "Noisy neighbors."

By the time Hazel and Maxie had cleaned and changed, and the oatmeal come and gone, the pilots were converging for the meeting they had put off the night before—discussion of the route and the draw for Lap Three. It was time now. The mechanics were beginning pre-flight checks. Even Stevie's airplane was fixed and ready to go.

Any minute Hazel expected some word to come through, something to go on. How she wanted that before any of them took off. A race official brought out the box with all the numbers in it, set it on a table under the refreshment tent, and waited. While Eleanor went off to talk to her press contacts, the pilots deliberated over Hazel's map, discussing the particularities of what lay ahead. The weather would be hot and dry again, the terrain, inhospitable desert. Once again their course angled to the southeast, first crossing the Gila River, then keeping east of the Santa Cruz. Skipping Tuscon, except for emergencies, they'd have to cross the San Pedro and angle south of the Dragon Mountains. Their destination was Douglas near the border of Arizona, a pit-stop at a small military field. It was important not to overshoot Douglas and end up in Mexico. From there, they would fly across New Mexico, aim for the invisible border of Texas, mesquite land, and El Paso for the night.

The general concern was over what press might lie in wait for them in Douglas, even though Eleanor was asking for friendly protection. Even so, whoever arrived first would receive the brunt of attention, and needed to be ready with quick answers. What to say for them all? In an unusual turn, Pamela wanted a news blackout until all the pilots were in. Even though she had a way with reporters, she too had had her share of harassment. She was shouted down. Impossible. They had to have an agreed upon statement. It was empty arguing to delay the real task at hand, but they consented to the following words: "All the pilots want a chance for the latest updates on Alexis Laraway before making individual comments. As far as the race is concerned—we will continue. The contestants are of one accord."

And then they sat, brooding over their coffee.

The official cleared his throat, "Ladies, we must get this done."

They ignored him.

Slowly, with a look of resolve, Hazel stood up; they all stood up, sluggishly circled around the box. She stepped forward, said in a tense voice, "This isn't easy for any of us. By drawing out a number, we admit to something. We admit to loss and we don't want to—because we don't know anything of any certainty. We admit not knowing where Alexis is...." Her voice grew hoarse, "We admit that we have to go on in spite of her not being here, in spite of not knowing what the search party has found or not found. We know that it's taking too long, that if they were not able to spot flares during the night, Alexis may be seriously injured. It's possible that her airplane will be too damaged to stay in the race, or if reparable, will have to catch up. Whatever the outcome, I believe, I really believe that we must be strong, must persist." The snapping of a camera startled her. "...We have to go on. I believe she wants that from us. So I'll start because I need to believe in what we're doing. If you get the lead-off and are at all uncomfortable with it, I'll take it."

"Press on!" Maxie yelled from where she stood, her head hanging down but her fist jabbing the air.

"Yes!" Stevie took up the cheer though her voice was thin from her own personal discouragement. "Press on."

Everyone's hand was up. On that note of solidarity, Hazel dug her hand in the box, and quickly pulled out her number. She shivered as she opened the folded paper. "Thirteen. Go on, then." She fought back tears, holding up the paper for everyone to see, then turned away.

*She was last in the draw. Oh, would that Alexis would be able to catch up, in that fourteenth, open spot.* The only consolation for picking the last spot for the day was that she might be able to catch a bulletin before taking off.

Glancing up she saw Eleanor walking toward the tent, a look of grim determination on her face; Vera went out to meet her, handing her something. What, film? Together they turned and walked back into the field house.

Squinting against the glare of the desert morning, Hazel shuffled out towards her Travel Zephyr, using a blanket for a coat. How odd to be shivering even in the warmth. It was time to think about flying. Already those in the first half of the draw were firing up their engines. All repairs had been completed, all the airplanes ready, and the checks in process. But what a different mood from yesterday when everyone had been smiling, eager; now everyone moved through the paces mechanically—no banter, no small-talk. She watched Lila Wilczynski who had drawn the lead, take last minute instructions from Frank before he climbed into a lead escort plane. He wants to be there when she gets in, protect her from the press and any news, brooded Hazel. She would have wanted the same.

Hannah and Marsha were performing cockpit checks, next to follow.

Dressed in damp coveralls, Vera found her shortly before the lead crew was to head out. "I have the morning papers for you. The coverage is left over from yesterday. Here's the Extra."

Hazel peered at the print, scant information which she already knew. *Search on for downed pilot. Area of search widened to include the Gila Mountains. National Guard may be called in.*

"And take a look at this," Vera handed her a single sheet which she had torn out of the newspaper.

Hazel looked at the article, featuring a piece on R.Q. Taggart:—'highly respected for his pioneer work on fuel-saving devices, now being widely tested, especially on heavier, transport airplanes, he looks to an expanding company and fleet of both transport and sport airplanes.'

"No, look at the picture."

The picture showed a smiling Taggart—that same humorless smile—standing on a runway, a light-colored Rearwyn in the background.

"The wing, Hazel. The number—NC-060." Vera tapped the picture. "That's the number I saw on the blackboard."

"True," Hazel said, folding the paper into a smaller rectangle. "So that explains that. He flew ahead of us to Phoenix, probably to set up publicity for Jo—and himself, obviously. I don't think he wants to hide any motives, or why let his picture and airplane be splashed across the paper?"

"Perhaps. But note that he has recently hired a mechanic by the name of Sylvester 'Sweeney' Crawford whom he has designated as his engine man...and the Rearwyn he flies is a two-seater."

"Sweeney?" A jolt run up Hazel's spine. "Alan wanted to talk to me when we got into Phoenix. Taggart may be innocent enough, but I can't say I'm comfortable with this Sweeney. I just hope both of them clear out now. Usually sponsors meet up or accompany pilots towards the end. It does bother me that Taggart hasn't become part of supportive crew if he intends to go the whole route, unless he meant only to come this far."

They began unsheathing the Zephyr, Hazel tucking the clipping into her pocket.

"I wouldn't count on it," cautioned Vera as they folded up the tarpaulin between them and stowed it away. "Al won't be able to fill you in, well, not if

Alexis is indeed out of the race. But if there was something important, he'd tell Gus, wouldn't he?"

"Affirmative. Depends what's happening out there. Gus will come as soon as he knows there is other support. I'll feel a lot better when he gets back." Folding up her blanket, she handed it to Vera. "Know where this goes?"

"Keep it. You're going to be needing it tonight again," Vera rested a hand on Hazel's shoulder. "I can hear the C-200. That's for me today."

With a wave, Hazel let her go.

As she pulled on her mismatched gloves, she looked up in alarm, but Vera was gone from view. Her camera! Damn, it had gone down with Alexis, and Vera hadn't said a word about it.

With no news before take-off, Hazel flew her lap as always, keeping constantly vigilant of the wind, her compass and her altitude. But this time there was a difference—never before had someone else's accident weighed so heavily on her heart. She just hoped that Alexis was all right.

She thought of what Jo had said about the winds; thought of the nagging mechanical problem that seemed to baffle Al and Al. She couldn't help but wonder whether there was any way someone could have tampered with the airplane. Something subtle, not immediately noticeable. Something done back in Santa Monica? But why? Why pick on Al and Al? It was absurd.

Distracting herself from worry, she remembered how it had been on her twenty-two hour solo—how her mind had started to create a separate reality above and beyond the incessant noise of her engine, above her conscious control, something she had not found in herself on these short laps. How startled she had been when Jo appeared to port to fly the refueling plane in tandem with her, one wide circle before they began maneuvers. How exhilarating that had been—a break from the monotony. How sluggishly her body had seemed to respond at first, how cramped her legs on the rudder bar, until the excitement took over. Then came the precision of each step, and the dangerous position of Jo's plane directly above her as she and Jo connected the fuel pipes, then keeping pace as the fuel flowed from one tank to another with the help of gravity. How many times had they practiced it, talked it through, and it still felt unpredictable and dangerous.

She couldn't help being a bit angry at Alexis as well as worried about her. Flying was always unpredictable, but Alexis must have felt something going wrong before she went down. She should have turned back... Damn...I should have listened to what she and Al were worried about more carefully, thought Hazel. I should have told her to ask for a delay, even told her to withdraw. But how can one possibly know? What more could I have done?

Of course Hazel knew that during any race, some catastrophe was inevitable. Men's Derby crash-landings were common even on the first lap. But for godsake, this was the *first* women's Derby. They had to establish credibility. They had to be careful. She hated to think what the press would say about a woman who went down.

Circling the Douglas airfield, she saw that not all the planes were in, even though she had taken off last. So taking advantage of a tail wind part of the way had paid off. Neat rows of military airplanes lined the runway like some sort of honor guard. She couldn't see a crowd, just mechanics moving among the airplanes, making the scenario look ordinary. But she knew the press had to be lying in wait, news or no news about Alexis. She braced herself for landing as though the runway were an oil slick.

By the time she had taxied to her ground position, the signalman dropping his flag, so telling ground crew to push her off the runway, she could see a phalanx of race officials and military personnel waiting. Immediately sensing trouble, she jumped out of her cockpit into the center of the escort. "This way, Miss Preston." One of the officials pointed as someone else took her by the arm.

Behind them in a roped-off area, guarded by cadets, was a cluster of spectators—by the looks of the notepads and cameras—reporters. Well, there was something to be said for the timeliness of this pit-stop—military security would be more than enough, and civilian crowds kept off the field completely.

She felt the uncomfortable crunch and jostle of men all around her, the persistent calls from the reporters; she protected her face with her hands as awful words rained down upon her: "Miss Preston, Miss Preston! Will Miss Laraway's death change your mind about continuing the race? Miss Preston—"

"No questions, no questions." Barked the official.

Hazel choked convulsively at the shock of those words so casually, so callously tossed her way. How long had the reporters known? As her escort pushed their way for her, even they could not protect her from voices.

"Excuse us, gentlemen, please...." All of a sudden she was shoved past some more cadets, and through a door which was slammed shut behind her.

Before her, in what looked like the officers' lounge, sat most of her companions in this stuffy sanctuary. Some of them hunched over a conference table, a few lay on cots which had been provided, or else collapsed like Maxie in one of the leather armchairs. Her eyes were closed but puffy and red from weeping.

Hazel stood, unable to move forward, still absorbing the shock, the unreal knowledge that Alexis was dead. Her vision blurred. Stumbling forward at last, she slumped into a chair at the table. There was a bad smell about the place, a smell that replaced the fumes that still clung in her nose.

The smell—it seemed like the smell of death. What was it? She sat staring at the shiny, smooth wood of the table.

When Hazel was finally able to look up, she was met by Jo's somber grey-blue eyes, and took the cup of coffee that Jo extended to her. Strewn in front of her were newspaper Extras. She reached for one as she brushed the damp hair off her forehead. Everyone maintained a dreadful silence, a silence which indicated they had already said enough.

Only as her mind cleared did she realize that the smell was from the polished leather of the chairs, and stale, strong tobacco scent clinging to everything. This was not a place women usually came to, a foreign place which certainly offered no comfort now. Under normal circumstances she doubted the women pilots would have been led here—more likely to the cadets' dining room. No doubt they had been put here because, under the circumstances, nobody knew quite what to do with them.

The large print before her eyes blurred, her head beginning to throb with pain. There was a picture too—must have been taken first thing in the morning. Someone from the press had been there that early! They *knew.* The Travel Arctic, if that's what it was, lay in a smoldering heap, unrecognizable. But she could make out an unmistakable part of Alli's registration—05, as well as they 8 which identified the aircraft all too boldly as part of the Derby. The headline read: *Derby Pilot Killed Near Gila Bend. Body Found Near Wreck.* Another read: *Derby must be Halted.*

"Tell me, Jo, didn't she jump?" Hazel asked in a low voice, turning the papers over so she didn't have to see the picture any more.

"Yes Haze, she jumped."

"Didn't her chute open?"

"It opened."

Pushing aside the cup of coffee, Hazel sighed, more like a sob. "Then why?"

"She must have jumped too late. The chute may have tangled and opened only below a thousand feet. They found her about a hundred feet from the plane—Gus and Al did."

Hazel hid her head on her arms, sprawling over the table. She could feel Jo's arms around her, head on her shoulder.

"Listen, Haze—Lila and Eleanor have been speaking to the press every fifteen minutes. We need your help to make a statement so we can get out of here."

"Of course. I need a drink of water." Hazel sat up. "Where's Vera?"

"She's with them too. They should be back any minute."

"And what's Jenney saying?"

"She and the Board of Sponsors are behind us all the way. No one is backing out. We do have an oil man threatening to close down the stops in

Texas by personally vowing to put airplanes on the runways. His statement reads, listen to this: *The pilots of the Girls' Derby have proved that this type of challenge is too perilous for them to handle. Without our guidance they are foolhardy and incapable. It is an abomination that husbands allow their wives to partake in this event. And if these girls can't stop themselves from this folly, it is up to men like us with common sense to see to their welfare, to stop fuel supplies and shut this race down ourselves."*

Hazel snorted in disbelief. "Damn—I bet Frank and Sam will have something to say about that! How serious a threat is this guy?"

"The National Air Exchange is seeing to it, but—"

The door opened to a group of people who pushed in hurriedly—Eleanor, Vera, Lila, Frank and Sam.

"...no, absolutely not. Fifteen minutes," Eleanor was saying as she shut the door. She turned to the pilots who all sat or straightened up. "Hannah and Nancy are fine. They were both too low on fuel to make it here and are being assisted in Tuscon."

"But we refueled adequately last night," protested Hazel.

Eleanor shook her head. "Apparently Hannah had some sort of clog in her fuel line—vapor lock. And Nancy was on her reserve tank when she started out, then when switching, couldn't get the gravity feed to work. They are both new to their airplanes. I think they were nervous. They are coming along now."

"And when do we take time out for Alexis?" Maxie demanded, standing up. "It was one thing to be told the news by a reporter, quite another to hear pretentious drivel quoted in the papers while shut up in a hot room in the name of privacy."

Pamela Christy roused herself up from her cot. "Exactly. I think we should make a statement all together on the runway before we go—in our behalf and in honor of Alli. A statement strong enough to keep the reporters busy. A big gesture."

"A good point," Eleanor acknowledged, her voice hammering through the numbness they all had in common. "Frank, could you have the Monocoupe moved out of it's spot? To have the first space open would make Alli's absence clear. Sam, could you see if a microphone could be extended that far?"

The two men nodded, ducking out of the room.

'Sarah watched her husband's exit, then said, "All right, ladies, we have the meeting to ourselves. Let's resolve the scandal aspects of this race, and make sure our statements keep things in the proper perspective. I, for one, would like to remind the public that we women had to achieve the same level of flying to enter this race as men pilots do, and that we are here also because of the enlightened men in the field who know enough to support us."

There was a buzz of consent, a silence.

Hazel who had been brewing for sometime, now spoke, "I want to know why the press knew this morning, but we didn't? This really bothers me." She saw Eleanor shoot a glance at Vera, then snapped, "You both knew?"

Eleanor took a deep breath. "I received a call from Lockheed—while all of you were drawing for position. They were determined to keep a news blackout until we were underway. I agreed because I didn't want anyone to lose nerve."

Hazel turned sharply to Vera who shot her a brief, acquiescing glance. So they had both known, and Vera had not said anything as they unsheathed the Zephyr that morning. Not a word about Alexis being killed or even about her camera. She didn't know whether to be furious or grateful, either way she was unsettled. Around her she felt a similar perplexity. At length she said through her teeth, "In the future we must know *everything*, all of us. Waiting all night was absolute torture. Flying here was torture—but then to hear it from a stranger—! We could each have had the whole flight here to prepare ourselves to face them—"

"I'm sorry," murmured Eleanor, hand to her forehead, "I'm sorry...I did what I thought best...."

"Hear, hear," Maxie cut in, wiping away a sniff. "I wouldn't have been able to take off if I had known. It isn't going to be easy now."

Again there was the buzz of conflicting opinions. Hazel sat back down in her chair, exhausted—I don't want to be spared. The blunt truth is better—somehow easier to bare. Knowing the truth would make it easier to take some action.

She banged her fist on the table for attention. "I think it's important that we work as a team. We haven't even reached the halfway point! I don't want things kept under cover, I'll tell you all very bluntly—check and double-check your airplanes prior to departure. We don't know yet what caused the accident, but you know Louise here has already felt pretty peculiar about what happened with her cables. Alexis' death may not be the end of it."

A babble of alarm and denial arose.

Hazel put up a hand for silence. "Al told me there might be an element of betting going on among ground crews at any or all local stops and who knows what else. We've heard about it in the men's circuits. He was going to fill me in more, and I did not get to speak to him last night. Gus will tell me what he has to say. I just think we should be vigilant, that's all. An oil man has threatened us with cutting off supplies to stop the race. There will be others."

Maxie's deep voice cut in. "No harm in playing safe, but let's keep sensible too. We're all under stress. I don't see what harm betting can do—"

"No, she's right," said Eleanor. "We should be careful. Air races are relatively new but somehow there is always the old horse-race element. The Robertson case a few years ago is very much a reality—there were no fatalities, a lot of unexplained events, and some serious injuries. Evidence of betting was proven, and that some tampering was clearly linked. It happened—"

"Not on this circuit!" Jo bristled openly. "The idea is intolerable. Talk about keeping sensible, Maxie is right. All the press needs to hear is that we're all jittery about getting into our airplanes for fear that someone's betting on us, and might interfere! I don't believe it. Maybe in a few years, there might be serious betting, but face it, the race has to have some credibility before that happens. Right now it's a matter of public debate whether our sex is even capable of finishing a race!"

Who was it that gave half a laugh then? Hazel wheeled to see Stevie and Marsha sitting together forlornly on a couch. It was Stevie who had laughed, no, not a laugh—it had a sound too full of irony. Stevie said, "We can't function if we're to think everything that goes wrong could be foul play. I'm still in the race with all my troubles and I blame my woes on factory assembly and my own inexperience mechanically. I certainly wouldn't bet on this race if I were a gambler."

Maxie who was nearby, thumped Stevie on the shoulder. "I would! I'm betting my life on it. Alexis did for Christ's sake. We're going to make a damn good showing. Come on, kids, the odds are against us as it is. There are always some things going wrong in any race. Even if something goes wrong on the next lap, does that prove we're sabotaged on purpose? Every little thing?—No, we can't let our fear get the better of us."

Hazel slumped. Fear? Yes, I'm afraid. And suspicious. I take us seriously enough. But perhaps Eleanor is right—sometimes you keep silent out of necessity. She clenched her jaw. Why had she said anything? She sat back in her chair, knowing she looked foolish, sensing their sympathy as they excused her comments as a show of personal fear, the ordinary jitters. Well, at least she'd spoken—she could not be blamed later for having said nothing. But she certainly wasn't ever going to feel easy until she knew exactly what had happened to Alexis.

"I agree with Hazel," came a strong but husky voice. It was Louise Gibeau, standing with her hands in the pockets of her riding britches. Short, plump with bangs that almost hid her eyes, Hazel found it hard to think of her as a dare-devil. Unassuming and not at all talkative, she cleared her throat now. "I want to say that I am a precision stunt pilot, very sensitive to my aircraft. I can't afford not to be. I noticed that my wing cables were all eaten through. No, they didn't snap from strain. I have an officially confirmed report that it was acid that had eaten the cables away to the point of danger. Why? I had this passing thought that maybe someone didn't want a Canadian in this race. Then I think, how silly. But Alli was complaining about something wrong. And it makes me wonder, you know? She was also from out of the country. It makes me think that Madelyn, being from Australia should be extra careful."

"Me?" Madelyn Burnett-Eades who had been sitting behind some of the others and brushing up her hair, getting ready to put on her helmet, jumped. Voice tight, "That's absurd—"

"It can never hurt to play safe," Eleanor said firmly, motioning for everyone to calm down. "We also need to keep level-headed. Now, I suggest we compose ourselves for the press conference and our next lap. First we need to look at the map—some changes...."

At 12:50 p.m. the Derby pilots walked in a single file out of their retreat according to the draw for the next lap. How calm and determined everyone looks, Hazel thought. Her own face felt like a pasty mask covering her inner turmoil as they all walked without a word, passing reporters who hung back in surprise and deference.

Out in the pitiless sunshine, in the space vacated by the Monocoupe, they stood in a circle—some with bowed heads, others gazing stoically, boldly ahead. The local Air Exchange official called for a moment of silence. Near Hazel, someone was still weeping—trying to hold back. She did not look to see. It wasn't Max. Directly opposite from her, Hazel could see Stevie, gaunt and pale with that shock of dark hair covering one eye; she was holding Marsha's hand. Marsha looked sickly too—deep blue circles under her eyes—and even though she was one position away from Stevie in the draw, she had exchanged places with Madelyn in the circle. Hazel remembered Alli's last words to her, "Do give some words of encouragement to Marsha, won't you?"

Instinctively, Hazel closed her eyes and reached out to clasp her neighbor's hand—not Jo's; it was Pamela who stood next to her and squeezed her hand back. How odd—a woman she had hardly spoken two words to and loved to ridicule.

Eleanor took over the microphone, not knowing or caring that her words were being carried on radio stations across the country live and unquavering: "We, the pilots of the First National Women's Air Derby, take our places on this airfield in Douglas, Texas, to acknowledge the passing of one of our own. At this moment two other pilots are tending to mechanical problems elsewhere, so they cannot be with us. They are doing the job of every contestant—running a race thoroughly by taking care of matters within their control. In every race there is a margin for error: mechanical, human and due to the elements. Right now, we don't know what factors played a part in Alexis Laraway's accident. But each of us here can fully appreciate that Alexis did her part with dedication and precaution, just as she would want us to do ours. She was like a warm wind from Alaska, bringing friendship and good faith to our common purpose. In a passing comment she made to me before we began this race, she likened our flight to that of the migratory wild geese, invisibly in formation, yet unified. This is what we intend to continue doing. It's in our blood now; you might even say, instinctive. We owe her that much—"

She stopped there abruptly, folded up her notes and stuck them in her chest pocket. The race official immediately declared that the draw was on. A moment of disorganized silence followed as the women began to move about, still in a daze. Mostly, they took to clasping each other in small groups, then moving to others, and on to their airplanes. Hazel found herself caught up in the momentum, hugging her fellow pilots. It was time to regain strength.

"Tell the press to keep away," Maxie's voiced shouted above them all, her hands waving in the face of a cameraman. "No comment, no comment, or I'll personally smash in some faces."

"Is that a threat?" A male voice taunted. Ground crew and cadets swept in to keep everyone but official personnel away. And almost like a stroke of luck, the first of the late escort planes circled for landing.

Hazel let out a sigh of relief; the last thing she wanted to see was Maxie engaged in a fracas with the press. Talk about distress!

Hope you're up there Gus. I could sure use you, she thought as she watched. It was indeed Gus—she could see the number, C-175. His landing caused enough of a commotion that the pilots could retreat to the safety of the airplanes and pre-flight checks. Hazel took the chance to avoid both Jo and Vera, running up to meet the airplane as it taxied in and stopped. Opening up the hatch, a bleary-eyed Gus leaned out of the cockpit, his usually kind and open face giving her a worn smile.

"Have you had any rest at all, Gus?" She asked as he jumped down.

"A bit." He said, though it was obvious he hadn't shaved.

"Do you think you can go with lead escort? I sure could use you running interference up ahead."

He nodded. "As long as I can take a back seat."

That was a telling comment. Almost anyone would rather pilot or navigate than sit in the cramped back seat.

"Tell me, Gus. Can you tell me? We have learned next to nothing from the papers."

He put an arm around her shoulder, as much for support as to offer condolence. "We found the crash site at sundown. Had to land on a road, then hike in. Pretty rocky going in the dark—lots of scrub. There was a bit of glow left from the fuselage to guide us, but the plane had obviously gone up pretty fast after crashing. Al went mad—hoping she wasn't in it. That's what we thought at first—that she had been.... But we found no evidence of a body and that gave some hope. We put flares out. I sent the Lockheed fellow to fly back to Yuma and give word of our position to company representatives only. Meanwhile the rest of us fanned out to see where she may have jumped, calling her name, looking for a sign. Al saw the white of the parachute...."

Overwrought he stopped; she could feel his weight upon her. He began to sob, his chest heaving, stuttered, "Al—Al held her and rocked her like a baby. Man, I've never seen anything like it." He composed himself, groaned as he stretched and turned his face into the fuselage, leaning with his hands up, his head down. She rubbed his back gently, gulping back her own tears.

Vivid images flashed in her mind, shaking her. Her brother Dewey's racing car smashing into a retaining wall, splitting apart as flames exploded. She remembered how long it took to run the half mile towards him, when she knew it was already too late. People said she screamed and was uncontrollable—if they hadn't held her down she would have leapt into the flames to retrieve him.

"Too late," she whispered. That's what they had said to her over and over. Too late. He's gone now. She remembered driving to his funeral, how she saw farmers cutting hay in the fields. How can they cut hay when my brother has died, she had thought. How can we go on with this race? she thought now. Alli is really gone.

She could feel the presence of others coming up to them and turned. It was the lead escort crew, somber and respectful, coming to refuel and ready the plane. Vera was with them.

"He's all right," Hazel said quickly. "Vera, I'd like him to go ahead, and have you switch to rear escort."

"Really?" Vera's face was drawn as though she thoroughly understood that they needed to talk, to mend things between them, but there wasn't time. " I'm less spent than he is. Can't I handle the press when we get in?"

Hazel waved a hand impatiently. "Then find someone in the C-200 to trade with you, if you want. I *need* Gus in ahead of me."

Vera eyes flashed but her expression remained tight. "I will." She wheeled around to leave; Hazel's hand stayed her. "I'm fully aware that you have lost your camera in this, I...."

Vera smiled slightly, one corner of her mouth, the lower lip trembling. Hazel wanted to grab her, to hold her, to crush her, to tear away those greasy coveralls and find those beautiful shoulders. The realization stunned her. Vera gently removed her hand, holding it for a moment. "Shh. It is...a loss— a cumbersome thing, sentimental but nor irreplaceable...Alexis was kind.... Talk to Gus. I'd like to be ahead with him. Whatever he has to say—I want to know. It may have been premature to sound an alarm, but you did right by us all."

Gus turned to them, his face the way Hazel was used to—a man unruf-fled. With a flinch to her jaw, Hazel nodded as Vera let go of her hand quickly, and darted off.

"You want to know about the betting." He stated, pulling out a log book with the list of checks. Pencil between his lips, he began the routine, port side. He shot a question about the refueling to the mechanics on the other side of the C-175, then proceeded to make a tour around the plane. Hazel followed him, glancing at her own, waiting Zephyr.

"I just want to know if it's serious, Gus?" she said hurriedly.

"Don't know. Al thinks they do gamble late at night over card games—but that's how it's done or else at seedy bars, common enough on the men's circuit. No place I go, I'm afraid. I'm sorry I'm not a gambling man, Pres-ton—I'd stand out like a sore thumb if I tried. Al wanted to try and join a game, find out who the bookie was, how it worked—"

"But what does he think...about Alli's airplane?"

"He's baffled." Gus stopped at the tail rudder, inspecting the mechanism.

"Could someone have...tampered with it?"

"Al says he was with the airplane pretty constantly. We both slept in the hangars at night. Doesn't mean someone couldn't prowl, but Al thought by Yuma he had everything right. And both of them were with the plane then." Gus shrugged, at a loss.

"Well, no—they both came in for food."

He looked at her sharply, thinking. "How long?"

"Fifteen minutes...maybe"

"If Sweeney had been there, I might wonder." Gus didn't look up from his task now as he scribbled in the ledger.

Suggesting money, Hazel rubbed fingers and thumb together in front of his eyes.

"He paid someone—?" He looked skeptical, but didn't discount it.

"Do you know that Tag has hired Sweeney as his engine specialist? It's right in the papers." She pulled out the clipping and handed it to him.

Gus stopped in disbelief. "He's nothing but a hack! Tag can't be in his right mind." He pocketed the clipping.

"Well," Hazel shuffled her feet, feeling awkward, "I worry. I worry why Sweeney got so hot under the collar at Alan. I worry why Sweeney wanted to keep going east—"

"Ah, that is worrisome...Has Tag been about?"

"He was in Phoenix ahead of us."

"I'd better get this contraption rolling. Who's piloting? Where's Frank?"

"Seeing to Lila. She has lead—"

He pushed past her. "I don't want to see either Sweeney or Taggart up ahead, not on this circuit. If they have hooked up, I don't think they're up to any good."

A flood of relief hit Hazel—she wasn't alone in her point of view, but then, she also knew Gus simply had no use for either man. "They're not dangerous to us really, are they?"

He looked at her meaningfully, scratching his bristly chin. "Sweeney is a user. He'll use any opportunity for his own ends. It's one thing to be using other guys when they're playing the same way, but not here, now...? I think in Tag, he's got somebody just like himself. They could be using the race for a betting scam, creating favorites by eliminating competition. Alli was flying a Beech, yet she came in as an independent...you follow me?—easy target. For now, I'll assume she had an accident, but I want to find out why those two are flying ahead. Now I know Sweeney wanted to get back on escort with us, but Tag never took us up on his seat! Why the hell not, I want to know. I mean, what's he up to? Look, I have to be off in five minutes." He shouted louder, "Frank Wilczynski! We're firing up, old man."

Frank came running towards the airplane, pulling on his jacket, 'thumbs up' to Lila who already sat in her cockpit, ready. He had the map and coordinates, called out, "Hey Gus—we're to El Paso. Thunderstorms to the east so we can't go to Pecos!"

Gus leaped up into the pilot's seat. Hazel watched, worried.

"I'm not tired anymore." He growled in answer. "Now get to your checks, Preston."

She darted backwards as he opened throttle and the others crammed in, pulling the hatch closed.

Within moments they were underway, roaring down the runway.

There was something unnerving about his take-off, something fierce, almost reckless, totally unlike Gus, and it made her swear under her breath.

"Aircraft approaching." A voice warned through a megaphone. Lila had to wait behind the readied C-200; Hannah was coming in. On the horizon to the west came another airplane—Nancy.

*Douglas to El Paso*

With the threat of thunderstorms moving in and the uncertainty about stops in Texas, the pilots flew northeast again, crossing the Continental Divide with Mt. Riley, at six thousand feet, a point of reference. Keeping that to the north while following the railroad to starboard, the course then lay towards the Rio Grande. It seemed like a miracle when everyone arrived in El Paso without a hitch.

Hazel landed to find the field house being draped in black. "I hadn't known that was customary," she said upon finding Gus as she climbed out of the cockpit. "Is that thanks to the local Exchange or the Board?"

"Don't get all choked up," warned Gus. "Compliments of Mr. Blaine,

70

the oilman who'd love to close this race down, thought he'd get all you contestants too overwrought to carry on or something. Pure publicity and self-serving. He doesn't have the clout he'd like to stop fuel supplies, but he's full of wind, and the newsmen are all taken by it."

"He's here?" Hazel bristled.

Gus sounded weary as he spoke, "No, I'm afraid he's as elusive as Tag. Maybe we'll be lucky enough to have a show-down in Fort Worth. Anyway, it's not being put up, it's being taken down. Maxie got all in a furor and began ripping it down herself, saying she wouldn't stand for pretenses. The newsmen have been having a field day with that too."

"Good for Max," Hazel cheered. "And how is everyone else about it?"

"All in agreement so far. Late-comers won't even have to be bothered with it." Gus smiled then. "Eleanor has made a statement."

By dusk the thunder clouds rattled over the airfield, but all the aircraft were safe on the ground and sheathed. In an appropriate and unspoken gesture to Alexis, Lila had left the first parking place open. After supper Hazel stood in that gap watching the dramatic movement of color in the sky. She was waiting—she knew she was waiting—for one more pilot to fly in. It was as though she could hear a sound, just barely, the drone of an airplane that must, within moments, be visible—white and burnished red.

The sky flashed with deep reds against the storm clouds in the distance. For a moment she felt as though she had moved to a place beyond pain and time.

Time, yes. She had flown swiftly and *made* time this day, slicing her margins to take a slight, tenuous lead. How was that possible when the flight had weighed upon her like an eternity? And with the threat of bad weather, she had been very aware of the parachute curled against her spine.

In the twilight she heard the crunch of footsteps behind her and swung around expecting to find Vera. "Jo!—I thought you'd have gone to one of the guest homes by now...."

Jo grumbled, "Don't you wonder that Texas has chicken ranches instead of steer? I can't believe every dinner we get is chicken!"

She put an arm around Jo and a perfunctory kiss to her forehead. "But your belly's full. And it was in a different form again. A Spanish chef, Maxie said—she says Mexican cooking has yet to be appreciated in this country—refreshingly spicy. I didn't mind crying one bit. It did us a world of good." She then decided on a mild apology for taking the lead. "I didn't expect to make such headway today. The thing was though, all I could think about was getting away from Douglas. Fast."

Jo responded stiffly. "I have female complaints today. Remember I told you I felt so heavy? Odd thing is, since the news about Alli, my bleeding has

71

stopped just like that—" She snapped her fingers—"I'm a wreck and need a good night's sleep."

"But your engine ran well, didn't it? You kept your speed?"

"Yes, but with the storms moving in, I had to rely on other tactics. In fact, that is what Tag has been consulting with me on. I just got off the telephone. I am beginning to see his method even though he didn't tell me. He flies ahead, then relays weather conditions and the best route, while testing the limits of his engine, leaves me orders for what to check...."

Hazel balked. "He flies ahead as a tactic? How much ahead of us?"

"Yes, by at least half a day." Jo became defensive, moving away as they walked down the line of airplanes. "It's not against regulations—"

Hazel hit her fist against her head. "Oh, don't give me that line again. Yes, yes, too bad *we* didn't think of it—a scout sent ahead, providing last minute instructions." She jostled Jo in a friendly way to keep the conversation going. She very badly wanted it to continue.

"No one's saying you can't put it into effect! Haze, this isn't an Air Tour, this is a race. We're making sales, we're on the edge—" her voice dropped as though she had suddenly remembered Alli, then spoke quickly, "Anyway Tag's instructions are specific to my Cygnus-311. He told me to ease up this lap."

"Will he do engine checks personally then?"

"In Fort Worth. He also wants me to have a mechanic from there on, now that Al's seat is open. He's petitioning the Board. Lockheed was going to put an extra Crewman in, but he says there should be a seat open for him—"

"And he wants to put in Sweeney Crawford?" They had come up to Madelyn's Bullett where Hazel grabbed the propeller, unconsciously testing for any play in the tension; it was tight.

"Exactly." Jo stopped. "How do you know?"

"I read the article on Tag," Hazel shrugged, letting go of the propeller. "The rest is assumption. I don't see how it will be accepted. Sweeney was asked to leave the circuit."

"He wasn't expelled!" Oh boy—Hazel could hear Tag's words coming out of Jo's mouth. "He was relieved by Maxie because they couldn't get along, and there were no seats for Tag's consideration later because you had put Vera Davis in very tidily even though he should have had priority."

"Wait a minute. He could have had the seat. He didn't take Sweeney on until after the race started. I don't see how he can start complaining now." Hazel didn't like it, not at all. She would have to call Gladys Jenney and keep Sweeney off. She was about to announce that Sweeney was nothing but a hack—but she didn't want to get into a shouting match with Jo. It was nothing she had ever done before. Besides, what did she know about Sweeney—not enough. She looked at Jo squarely. "I can't stop Sweeney from checking your engine, but I don't want him as part of the escort, and will speak to that effect."

"You what? You have no right!" Jo stormed. "There's no reason—"

"You don't think the fact that he has no use for women is a reason? I want a totally supportive escort."

"I don't care what he thinks about me or us—he likes airplanes and he's working for Tag who thinks he is a good mechanic. Anyway, if we cared about male attitude we wouldn't be flying. If you petition Gladys, I shall protest—I have to. Anyway, I think I can deal with him better than Maxie could."

"Do you?" Hazel said dryly, but she was furious. Jo was the one who was supposed to care about doing things right, a stickler for safety. Hazel felt she no longer knew this woman. Maybe she had never really known her. How could she talk so casually about Al's place being open? She was about to begin a lecture on betting, and that Jo had no reason to trust Sweeney an inch— and perhaps say much too much, when Jo interrupted.

"Look, I came here to fetch you away from this blasted airfield. You must get away. There is life beyond this, you know. Now, a wonderful Mrs. Cannon is waiting to take us to her home. You need to get some rest, some perspective, for Christ's sake. Besides, you could use a good bath—you smell to high heaven! We can do a laundry too."

Hazel had always been eager to go with Jo anywhere, and Jo always the reluctant one, setting the terms. Now, too suddenly, Jo seemed to be pursuing her! How odd that Jo's coaxing did not disarm her as it always had in the past. "I'm not going. All right? We'd end up in separate bedrooms again. I'm going to stay here like the crew. They give us buckets of water to wash with. That's the kind of bathing I grew up with, and it will suit me just fine now. I'm too...too rattled to go off and be someone's house guest. I want to be able to breathe. And I don't think you and I should keep company right now." The finality in her voice startled even herself, as did the realization that Vera would be there along with the crew.

Jo drew away coldly. "Fine, suit yourself. Just keep out of my business too. Good night."

Hazel said nothing as she watched Jo retreat towards the buildings of the airfield, angry at herself now for alienating Jo further when she should be gathering her into confidence. If her hunches were right about Taggart and Sweeney, Jo was in trouble too. And, after all, having Sweeney openly on escort might not be such a bad development. It might actually be better to have him in view. And perhaps she should send an advance escort, one lap ahead too, just like Tag was doing. Keep up with them.

As for Jo's insensitivity—how could she actually have said, 'Now that Al's seat is open,' so coolly? Damn. Hazel hurried towards her own Zephyr, intending to set up camp, Jo's words repeating in her mind. Where was Vera? Was it possible the Arctic had been tampered with just to get Al's seat? She couldn't quite bear it. She wanted to talk to Al now—badly. Was Alli's crash more than a simple accident? Alli's death may not have been intended, but what if her plane was meant to fail? And why? Why the Travel Arctic? No, no, not just to get Al's seat. There were other ways to get a new seat assignment. No, that didn't make sense. Yes, the betting. It had to be the *betting?*

In wartime 'dog-fighting' the operative method was sneak attacks from behind. In the Robertson article, Eleanor had explained that on the circuit, 'dog-fighting' meant sneak attacks from behind too; pilot and crew sabotaged competitors under cover of darkness or in unguarded moments, to up the ante in betting, or to assure an outcome. Hazel's jaw flexed as she tried to think it through. The Travel Arctic was a Beech Aircraft, one of three including Hannah and herself. As far as other Wright engines went—there were Stevie and Nancy's. Marsha with her Spartan and Sarah Morris-Newton's Taperwing used Beech parts. Was the Arctic an arbitrary target?—eliminate some of the competition? What about Lockeed? Eleanor's Vega, yes, but Madelyn, Pamela and Lila all used parts and services supplied by Lockheed. Lousie Gibeau used neither company, nor did Maxie. Nor did Jo; Tag bought parts independently of either company. Three fliers out of the lot had absolutely no company connection, a definite minority.

*Why Al and Al?* Had Sweeney simply thought Alan was a sucker? Or because Al didn't help him get a seat? Why would Sweeney have even approached Al, if Tag had already hired him? Obviously, it was later that Tag took him on. Or was it because Sweeney had found himself bumped unexpectedly that Tag had started this business of flying ahead? Why did Gus distrust Sweeney so, realizing that any and all of the men on escort or grounds crews had a history of one sort or another together, while the women pilots flew in all innocence. What did she know about personal enmities when she'd only had her first glimpse from Gus.

Her thoughts swirling in confused speculation, Hazel arrived at her aircraft to see that a ground cloth had already been put down under the starboard wing—the side with a view to the rest of the planes, all down the runway, hangars lit up at the end. She would have preferred the side facing away from everything, but that wasn't the purpose, after all. Blankets, secured with rope to the wing and landing struts, provided a wind break. An unlit lamp sat on the ground well out of the way of the wing, a box of matches beside it. Vera had obviously wanted everything in order. Hazel had to commend her—this woman was serious about security. Fetching the blanket from her fuselage locker, she went to sit in the make-shift tent, lighting the lamp. Perhaps Vera would return from wherever she was at the sight of the beacon. Where was she? After all of the hubbub and swarm of people to placate at dinner, after all the condolences given and received, the telegrams read or sent off, she was glad for the prospect of finding time with Vera—alone.

Alone? Had she actually thought that? Of course, she wanted to figure out what to do.... Hazel drew back from her need for Vera's presence. She had never wanted anyone but Jo. How was it possible now—?

"There you are!" Vera arrived, the glow of a cigarette preceding the dark form of her body. She crunched the end out underfoot before coming closer.

Hazel jumped up, flushing hotly, as though Vera might discover her naked thoughts. Vera came up to her, the lines of her face softened in the suggestive lamplight, her green eyes glowing. Standing stiffly, Hazel could not suppress the foolish grin that came to her lips.

Vera raised an eyebrow. "That's the first I have seen you smile today."

Hazel muttered, suddenly somber, "It's been a hard day." She found herself backing against the Zephyr's fuselage, bumping the back of her head.

"You and that knot in your jaw," Vera approached her, fingertips caressing Hazel's jawbone.

How stiff Hazel felt, how wooden with restraint, all her loyalty to Jo, all her better judgment reining her in, while she wanted to melt into Vera.

"Hazel—come rest with me."

"I can't—I'm not tired." Hazel put a hand up to stop Vera from coming any closer than the few inches that were left between them.

"Oh," Vera stepped back, "Of course. Oh please, don't mistake my intentions—I'm sorry. I just want to rest with you and keep watch—to be your comrade in arms. Look, I know you belong to someone else. Belong—it's not the way I usually talk, but it's to the point isn't it? I won't deny that your friendship with me isn't important—I couldn't bear to destroy that. I won't admit that I'm terrifically keen on you; we could call a truce on that. You are so shy, so correct—"

"Vera, I'm not—I'm not shy or correct." Hazel caught her by the shoulder, turning her. She didn't care to hold back her passion, in fact, it broke loose in spite of herself. Like the Zephyr seeking out and throwing itself onto the winds, she let herself go now, finding Vera's mouth with her lips.

Vera pushed her gently down to the ground. Hazel could feel those hands, stronger than she imagined, coursing along her clothes in search of buttons, of loose, untucked places. Vera's hands slipped under her shirt, the warmth coming to touch her skin. With urgency, Hazel undid the top of those blasted coveralls, her lips seeking the beautiful chest, then again Vera's mouth, hands fumbling until she squeezed the yet hidden breasts. Ah, what breasts—full, magnificent—

Vera's hands had found Hazel's stomach and hips. What strength Vera gave her—so much that Hazel was baffled by it. In such enveloping, such demanding strength, her body was pulled closer. And then Vera was on top

75

of her, pressing through their clothes against her, hips pushing. Land Amighty—Hazel gasped in surprise, her mouth smothered as Vera's tongue probed to play with her own—I'm supposed to be on top. Aren't I?

Pushing Hazel gently further into the corner of their lean-to, Vera's hands stroked her hips, fingers finding a way beneath undergarments.

"I want you," said Vera into her ear, biting it. "If it's only tonight, I don't care. I want you. Let me inside you."

"I don't care either." In jubilant release, Hazel loosened her pants, glancing around to make sure no one was nearby. She felt as though she were swollen to bursting between her thighs, wanting Vera to find her there with those sinewy fingers, a hand full of them. Vera's pubic bone pressed against hers in rhythm, building rhythm.

"I want my mouth on you, Hazel—"

Here? Right out under a wing on the airfield? It was sheer craziness. How she wanted it—Vera! As if anticipating, Vera's mouth began to move down Hazel's body, her lips touching, finding Hazel's tingling nipples. Already Vera's fingers dipped into Hazel, encouraging complete desire, lips and tongue nipping and licking her taut stomach; Hazel could only bear it because she knew she would yield soon, melt into this woman's passion. How she wanted—

A noise stopped them. Someone in a motorcar roared onto the airfield, bright head lamps pointing directly at the lean-to, the auto coming full speed, weaving, careening.

The two women froze for a long second in mid-groan before Vera threw a blanket over Hazel; crouched. "Watch out!"

Rallying, they rolled under the airplane to the other side, ready to run, Hazel pulling her pants, like a potato sack, up to her waist. She hardly had time to fathom that the vehicle would crash into the Zephyr's wing, when at the last moment, the car spun away, tires screeching to a halt.

"Ha-ha! I knew I'd find ya!" Came a loud, boisterous voice amid curses and kicks as the driver climbed out of the open seat. "How did you like that ground loop?"

"Yeah, but did she know what she'd find us doing?" Vera moaned under her breath.

"Max! You mucking-dame-rag you—you scared us out of our wits!" Hazel called to her, still tucking in her shirt as she and Vera walked round the Zephyr's tail.

"Yeah? You weren't asleep were ya? You weren't—!" Maxie stopped there and laughed from behind the blinding lamps.

"Ma-xie," Hazel chided, thankful for the darkness.

"Hey, Preston. I've got a joke for ya. What crosses the airfield to get to the other side?"

"I don't know. Come on, turn those things out."

"A chicken dinner!" Maxie roared with laughter, managing to turn off the lights as she stumbled about, then ambled unsteadily towards the lean-to. "Hey, wanna arm-wrestle, Preston? C'mon, c'mon, I need some action. Feel my muscles, c'mon, feel my muscles. We'll use the hood here, it's even warm—"

"Max, not that. You know I'm no match for you. How did you know I was here?"

"Jo, my dear, Jo, who is so blue, blue without you."

Hazel could hear Vera suck in a breath. "She *is not*, Max—"

"Oh please, please don't act guilty. Hey, when I found out you were camping here, I knew I couldn't stay in a nice clean house. I thought I'd make our presence known on this filthy field. Nice people, nice people though—let me borrow their car to come and check on things. Overcompensating for our grief, perhaps? Well, I wasn't going to refuse."

"What else didn't she refuse?" Vera whispered.

"C'mon, Preston, feel my muscle, feel my muscle!"

"Maxie, you're drunk." Hazel walked out to her, took her by the arm. "I feel it, I feel it, hard as a rock always."

"Yeah," drawled Maxie, her voice like smoke, a fierce gleam in her eye. She pulled out a flask from her pocket.

Hazel took it from her, removed the cap for a sniff. "Gin. Where did you get hold of this stuff?"

"Please, don't ask...I had to have some. How do these damn idiots expect us to survive this race, especially at a time like this? Sometimes you have to give a little, ya know? Alli was my friend." The last words were uttered with a deep sob of despair.

"I know." Hazel pulled Maxie close, hugged her gently as she kissed her damp forehead, leading her to sit down under the wing. "Your secret is safe with us, hon. All our secrets are safe."

"Have some gin." Maxie wiped the tears from her eyes.

A flash of lightning startled them all; in the bright flash, Hazel saw the look of conspiracy on Vera's face. Thunder boomed in the darkness which followed, and then the rain began spattering. Hazel uncapped the flask. "Then I shall offer a toast to Alli. One good, stiff belt." Yelled into the ear-splitting crack of thunder, "Goodspeed, Alli!" Throwing her head back she took a big gulp, then passed the flask to Vera.

The rain fell, warm. Hazel ran out into it to pull the car's cover over its open seats. Head tilted to the sky, she laughed, a frenzied, desperate laugh while Maxie fell, passed out, in the lean-to. Vera covered her, tucked her in; sat huddled in a blanket, shivering.

Hazel came back for cover, feeling too sober for the gulp of gin she had swallowed and the hot passion she had let out. Everything about the day hit her as she looked down at Maxie, gently rubbing her friend's back. "I suppose we ought to get some rest too."

On the other side of Maxie to her left, Vera nodded. The harsh reality of the day came back to haunt them as they each sat in silence, the drizzle falling, hemming them in their miserable shelter.

"I'll keep watch, Hazel. Sleep a bit." Vera said finally, leaning across Maxie to grasp Hazel's hand.

"All right—but only if you stay close." Hazel returned the squeeze.

"I'm not going anywhere." Vera started to retract her hand, but Hazel wouldn't let go. Lying down she kept Vera's hand on her breast, and allowed herself to fall into a ragged sleep, trying not to think about Jo.

*We may not be visibly in formation but to me, I see us like a flock of wild geese migrating together. If someone takes the lead, it's to break the wind! (laughter)*

Alexis Laraway        *—from a Journalist's Notebook, E.W.*

# 6.

*El Paso to Pecos*

Early in the morning Vera elected to drive Maxie's borrowed car back to its owners, leaving Hazel with buckets of water and coffee to rouse Maxie. As Vera climbed in the driver's seat, Hazel was beside her on the running board. With slanted eyes still sleepy, Vera said with urgency, "Maybe it was best that Maxie was chaperone lying there between us, before we lost our heads entirely. We can still call it quits and not regret anything."

Hazel bent to take Vera's hand in her own, fingers entwining. "I don't want to call it quits. Vera—when we fly, most decisions are impulsive, for better or worse. I have to trust myself to make the right decision in these moments. Do you see?"

"I might, except that I must warn you...this race is a short term affair, a set-up that people leave behind when it's done, going back to their real lives. And worse ...Alli's gone; we are reeling from that shock. I know—some of us know, how people die flying. Believe me, I've seen it. And every time I walked out on a wing...you're on the edge of eternity, which way will you fall...back into life for a while? How can we ever trust any feelings when we hang in such a balance? Look, if Jo were not in your heart, we could be as giddy as we want. But whatever you do now, you'll lose something. I already know...how I will feel when you turn away from me."

"You know the only reason I can stand the race now is because of you," Hazel spoke hotly, her grip tightening around Vera's hand. "We can sort ourselves out when the race is said and done."

"An eternity till then?" Vera's face softened with affection but she looked down at their hands sadly. "I know that Jo might need you any moment, and then I'll become the villain."

"Please don't—" Hazel's jaw was set. "Whenever I can find the moment, I want to be with you. With Jo I feel constantly tethered. With you I feel the sky...."

"Like flying in open cockpit?" Vera laughed easily then, undoing Hazel's fingers from her own. She sat back with her hands gripping the steering wheel. "I certainly hope that feeling comes to you often, because I'll be there." She looked away. "As if I could do anything different." She looked up and smiled. "Come on, I see Maxie sitting up. Let me leave so I can be back."

"Yes, get back soon—I'd really like Gus to get an advance escort to catch up with Tag."

"Oh, don't fret; he'll be waiting in Fort Worth quite openly for engine checks, remember? The point is to keep track of him. And as long as we are watching the airplanes, there's nothing he can do. I'm not going to leave the field—I'll be everywhere with my camera. Now off you go."

Letting Vera start the engine, Hazel stepped off the running board. Spying a folded newspaper on the back seat, she took it at the last moment before Vera sped off. Yesterday evening's paper. No wonder Maxie had needed her drink—Alexis Laraway's stark obituary was surrounded, no, squashed almost into insignificance, by articles on the race, pro and con. Damn that Mr. Blaine rattling on and on: *It was a mistake to ever allow ladies behind the steering wheel of the automobile, must we now be menaced by them in the air as well?* Why on earth did the papers bother with him? No wonder Eleanor had to bend over backwards to create positive coverage, when this kind of stupidity got paraded across the pages in an instant.

But what was this, then? Hazel refolded the paper to get a better look: Maximillian Schulz, on behalf of the Board of Sponsors, rebutting the oil man—obviously before news of Maxie tearing down the black ribbons!—and getting some bold type to say it:

**Ladies Derby Will Continue**...*It's about time Mr. Blaine met these young ladies; a pluckier, more determined bunch he'll never be more fortunate to know. How can he so quickly forget that our own mothers came out west in covered wagons? Did they menace the trails when they took up the reins or helped till the land?*

Hazel had only met Granddaddy Schulz with his unruly white hair, his large, almost overbearing presence, as the race was being organized . He was a man used to getting his way—would not tolerate obstacles or hindrance to his decisions.

"Hey Max," Hazel greeted her friend, chuckling, "how good of your granddaddy to come to our support! I've just been reading—"

Maxie groaned, hand to her head, "Please, spare me; it'll give me a headache."

Great popcorn clouds loomed like mountains above the haze to the east. Even though they looked majestic and fixed, they were moved by winds across the designated route. The weather caused an hour delay before Pamela could lead the draw in her red Bellanca.

The course would skirt the northern edge of the Diablo plateau and the southern end of the Sacramento Mountains, on towards the Pecos River. The pilots would leave behind the Rio Grande, with Pecos a short hop away, then bee-line for Fort Worth. Midland was also offered as a brief check-in, but lagtime would be kept to the minimum. As soon as the bulk of the draw was in, the pilot in line would proceed towards a late lunch in Abilene.

Hazel was in fourth spot this time, behind Eleanor; then came Nancy who was solidly part of the pack now. In fifth came Madelyn, then Maxie. She would not be able to keep track of Jo who came near the end. The consolation was that they could keep out of each other's way; Hazel needed that.

Now pulling on Jo's tight, left glove made Hazel's hand ache. Though I have no regrets, no regrets, she tried to convince herself. But it would be hard to look Jo in the eye now. Not just because of Vera. What if they did expose Sweeney or Tag or both? What if they actually were dogfighting or worse and had been involved in Alli's crash? She didn't want to think about what that would mean for Jo who had been ignoring all the warnings. After all, Jo was as capable as anyone of seeing what these men were. And Jo was the one who had defined this as rivalry between the two of them—had traded gloves!

When Hazel found Pecos it was just as it had been described, a strip of desert cut in the mesquite. A very narrow strip at that, but long enough. Tents were pitched neatly to one side for shelter but in the sun; they'd be like ovens. The only thing she didn't like about what she saw in Pecos were all the motorcars. People had come for miles around to park their autos haphazardly along the runway while they watched. Hazel could see the escort Beech C-200, standing ready to assist; the C-175 took off just before she came in.

She landed her craft, finding relief in the final flare-out of her landing. Again she had made good time, had her pace. It would be good enough. All she had to do was keep it steady and let Jo try all she wanted to keep up.

The usual press occupied a tent, waiting, pens poised as each pilot came in. Could Hazel detect disappointment on their faces—this time no major disaster. Wasn't it enough that Nancy provided them with a ground-loop and minor damage?

It was Maxie who provided an event for them. Already waiting for take-off, goggles up and sitting in the cockpit of her Zephyr, Hazel watched Maxie ever so gently glide in on the wind. She waited for the Curtiss-Robin to land. As the wheels touched the runway, Hazel caught a movement to the side. How could it be?—a motorcar was driving at an angle into the field—much too close! There was no way Maxie could see him, her peripheral visibility cut by both the huge engine casing and her starboard wing. Couldn't the driver see the airplane coming in? It was his responsibility—couldn't he see? Why, he'd have his head sliced off!

Frantically, Hazel unswaddled herself and stood up in her cockpit, yelling to ground crew who swept along the runway waving madly at the car. They leapt away just as suddenly as the machines got too close, much too close.

Too late. The tip of Maxie's starboard wing crumpled against the rear of the car, the impact forcing her to spin almost completely around. The fuselage listed to port so that the remaining wing scraped along the ground.

"Miss Mack," sobbed Hazel, leaping down, running like others to crowd around—officials, reporters, mechanics and onlookers.

Maxie stood up in her cockpit, parachute and helmet still on, looking stupefied but unhurt. She gazed down upon her beloved 'Mackie,' all folded up, and then at the deeply ripped soft-top of the Ford below her.

"Max, Max. Come with me," Hazel commanded, holding an arm out .

"Clear the runway, clear the runway," called the grounds foreman.

Maxie clambered down, but marched instead towards the motor car, yelling, "That filthy ass better not be hurt 'cause I'm going to smash his face in—" She stopped abruptly. "Hey, where's the goddam driver? There's no goddam driver." Frantically, she began to look on the other side, as if sure he was trying to get away.

Dumbfounded, Hazel could also see there was no one. A quick glance told her that the car had rolled over relatively flat ground but coming off higher ground, guessing that it must have been left in neutral with the motor running until it stalled out. There were other cars lined up in that direction, curious people coming forward, but no one came to claim the car.

Someone yelled, "Where's the owner of the vehicle?"

A nervous official, reporters at his heels, came up to her, panting "What happened here?"

"A runaway motorcar, that's what," Maxie bellowed. "There's no goddam driver!"

"There will be no swearing, no swearing, Miss Schulz. This is a lady's race."

"Oh, for godsake," muttered Hazel, trying to pry Maxie away. But Maxie was not to be moved. She stood staunchly with her feet apart, hands on her hips, eyes blazing so that Hazel moved back a step or two, and braced herself.

"You've got to be kid—" Maxie began and then stopped short as she spied the reporters. Suddenly, turning on her heel, she pulled off her helmet and gloves, walking away without another word. Hazel could only pad after her at a quick pace.

"The only reporter I'm talking to is Eleanor. Tell 'em that!" Maxie growled under her breath. "And if I swear, it's damn well off the record!"

"She's already on to the next stop!"

"I want her here now. I could've been killed. Where the hell is ground security?" Maxie stopped without warning, grabbed Hazel's collar as if to lift her off the ground. "Why me, Preston? Why *me*? What's going on? It was done on purpose!—I'm sorry, I guess I never really took it all seriously before...I bet it had to do with my granddaddy's sweet ol' article, didn't it? Didn't it? Or because I tore down the ribbons?"

"Max—" Hazel knew it was impossible to console her. For Maxie the race was over; it just hadn't quite occurred to her, hadn't percolated through yet, wrapped up as she was in protective shock.

Maxie turned to her, eye blazing with something other than rage. "Odd thing. Back there...when ya touched me on the shoulder...I turned—I thought I'd be looking Alli straight in the eye. I actually heard her voice! She said, 'Skip it, Maxie.' Then I saw you there. Can ya believe that?"

Hazel nodded, trembling. They stood in silence a moment, then Hazel took Maxie's arm and they walked away from the hubbub, away into the mesquite, still in full regalia. "Listen, Max. What are we going to do? I did arrange for security on *parked* airplanes, but we've been outdone. I don't know what to think, whether Mr. Blaine is connected with this, or...see, if Sweeney came through here ahead of us, did he pay some lackey off again? Someone to conveniently pick off another independent entry—Or if he's the lackey, then it's more likely Tag—"

"Sweeney...*Taggart?* Oh, better hope it was just an accident," Maxie moaned as if her pain was finally hitting her. "It had better be that Mr. Oily, then he and my granddaddy can shoot it out at high noon for all I care, but if it's someone along with us, getting to us—Oh, poor, poor Jo. I'll skin him, I'll skin Tag if I find out he's behind this. Oh, how can I—I'm out." She began to storm back to the airfield with a vengeance. "I'm going to get to the bottom of this; mark my words. If they set up something to cause Alli to crash...it was murder. Alli was...."

Hazel grabbed her. "Easy on. *Think* a minute. You don't know this wasn't a stupid accident. There is no report yet, official or unofficial, that points to any tampering with the Arctic. We have no evidence, no proof, nothing!—except our suspicion, our hunches."

They stood helplessly under the blazing sun, the sweat soaking through Maxie's black shirt as she pulled off her flight jacket and parachute. "We ain't wild geese," Maxie said glumly, "more like ducks in a puddle.... Preston, what would we do if we were fellas out here on the circuit?—with all these supposed accidents. Louise, Alli and I are all independents—maybe security better be tightened on all remaining independents. I mean, why us? Easier to get rid of because we don't have company ties? All this to advance the few that are left? Maybe to advance Jo as the ultimate independent? Now wouldn't it seem likely that the next step, whoever is doing it, would be to pull a few wires on the Rearwyn? Hm?"

"Maxie!" Hazel looked at her shocked. "There are always some real accidents in any race."

"Well, that's how it's done. We'd better think of something, or you had

83

better start slowing down, old girl. This tamperer will take you on sooner or later, company ties or not, mark my words—I should have marked yours."

A ground crewman was sprinting towards them. "Miss Schulz, ma'am, the officials want you. They found the owner of the car—drunker than a skunk. Doesn't know his head from his tail."

"At ten in the morning?" Maxie slapped her thigh in disbelief.

"The police are questioning him now. Can't remember anything."

"Too fishy." Hazel scowled.

"Some folks have been camping out all night to see this," he shrugged apologetically, then added, "The officials want to know if you're going to take off now, Miss Preston."

She looked at him squarely, a local rag, and thought, I could be looking at the very culprit. "I'll be along presently." She dismissed him with a wave of her gloves.

"I'll see to this mess," said Maxie. "Dang, I'll have to cable my Grand-daddy and soothe him first or he'll be out in full force to take vengeance. That's all I'd need. He'll take it as a personal affront, you know. He'll expect it to be a personal enemy, won't dream he made a perfect sittin' duck outta me. Then I got to get myself on that rear escort plane and see you in Fort Worth. Isn't Al's seat still empty?"

"We put someone in this leg, but Tag has petitioned to put Sweeney in."

"Sorry, seat's taken. I'll telegram Jenney from here. I'm heading up tighter security with Vera. Won't Sweeney be surprised to see me?"

Hazel grinned for a moment. "What will you say to Jo?"

"I'll tell her my accident was no accident, that I feel independents are being targeted and that she'd better watch out. That I have to have the seat. That's all. She's not going to fuss with me the way she does with you, I'm too big and pushy. She may not want to believe me but she'll hear me out. And I'm going to find a way to stop whoever is messing up this Derby. We have to. I may be out of the race but I'm not leaving the circuit. I owe it to Alli."

Hazel walked toward her own plane then with trepidation. For one thing she had not been paying attention to the Zephyr these last minutes—what could have been done to it while she was talking to Maxie? But in broad daylight with other pilots and crew near by? Still, even though she had done her checks already and had never before thought such a short interruption would change things, should she simply swing into her cockpit seat without care or thought? She nervously did a cursory inspection for the obvious. Her time on the ground had taken too long, so she hurried to be on her way. She had to reach Vera up ahead.

Hazel flew, her mind churning along with her propeller. Look, she admonished herself, I'm no fool. I saw plenty of accidents on the race circuits back in the days with Dewey. Accidents were accidents time and again,

84

proven by the experts, even when racers felt that circumstances were odd. Now I know Dewey's crash was an accident, don't I?—he hit an oil-slick. And I know guys had to be betting on him because he always joked about it. But I always *knew* it was an accident. Nobody went out and poured oil there; it had even been cleaned up with sawdust and other autos had already passed. He simply took the corner too close and hit the drain-off.

Even thinking about it now made her head shake in disbelief. He simply took the corner too close. Disbelief—that was it, that part never went away.

She began to go over the aircraft problems so far, wanting to be reasonable: Now look, okay, so Louise finds her cables all eaten through—maybe something that happened while it was in shop. No explanation we know of, but in part because the Moth was a last minute substitute, because she couldn't get her plane into the country. Was it pulled out of its hangar without a thorough enough going-over?—even though she tested it before the race. But she feels funny about it. And Alli?—an accident. Maybe she hit those down-drafts like Jo suggested. Yet she was complaining of a problem which Gus says Al thought he had resolved by Yuma. But maybe not. And Maxie?—no way, no way was that an accident! It just seems too ridiculous. I feel funny about everything because of two simple facts: one, Al tells me there may be some betting going on, and, two, because I don't see that Taggart has been dealing with us in an open or even friendly way. Why?

Skimming the tops of the clouds as though they were a fog on a bottomless lake, Hazel kept to a level thirteen thousand; she knew where she was in spite of her gauges because of the nip to the air and her need to breathe slowly. She would make good time at this level, but could not help wondering about Maxie, and about Maxie meeting up with Jo. And how Jo's flight was going.

With quick mental calculations and eyeing her compass, she changed her course by degrees to the northeast. Again she went over her coordinates. She had overcompensated as she banked, was slightly off course. Steady, she commanded herself, trust the compass. It was all she had to go on for the moment as she was above the clouds. From time to time she caught snatches of the land below where the clouds parted or grew thinner. Otherwise there was just the endless horizon, sky meeting cloud. There was no place else to be—and it brought her back to the moment, the reality of why she flew.

To go below the clouds would have put her in return lanes while bumping into crosswinds, and the foggy layer itself was too thick to stay in very long. Just above the clouds, she found a protective bubble. A less experienced pilot might climb the sky more and do battle with higher, gusting winds from the southeast.

How that first lap seemed like such a lark now—an afternoon outing as she had arched across the rippling desert heat. The weather conditions had changed as they moved away from the coast into shifting winds and rain-storms.

But for the moment the thrill of this airborne life took hold, moving her beyond her worries. With wings trembling to the beat of the engine running smoothly, and her feet holding the rudder steady, she sought the best course, took on the winds, thundered across the vast white-capped ocean of clouds. It was good to be alive like this. Too good. Like Vera said—going to the edge. Now she appreciated this easy flying like a sailor who has weathered enough of the sea to appreciate a good wind, because that sailor knows an inevitable storm is brewing in the distance somewhere.

Glancing over her shoulder to watch the cloud spill upward in her wake, she felt a resentment surge through her that these simple joys could be threat-ened by forces other than the menace of weather. The tension settled in the tendons of her lower jaw. She ground her teeth with determination; she had changed. Now she had no room for fear anymore. She would dare to indulge in this speed and power, dare to enter this infinite blue ether and survive it.

At the moment it was the only thing she could care about.

It was one way she could mourn Alexis, a way to let her go. Because this too, was what Alli had especially loved. And what Maxie loved.

Setting her course for Fort Worth across the Brazos River, Hazel sud-denly let go of the confusion she felt about the race as if she were diving through the calm, still eye of a tornado that sucked her onward, downward. A sentence came to mind. "The more competent I become, the more risks I take, the more protective he gets." Lila had said it about her husband, Frank, during an interview with Eleanor.

Why did that come to mind? She chewed it over and over. *The more com-petent I become*, hammered through the center of Hazel's brain, in tune with the rhythm of the pistons that shook her frame. There were two kinds of pro-tection, weren't there? One had to do with chivalry—protecting the weaker, the dependent. The other had to with domain—like with Mr. Blaine wanting to shut the race down, keep women fliers out of the skies. Why? Because we're good enough to be a threat? Was someone tampering with airplanes to intimidate them?

As she banked for her final descent, Jo's words came back, "…we're aber-rations of society." Was that all they'd end up as, for all the work? She couldn't tolerate the thought.

She climbed out of her cockpit, down the wing-step into Vera's arms.

"How was my time?" Was all she managed to mutter as Vera helped unbuckle her parachute, then led her to the pilot's quarters.

"Four hours and forty-seven minutes total!"

"Good." Hazel was spent and hungry. And what did her time mean? Not much until Sarah and Jo came in. Eleanor was no longer in the top margin, only able to keep in the 130 mph range. Hazel had serious doubts that Jo would be able to keep the Rearwyn at much more than 140 mph. If Jo could do better, then it would be a test of the winds because Hazel was keeping a smooth 145 mph, the engine purring all the better each lap. Not asking directly, but by keeping an eye out, she knew that Jo had changed sparkplugs for the start of this last lap. A precautionary measure? She turned to more immediate concerns. "Vera, did you get a radio message from Pecos?"

"Affirmative. Gus and Eleanor want to confer as soon as you've got your breath back. Obviously, everyone is pretty upset—accident or no, this sort of thing can't happen again. A driver who leaves his car to roll onto the airfield and turns up lying drunk someplace else?" Vera shook her head as they walked into the field house.

"Where is Tag? I saw his airplane as I came in, clear as day."

"He's here, waiting for Jo, but we have security in place. Sweeney is with him. There's a telegram for you. I'll fetch some water, juice?"

"Anything will do." Hazel picked up the telegram from the airfield clerk.

*Open seat in debate. Stop. Sponsor requests priority. Stop.*
*Need more information. Stop. Gladys.*

Well, at least the decision was still open. She knew Gladys Jenney would stall as long as possible if Hazel, as a top organizer, made a request. Maxie's telegram would meanwhile be on its way, if not yet received. Hazel decided to send a second appeal:

*Seat for Maxie. Stop. Security measure. Stop.*
*Too many accidents. Stop. Need Maxie. Stop. Hazel.*

There, that ought to show how important the seat question was without naming other names. Hazel wanted to put a call through, but somehow didn't trust that she could find the privacy she needed. The telephones were always out in the open, people around. A chance for privacy could come before long; she would just have to wait it out another lap, if she could.

"Excuse me, ma'am," said the clerk as she paid for her transmission, "I made the wrong change for that other lady, would you mind giving it to her?"

"Who?" Hazel looked into the young man's earnest, if not embarrassed face, as he held two coins out to her.

"The one with dark hair who came in with you. I overcharged her."

"Oh sure, sure." She played with the coins in the palm of her hand, slipping them into her pocket, smiled slightly so he could relax.

Slumping onto a bunk along the wall which usually served a mail carrier between stops, Hazel closed her eyes. Strategy weighed heavily on her mind like a balm against a deeper pain of loss: if I keep doing well, will something happen to me? Is Taggart behind any of this? Should she let Jo set the pace? Or Sarah? What danger was Sarah facing to be in the top margin too? Would it be best to think of the endeavor as a tour not a race for the sake of them all?

Vera brought her water, even sarsaparilla tea with sugar in it.

"Oh, here's your change from the telegram clerk," Hazel rummaged in her pockets and handed Vera the coins. Vera's startled, flustered reaction caught Hazel by surprise. "It's all right, Vera, he seems very honest—an honest mistake."

"Oh well, I just don't think he should have bothered you with it," Vera said hurriedly, regaining her composure, "especially since it didn't matter—just a telegram to my mother that I'm fine. Didn't want her to worry about me with all this…. I need to go keep an eye on things…. I'll be back in ten minutes. Rest now."

Hazel sank back, watching Vera, until her eyes closed of their own accord. The vibration of the engine still echoed in her hands, up her arms, tortured her all the way into her disconcerted heart. She fell asleep waiting for the rest of the draw to come in, and the particular drone of the Rearwyn which would surely wake her up. She wanted to be out of the way and busy somewhere when Jo came in—until she'd at least had a chance to talk to Maxie.

Did she hear the Rearwyn come in? It was as though she heard it every few minutes as she tossed in a restless sleep. Was she sleeping?—no, she was awake, listening. Where were Tag and Sweeney?—just standing about in the open? She couldn't rest; she sat up on the bunk, then fell back onto it. Maybe just a few minutes. It would be a long time before she rested again. Vera would come rouse her. Knowing that, she let herself sink deeper.

She could hear the drone of an airplane, but it was falling from the sky. A white airplane with burnished red. Jump, she called, jump! But it was Jo who was falling out. She ran to help. Why wasn't Jo pulling the cord? Jo was falling. Why didn't the chute open? Too late! Make the chute open, Jo—

Someone was shaking her shoulder. Hazel sat up suddenly, expecting relief, expecting Vera there. Sweet, familiar hands. But is was Jo who looked into her eyes, that face pale and tired.

Hazel rubbed her head, a knot of dread gripping her heart. Jo was the last person she wanted to see, but she managed to say, "I didn't hear you land. I thought I would hear you."

"I'm sorry, I didn't know you were asleep. You were groaning—"

"Was I?"

"Are you all right? I wouldn't have disturbed you…. I had to see you. I need to talk." Jo's face, so close, looked drawn.

"Something the matter?"

"Can you walk? Can we walk somewhere? All these people around makes it difficult…."

"Sure." Hazel stood up, her head reeling. She didn't want to talk. "How's your engine holding up."

"Fine, fine. Let's go out this way. We can walk up the road a bit. I have to go see Tag shortly. He's checking things over with Sweeney."

They walked out of the airfield building onto a gravel lane, bordered on one side with a dry creek and a row of cottonwoods, stockades on the other. Hazel squinted against the sheer, late afternoon sunlight, her vision blurry. Jo's silken hair was still plastered down from wearing her helmet, and the lines from her goggles still showed red around her cheekbones. What could be so urgent? Hazel didn't want to guess; she just wished Eleanor or Maxie were with her. Land Amighty— it had to be about *Vera!* Jo was going to talk to her about Vera.

"I want to know what's going on." Jo took her arm in a way that she hadn't in a long time—hooking her elbow so that her fingers clasped Hazel's forearm, near the wrist. Hazel had always loved that, how Jo's last two fingers would tuck in under her shirt-cuff. Today it cut to the quick.

"What?" Stiffly, Hazel put a hand onto Jo's, holding her there.

"Maxie. She says she's coming along as security, that you have agreed to her taking the open seat."

"Yes." Hazel wanted to sigh in relief—she could handle this issue. "Can you blame her after what happened in Pecos? We need some control over what happens at the airfields when we come in. If anyone can, she's the one to go ahead and see that people and autos are out of the way."

Jo stopped, incredulous, as if that disbelief had swept her along the whole lap. "Why are you determined to prevent me from having the support I need? Why can't she replace one of your company mechanics? You have enough of them. What gives you the right?"

Hazel remained silent for a moment. True enough, it was what she might have done in other circumstances, even though she could justify the pro-rated need of Beech escort for the number of pilots needing Beech service. What she said was, "There's nothing to prevent such decisions in the regulations— as you like to remind me. Am I right? I have this whole race to keep intact—"

"I told you I would protest! He is my sponsor's mechanic, and he is my only crew. That is priority Hazel, I need him, I need someone along."

"Sponsor priority ended with the first deadline. We've already fired Sweeney once from this circuit. I think it's better that he stayed off." Hazel looked at her friend as calmly as she could, considering her inner turmoil. "I happen not to trust him, and I certainly don't want to entrust you and your airplane to him when I suspect he's part of a tidy little betting scheme. You can have support from Beech crew—"

"And what makes you think Sweeney has anything to do with gambling if there is any. What possible proof have you? You don't know he's doing it—"

"Al's word on it is all I need until I know more. He wouldn't have said anything to me about it if he wasn't sure. And now he's conveniently out of the race. A bit too worrisome a fact for me. This is a preventative measure. I'll give you a mechanic. I'll help you in any way I can. Too many unexplained things are happening to us. Didn't Maxie tell you what happened?"

"Yes. A drunken driver leaves his motorcar unattended. I fail to see any connection to Sweeney. What makes you think he could possibly be responsible?" Jo's face was flushed now, the goggle lines becoming white. "Has Alli's death affected you so badly that you can't make sense? We're all under a terrible strain, for goodness sake. But you are going off the deep end! I think you're just looking for some scapegoat, some reason, some excuse for Alli's accident. Someone to blame. And influencing others, to boot! Of course, they will all listen to you. Maxie's airplane careens into a runaway auto, and you say, 'oh Maxie, it's a conspiracy—this was done on purpose.' And your nice new photographer friend there, all agog over you, running around with her camera—conveniently reflecting your panic and taking pictures of everything in sight."

"What do you mean, everything?"

"Just now, when I came in. She was round Taggart and me like a hornet while we're trying to confer."

Hazel had to laugh, releasing her irritation at Jo. "Yes, she is taking pictures of everybody as they come in. You should be pleased. Aren't you the one who wanted publicity? This is the first time you've met up with Tag. Here: a picture of Taggart conferring with top contender."

"Well, it was annoying and ill-timed, as though she were trying to find out how my flight went. To inform you, I suppose." Jo walked, arms flailing in agitation, her blue-grey eyes flashing.

"Why? Do you have something going wrong? Pushing the engine a bit? Was he pressing you?—Look, if I want to know what your time is, all I have to do is look at the official roster. I don't need someone eking out information for me—when I can find out for myself how often you're changing spark-plugs." Hazel turned to Jo sharply. "Who was annoyed, really? You or Tag?"

Jo paused a split second. "Well, he was, yes. Yes, he was very undone. None of us like cameras up in our faces. It wasn't an odd reaction. Like any of us he likes planned press coverage. He asked her to leave."

"And you didn't introduce her? No. And until that point you didn't care, perhaps were even flattered?"

Jo spat, "I had barely climbed out of my airplane. I had things on my mind. It's a vulnerable time as you well know. You just want your crew at that time and some well-earned privacy. You even expect some protection, don't you from Gus? From Vera now? You did put her up to it, didn't you?"

Taken aback, Hazel squared her shoulders. "What?—Wait a minute. Slow down here. I didn't put her up to anything. I'm not intending anything except to have Maxie help out on security for the remainder of this race. Vera is another matter—she is simply taking pictures for the record. I put her up to that much, yes. Why are you so up in arms?"

"Because it seems to me you are interfering competitively. Can't you stand it that I'm doing well? It is as though you want me to fail, have to find something wrong with my particular sponsor, my particular mechanic! You can't stand it that I can do this on my own, and maybe beat you at your own game. I can't believe that you actually expect me to use *your* company mechanics.

"My game?"

"Yes, your game. Miss Showcase for Beech Aircraft! I'm the thorn in your side, and you're sowing discredit at every chance. Don't you see how Beech dominates? You want *to provide* me with a mechanic? Don't you see that Tag would never let a company mechanic touch his airplane? Who has the real motive here to fix the race, to interfere with independent sponsors? Beech wants the monopoly, or at least to squeeze the upstarts out. Don't you think they would like to know everything about Tags design? Tag's whole future rest on how this airplane tests out. Do you think Beech or Lockheed want him to succeed?"

They had reached the creek, and were standing in the scant shade of the cottonwood, the hubbub of the airfield at a distance to their right, and across the road came the lowing of steer crowded into small paddocks. The smell of the animals filled the air, a stench that made Hazel come to, alerting her to how pent up she felt, how tense with restrained anger. It was fear she smelled.

She spoke quietly, "I don't think so, Jo. Smell those animals? They're in a panic because they're going to slaughter. In all honesty, I think our race is in similar straits unless we take serious precautions. I really don't give a damn if you win, if it's a fair test. But let it be a fair test. No, I can't prove anything, but I want to find out what's going on, and *I don't know how to*. Until Al has settled matters over Alli, he can't help us—he's too conveniently out with little chance of catching up with us. If I could pretend I was a man, I'd go find out! I can't go to the bars Al is used to from Alaska and might have been able to scout out—bootleg and unwashed men dealing dirty. But I can't! Not only am I a woman, I'm busy trying to fly a race, and keep us all from any more 'accidents'. Don't think that you're immune. If you don't make the showing these gamblers might want, you could just as simply be helped to lose as win. Don't you see?—it's money. Manipulating the stakes. It's dog-fighting with a twist—something new at our expense."

Jo gave her a cold, hard assessing look, whistling under her breath. "Where on earth do you get this theory?—A comment from Al and the knowledge that Gus personally dislikes Sweeney...Have you plain lost your perspective on things?" Jo's shoulders drooped then, as if her weariness had hit her. She sighed, "Look, if you suspect Sweeney that badly, no, I certainly don't need him on escort. Let Maxie look out for us. If it would ease your mind."

Hazel reached out, but did not take her hand, relief flooding through her. "Yes, would you do that? If you don't want company crew, I'm sure we can get Frank to help you."

"Well that's settled then." Jo turned to walk back towards the field.

"There is something else...I don't want Taggart running ahead of us."

"Tag? What could possibly—? Are you insinuating that he's in on—?"

"Just take as good and hard a look at him as you did me a minute ago. That's all I ask, Jo. What are his motives in this race? What kind of a sponsor is he for you, for women pilots—?"

Jo laughed outright, her head tilted back, but the notes, so usually melodious, came out sourly. "God forbid! All right, I'll take a scrutinizing look. And then you do something for me too, tit for tat. I'm not blind, you know. I'm not stupid. I can't for one minute believe that Tag is in any way suspect, any more than there should be any truth to your amorous designs on Vera. Right? Night watch on the airfield and all? What is the real need for you to camp out? You will take a hard, close look at that."

Hazel could not speak. The half-second that demanded a quick retort passed. The seconds became a long pause. She could feel the fences closing in around her, the gates snapping shut, locking in her wild and beating heart as it pulsed through her brain. She could feel her feet pawing the ground, breath sharp and painful, a stifled cry. Anything she said would give her away. What was the truth? Could she deny half of it?—*no, there is nothing between Vera and myself*—and not the other?—*but yes, Taggart is a dangerous man.*

Jo's voice quavered slightly. "Yes. I thought so. We might as well be honest about what worries us; I knew she had designs on you from the start, perhaps even before she met you. A hanger-on who is here to flatter you, use you, drive a wedge between us."

Hazel snorted, "That's ridiculous!"

"Is it? Oh Hazel, you are good at so many things, organizing tasks, putting things in order, seeing a job from beginning to end, but you don't read people very well. Maybe that's what I found refreshing about you when I met you—right from the farm, full of integrity and good will, but not sophisticated about people. You don't like the way Tag handles his part in the race, so you immediately suspect him of being up to something, when you really don't know him at all. Why don't you apply the same rule to Vera?—simply because she charms you? Look, it was no mistake that I sent Maxie off to find you. I knew she was drunk and should not be seen in polite company. Who do you think got her the motorcar and sent her to you? Darling Haze, may both of us be wary of flattery and the taste for glory. This isn't child's play. We are in competition. We are fierce competitors, but lets try not to be enemies. I want to believe that isn't possible" She held out a left glove to Hazel. "Perhaps you should take this back."

Stupefied, Hazel slapped her empty thigh pockets. "I don't have my gloves with me."

"Sometime soon, then? Come on, we'd better get back. There is a lot to tend to." Jo's voice was almost cheerful, if it weren't for the flat echo of grief.

"He can't come to Independence. I won't let him come to Independence." Hazel said stubbornly, following.

Jo turned at the reference to Hazel's hometown, the next upcoming pitstop. She cocked her head slightly and smiled. "The uninvited guest? Don't worry, he probably wants to go on to St. Louis anyway. And if Sweeney can't have a seat on escort, Tag's going to have to fly ahead with him."

"Yes, he would fly ahead anyway." Hazel said, feeling uneasy. She had won her point, yet something was still horribly wrong, twisted; somehow Jo had indulged her, yet it still made her feel stupid until she didn't know what to think or feel.

Jo was practical, had always been like that, didn't panic in tight moments. A steady-on sort, wasn't she? Hadn't Hazel felt that, indeed appreciated that on their refueling maneuvers in Florida? Wasn't Jo right about things? Usually?

But not always, not always. She too had blinders on about obvious things—their own relationship, for instance? So cautious to the point of fearfulness? Or was she just being realistic and sensible as she liked to claim?

Oh, how could she be reliably sensible about Taggart? Was she? If she could so easily see through to Hazel's feelings for Vera, could she not also see Taggart for what he was? Or was Hazel herself wrong about Taggart? Maybe he was being fooled by Sweeney too.

In parting, Jo kissed her lightly on the forehead with a jaunty face-saving smile. Hazel nodded a farewell, then turned towards the Zephyr. Perhaps if she rummaged there, stowing away things, checking vital fluids, she could be alone and preoccupied. How she hoped Vera would sense enough to stay away for the moment. Yes, even though Hazel's body shook with doubt and desire at the same time, she didn't want to see Vera. 'If we could be giddy…' Vera had said….

Hazel found her gloves in her fuselage locker, Vera having stowed them there. Clutching them in her right hand, she slapped her left palm, studied the stitching on Jo's. The seam all along the forefinger and thumb had been strained to the point beyond endurance, and now the stitches were coming out. How could she return such a glove? She would have to buy Jo a new pair—for it was Jo who was calling a truce now.

Staring up at the golden words, *Press on Preston*, emblazoned upon the bright blue of the Zephyr, her mind began to clear. What's in my control? she questioned: to fly my airplane if I can. Then understanding hit her shattering what she had thought was Jo's call for a truce—Jo was agreeing to have Maxie along for security—oh, the reason was so simple Hazel had to laugh as she slapped those golden letters with the gloves, one sharp smack. Jo wanted Maxie to keep night watch either along with Vera and Hazel, or else to create a situation in which Hazel would have less reason to refuse hotel accommodations. *Rot, how I've been had!*

At dinner the pilots were served broiled beefsteaks.

"Ha-ha," Maxie gloated. "I knew those weren't four-legged chickens in those stockades, eh?"

"Affirmative." Hazel sat next to her morosely, not touching the food.

"Hey, kid. Ya'd better eat. It's another long haul tomorrow and you don't want to pass out up there."

"Potatoes will do. I can't eat something that I know has been penned up and its heart broken."

"Good God, girl." Maxie stopped in mid-bite, hand on Hazel's back. "What's the matter with you?"

Hazel glanced around at the long crowded table, Jo down at the other end with Taggart to one side and Eleanor on the other. Most of the pilots were there except for Marsha who had taken ill again, been ordered by the doctor to go to the hospital for examinations. Stevie of course, had taken to her side. Also notably absent was Vera who said she'd keep to the airfield, take dinner with the crew.

Leaning against Maxie as if in mid-jest, Hazel smiled weakly, sniffed, "Pilot fatigue. Don't give it another thought."

"Uh oh," Maxie's voice dipped to her deep quiet tones. "You talked to Jo, didn't you? I was hoping you would wait and let me do it with you."

"I had no choice. She came to me first. Too bad—I didn't think she'd do that."

"What—she still going to contest the seat? She swore up and down she would when I talked to her. Said I was all bent out of shape about Sweeney and all."

Hazel shrugged, took a sip of the bitter lemon she had ordered. "She won't suspect me of being up to mischief with Vera, if I don't suspect Taggart of being up to mischief with the race."

Maxie's lower jaw dropped; she took a quick gulp of her water as if sickened. "That hardly compares."

"Thanks, Max. I needed that reassurance." Hazel snorted.

"Preston! Listen to me. It doesn't bear comparison. We have two separate issues, one has to do with your heart, the other with the race which affects a lot of people. It has to do with us wanting to know more about Taggart, and what Sweeney is up to. Why are they flying ahead? Is it simply tactics, or are they doing something that affects us? There he is, eating at the same table as us for the first time since the race started, a sponsor—a betrayer? You are uneasy about him. Why? Let's start with that."

Hazel thought for a moment. "Well, he doesn't go by the rules we organized. Okay, so he's a maverick, he resents the company presence. I can forgive him that. I'm a main organizer, along with Jo and Eleanor, and yet he has never conferred with me, not even once. No communication. Only through Jo, and what I hear, I don't like. But I can deal with that too. He hires on a mechanic we dismissed, someone Gus has no use for, and that's when I start feeling real bothered. Jo says I don't read people well, perhaps not—but I do go on my horse sense, farm girl that I am. I feel terribly uneasy about that man, and I trust that feeling in myself. Now I just need a way to find out what is making me feel so damn suspicious. I want to know for my own sanity, what he's about. And I have to watch Jo being at his mercy...I don't like it. I find it disturbing."

Maxie shrugged. "How is there any way to remove all doubt? Let me hear what Al has to say. Do you realize he has barely had time to make funeral arrangements for Alli? And we still have to find out how the betting works." Shaking her head, she continued eating voraciously, as if soon she were bound to find an answer. With her mouth full she waved her fork. "You'd better sort things out with ol' Veree back there on the field though. Something turned sour pretty quickly between the two of you, huh?"

"Why? Did she say something to you?"

"She didn't have to. You've both kept to opposite ends of the field as if your movements were choreographed. What are you going to do about her?"

"Beats me, Max."

Maxie pointed her fork again, this time directly at Eleanor. "I think we need to talk to that one. She's not sitting next to Taggie for nothin.'"

Hazel shot a glance towards the other end of the table. No, by god. Eleanor looked up at that moment, the briefest glance, as she continued to conduct her interview, pen scribbling between bites of dinner.

It was then that a commotion erupted at the door, and a messenger from the hospital arrived to say that Marsha Banfill was diagnosed as having typhoid fever, was in serious condition, and would have to withdraw from the race. All pilots were asked to write down what they had eaten and drunk over the last few days.

"Land Amighty—we've been eating the same food." Hazel had even less appetite now than before. She felt her head to see if her inner heat might not be a fever.

"Yeah, chicken." Maxie pushed her plate away. "All it takes is one bad piece or some infected cook."

"Well, there goes another independent. I suppose if I go by Jo's appraisal of the situation, I'm not supposed to blame it on a deliberate conspiracy."

"Ha." Maxie's large chest heaved as she sprawled back in her chair. "The way I see it, is we have an airplane without a pilot. Very tempting, very tempting from my point of view."

"Max, of course! You could complete the race as a pilot. Let's talk to her sponsors right away. They're the clothing-store couple, right?" Then Hazel laughed her first real laugh in awhile. "Max! You get a whole wardrobe as part of the deal, make-up too! Dresses and accoutrements for airplane travel. I love it."

Maxie looked down at her black riding pants, her western-cut boots. "Can't I start a new fashion?"

Hazel slapped Maxie on the thigh. "Come on. Let's go talk."

Finger to her lips, Maxie beckoned Hazel to wait. "What about the open seat then?"

Hazel shrugged. "Beats me. Sweeney is going to keep being along anyhow. Maybe we were right before—better have him in view at all times than out of sight sneaking behind your back."

"Preston, I have already been scratched from the race. Let's leave it that way. You know my Granddaddy would love to pull strings to get me back in, and I don't want that. He's taking all this pretty personally as it is, but I've got him all busy to receive Miss Mack, sans wings, by rail. No, I want to participate unofficially if we can get her sponsors to agree—I mean, they've done all this advertisement—I want to complete the circuit but I want to fly ahead one lap. How about it?" She tilted her head, her thick black eyebrows raised.

Hazel looked at her fondly. "Max, you are terrific. We'll arrange it. We must. Let's go get Eleanor—she's great at this sort of negotiation."

As the dinner group dispersed, Maxie and Hazel wended their way over to find Eleanor, and explain their thoughts.

"We need to make some telephone calls then," she said efficiently.

"Ellie, you have access to a private telephone?" Hazel was curious. "How do you do it?"

"Ah." Eleanor paused mysteriously. "You go to the switchboard operator, plug directly in and use a set of headphones. I always do that at the local newspaper. Operators are usually women—they understand and can be most helpful."

"Lordy, Ellie, you're always so on top of things." Hazel said, impressed.

"Am I?" Eleanor stopped abruptly, blues eyes twinkling in spite of her serious attitude. "This way, ladies."

96

"So you don't think I'm nuts then—?"

"Yeah, what did you learn from Taggie?" Maxie cut in.

Eleanor waited a few paces as they made their way out of the airfield buildings. "We have to go to the local press office. Now to find the cab, they were going to send out for me, ah, is that one? I have to file my race updates and my story on Maxie, but I don't think I can use anything on Tag. Let's go.... Taggart is a cool customer. No, at first look, he is a humorless, innocuous sort. Thin lipped. Hard. Doesn't respond to conversation. You'd never know what cards he was holding. I asked him how he thought the race was going. Hard to say; he tells me. Nothing. Then I start talking about the odds, I start throwing in all the betting imagery and language I can think of...." They climbed into the cab that drew up, the driver sticking his head out the window with a 'Miss Wilson?' Eleanor waved her hands at her friends to indicate she wouldn't talk. Hazel sat in frustrated silence.

Maxie's patience gave out first. "And?"

Eleanor tossed her head, glancing at the driver, then turned to lean closer to the others. "He got very twitchy—smoothing his hair, scratching his neck, giving me a patronizing smile. I think any stronger reaction is going to be dumped onto Jo who already seems tense, if you ask me. She's going to take the brunt of him and filter it to us, one way or another. More to the point, I received a telegram from a colleague who is doing a bit of research for me on Tag, saying he found a few interesting facts—I need to call him and find out what they are. I had it on my mind to talk to him even before you approached me, so we have business to do here. Who do you want to put calls through to—Gladys and the Mortons, correct?"

With Eleanor's guidance, they made their way through the office at the newspaper, a small frontier atmosphere with two typewriters and the typesetter, the editor obviously a one-man show and overworked, who waved them to the switchboard at the back of the building.

They called Gladys Jenney for Al's whereabouts with messages for him, asking that he be available with her the following night. Jenney had no news on the accident report, only that Alexis' body was still at the embalmers, that Al was making arrangements for her to be shipped to their hometown in Oregon for a private, family funeral. Jenney would arrange public memorial services in California and New York for early September.

They called the Mortons and bargained for Maxie to take over the *Spartan* unofficially, so that upon Marsha's recovery, they could still proceed with the tour she was going to do for them. Depending on the timing, they wanted Maxie for a substitute on that tour if Marsha could not fulfill her obligation. Maxie swallowed hard at that, crossing her fingers that Marsha would be on the mend.

Eleanor looked up at Maxie crowding in on one side of her, after listening intently through the headphones, said very soberly, "Portia Morton wants to know your dimensions, please."

Maxie groaned, and Hazel on the other side held back a guffaw.

"Tell her anything Marsha can get into I can squeeze into myself." Maxie gave a sharp, dismissive swipe with her hand in the air, looked at Hazel reproachfully. "I ain't wearing anything else but my own apparel, I can tell you that right now, Preston. I'll fly their little airplane anywhere they want, but that's all I'm modelling."

Eleanor looked at her again. "And don't forget the banner on the last lap...."

"Banner?"

"...yes...yes...I'll tell her. Maxie, there is a banner behind the seat. Attach it to the tail—you know...it says 'Morton's Apparel Salutes Derby.'"

Maxie rolled her eyes. "Don't that beat all."

Next, from Eleanor's colleague came the nitty gritty, if her grunts were any indication. She replaced the headphones most abruptly when she was done, pulled out the plug, and nodded gratefully to the night operator on duty. That meant signing her autograph too, and all of them taking the small-talk, the flattery, the sincere admiration, before they could hasten outdoors and to privacy, Maxie stopping to light a cigar in the open air.

"Something interesting, my friends," said Eleanor. "Apparently Tag was a junior engineer on Wright engines some years ago. Bright and ambitious. Little known facts, hm? He was dismissed due to breach of contract. My source pursued this, talking to the lawyers involved. This breach was one of confidence. Apparently, our boy was gleaning information but not producing design work. There was no further legal action but apparently he threatened a suit against Wright and Beech for stealing *his* design, adapting it and crediting others. If you took his story, you would be left thinking that much of the basic Wright design came from him. Meanwhile it was clearly established that the Wright engine had already been patented before he worked on any projects, so his lawyer advised him to drop legal action."

Sticking her hands deep into her pockets and arching her back, Maxie blew out a deep puff from the cigar stuck at an angle in her lips. "Wahl, I'll be dog-goned...a fallen angel?"

"Give me a puff," Hazel beckoned with fingers waggling. Taking the cigar, her hands shook as she inhaled, trying to focus her thoughts. "Jo said he is very protective—doesn't want Beech Company mechanics around his airplanes. Has he simply taken a Wright engine and adapted it, perhaps adding his fuel-saving element—or tuning it to take a slightly different mix? It's easy enough to buy Wright parts, assemble ones's own engine from various sources of parts, or hone them himself if he's a trained engineer. I know that in the model Jo is flying, or shall we say prototype, he is going for a more high-powered engine in the lightest body possible, reinforcing the framework for stress. And frankly, when I've watched her coming in from test flights, it looks well-balanced. But on this long-haul, I have my doubts. He has to have doubts too, and he has a personal grievance against Beech. Now at least we know why. What his motive might be—he has to prove his design. Come on, let's get back to the airfield and take a look at the Spartan."

"Wait a minute." Eleanor frowned, looking at them in alarm. "Motive, you say...he, my source—said something about the design controversy—it wasn't specifically engine design; he did say something about fuel efficiency, but he also said '*exhaust system.*'"

Hazel handed back the cigar to Maxie, eyes narrowing in the wake of the smoke. "He's an expert on exhaust systems then? Back in Santa Monica, remember, Al and Al had exhaust problems...something Al tried to catch in San Bernardino and didn't solve. Tag had all the time in the world to do something to the exhaust of the Arctic in Santa Monica. The Rearwyn was *right next* to it....that...that morning when Vera first came to take photographs of me! Damn! I was walking around in the space where the Rearwyn had been, starboard tip to port, and I remember now, seeing that white fuselage as I looked up—" Hazel closed her eyes to recall the image. "It was the *Arctic*! Who was on the other side? Lord. Not a Beech...something in CW Tag didn't care about...? Then Vera called to me and she was setting up her camera further along in front of my Zephyr. Let's go—maybe she'll remember...."

"Even in the dark it still looks like a Christmas ornament," said Maxie, appraising the green, red and gold Spartan. She was looking at the golden, promotional lettering along the tail end of the fuselage: *Morton's Apparel for Ladies—in step with the modern woman.* Unsnapping the canvas cover of the cockpit, she climbed in, snuggled down into the seat, her hands running over the instruments.

Eleanor, with a foot up on the wing, and leaning over her knee, yelled up, "How does it feel?"

Hazel strolled around the front and back, feeling the propeller, remarking upon the fact that in this model the pistons were not in the usual circle behind the propeller and, though a sports plane, didn't have a self-starter, but Maxie was used to that.

"Hot damn," Maxie grinned down at them, "it'll have to do till I get my Mackie back, if I keep my elbows in and my knees together. Uh oh, can't do that...there's a stick in the way. Ooh..." She accepted their groans, then tried to be serious, "We'll see how the precision of this piece bears up. Isn't its strength supposed to be in the cut of its wings, that peculiar curve to the fuselage? I can't believe Marsha flew this thing with a high fever, and still kept her time so well."

Vera arrived at that moment with a lantern, urgency on her face and noticeable relief. "How did you come out here without me seeing you?"

Eleanor hunched her shoulders. "Just walked out from the building—"

"No, remember we cut across from the path," said Hazel.

"Well, then you're lucky, or else my scheme is not fool-proof! I put trip wires at random all around the airplanes."

"Trip wires!" Maxie's laugh came rolling over them as she heaved herself out of the cockpit.

"Well not entirely random...certain airplanes. I wasn't worried about the Spartan." Vera went to stand on the other side of Eleanor as Maxie jumped to the ground. Hazel kept to the background.

"Well, perhaps now we should worry about it..." Eleanor began to fill Vera in on the latest developments, finishing with, "...and so Maxie will fly out ahead to watch for trouble, keep tabs on Taggart. We'll put Sweeney in advance escort with you if Jo goes in the first half, or else with you in rear. Do you think you can stand that?"

Vera sounded very business-like as she said, "I may not like it, but I intend to make him as uncomfortable as I can—the two of them. I think the more we just hang right in there with them, the better. The horse can't kick you if you stand right close to its side."

"I think the discomfort has already been noted," Hazel ventured. "I have already heard a complaint through Jo about your photography session!"

Vera shrugged. "What can I say?—He's so photogenic."

"Yeah, I know but I'm supposed to tell you to back off." Hazel's tone was apologetic.

"Twenty feet instead of ten?" Vera's mouth tightened at the corners. "Sure, I can do that."

Maxie interrupted. "Say, Vera. Do ya remember when you first took pictures of Hazel in Santa Monica? We were wondering if you remember how the airplanes were lined up...Do you have pictures from that day?"

"No, no I don't. I send all my film home to my mother for developing later because I don't have any facility here on the circuit, nor the time."

"Do you remember where any of the airplanes were that day?" Eleanor pressed. "What order they were in the line-up?"

Vera shook her head. "No, I've seen so many different line-ups by now, I don't know who was parked where. I might have pictures—I did take pictures of the airfield that day—a row of propellers, angles, things like that. Perhaps I could telegraph my mother to develop those. Would it be helpful?"

Eleanor shook her head. "It's circumstantial now, but it might be good to have, if anything, to bear out Preston's memory here, and show that there was opportunity for Taggart to tamper. It could be that the Arctic was right next to the Rearwyn for those days prior to the race. We want to know who was on the other side."

"Wait a minute—I think the Monocoupe was—green and white. I remember wishing I could photograph color. I remember—because the Rearwyn was gone, I saw two rows of airplanes, not a single row. And as I passed the end of the first row, I remember the green and white. And that it was a lightweight plane."

"A CW just as I thought," spouted Hazel. "Lila hasn't had a lick of trouble."

Eleanor put up her hand, a cautionary gesture. "That might explain one side. Are you sure that's not what you saw, Preston?"

Hazel curbed her sudden irritation. "No. The Monocoupe is more green than white, and I was walking towards the ocean-side. Were you, Vera?"

"I can pretty firmly agree to that. I was walking towards the ocean—looking for the Zephyr."

Maxie sighed, hands in her pockets. "What does it give us? Not much. I just know that Alexis was not having any problems. Then, between her flight from Alaska and her first lap, something changed. Something that had to take a bit of time to do. What's our next step?"

Eleanor made a few notes before tucking her pad and pencil in a pocket. "I want to start putting it all together, the research my colleague did for us, the picture. I wish I could question the driver of that motorcar some more, but our hands are tied during the race, unless we catch Tag or Sweeney in the act of snooping or tampering in next few days. For the moment, our survival is what we need to take care of. What will hold up in a court of law may take longer to prove. We'll see. Vera, can we wire your mother and see if she can develop those first pictures?"

Vera frowned. "Oh dear, I just remembered—she won't be home for another day or so. She was going to visit her ailing sister."

Eleanor suggested, "I suppose I could call my contact again and see if there are any publicity pictures from the days prior to the race."

Maxie snapped back the cockpit cover on the Spartan, then scooted down. "Well, I may as well get my things and stow them in the locker here. Let's see. Yep. Looks like Stevie has cleared Marsha's things out. Ellie, I'll come with ya."

Hazel, having a feeling that Maxie was deliberately clearing out, said, "And leave security to us?" In a way she was terrified that Maxie was going off, leaving her alone with Vera. The emotions she had been keeping at bay surfaced with renewed intensity.

"I think you can manage," Maxie muttered as she shoved passed Hazel to march off with Eleanor.

A few feet apart, Vera and Hazel stood silently, not looking at each other.

Finally it was Vera who spoke, "I have a place set up over by your airplane. Let's go there. I'll get us some warm water."

"You don't have to look after me," Hazel said too quickly. "I can get my own water."

"It's no problem...." Vera backed away as they both started to walk towards the Zephyr. She added, "This way is clear, no, don't go there, you'll—"

"—trip." Hazel finished as Vera grabbed her shoulder to redirect her. Now they were face to face, and only a few inches apart. Hazel couldn't help but grin, melting as her arms swung around Vera, clasping her so urgently that Vera was thrown completely off balance, was completely at her mercy, her camera swinging from her shoulder and banging against Hazel's hip. Letting her feet touch the ground again, Hazel ushered her quickly to the other side of an airplane wing. "Put that darned lantern and camera somewhere else."

Vera did, but she came back with full strength, pushing Hazel into the corner where wing met fuselage. "This has been unbearable. Where have you been for so long?" Hazel had no chance to answer as their lips met, Vera pressing her even further into the corner with her hips.

Hazel broke gently away from the kiss. "Jo knows what may or may not be happening between us. But it's all wrapped up with everything else, I've given up trying to sort it out."

"I see. But what does it change?" Vera did not move.

"Very little, except she likes the idea of Maxie on security so that we'll behave ourselves. Only thing is, I don't think Max enjoys playing chaperone—so we aren't saved from ourselves at all."

"Should we be?"

Hazel sagged against Vera's strength, maybe just to see if it was there. She could feel Vera's hands moving around her back, down to her buttocks; fire came from those fingertips which tugged to loosen her pants. Hazel undid her belt for Vera, letting those hands move between layers. She liked being pressed into a corner, support from a bi-plane's lower wing allowing her pelvis to move against Vera's.

How sweet the ache, how terrible the longing, how frustrated the passion, Vera's hands stroking up and down her thighs while her mouth played along Hazel's neck and shoulders.

"Can I get my hand inside you here?" Vera asked, warm breath along Hazel's cheek as she moved her hands further, reaching through more clothing. "Ah, that is what I want, yes, can I?"

Bracing against Vera, Hazel spread her legs, pulsing, swelling to take Vera's fingers, her whole body tingling with want.

"I want you on a bed, a real bed," whispered Vera. "I want you without your clothes and my mouth sucking your breasts, your sex. I want you completely, sparing nothing. I want your desire at my mercy. Yes, like that I want you. I want you on very rumpled sheets."

"Rumpled?" Hazel gasped, opening herself to take in as much of Vera's hand as she could, the heel of Vera's palm rubbing her as the fingers slipped in and out. But she knew this would only tease her, drive her mad.

"Yes, very rumpled." Vera laughed into her ear, licking her there with her tongue, pushing against her at the same time as bracing her from behind with her other hand. "Hours and hours of being rumpled."

"We must go. We can't do this here." Hazel protested, eyes closed.

"Why not?" Vera pressed against her more firmly, not letting up. Hazel could feel Vera's pelvic bone moving against her, Vera's breath quickening. "Release yourself to me—you can—you can."

Their mouths found each other, perhaps to stifle their moans, then Vera broke away, perhaps to concentrate on her hand, on coaxing the climax she wanted from Hazel. She began whispering, "Come on, Hazel, come on. Give yourself, darling. There is no car careening towards us this time. That's right, swallow me, come on. Why do you think I strung up wires everywhere? I am your security. I am—" As if her whole being were swelling, billowing outwards, Hazel caved in against Vera's hand, pulsing as Vera slowly slipped away. Vera kissed her, kissed her, mouth open, crushing against her. Hazel was delirious from the strength. She wanted to cave into it again. Pressing against Vera who was still moving urgently against her, she kneaded Vera's back, encouraging the power to wash over her, until Vera moaned in her ear, and relaxed, spread eagle upon her.

"I think the airplane is moving," Hazel said, regaining her balance. "This isn't a heavy plane—whose is it?"

Still clasping her, Vera rallied ever so slightly. "Gold and black, I think—must be Stevie's Eagle."

"Oh good," Hazel sighed, "she wouldn't mind."

Head tilted back, Vera laughed, not letting go of Hazel's hips. "So help me, I want you without your clothes. Do you think we'll ever find such a time or place?"

"I don't know. I do know that the next pit-stop is my home-town, my family farm, in fact. They have mowed a whole field for us...."

"Your childhood home?"

"Yes."

Vera moved her hand between Hazel's legs again, fondling her. "You're oozing with desire and you want more. I think that if we're going to a place you know so intimately, you'll know where we can find a safe hide-away for awhile."

Hazel caressed Vera's hair, brushing fingers through it. "Yes, yes I can.

The hayloft and barn is at our disposal, but that is for everyone. I think I know where we can go."

"Good—Maxie will have to do security for awhile."

"Security? You're talking about my home turf. I have three big brothers who are not going to let anyone near the airplanes if I say so. We might even get a night's rest. Good home-cooked food at any rate. My mother and all my aunts will take charge. They've had plenty of training on church picnics. This will be my father's triumph—he's a barn-stormer from way back. To have one in his own barnyard!"

"No chicken, I hope."

Hazel chuckled. "More like my grandpa's smoked ham. And pies of every description. There is going to be such a hub-bub that it will be difficult to get away, if, and only if I have paid my fair share of attention to everyone."

Taking out a handkerchief, Vera wiped her hands, holding the cloth up to Hazel's nose mischievously.

"You filthy rag!" Hazel declared, genuinely aghast.

"Exactly." Vera carefully folded the handkerchief and put it in her pocket. "There—for safe-keeping, my love."

Hazel was heady with the thrill of this woman's love-making. Had there ever been anyone so full of zest, sensuality and beauty at the same time? This woman pursued sex the way Hazel flew, right to the keen edge. With the promise of flying by day and Vera by night, Hazel thought her world had to be about as complete as she could ever want it.

*Just because I am a small person and need a cushion on my seat and extension blocks on the rudder bar doesn't mean I can't fly. But I do find that the more competent I become, the more risks I take, the more protective my husband gets.*

Lila Wilczynski　　　—*from a Journalist's Notebook, E.W.*

## 7.

*Fort Worth to Tulsa*

In the morning, as far as Hazel could tell, there had been no tinkerers, no takers during the night. She only roused slightly from her hard bed on the ground to see Vera slipping off to take up all her trip wires. Still tightly wrapped up in her blanket, Maxie's breath came in the strong, even measure of sleep. Hazel sank back to doze again, recalling Vera's arm inside her clothes and around her body all night, recalling her own hands touching Vera's nakedness, the feel of those round breasts, the curve to the waist, the full yet muscular hips.

She might have been able to bask in the memory if it weren't for the thought of Jo in the back of her mind. How long had they been lovers?—off and on for two years. But the guilt she felt couldn't outweigh one thing— never before had sex been brash, so splendid. With Jo it was always as if she had to contain her passion, as if trying to fit in clothes that were too small. At the time she hadn't really known this because Jo was her first love, her first experience and at the beginning, that alone made her happy. But Jo always seemed to be looking over her shoulder, afraid someone would know, would see, would condemn.

With Vera, Hazel saw what she hadn't known was possible. Hazel sat up, these thoughts too strong to let her doze any longer. Pushing her hair back, she looked at the sky. At six a.m. it was blue over the airfield, but low, nimbostratus clouds were moving in from the southeast. Rain was certainly on the way. She shook Maxie awake. "Time to get rolling Max. Looks like rain will catch up with us before long."

Maxie rolled over and sat up groggily, peering at the day. She didn't say anything, just began to unwrap the blanket and fold it up.

Before long the other pilots began to appear on the field as if the upcoming weather was foremost in their minds too. Hazel observed Taggart arriving, making straight for the Rearwyn where Sweeney already had the cowling open. God, what a crew to have, Hazel ruminated. Oh, it wasn't that everyone had to wear starched coveralls to be trustworthy, but Sweeney did look more like a carnival man ready to crank up a tawdry looking carousel, than a

105

mechanic in charge of a highly secret test engine. And Tag—well, he was a bit crisper around the edges, hair slicked back. He had a hard look about him though. Going about her business, she kept an eye on them, watching when Jo arrived for pre-flight checks. If her body said anything, Jo was tense if not angry about something. Hazel couldn't see Tag's face; funny how he kept out of view. Well, there was only one way to deal with him if he never came forward to be part of the Derby openly. Go to him. Hazel smiled at her brewing plan. Where was Vera? It was time for some picture taking. Within moments Hazel had rounded up the photographer, and invited Sarah along for good measure along with her husband and mechanic, Sam, as well as Gus who looked at her grudgingly.

Approaching the Rearwyn, Hazel called out to Jo. Damn, but did that engine cowling fall shut fast or what? The two men turned in surprise at the party, Jo shooting Hazel a dirty look, saying, "Haze, we're in the middle of a conference. We don't have time—"

"Oh, this won't take long—a publicity photo of the current top contenders, and supportive crew. Good morning, Tag." Hazel put on her most jaunty air. Well, why not address him in the familiar—if he was going to be present on the circuit even in his obvious absence, at least let it be face to face.

He gave her a silent if not resentful nod. Oh, but he's unreadable, right Jo?—Hazel reminded herself.

And before anyone on the Rearwyn crew could rally, the airplane had become the backdrop as Vera lined up the three pilots in front, and ordered the mechanics to the back. Well, I'll probably get hell later, but I got what I want for now, Hazel thought, grinning for the camera. "One more, Vera," she said, as the group began to break apart, "I'd like one of Tag and myself." She turned with outstretched hand to shake his, looking at the camera with a smile, and then directly into Tag's shuttered eyes. He looked uncomfortable, even put out, but took her hand. She could feel the iron in his grip, and something sharp against her palm from the ring he wore. She said, "Thank you. I'm glad to make your acquaintance at last. If you need anything from me as an organizer, please let me know. And may the best team win. I'm looking forward to the rest of the race."

"Much obliged," he said colorlessly, obviously pushing a plug of tobacco into his cheek so he could mutter, volunteering nothing more. But were his ears red or were they always like that? Was he angry?

"Yes, how about a friendly bet here…."

"What?" He took his hand away sharply, looking dumbfounded. And why did the palm of her hand smart?

"Yes, I'm going to bet on my Zephyr, of course, and you the Rearwyn. Whoever wins buys the bottle of bootleg for a celebration drink. Are we on?"

"Hazel—" Jo interrupted, a definite reprimand.

"Well, are we?" Hazel persisted.

Taggart shrugged, a faint twist to the right corner of his mouth which she interpreted as a smile. "Strong drink on a ladies' circuit? Only if you say so."

"Are you in too?" Hazel turned to the Morris-Newtons as they nodded.

"We don't drink though," Sarah apologized.

Sam added for clarity, "We feel it impairs our performance and we need absolute precision when we're doing disaster relief. But we'd be happy to provide buckets full of ice-cream all around."

"Good enough," said Hazel satisfied. "Of course, we don't know what can happen in this unpredictable race, do we?" She looked pointedly at Tag. "Some one totally out of the top margin now could surprise us all! What do you say?"

He drawled slowly, as if toying with her and enjoying it, "I think ice cream sounds just about right for this race."

She wasn't going to forget his tone, no, even as she made everyone shake hands all around, Sweeney leaning against the cowling as though defying anyone to suggest a friendly look-see.

"What the hell was that about?" Demanded Maxie as they came past where she stood near the Spartan. All suited up, she was waiting for Tag to take off.

"I'd like to know too," said Gus in his quiet voice as he took up pre-flight checks in earnest, so that he could hurry off to the crew plane. "If I didn't know you were up to something, H.P., I'd say you made a darn fool outta yourself."

Vera began packing her camera up, taking cues from Gus.

"Well, it's the only way we're going to see him face to face. I wanted to see him, thought I might get a sense of him," said Hazel as she opened her right palm to notice a long scratch. She had a feeling that no one else had received such a mark when shaking his hand.

"And did you?" Vera asked.

Tucking hands under her armpits, legs apart to show more confidence than she felt, Hazel bit her lower lip. "I'm thinking about it. I won't hold you up any longer, Gus..."

He waved and headed off to check the C–175.

"I must go too." Maxie pulled on her gloves.

"Yes, please," urged Hazel, "keep an eye out on him, would you?"

With Stevie waving to her stoically, Maxie took off in Marsha's airplane about ten minutes after Taggart. Madelyn was to lead the draw, then Eleanor who was pleased to have drawn second position again. She liked getting to the next stop, dealing with the press before the other pilots came in.

Leaning with one arm against her prop, Hazel stood sipping the last of her coffee that Vera had brought over before she had joined the C-175 crew escort.

Just before jumping into the C-175 pilot's seat himself, Gus loped back to her, handed her the Zephyr's ledger, having completed his checks. Under his breath, he commented flatly, "Don't push it today, Preston."

Startled, she about spat her coffee. "Why not?"

He shrugged, almost apologetically. "Just the weather. Let the competition do itself in. Now I must be off."

The shock of his words hit her as she climbed into her cockpit for instrument checks. It was a plain reminder that the race was still in Jo's favor as her overall time was the best so far. That he had waited to find a private moment to give her advice, gave his simple words deeper meaning—a warning. That meant two warnings if she considered the scratch still burning on her palm. Oh, she could be sensible and take the hint, or she could dare to ignore it if she wanted to. She could easily clock 156 mph. in her little rat-trap. Couldn't she run the race as she chose? She'd be damned if she would let Taggart control it all. Why not challenge him to jump out at her and say boo? She'd be ready.

To top it all off, there was Jo, one position ahead of her in the draw, just out of reach with Hannah in between. Hazel watched Jo from a distance, warily. The very luck of the draw was like a taunt. How Hazel wanted to chase the Rearwyn.

She watched the first half of the draw take off in succession, wondering whether everyone would be able to take off before the clouds and rain came. Radio reports had assured open clouds over Tulsa.

Before she knew it, she was firing up her own engine, its power running through her body so that she trembled with anticipation. The sky was hers as she climbed, the blue and gold of her wings glinting in the eastern sun which would be eaten up by the cloud bank in moments.

No, there was no way to beat the clouds, unless she climbed. First the wisps of fog curled about her like tentacles, then danced away like dust in her wake. I must get higher, she thought. She tried to find the sunlight but going through the cloud layer was like scaling a mountain that moved. A blinding whiteness buried her—these were more than just stratus clouds, reaching well up to ten thousand feet. Soon she could no longer feel the sun, much less see the tip of her wings. Keeping watch on her compass she steered north, true north. This flight would demand dead-reckoning: the compass and the clock.

The cloud cover thinned, an opening between layers, where it was drizzling. She was sandwiched between the black floor of clouds below and a ceiling of grey ones that splattered her. Air pressure pushed down against her wings. Steady, steady, she commanded herself as she dove through a wall of fog again, bracing herself for some inevitable barrier. Instead, the cloud was ever yielding. Didn't it part for her? Crossing a field of clouds she felt no lightning lurk there. She herself was the charge of power, madly finding her way. Again she tried to gain altitude in the bone-chilling, drenching air.

She could not reach thirteen thousand because of the pressure. Of all times, she needed this lap to push her speed, had to find a comfortable lane. Jo had been pushing the Rearwyn, but the Zephyr had not even reached its potential yet. Gus had said the Zephyr could reached 170 mph. under the right conditions. Hazel set her jaw. The right conditions! With a calculated recklessness setting in, she began to push the plane—150, then 160 mph. If I can fly this fast, then I *will* fly this fast. She was not going to let Taggart fix her race, not while she had any control at all.

Snatches of blue sky played above her, only to be swallowed again.

There was no Red River to pinpoint, none of its north or south tributaries. It was one thing to do battle with the elements, quite another to find Tulsa somewhere in the thick of it. After yet another calculation, Hazel began her descent based on her speed and time in relationship to the compass, beginning to regret that she had chosen acceleration. What if she had overshot her mark? Her radio receiver announced only static, no homing beep, so she wasn't within range. Where was the supposed opening in the clouds?

Descending to five thousand feet only brought her into the bowels of the storm, like a fly landing in soup. They should never have flown with these conditions, at the same time, she knew they would all be driven to stick with the schedule.

She began to circle, backtrack, trying to locate the Arkansas River. By her calculations she should have reached the airfield. Still no river—she could see buildings, clusters of them—farms. But no river. Spotting a road, she swept over it, looped back, thinking to land there and recoup. Her better judgment told her she would be mired in mud.

Then by sheer chance, while making a wide bank to the east in hopes of catching the river to port, she caught the shape of low-lying buildings beyond the corn fields to starboard. No, not barns, hangars! How could she have missed the river? She could distinguish airplanes through the mist. Then she saw the beacon light, blinking on and off. How faint it was through the grayness. With a yelp she swooped up like a swallow and made her approach as the homing beep came in faintly over static.

The Zephyr's wheels touched the wet field and she could feel the aircraft slipping as she fought to control the rudder and break the rush of air. Forced into a ground-loop, her wheels skidded as she made a stop sideways. She knew she could have done a lot worse.

With the weather, there was little pressure from onlookers or the press, and all the pilots seemed to be taking the rain in stride. The mail-carrier's bunkhouse was quiet, almost everyone eager to collapse and catch a few minutes of sleep. A fire in the small coal-stove warmed their spirits as they lined up helmets and gloves to dry out.

Everyone made it in except for Pamela Christy. Word came in that she had chosen to wait for better weather less than an hour out of Fort Worth.

Hazel conferred with Gus briefly before taking cover. He took one look at her time and berated her, "Don't flirt with your mortality. Let her do the pushing. I worry what Taggart has in store up ahead for Jo and his plane— especially since she's doing so well. Do you see? Anyway, her engine almost drowned out on her, and she could only maintain 140 mph."

Helping him sheath her airplane from the drizzle, she asked, "Gus, do you think he really has an adapted Wright engine in there?"

He laughed. It was about the first time she had seen him laugh in days, and she had always taken him for a relatively happy man. "Doesn't *sound* like it to me unless it's *very* adapted. But I wouldn't put it past him to do something like that. I frankly don't think he has what it takes to design a completely new engine, but ya never know. By the way, she had the spark plugs changed again. Something is wrong with that engine whatever it is."

"He's going to try and do something to the Zephyr if he has a chance, isn't he?"

Gus shook his head. "I don't know. I've been on a number of race circuits—he and Sweeney have worked on the same crew before at least once. On the Florida to New York race last season there were unexplained failures on some of the planes. A Beech crewman came across the two of them hanging about one of our airplanes very early in the morning. The cowling was up, so you can't say they weren't doing anything. They said they were just looking, but even that's fishy. The crewman was a poker buddy of Tag's from the old days, so it was kinda like, 'Come on fellas, beat it and I won't say anything.' The plane in question had no problems, and the only reason Bates there told me about it was because he was scared. He had to get it off his chest to someone. If they threatened him, he didn't say, but after that race, he quit as crew and went to work in the factory. Now why?"

"That's a comforting story, Gus. I wish you'd told me before the race got underway."

"It didn't occur to me. It was hearsay and I didn't know they were going to hook up on this circuit. It was only when they *did* that I remembered. I might have had more presence of mind if Alli hadn't gone down. I mean, I had just gotten over all the pre-race details, just underway here—"

She didn't want him to apologize, and put up a hand for him to stop. "Where's Sweeney?"

Gus pointed with his thumb towards the hangars. She could see Vera standing at the edge of one of them with her camera, perhaps waiting for a break of sunlight. "Preston, they know darn well we're keeping tabs on them. I told Maxie I thought she shouldn't go all the way to Kansas City alone. Look, I know she's self-reliant but may not know what she's up against."

"They'd harass her?" But Hazel didn't doubt it.

"She has already had one accident—"

"She'll stick with race officials and the society ladies." Hazel wanted to ease her own mind about Maxie's safety, wishing she'd had a chance to warn her about the hand shake she'd received. "Have you talked to Frank or Sam at all about all this?"

"Yeah, they asked me about Al and Al. They don't know Tag at all, but they know about what kind of things happen on the circuits. Both of them have their noses under their own cowlings—they're doing this race for their wives but it's a vacation. They don't take it very seriously and don't see any reason for foul play here. What I mean is...they laughed."

"You mean they see it as a dame's race." Hazel finished dryly.

He cocked his head, a slight shrug of agreement from his left shoulder. "Yeah...more like a tour."

Hazel folded her arms so that she wouldn't flail them about in anger. "Sam should care a little that Sarah is in DW and in the top margin. Her airplane may prove easier to get to than mine."

Gus put a hand out, thumped Hazel on her right shoulder. "Sam is military, don't forget. An officer. Tag hardly wants to take on the Air Force which Sam would set on him, if he got annoyed."

"Oh." Hazel's mouth tensed. "Might not stop him. You wait and see— it'll look like some simple accident. The kind that happen in a dames' race."

Gus added quickly, "Look, I know if I need to call on Sam, he'd help out—he respected Al, you know. They conferred a bit before the race, friendly-like. Sam says he has had no trouble with Sarah's Taperwing. He wants to know any further news that comes through on the Arctic. Come on, you'd better get inside a bit and dry off."

She left him to join the others by the coal stove. Jo was on a bunk with her face to the wall, shutting herself away, perhaps because she knew that her time on the lap was sluggish. There weren't any more bunks available; once, Hazel would not have hesitated to join Jo, stretch out beside her. She chose instead to sit on the floor near the stove, back against the wall next to Madelyn who nursed a mug of coffee between her bent knees.

"You look like you need to get closer to the heat." Madelyn's friendliness was appreciated. "Any break in the clouds out there yet?"

"Maybe within the hour." Hazel took a sip of the coffee that Madelyn passed to her. "Thanks." It was more like black bile than coffee. She swallowed it and thumped her chest.

"Stevie has problems again. She doesn't want it to clear too soon so she can get things adjusted. Jo thought her engine was going to drown out. You know, Hazel, my engine was hissing too. I didn't do very well. I hear Pamela landed in a field."

"Lordy, I hope it wasn't a corn field!" Bracing, Hazel took another swallow of coffee. "But then, her Bellanca is a fair-weather model."

"Whose isn't?" Madelyn exclaimed, but her voice was low.

"I suppose if I'd had to ditch my plane in the Atlantic like she did, I'd be a little shy of rain." Hazel passed the mug back.

"Yeah, the farmer even pushed her airplane into a barn. Can you imagine? Talk about royal treatment!"

"No, rural treatment!" Hazel laughed.

She felt Madelyn's hand clasp her knee tightly. "I was terrified up there. I began to worry about what Louise said—how I'd better watch it. I couldn't shake it. We must be careful what we put into each other's heads."

"You couldn't be more right." Actually, the words shook her to the core. Hazel took another sip of coffee, and said quietly, "In all honestly, I was afraid too. The reports weren't accurate at all, but at least visibility was okay at a thousand. That's the only reason we could land safely at all."

Madelyn took the cup back. "Hannah has gone out to see to things with crew—blocked fuel line again. Luckily she got her reserve tank to work."

Poor Gus, Hazel thought, he'll stay damp helping out on that. Hmm…if Hannah is delayed…. Hazel sprang up, shuffled to the window to look out, one simple thought kindling within her. What if Hannah were delayed? Oh, better not wake up, Jo hon, rest up. If Hannah is delayed, I get to chase you.

Someone tapped Hazel on the shoulder. There stood Eleanor, that wide charismatic smile on her face as she pointed. "See that brightness? Sun's about to come through soon."

A smile surfaced readily to Hazel's lips in response. "Yes, so it is." She could almost believe the race was on the level. It always felt that way around Eleanor, even in the worst moments.

Eleanor thrust a newspaper article into Hazel's hands. "Here, read this while you wait. It's what I wrote up about Alli. You can keep that copy."

Hazel read: *The best way I can eulogize Alexis Laraway is by way of anecdote. I remember before the race began, Ruth Stevie Lamb was experiencing difficulties with her Golden Eagle, and had been working for many hours without stopping to eat. She was frustrated to extreme, a friend, Marsha Banfill, trying to make her take a break. Along came Alexis with a platter of cucumber sandwiches for the general cause. Announcing her 'tundra specialty' she had Stevie laughing within minutes.*

*I brought up the incident to Stevie last night. She nodded, remembering, "She called me Li'l Lizbet Follensby, you know, of barn-storming fame. I guess she was a great heroine when Alli was seven or eight. Li'l Lizbet was less than five feet tall and would do acrobatics out on the wing of her beau's Curtiss Pusher. She was known for her temper and her habit of pouting if she didn't get her way. Her boyfriend would offer her mink stoles, candy, a night on the town to get her to perform. It was all part of the show. She got so good she could do air to air transfers, dropping from one airplane to the next below. But an air show Commissioner in Detroit put an end to her act when another performer got killed doing the same thing, and put her out of work there. She moped for weeks but it didn't work on the Commissioner.... Anyway, that's what she called me—'Come on, Li'l Lizbet Follensby, don't you pout. Have a sandwich.' I couldn't turn that offer down.'*

*It's not that Alexis, like Li'l Lizbet and the rest of us, wasn't aware of the dangers a career in aviation meant, but she was determined because she also knew the joy of flight, that boundless sense of freedom in the sky, that sense of power and speed, that sense of breath-taking awe at seeing the land unfold so far below.*

*She will be most sorely missed at all the Alaskan outposts where she was a weekly and monthly link to the outside.*

*Every pioneering effort demands the willingness to sacrifice, as well as to persevere. I think of others like Julia Tuttle lost over the Atlantic, Jody Danvers lost over the Pacific, and Sunny Cooke who perished when out for an afternoon joyride, all of them trying to attain their private dreams in flight while paving the way for the rest of us. Yes, even Li'l Lizbet Follensby who fell from her airplane seat in 1915 as she prepared to perform—her accomplishments should not be underestimated or forgotten.*

*I can only hope that Alli's sense of exhilaration and triumph crossed over with her beyond those last minutes of alarm and fear.*

Hazel sighed deeply as she folded the article carefully and slipped it into her chest pocket. Eleanor had moved away to talk to others. Hazel turned to stare out of the window, remembering the cucumber sandwich, cool and succulent, Eleanor had brought to her that day in Santa Monica. Sandwiches Alli had made. And she didn't even like cucumbers.

She ruminated over the words 'willingness to sacrifice.' More like a lamb sent to slaughter. If Alli had gone that far for them all, they owed her the fact that they owned the race. How, Hazel wondered, how can I allow Tag to somehow mess with the Zephyr just enough that I can still out fly the problem? Do what Alli couldn't.

One thing had become clear—she wasn't going to let up for anyone, she was going to fly flat-out the way she was meant to in any fair race. No matter what, she'd make it. Madelyn's words came back to her: 'We must be careful what we put into each other's heads.' No, she would not act out of fear, but persevere. Even if she died doing it.

A woman with a mission, she went in search of paper and pen, found a corner to sit in. She wrote three notes, the same: *Tulsa. I am concerned that the race is being influenced by a betting scheme involving sabotage. I am aware that at any moment, on any lap, I might be confronted with intended malfunction. I will fly to the best of my ability to overcome the obstacle. If I should fail, my death and Alexis Laraway's should be investigated. Gus Henderson, Eleanor Wilson, Maxie Shultz and Vera Davis all equally share information that may help. What we have gathered so far is speculative, and circumstantial. But my death would mean hard evidence.*

She did not add: I'm writing this because I'm afraid.

Buying envelopes from the postal clerk at the airfield, she sealed the notes. One she gave to Eleanor, one she kept on herself until she could give it to her family. Tapping the last one against her cheek, she strode out on the field. She had written it with Gus in mind, but it now made sense to give it to Vera.

She found Vera taking pictures of the airplanes gleaming in the sunlight as clouds broke apart. All about crew were mopping up cockpits.

"I shall title it, *After the rain* ," Vera said by way of greeting, letting go of her camera so that it swung from its strap when she saw Hazel's sober expression. "Uh oh."

"Not to worry, Vera," said Hazel, cracking a smile. "I have a sealed note I'd like you to keep for a while. Do you mind?"

"A sealed note?" Vera looked startled. "Sounds serious. Is this to tell me off. Or a love note? A farewell?"

"Just keep it till later. Would you? Just in case something happens to me."

"How morbid! Nothing's going to happen to you." Vera snorted.

"Yes, well, Alli might have said that at some point, too. Maybe it's because I just read Eleanor's eulogy. Here, keep that too. Did you ever know Li'l Lizbet Follensby?"

Vera smiled, her eyes gliding off as she pocketed Hazel's envelope. "Lizbet, yes… she was big time. I was just starting out when she died. She didn't lead a very happy life, but then neither did I. Maybe we kept doing those acts in defiance of being miserable and wretchedly poor. To be somebody! I know she went mad about jewelry…real or junk, it didn't matter—like a starving kid after candy."

"And you?" Hazel asked gently because she saw the pain flicker in those slanted eyes.

Vera stood straighter. "I've always liked dollar bills myself—cold cash, you could say. It's the only way I could buy my way out of the pit—" She stopped as if she had said too much. "But it's true, isn't it?"

"I suppose." Hazel stuck her hands in her back pockets, leaned back to look at the widening patch of blue sky. "Depends who is paying the money and what you have to sell of yourself to get it…A bit of your life everyday?"

Vera fell silent. "Look, I have to go help—but I'll tell you, if I had gone

114

the way of Lizbet—as far as I'm concerned it would have been a job well done. She did honest work and was cut short. I happened to carry on—for no good reason that I can think of, any more than there was a good reason for her to fall out of her airplane. Sometimes I wonder if she didn't have it easier that way." She turned away to leave for the C-175.

Hazel, stunned by this outburst, begged, "Wait up. We can't part like this."

Vera turned back to her, a faint smile on her lips. "If I had a moment in which to kiss you, it would be now, dear Hazel. Later...." But her hand reached out to touch Hazel's lips briefly—slowly from one corner to the other as if to tell her to be still. "Thank you for the article, and I will keep your letter safely tucked away."

## Tulsa to Independence

At last! Yes, that speck on the horizon had to be the Rearwyn. It floated above the clouds at degrees to the northeast. Had to be Jo. The temptation was too much. With a hoot of abandon, Hazel accelerated, opened throttle, watching her speedometer. She let loose, pushing the speed up, steady at 158.

She would keep up with Jo, close the gap just enough not to lose time circling while Jo landed. She would keep on her tail all the way to Independence.

Everyone came to the Preston farm to see their home-town girl land in her blue and gold airplane. It was almost as big a do as the county fair. Old man Preston was putting on a barnstorming show like he hadn't done since before the War. The town had even kept its Fourth of July fireworks for the occasion.

When Hazel had flown through in June, she had stood with her father at the edge of the large hay field, the grass just ready then for the first cutting. Measuring with their eyes, motioning with their hands, they had imagined the field all cut and ready to host a flock of fliers. She remembered how much she had wanted Jo to see this place, how they had quarrelled over the route, Jo wanting to go through Wichita.

Now when Hazel took in the farm with a downward glance as she circled in preparation for landing, she could feel the tears of joy and pride well up. For one thing the old water tower, instead of sporting 'Preston,' had been repainted with 'Hazel.' As the wheels of her Zephyr touched the ground, she trembled with relief. They were here, the race was actually happening after all the dreaming. Then the tears began to fall. She cried out of exhaustion, out of spent nerve. She found it hard not to believe that her speedometer hadn't been broken. Surely she had broken time, shattered it. She found herself crying her heart out. Crying for what she had lost along the way, and for what she brought with her. Perhaps it was the safety of her mother's lap she was

115

remembering and which allowed her to cry now.

She wiped her eyes as she took off her goggles and climbed out. For once she was grateful to have people crowding around her airplane. She would let herself drown in people here, anything to keep away from Jo, anything to soothe her nerves. Let herself sink into the hugs of her mother, her father and all the rest.

Under fair skies, a community picnic supper was set out on trellis tables under the long shadows of the oaks and elms. No hurry about it though, as there were many people waiting to dish up, and Hazel wanted Hannah to come in, bringing up the rear, before she piled her plate up. There was plenty of time to roam about the farm, catch up on news with people she knew as the sun sank in a wide western sky. Her brothers took to showing the airplanes off, men poking their heads into cockpits and engines—all except the Rearwyn's where Sweeney kept a solitary vigil—women clustering around the pilots who represented many a hidden dream. The town band had come to play tunes while the children ran around like squealing piglets, begging for turns to sit in a cockpit.

Later, as Hazel was piling her plate with apple pie and home-made sugar ice-cream, anticipating the first luxurious bite, she turned to find Jo looking sternly at her while holding a plate of food.

"Haven't eaten yet?" Hazel said lightly to hide her surprise. "I didn't see you coming. Join me?"

"It's for Sweeney."

"Oh, tell him to relax, nobody's going to bother your airplane."

"He has his orders." Jo retorted.

"Well, you relax then, come have dessert with me."

"You must be kidding—"

"Why? I've always wanted to bring you here to my home. And here we are. But maybe that doesn't matter to you," Hazel fidgeted with her fork as she cut into the pie. "I mean, maybe I'm just being stupid but it's like a treasure I've wanted to present to you for a long time now. Funny though, sometimes you save up something, and when you give it, the recipient doesn't even see it, hardly notices or cares."

Jo bristled. "Why don't you present it to Vera then? She seems quite willing, and it won't be the first treasure, will it?"

Hazel stopped in mid-bite and set her plate down on the trellis table. She could feel her hands trembling.

"At a loss for words, Haze? Don't try and defend yourself. I thought we had an understanding. But it seems as though we don't. You are romancing Vera, so I don't see how you can stand there, all giddy. Oh yes, it shows all over you. Now tell me you've been saving all this for me," said Jo with a sweep of her hand.

116

"Well, I was," Hazel answered, her tone brittle. "I wanted it all for you."

"I think I should advise you that some of the other contestants are whispering about you and Vera staying on the airfield. It doesn't look good. Not at all."

"Damn it, we're keeping security. Maxie is there too. Anyone else can come and help out too."

"Look, you can't go around thinking you're fooling everybody, least of all me. I thought Maxie would keep you in line but it looks like she doesn't give two hoots whether you're making out with Vera. Why should she?" Jo was dangerously close to shouting. Only her instinctive caution and sense of people nearby kept her from unleashing her fury.

"Yeah? And why should you care what I do? You've all but admitted you don't. Frankly, I find your idea of competition unbearable. I'm just trying to have a bit of a good time on this godforsaken circuit—"

"Oh? Well good, that's very good, Haze. You go right ahead. I thought you had a bit more backbone than that, but I see I can't count on you." Jo's head tilted back as she laughed incredulously. "Ha!—You are one for living notoriously after all. At my expense now, I see. I just didn't dream you'd take up with someone at the drop of a hat."

"Drop of a glove, don't you mean?" Hazel cut back, icily. "Sorry to have let you down, but I hardly thought it mattered. I'm tired of being written off, you see. Yes, I do like to be around people who accept me for what I am, no pretenses. I wanted it to be with you, damn it. You have done nothing to encourage me. Well, I can't live like that. I don't live notoriously; I simply live about as honestly as I can."

"Honestly? How can you say that to me when you're getting involved with someone behind my back and pretending it's not happening."

Exasperated, Hazel stuck her hands deep in her pockets for fear she would start flailing them about in wild panic. "I guess it isn't behind your back if you know so much. Besides, all you're worried about is that others are whispering—and so, how will that reflect on you! Well I say, never mind. It doesn't have to reflect on you at all from here on. Let's just consider ourselves the competitors we are for the rest of the race, and nothing more. If you feel like talking things over when we're done, fine, until then, just keep clear of me, and it won't damn-well matter a hoot."

Jo stood back on her heels, her eyebrows arched in surprise as if she hadn't expected such an onslaught from Hazel who could plainly see the hurt and coldness in those blue eyes. Then Jo turned abruptly, and walked away.

That's the first time I've let her have it, Hazel thought, picking up her plate of pie without any appetite left. She poked at the rapidly melting ice-cream, her heart heavy and at a loss because she wished immediately that she hadn't said anything at all. Looking up, she watched Jo moving through the crowd towards Sweeney in the gathering dusk. Brooding, she watched as men from the town began to set up the fireworks. Why couldn't she have said that she was simply glad to be home? She needn't have confirmed Jo's suspicions so easily. Shrugging the episode off, Hazel gave in to her delicious dessert and the festive mood around her.

"H.P.!" It was Eleanor hailing her with a businesslike wave. "We need to get to a switchboard, remember? Gladys is supposed to be tracking Al down, and I said we'd put a call in by eight-o'clock here."

"Sure," Hazel said, coming to out of her pleasant delirium. "I'll borrow an auto and we'll go over to Doctor Turner's place. His wife, Dot, is the switchboard operator. The locals say, 'Who do you want, Doc or Dot?'—anyway, I'm sure she wouldn't mind a visit."

The two women made their way to find the motorcar belonging to Hazel's brother, then surreptitiously drove off to the doctor's house, Hazel telling her brothers to spell crew, but keep a sharp look-out on the airplanes and Sweeney.

Hazel's last glimpse of Vera as she drove off, was her doing cart-wheels with children on the lawn. She smiled to herself, thinking of the old tree-house down in the apple orchard. If none of the boards were too rotted out, they'd have a fine haven.

After embraces and exclamations, and thanking the good Lord for a fine view from her window, Dot Turner ushered them into the doctor's study with its shelves of medical books, its large wooden desk and handsome cherry swivel armchair. Hazel took the seat, put her feet up on the desk, fingers playing against each other as she waited for the call to get through.

Eleanor sat on the edge of the desk, one leg up, arm resting along her thigh, her hands clasped in front of her. "This is when I miss Maxie," Eleanor mused.

"This is when I miss her cigars," Hazel countered, grinning apologetically.

"Ah." Eleanor gave her a nod. "I think we should put a call through to her in Kansas City afterwards too, don't you? Make sure she's okay?"

"Affirmative—" The heavy, black telephone on the doctor's desk rang. Hazel stretched to answer it.

Dot's voice announced that the call was through, and then Al's voice crackled on the line. His voice was flat, belabored—It would take days if not weeks for the Beech experts to sift through the debris. Hazel explained to him what they thought about the Arctic's position next to the Rearwyn before the race. The static on his end of the line made Hazel think she had lost the connection, but his voice came back: tampering with the exhaust system would have taken some time, maybe someone had succeeded in sticking something up in the pipe or in a valve that would create a blockage, but then the resister valve had been replaced, but still, a severed or loosened bolt in the wrong place could throw things off. He didn't discount that something had been done by somebody. "...especially, if it's tied up in a betting scheme. I have more information on that...if you're ready."

"Go ahead."

"Well, I spoke to a fellow here in Santa Monica, someone I knew back in Alaska. He was at the airfield before the race and said that he was told that he could place a bet on the race. He's always ready to gamble, so he was game. Anyway, the bookie is right along with you," he paused, "—a woman."

"What, one of us? One of the contestants?"

"No," he said slowly, "the photographer."

"What?" The words hit Hazel like a sharp box to the chin. She could feel it in her jaw. "Are you sure?"

"He was told to look for 'the dame with the camera'—those are his words. She would give him the odds, take his money. So he did. He told me because he came to give me his condolences, saying he had bet on Alexis."

"Go on." Hazel didn't know if her voice cracked. She put her hand out to hold Eleanor's

"He gave me the stub because he said it was useless to him but if it could be of help to me—well, the winnings are to be paid at each stop after the race is over. Once again, by the camera woman. His stub has the word 'FIDO' on it. He didn't know who else was working with her but she has to be working with someone. I could wager myself that you won't find any film in her camera."

"But she has been taking pictures and helping with security!"

"Have you ever seen her load or unload her camera? We haven't found much left of the one that went down with the Arctic."

Hazel wracked her brain. Had she ever seen Vera with film? Well, there was that one time behind the field house—where had that been?—when she saw Vera rewinding film. But that could have been for her benefit. She also remembered Vera stuffing a brown packet into the camera case—the money? She remembered looking in the big camera case too—it had looked real enough. And Vera had used it. Then there was the telegram Vera had sent off—both times she had had a similar reaction to Hazel, surprise. Hazel slapped herself on the forehead, stammering, "I don't know. But she has published pictures. I mean—Eleanor knows her work, if anyone. Al, is your friend reliable?"

"Frankly, Hazel, I don't rely much on anyone right now, but he has had no wish to see me harmed. He came forward—it was an incidental piece of information that I wouldn't have found out unless I found myself back here."

"Look, you keep that stub safe, Al, it may be evidence...I want you to tell this to Eleanor who is with me. I want her to hear it from you directly, not from…me." The last word hardly came out as Hazel handed the receiver silently to Eleanor. Pushing hard away from the desk, she let the wheels of the swivel chair carry her motion through, so that her feet thumped to the floor. A heavy knot constricted her throat. Leaning over the arm of the chair, she opened the office window, wanting gulps of air. She'd be damned if she was going to throw up her fine supper.

Vera! Impossible. It had to be someone else. Wasn't there anyone else with a camera to blame? Vera working with someone? Vera working with Sweeney or Taggart? Impossible. Rubbing her right palm she was reminded that anything was possible. But hadn't it been Vera who had clued Hazel into the fact that Taggart was flying ahead? Hadn't she indeed—but why?

Hazel focused her attention on what Eleanor was saying.

"Well, I know of at least three pictures that I had published along with some articles. She showed me others. Maybe they weren't hers…yes, a few months ago, yes, on an airfield. She approached me, wanting to know if I could use her work. She seemed genuine. People are always urging things upon me, favors, direction, contacts. I took her on because I liked what she showed me, and also, Mr. Schulz recommended her to me, said he had seen her work…all right, Al, thank you. We are thinking of you, you know, aside from this business. Will you be available same time tomorrow night? Good. We'll call you from St. Louis. No, she's flying Marsha's Spartan—going ahead to keep track of Taggart. Fine…yes, and I will telephone my researcher. We may find out more about her background. Thank you…tomorrow then." Eleanor let the receiver fall heavily into its cradle. With her cheeks puffed and her lips round, she blew a long, silent whistle. Gaze turning to her companion, she said nothing.

Hazel gestured helplessly. "There is only one dame with a camera. What about the film she gave you, you know, in Douglas? She took pictures of our meeting!"

"Oh, sure, she takes pictures. One of them was published—you were making your speech, or remarks. I missed that part." Eleanor sat with her perched leg swinging slowly. "She only has to do it some of the time. I don't doubt a bit that she is a photographer. His friend—his friend said that she laughed when he placed his bet, said, 'That's what we bank on, you fellows who bet on the long-shots.' Now why? Going into this race we were all long-shots, except for you, perhaps. Alexis had just as good a chance as Hannah, Sarah or myself—if you go by experience she was certainly a match for me or Jo. Except that she isn't as well-known a name, that's all the difference I see."

"I asked Vera to talk to crew in San Bernardino, not before. He placed the bet before that…I don't understand how the betting works. Don't you usually bet on a race before it starts? Why is she still taking bets?"

"I don't think there are any givens to betting on air races. It's a brand new field. I would guess from the little I know, that you bet on the factors of each given lap. As long as you have the right date on your stub, the lap number, you can collect your winnings accordingly."

Hazel was glad that she was sitting because she knew her knees would buckle if she were standing. Here they were, talking like this about Vera. She hung her head in her hands, moaning.

"What?" said Eleanor evenly.

"Damn, you know I've been quite keen on Vera!"

"Yes, I think I detected that. And not one sided—she seems avid about you too."

Hazel gasped, "I put my trust in her, El. Everything we know, she knows!"

"Not quite," Eleanor reminded her, pointing to the telephone.

Hazel slumped in the chair. "I don't know what to think...I can't think. This is an extreme blow, do you understand? I can't bear to think she might be in cahoots with Taggart. No, I don't think she is, I can't—"

"Well, let me put a call through to my colleague. If there is anything to dig up on Vera, he can do it." She walked to Dot in the other room and asked for the next call, then came back and sat where she had been before.

Hazel began to shiver. If this is true, *I've been had.* The thought was unbearable. What was Vera—*married* to Taggart or something? Or *Sweeney?* Was there a scam in the works, a confidence game? Or was Vera desperate—is that why she had aroused suspicion over Tag? To deflect any attention from herself because she wasn't working with him but someone else? The thought made her sick. Jo's words came back to her. 'She had designs on you before she even met you.'

"El?" Hazel tried to find her weak voice. "Vera and I have made love."

Eleanor's eyebrows went up ever so slightly.

"It's one thing to admit that I cut out on Jo. Somehow my conscience could deal with that though it has been troubled...probably not as much as it should be. But do you understand—I let her into my confidence. I, I think I'm in love with Vera." She slapped her hands down on the arms of the chair, pushing herself up into an agitated pacing. It seemed that her knees were no longer going to give under her weight. "How can I be so gullible? If this is true, how can I ever trust again? Trust my own judgment?"

"Hazel, we take each other on faith all the time. And every time we take off." Eleanor followed Hazel's movement with her eyes. "And don't forget, I sent Vera Davis right to you. I believed her too."

Hazel shook her head. "There must be some mistake. I can't take it."

"Well," Eleanor offered, "I think it's time we got professional help."

"Professional help?" Hazel stopped short. "Police?"

"Well, I was thinking more in the line of a detective. Either my newspaper source or Lockheed could help us. This is over our heads. In any case we may need some quick back-up. Some of us are in real danger—any of us that are informed...and frankly, you."

Hazel slumped into the chair again. "I suppose you're right."

The desk telephone rang, and Eleanor picked it up. "Yes, thanks. Hello— Sheldon, yes. Eleanor here, I need some more research from you...."

Hazel listened, feeling colder by the minute as Eleanor relayed information about Vera. Jaw on edge, her heart plummeted. Vera had been her very security—what, just waiting for the right moment or signal to fix the Zephyr? How easy...take the pilot into your confidence, take the pilot completely, oh yes, any way you can, then knife her, up close and personal.

When Eleanor finished she walked over to Hazel and crouched beside her. "I think we should ask the doctor to give you something. You look awful."

Hazel swiped the air. "No, no, I'll be fine. What does your—Sheldon recommend?"

"He'll have someone talk to us in Kansas City. There'll be someone in place by then. All we have to do is get that far."

Hazel groaned. "But what should I do? How can I look her in the face, and not say something. She'll know something is wrong. Damn—I feel so used. If she is involved with Tag, she must have told him everything, all the way along, everything we know and fear."

Eleanor cautioned her. "We don't know yet, how and if they are connected. Maybe the betting scheme is something quite separate, something Vera is doing quite independently, or with someone else entirely. You see? Maybe that's why she has been so helpful. Maybe she has her money on you! I think you need to keep as friendly as you have been, for now."

"And make love to her?" Hazel gulped. "Oh, Ellie, do you know we were supposed to meet tonight someplace on the farm. My body has been wracked with it all day. I can't bear it. And just when we were leaving there, she was doing acrobatics with the children. Does that add up or what? How can I make love to someone who may well be an accomplice in Alli's death."

"Well, you could put the meeting off but keep her interested—"

Hazel hid her head in her hands. Why didn't the tears flow now? "I feel like Al—who can you rely on?" She clutched Eleanor by the collar. "Ellie, it was so *good*. How am I going to live with that? How can sex be so good and not be on the level?"

Eleanor stuck out her lower lip, jesting just a bit. "I'll let you know if I ever find out. Besides, maybe she *was* on the level sexually. Come on, hang in there. Let me put a call through to Maxie."

Hazel nodded. What could she do, get caught up in the push and pull of family and community, so much so that she could keep clear of Vera? How could she tell her that she had found no place for them to go? On the other hand, how could she go through with it just to keep Vera's confidence? The shiver in her body told her she could—she could very easily keep the tryst. She could use Vera too. She could, but she didn't know that she could live with it after the race was done.

Then she remembered the sealed letter she had entrusted to Vera. Biting her lip she wished she had given it to Gus. For all she knew, Vera had already opened it.

After what seemed like an eternity, Eleanor came back into the room with a glass of water and a shot of brandy. She held up the brandy. "Compliments of the doctor. I said you had had rather a shock about Alli's accident report. And I just talked to Maxie—luckily she was right nearby, had just seen Tag leave with some cohorts or other. He waved to her as he left. She thinks you should get the camera and take a look inside."

"What? I might expose her film."

"If there is film inside, yes, you might expose it. Perhaps one day you can pay her back. Meanwhile, I think you need to know whether she has film in it—as in right after taking pictures."

"I'll try. She always has it around her neck. It's not something she lets out of her eyesight."

"Doesn't that make you wonder?" Eleanor drank the water while Hazel sniffed the brandy.

"Well, not in light of losing her big camera. But if she knew that Alli's plane was sure to go down, it had to be a shell. We haven't seen any pictures from the beginning of the race. I thought she handled that loss pretty philosophically. If the camera wasn't genuine, you might think she'd make more of a fuss—as a cover."

Eleanor finished her water with a gulp and put her glass on the desk, clearly coming out of her own thoughts. "You know, you shouldn't be too ready to discredit Vera. It's Jo who is connected to Tag. We feel protective of her. It could be that Vera is somehow stuck in a similar situation."

"You mean out of some sort of desperation? If it's true, then Tag knows how to take advantage of women, doesn't he?...And I sure know how to pick 'em. It is hard for me to swallow about Vera—she seems like such a free spirit, strong in herself. I can see Jo's vulnerability to the situation; I know her ambitions. But I don't know Vera's. Maybe that's what I should seek out."

Eleanor nodded, pursing her lips. "So what are you going to do H.P.?"

"Whatever I can manage."

"Good. I'll be settling up with Dot. Let me know when you're ready."

Arriving back at her family farm, Hazel welcomed the distractions and inquiries that she would usually have found tiresome. What she might have reacted to with impatience and efficiency, she now welcomed and harbored, taking extra time to listen, to answer. She wondered if she had ever moved so slowly. It was a surprised Hannah, with an ear full of complaints against Beech, her assigned Travel Air and the fuel-line problems, who found a most receptive Hazel. Together they went over what possible solutions had not yet been tried. Once, Hazel might have fumed how Hannah had been saved a great deal more trouble keeping the Whirlwind out—the more complex the airplane, the more complex the problems—but she said nothing of the kind, and asked Sam Morris-Newton if he'd mind assisting Gus with replacing whatever parts Hannah desired.

While she was listening to Louise Gibeau regale the children with stories of her stunt-flying, Hazel discovered another cheering fact. The next day had been declared a school holiday. Children had come from miles around for the event and the promise of watching the draw take off in the morning; already she could see that blankets had been spread in the orchard, on the lawn, even on the airfield where her brothers were camping out. The notion of a tryst became ludicrous.

As the first of the fireworks went off, Hazel climbed into the haymow, throwing open the upper doors, feeling like the child she had been years before. Some of the other pilots were coming to rest, amused and delighted with their accommodations. Among them she could hear Jo's comment on the fact that the married couples were going to the local inn, along with Louise who was susceptible to hay-fever, and Pamela who said she, "couldn't bear to spend a night on straw."

As Hazel leaned out to secure the haymow door, she caught the whiff of cigarette smoke, and knew that Vera lingered below. Seeing that Jo was distracted, Hazel climbed quickly, if reluctantly down the loft ladder, and hurried out the rear barn door. If she were fleeing Jo, she also knew that it was nothing else but desire that drove her to Vera when her better judgment told her avoidance would be far better.

Peering around the corner, she saw Vera's dark form leaning against the barn, watching the fireworks, and yes, the tell-tale glow of the cigarette end.

"Do you want to burn down the barn?" Hazel called softly, accusingly.

Vera moved abruptly, hurrying to her.

"We can't talk right under the haymow, come on." She grabbed Vera by the arm, escorting her around the chicken shed and finally to the smoke-house, looking about her stealthily. This was the least likely place for anyone to intrude. Wasn't everyone out on the lawn or on the porch?

"I thought you'd never come," Vera gasped. "I began to think something was wrong."

"Wrong?" said Hazel too quickly, pushing open the smoke-house door which squeaked on its hinges. Good, it was dark. "Put out your cigarette!

124

Come on, put the camera down...I haven't even visited my mother yet, with every second cousin showing up—" She pulled Vera into the shed and closed the door, smothered her with a kiss. No talk, no talk—she would engulf this dangerous woman with passion, pour her fear and distrust into demanding caresses, loosen clothes, find those full breasts, the hardened nipples. Vera responded with an honest, spontaneous moan, as she braced herself against a stack of hickory wood and the wall boards, holding Hazel tightly.

Coveralls had to be the most practical clothing to take off, Hazel thought as she stripped Vera down, hands slipping along her hips. I have not known your nakedness, Hazel thought, but I find out other things about you instead, things I don't want to know. All I want to know is your nakedness. Underwear pulled to expose her thighs, Hazel's lips coursed between Vera's breasts, slowly down to her firm stomach.

"Hey," Vera protested, her arms around Hazel's head like a crown. "Not that now. I don't suppose there's a bed in here."

"Shh," Hazel became insistent, her hands securing Vera's hips, her lips parting Vera's swollen labia. Dropping to her knees, she began to knead Vera with her lips and tongue. This is my lover, she thought, this is who I want. What had Eleanor said?—'maybe she *was* on the level sexually.' For the moment Hazel didn't care—she just wanted to make it hard for Vera ever to forget this, because she knew she wouldn't. She had never wanted anyone like she did Vera, but what had been free, was now tangled up in fear and doubt. Her tongue begged for truth.

And then Vera came—too fast, too furious—trembling, stifling her groan; she laughed into Hazel's ear softly, fingers caught up like a comb in Hazel's thick hair. "...Help me with my clothes. Come on. Where are we anyway?—smells like smoked salmon in here."

"More like ham—we're in the smokehouse." Hazel began to pull Vera's sleeves back onto her arms, and button the coveralls.

"Hm, well it reeks. Oh Hazel, I wanted a real bed with you, a real night. I'm so happy tonight, full of summer and all the children laughing. I saw the Newtons leaving for the hotel and I was envious. I can count the days I've known you on one hand, but it is a complete life. Can't we go somewhere— I'm not done with you. I'm so foolish—I wish I could marry you Hazel."

"You what?" Hazel reeled from the shock in mid-button.

"Oh don't take it wrong, please. I never wanted to marry anyone before. Maybe it's because you brought me home. Oh, I know you didn't bring me—you brought all of us. But I suppose I pretended just a bit. I talked to your mother, well—I helped carry out food. She is tall like you, that same kind of hair, silver in it now—you have her looks...all except for that lump in your nose. And she didn't know me from anyone. I wanted to tell her I loved you. Instead, I admired the fruit pies. She said you couldn't cook!"

Wait a minute, Hazel steadied herself. Why is this woman talking like this? Was it honest sentiment or manipulation? Until today Hazel would have eaten it to the very core. Yes, she knew she wanted to be close to this woman, body and soul. She could not speak, but enveloped Vera, could hear her heartbeat.

"Don't be alarmed," said Vera, rubbing Hazel's cheek with her own, her voice becoming ironic. "I know you have your career, and that it's foolish to marry a pilot."

"Oh? Backing out so quickly?" Hazel jabbed. "I mean, what are your plans once the race is over?"

Vera pushed her away slowly. "I'll take a train back to California."

"And?" Like hell, thought Hazel, you're flying back and stopping at every field to settle accounts, or are you a swindler?

"I'll see when I get off the train." Vera made a move for the door, bending to find her camera.

"No." With full weight Hazel blocked her, hips hard against her. "I work on the west coast too. Your life is airplanes and pilots, or are you going to photograph something else? What about the book you want to do? I've been thinking about the sponsorship I could track down for you."

"The book?" Hazel could feel Vera's warm breath quicken.

"Yes. I don't know what you think marriage is, but to me it means working on a whole lot more besides sex together."

Vera relaxed against Hazel. "Let's see if I can get any decent photographs first."

"Of course. You need film? Let me help you get film. It must be expensive." Hazel took hold of the camera case which already hung from Vera's shoulder. "I don't know anything about cameras, any more than cooking. But you can show me."

"Yes, of course," said Vera touching a finger to the end of Hazel's nose. "And you can help me find flying time."

"Good, then you'll have something to do when you get off the train."

This time Vera hugged her. "Don't make an empty promises, that's all I ask. You have a race to finish, or have you forgotten?"

Vera's body did not tense as Hazel thought she would, not at all, instead a great wave of sadness had washed through Vera from the way her body slumped, the way her voice changed.

Hazel just held her. Empty promises? Are we both pretending that nothing is wrong? Are we both relieved for the cover of darkness? In what way are we honest at all? What does she fear? And what has she done with my letter?

"You'd better wash up before you join the crowds, Hazel, you smell of my sex."

*This Derby is preparing me to take on a flight across the Outback when I return home. The only difference will be the lack of airfields with fuel and mechanics, not to mention that I won't find other women pilots. Flying will be terrifically lonely.*
*Madelyn Burnett-Eades*      —*from a Journalist's Notebook, E.W.*

# 8.

## Independence to Kansas City

Hazel stirred from her straw bed to check on weather conditions. Peering out the loft door she gazed upon the field of airplanes and couldn't quite believe the sight. As a girl out there raking hay with her brothers summer after summer, she had never dreamt of this other use for that field.

Then she looked over at Jo nearby, relieved to see her still asleep, feeling odd that she had slept here as though it was a spot she was still supposed to take, while Vera had taken to the opposite hay-loft with Nancy Saunders and Stevie. She felt as though she hadn't slept, as though the whole night Jo could smell sex on her, even though she had washed up and stayed about two feet away from Jo whose back had remained firmly toward her.

She wondered if it weren't for Vera whether they would have nestled close, whispered. Instead there had been a tense, thick silence between them. No touch. Nothing like she had dreamed about before the race. How many times had she dreamed of them here, always alone and intimate. Never had she imagined desperate lust with some other woman in the smoke house. Did Jo guess she had gone off to meet Vera?

But she and Jo wouldn't have nestled anyway, not with the others so close. No, that couldn't have happened anyway, not unless they were in a safe haven like Maxie's guest bungalow. Forget it.

Leaving the others sleeping, she made her way down the ladder and to the bath-house to stoke up the stove so that others would have basins full of warm water; she made do with tepid water from the night before changing into clean clothes, then headed to the kitchen to find her grandmother and mother.

If they had ever expected her to get up at four in the morning, help bake biscuits and feed the farm help as well as keep the household going, she had let them down terribly. She had also disappointed their hopes that she would marry a nice local farm boy—well, Gram's, anyway. No, she had never taken to 'feminine' tasks, even as a small girl. Oh maybe to gather eggs, or help pluck a chicken. You were always wild ones, the family would say, you and Dewey. This is the sort of place I might have spent my life she brooded as she accepted a cup of strong, black coffee, then put biscuits from the oven into a cloth-lined basket…if there had been more girls. One simply hadn't been enough at the end of a line of four boys. Maybe she had been spoiled on that account—the baby girl. Luckily for her, the older sons, Stan and Clancy, had kept close to home, helping run the farm and tractor business. And it looked like Tom would be back after agricultural school. Their wives fit the traditional mold and, certainly, all the little girls being raised now seemed quite sure of themselves as tenders of hearth and home. At least it appeared so from the examples of well-stitched samplers that Gram had framed. Somehow, she had been granted an exemption—she didn't know why, except that there seemed to linger, a tacit acknowledgement that she was finishing 'Dewey's business' even though he had never even come near an airplane.

Well, if it hadn't been for Dewey, maybe she would never have had a taste for adventure. Dewey, the inventor, the fabricater of dreams with that wicked sparkle in his eyes, always treated her like one of the boys. "You can do anything you want, Sis."

She remembered the time when she was sixteen; to her mother's great relief and her own chagrin, she had started menstruating in earnest, no more intermittent spotting. It was her first encounter with a 'sop rag'. In a foul mood she found Dewey out working on his motorized pump he had made out of old engine parts, so that when the windmill was becalmed, they could still pump water. He couldn't get the hand-crank going, so she took a turn while he rested. She could swear the fitting had been tight before she flew at it; just as suddenly, it flew back at her, smack in the face. It broke her nose. Ah, the blood, not thick, dark and coagulated like menstrual blood, but thin and red running like a well-spring. Poor Dewey, how terrible he felt—his sister's face changed forever. It took a long time for the swelling to go down, the dull blues and then browns creeping all the way up and around her eyes. He never lived it down, and no, she never did look the same. She was marked. In a way she took it on as a badge of courage, her own private stamp of womanhood. She began to lift her head more defiantly. She wasn't a pretty face anymore. Dewey's cohorts who had eyed her shyly at school, now looked at her with squinty eyes appraisingly, perhaps a bit afraid.

"Aw, don't pay them no never-mind," Dewey had said, arm slung around her shoulders. "You're still the prettiest to me." And she knew he had not understood.

Maybe that was when the rift between them began. She had always padded after him, though she knew she'd never be happy in his pit-crew for long, once he started racing. She didn't want to be just 'one of the boys at his beck and call,' as though that were some sort of privilege. She was going to prove to him that there was a place for her in competitive driving. He hadn't taken her seriously so the fighting had started.

He: *No way, it's too dangerous. Let it be my madness, not yours. I think you should drive, don't get me wrong, but not competitively.*

She: *You think I'm going to be happy on a tractor for the rest of my life? I'll find my own car, my own sponsors.*

He: *Look, Sis. You can't race. I'll stop you. Not because I don't think you can do it. Land Amighty, how would I look Mom and Pop in they eye if anything happened to you? It was bad enough when I broke your face. It's because I couldn't live with it...if something happened.*

Adding injury to insult, he had started to annoy her by sleeping with any pretty woman who came by to flirt into his handsome face. She had hated that, hated the women that came between them. He got to go to bed with them; she did not get to go to bed with them. It was a realization that stumped her, a confusion that exasperated her.

What no one knew, is that the rift between them had had no chance to heal. Now if she wept for Dewey, it was not that her hero brother had fallen, not that she had so much more to learn from him, it was knowing that they had unfinished business. And how was *she* supposed to look Mom and Pop in the eye? Is that why she had fled?

Her memory stirred her from her seat in the kitchen with its low murmur of her mother and Gram talking as they worked. She went with a sense of resolve into the dark parlor to look at family pictures on the mantel above the fireplace, passed up the one of herself at twelve with that pert little face. Picked out her favorite of Dewey standing smartly in his greasy coveralls. She still wore a pair of his overalls when she was in the shop, rolling the cuffs up.

He had never flown, but he always tinkered with machinery. Sure, he had talked about flying, the barnstorming events of their childhood. As a kid, what had those airplanes meant to her?—not much more than fireworks—a good ol' time. No, his passion was automobiles—women on the side. Was she more like him than she wanted to admit? Following in his footsteps. If Dewey had been around to take on the job Pete Harper had for him in the fuel company, would she ever have had the chance?—*Yeah, take me for the job, but my kid sister comes too* .

She took down the picture and kissed it tenderly. Yes, it was strange how things were connected, twisting and turning along the way, creating voids and yet also, new possibilities. Like Maxie writing Alexis up in Alaska to come fly in the derby, challenging fate. Dewey had dared fate everyday, and it had caught up with him. What was she inviting? Putting the picture back, she felt in her pocket where she had placed the last sealed letter. Pulling it out she slipped it under his picture: *Keep this for me, D., will ya? I'm in a bit of a tight place.*

Turning, she saw her mother's full figure lit up in the kitchen doorway. Mom didn't say much these days about flying, didn't say much to her daughter except farm talk. Hadn't said much since Dewey's death—not a thing about racing, about Hazel's flying. Now her mother said simply, "I'm glad you took a moment out for him. He'd be happy to see you today."

"You knew where I was going, didn't you?"

Her mother smiled and nodded.

The mood before take-off was festive—the school children cheering, the neighboring farmers all lined up with their cars, wagons and tractors along the road to see the planes take off. As she began her pre-flight checks, Hazel realized she felt invigorated by it all, the lovemaking and the danger as well. And she felt as though she were thumbing her nose at all unseen obstacles.

By the Zephyr Gus was wiping tools clean that he had laid out on the lower wing. He said, "I've tightened the belts up a little." His face looked more relaxed than she had seen since Alli's accident. He added, "I'm not going to bother to tell you to slow down, not with the engine purring like it is. Besides, you're not going to listen."

She shrugged. "Well, all I have to worry about are the small things that could undo me, someone switching dip-sticks on me so I get the wrong reading, an important nut and bolt removed here and there so my wing falls off.

His face grew pale, serious. "Preston, I'm not going to pretend that can't happen, especially if the Rearwyn's engine starts to burn itself out."

"Well, if Taggart, isn't careful, he's going to find both Jo and me out of the race, and some total surprise as the winner."

His laugh in response was dry. "I think I'll stick to air tours from now on." He paused. "I'm proud of you, Horse Power, that you're not buckling under. We'll see this through somehow."

She grabbed him by the shoulder, wanting to tell him everything Al had said, but only offered, "We're getting professional help, Gus, someone who can help get to the bottom of this—"

A figure caught her eye, and she hailed Vera, exclaiming, "Picture! Vera, you must take some pictures; will you—my family next to my airplane."

"Sure," Vera nodded, unlatching her camera-case while Hazel strode about gathering her clan next to the *Zephyr*, bringing her Gram out from the porch while her mother took off her apron.

"Now I want a picture of you too." Hazel made for the camera, motioning Vera to go stand beside the *Zephyr*.

"No, no," Vera protested vehemently.

"Why not? One for the record? You have to have proof you were on this junket. For the back of your book?" Hazel motioned her to stand more in the sunlight, pushed her into position. "Tell me what I should press—this one? Steady—don't move!"

What does she care, thought Hazel, when there isn't any film in this camera? I shall pester her to find someone in Kansas City to develop this film, and we shall see what she comes up with. "Yes, I'd like to get this done up, do you think we could, perhaps through Eleanor at the newspaper?"

She'd find some way to make Vera an honest photographer—keep her supplied with film, help her mail the negatives or have them processed. Sooner or later, she would find out if the camera was in working order or not. What if Hazel lost the camera somehow, so that Vera couldn't be identified, couldn't take bets?—she was frantic to correct any mischief, any flaws in the race and in this woman. She was completely smitten.

"See, that wasn't so bad." Careful not to handle it like a hot potato, Hazel handed the camera back to Vera.

"Well, I don't think you focused it. See, like this, but perhaps it was all right from my earlier setting." Vera pulled the small light-meter from the case's side pocket. "Well, and the light is always tricky."

"Hm," Hazel looked Vera over with the pleased air of a satisfied lover, enjoying it that Vera was flustered. "Well, if it doesn't turn out, we can always try again, and I'll keep this film. A personal thing."

"I don't like my picture taken," Vera said slowly. "Why do you think I am behind the lens?"

"Oh, why?"

"Some people like to swim, some don't." Vera explained without the quick smile she usually gave along with retorts.

The race officials arrived then, and preparation resumed in earnest. Pilots clustered on the field to draw for positions, having put it off the night before, this time out of pleasure not pain. Hazel found herself in fifth position for take-off, Jo near the end.

As Hazel completed her cockpit checks, watching the C-175 leave with Gus and Vera, she felt her blood racing, the nervousness coming back. She didn't want to leave this safe haven. Perhaps it was only Eleanor's wave as she climbed into the Vega that gave Hazel the courage to carry on.

On to Kansas City then, Hazel said to herself with her jaw set. Before long she was up in the air, making that extra, sentimental farewell circle above the farm, then left behind the farm's windmill and water-tower.

She set her speed at 150 mph and settled into her task, relaxing back into her seat to calculate her route. Reaching twelve thousand feet, she wound her scarf around her face and mouth to keep warm, and keep her cheeks from getting chapped. The air had changed since the desert, more humid, cooler. Carving her course high above the land, she mentally checked off the rivers according to her map—the Neosho, the Marais de Cygne—as she pursued a northeasterly route. Everything was routine; no wings fell off. The blue and gold of the Zephyr sparkled larger than life, surrounded her, carried her forward. It was a magical bird smelling of hot oil. If she didn't know any better she might have thought that nothing could spoil her happiness.

Kansas City was supposed to be a quick stop, but both Stevie and Hannah who had led the draw, were having the usual sort of problems. But Stevie no longer gnashed her teeth in frustration, cussing under her breath frantically, perhaps because Marsha was still tossing in fever. The question now was whether she could keep up and finish the race.

Hannah had changed her fuel line but it did not seem to help; for some reason she was still experiencing condensation. Hazel wondered if a bad mix of fuel, even before Hannah's use of the Travel Air, had left residual water in the system. By now Hazel also understood that Hannah was meticulous about maintenance and preparations; she felt guilty and responsible. Had The Beech Company in fact, taken on more sponsorship than it should have? Maybe she had tried to push things too much in her eagerness. Hadn't she convinced Al and Al back in December to go with a Travel Air? What a good sales job she had done—a tidy commission. Hadn't she encouraged Stevie to go with a Wright engine for extra power? But I did all that to create a better field, a better competition, she argued with herself as she went about as cheerfully as possible to keep up morale.

Eleanor caught up with her, with a nod to her head said, "H.P., I have a propeller man coming in for the next lap or two. Will you help me make arrangements?" The words were for Vera who stood nearby. Hazel left with Eleanor swiftly, but not before making sure Maxie was left keeping an eye on things along with Vera. It looked like she wouldn't have a chance to talk to Maxie alone.

"So this is it? Sheldon found you someone?" Hazel said as they bustled off to the press tent.

"Exactly. Let's talk informally as though talking shop. Here he is...."

Hazel stopped short as they approached the tent. A slender man in Lockheed coveralls stepped forward, a can of chewing tobacco open in his hand as he plugged a wad in his cheek. Did he do it solely for effect in his role? She wished they didn't need his help.

"My name is Gregory Fox, Private Investigator." The man stuck out his hand to shake theirs each in turn. "I have a man in St. Louis waiting for orders. What can I do for you?"

Hazel let Eleanor explain the situation.

Then he said, "Well, what we'll have to do then is have my man place a bet with this person. You'll know Harry because he's tall and stooped. Once he has made initial contact, he'll walk by where we're working and drop a quarter. I'll tail him so any deal will be witnessed. We may have to do this twice, get plenty of evidence before we make any arrests. The point is for us to tail this person until she makes the drop off—see who else is connected."

Hazel winced every time he said 'this person.' He was looking at her now in a puzzled sort of way, maybe sizing her up.

"I want to witness any transaction too," she said bluntly.

He spat out his tobacco on the ground to his left, shrugged. "I don't usually let a client in on my sleuthing."

"It's important. I need to see for myself."

He cocked his head, as if chewing the request over along with his tobacco. Was it Eleanor's insistent nod that convinced him? "Fine, but only if the timing is convenient, and you will have to do exactly as I say. It's a matter we need to approach with extreme caution."

"I'm a pilot," she retorted. "It's my training to be cautious."

His left eye twitched—a knowing wink. "Shall we take a look at your prop, Miss Wilson? It's a replacement isn't it—a Hele-Shaw Beacham—not responding to oil pressure? Let's see what adjustments we can make."

As the two began to walk away, Hazel asked quickly, "Are you an airplane mechanic?"

"He has been briefed, H.P. There is nothing wrong with my propeller."

A sadness washed over her as she watched their retreat. When she returned soberly to her airplane, she managed a smile in Maxie's direction. Maxie, bless her heart, kept conversation to chit-chat, and a rumble or two of hearty laughter over inconsequential, before scurrying to take off. Taggart was long gone.

How shallow I am, Hazel brooded as she pulled on her helmet and gloves, swung into the automatic, yet ever so vigilant airplane checks. Did I ever really love Jo, or have I taken her for granted, some shadow figure? Was it that I was put out when she claimed her place in the light so that I chased after someone else for pure thrill—for something I don't even know, and can't handle? Oh, Vera, how I want you to be real, not some false name, some false front, something to trip me up in my vanity. If I can't pick the right lover, let me be a cockpit hermit, and nothing more. Just press on.

Hazel was glad there was a race to get on with.

## St. Louis

Unscathed and remarkably successful, Hazel made her landing in St. Louis amid tumultuous reception and demands for interviews. Being successful had its serious drawbacks; she was torn between wanting to make contact with Gregory Fox and pursuing Vera to keep her so busy she would have to live honestly in her trade as photographer.

For the moment she was not in a position to choose her course of action. A minnow in the current, she was huddled off by the pressure and sweep of photographers and reporters towards the steps of a handsome brick building, hardly having had a minute to acknowledge Gus and leave the Zephyr in his hands. Where was Vera? Evidently, she wasn't jostling along for a vantage point with her camera.

"Miss Preston, Miss Preston, what do you think of St. Louis?"

Not an airfield like other airfields out in the plains—what had been remarkable? "Well laid out runways, great visibility coming in. The new hangars and building here are well-set back and speak to a future of passenger flight, especially that remarkable atrium. Most receptive winds too! What a reception. Thank you, thank you all."

"Any comments on your speed?"

"I'm pleased with my Travel Air Zephyr's over all performance." Her answers came out too flat; she could feel that her voice was tight. Was it from the cold wind on her throat on the flight?

"Any comments on the upcoming laps?"

"I'll fly them to vindicate Alexis Laraway, and to put up a good fight against Jo Russell and Sarah Morris-Newton." And nothing had better go wrong for any of us—

Suddenly Vera was at her side, waving away the reporters. "Thank you gentlemen, but Miss Preston has another appointment at this time. Thanks."

As if flood gates had been opened the current of people swayed towards the next flier coming in.

"What?" Hazel said as Vera grabbed her by the elbow and steered her through the imposing front door, through a large lobby with the arched glass roof that Hazel had seen from the air, and down a hallway to the opposite side of the building. She didn't move so quickly that Hazel missed a glimpse of Gregory Fox to the rear of the crowd. "Vera, where are we going?"

"For an exclusive—while the light is still good. Out here." Vera pushed open a bevelled-glass door to an outside terrace.

"What does *that* mean?"

"Look, trust me, Hazel. I managed to get some film from a photographer if I helped him with an exclusive."

"Film?"

"Yes, that's how I get film. Most of the newspaper photographers have extra that they get from the office, so I can get a cut-rate deal. Sometimes if I'm charming enough, they even slip it to me, gratis. This is an exchange."

Hazel stopped abruptly, but only for a split second because Vera was hastening her to the far end of the terrace where a photographer waited with tripod and camera, his back to the dipping sun.

*You charm them out of film?* The way you charm me? How simply you put it. "Usually people want my airplane as background. Why here?"

"It's called a portrait, Hazel. Here, put your helmet and goggles on. Your hair is a sight so you may as well cover up. Yes, and your gloves. He was particularly interested in your whole image with the riding pants and all."

"And without riding crop?" Hazel teased, because she was nonplussed.

134

Vera didn't miss a beat. "Yeah, and no winged horse—that part can be left to the imagination."

Hazel looked down at herself, never having noticed before how thoroughly ridiculous her outfit was. She had simply stuck to it because it was practical, and acceptable at some level by the public, so she didn't feel the need to change into a dress after each flight. Even Eleanor slipped from her baggy coveralls into evening dress when it was required.

Vera introduced the photographer and excused herself almost in the same breath.

"Hey, where are you going?" Hazel said nervously. "You can't just leave me here."

The photographer coughed into his hand, smiling in a friendly but business-like way.

Vera blew her a characteristic kiss. "Ted won't bite, and he knows not to use your profile...I have to get back to the airfield." Vera hurried off around the corner of the building.

As Ted told her how he wanted her to stand in front of brickwork, Hazel caught movement out of the corner of her eye. The private-eye had come out the glass door. He stopped briefly on the terrace, perhaps to observe her, or to light a cigarette, or both. Then hurried after Vera.

Has Vera set this up on purpose to get me out of the way? Hazel panicked as the photographer asked her to relax, soften her face. He said, "You can't rush this, Miss Preston. I get five poses for the film."

"How much film?"

"Five poses worth." He smiled back at her noncommittally, then hid behind his camera.

She tried not to chew on her lip. It had better be worth it. She cooperated so as to be done more speedily, but she chafed, because Vera was up to something. The thought was unbearable.

"So, I hear one of your nick-names is H.P., for 'horse-power.'" He was bantering with her, trying to get her to respond, to let down.

"No," she said tersely. Oh boy, not that line again. Do all photographers needle this way, or did Vera give him the idea? "I'm sorry, Ted, but I've just come off a strenuous flight. I don't think you'll me find anything but tense."

"You're doing just fine, H.P. I can see that in the lines around your eyes."

She bristled openly at his familiarity. "Only a few close friends call me that, in fact, Eleanor Wilson—I take it from her, you see...."

"Mm hmm." He adjusted the lens.

Land Amighty, I had better shut up. C'mon, take this definitive picture of a woman overwrought and undone.

When she was free of him finally, she tore across the terrace and around the corner as she had seen both Vera and Gregory Fox do. A wide alley opened between the building and new hangars for airplane construction on the right. She made her way easily at a fast pace out onto the airfield. A neat row of contestant airplanes sat about a hundred yards from her. Not everyone yet—Jo and the last of the draw were still coming in. A commotion still took place in front of the building.

Across the runway were the maintenance hangars. Vera was not obviously in sight anywhere, so Hazel made her way briskly towards her Zephyr. There she found Maxie sitting on a crate with a clear view up and down all the airplane tails as if she sat among a pod of beached whales. Engrossed in a book, she hardly looked up at Hazel's approach.

"Seen Vera?" Hazel was chewing on her lower lip in agitation again.

"Nope, didn't she go off with you?"

"Yes, for a bit. She said she was coming back to the airfield. Max, how can you be keeping watch if you're reading?"

Maxie held up the small blue book. "Have to stop after every paragraph with this one. A friend sent it to me ages ago—some up and coming writer. She's always bringing me books from European presses. This Modern Library edition came out last year, ever hear of her—Virginia Woolf?"

Hazel shook her head dismissively; other things were on her mind.

"Don't read much, do you, Preston?"

"Only manuals. Do you think she's onto us, Max? Given us the slip?" And Hazel explained about the photographer on the terrace.

Max stood up and stretched, placing her book carefully on the crate. "I haven't seen her, but ya shouldn't worry too much. Isn't that Lockheed fella keeping track of her?"

"I don't care, I've got to stop—" Hazel began to hurry off, didn't quite register the low, "Uh-uh, not so fast, rag," from Maxie, nor the black boot that stuck neatly out to trip her. Hazel fell headlong, and only came to when she found herself sprawled on the ground. For good measure, Maxie had tackled her too, arms around her waist, and so they were both down. It was Maxie's strength that jolted Hazel, a spine tingling thrill. She gasped.

"Sorry," said Maxie about six inches away, her big brown eyes apologetic but firm. "I care, you see. I'm stuck on this junket because I want to know what happened to Alli. Not to mention Miss Mack. I'm going to accept that ya lost your head for a brief second there, Preston. Look babe," now the tone was tender, "if Vera is honest to goodness clean, then there's nothing for you to worry about. She'll pull through any set-up just fine. If not, then you'll know. You can't save her—especially not from herself."

Hazel sat up sheepishly; Maxie pulled back and began to stand up as she dusted herself off. She then extended a hand to pull Hazel up, helped dust her off too. For lack of words, Hazel slowly took off her helmet, goggles and gloves, stowed them away silently. At last she turned to Maxie, "I won't believe it unless I see for myself. I can't...."

"Can't you leave the dirty work to the private eyes? That's their job. I would personally take it very hard if you interfered so that we couldn't get to the bottom of this. Look—" Maxie took Hazel into her arms, smoothed the wiry hair which stuck at all angles, "I've lost my head over the wrong person too. I followed a woman all across country by train once, then onto a ship for France. There were no first class tickets left. I had to go second class, sharing a cabin with an elderly widow. Never got to see my beloved on the whole trip because we were separated by decks and dining rooms. When I finally did sneak through forbidden doors, by following the maids, and found her cabin, she was most surprised to see me yet again, having thought she had left me behind in New York. Did she see my presence as a grand show of passion, of bold love? No, she laughed in my face."

"Had you made love with her?" Hazel choked.

"Of course! It was deliriously good. Is that what you think about Vera too? To the point you'd do *anything?*"

"Oh dear, Max. Were you really that foolish?"

"Indeed."

Hazel held her friend tightly, not quite sobbing into her shoulder, but thankful to hide her head a moment all the same. "What did you do the rest of the trip?"

"I pined away in my cabin so that the widow thought I was sea-sick and took to nursing me. We remain fine friends, and I always have a place to stay in Paris now."

"And your lover has evaporated."

"My lover has evaporated."

"Oh Max, I can't bear it. I know I've lost Jo in all this too. But it is over Vera that I'm undone."

"I think ya should take up flying. A sure cure."

Hazel tried to smile. "I've thought about doing that, Max." She opened her right palm, pointing to the scratch, "I wanted you to see this too. It's what I got when I shook Taggart's hand."

"Did ya now?" Max bent to inspect it. "Did you show Eleanor?"

"No, we've all been at such a hell bent pace and somehow, well, I wanted to show you. To admit it to anyone else, well—it ...has been unnerving."

"Hm, from something sharp he held between his fingers, a sharp edge on his ring. Was he wearing a ring? Might be trying to intimidate you, warn you about your place in the race. I'd say it reveals something quite clear about his character."

"You don't do that to a lady, do you, not even to a woman?" said Hazel evenly. "But to a rag—"

"Quite." Maxie ruffled Hazel's hair reassuringly. "'Nough said. Good thing you went over for the picture, after all. I think he told you quite a bit. Keep watch with me now and I'll read you from this Virginia person till the others get in. You just carry on and go to dinner like all is normal. If and when Vera comes back, I'll be right here."

They both eyed the next circling airplane—Jo was coming in.

As if on cue, Vera came bounding up with an armful of field flowers. "I couldn't resist!" She said, those green eyes beaming. "Wild prairie flowers for you, Hazel. A field full of them on the other side of those hangars. I know you had to put up with that photographer for my sake." Her lips puckered in a silent kiss that Maxie didn't see because her head had conveniently disappeared behind her book.

Hazel was confused.

She went off to dinner as soon as she could, knowing it was a convenient escape for the time being, leaving Vera and Maxie to get dinner from the crew mess and to set up watch for the night. Vera was happily festooning the Zephyr with her flowers so they could blow off in the morning when Hazel took to the air.

Foremost on her mind was finding Gregory Fox to see what he had come up with. He, in turn was waiting for word from Harry who had indeed talked with Vera, and knew she had taken pictures of crew in the maintenance hangars. Hazel could do nothing but join the pilots going off to a restaurant in chauffeured motorcars. Publicity for the Derby was one thing, and it would not stop. At least she knew where Taggart was. Loud and clear at Jo Russell's side, he was busy claiming that the Rearwyn would yet succeed. Was that a smirk on his face?

Late, well after all the niceties and well after dark, Hazel and Eleanor found a switchboard and placed a call to Al. Gladys Jenney was there but said Al had to change plans and go on to Oregon, was relieved that they had a detective to help. She assured them she would do what was needed such as calling in police protection—all they had to do was say when. They begged her not to be alarmed prematurely, but they knew she was agitated.

From Eleanor's contact, Sheldon, they learned that Vera Davis had indeed been a wing walker some ten years before, and that at one point mention of her in events had ended abruptly. She did have a valid pilot's training license, did not seem to be wanted by police anywhere. He had even tracked down the fact that there had been a photographic studio in San Francisco with the name Davis which seemed to have been a family affair, but more of an artistic studio than a commercial enterprise, and had ceased to exist in 1925, reasons unknown, nor could he determine any connection to Vera, other than her address seemed to be the same.

"That's if this is the same Vera Davis. What if she is an impostor using some perfectly innocent woman's name?" asked Hazel on the drive back to the airfield in a cab.

Eleanor shook her head. "Wing-walker and photographer? Seems like it would have caught up with her before this if that were true. No, I think she is legitimate, but definitely up to something."

"And exactly what, besides an amorous involvement with me?"

"Indeed. And with an avid interest in security. She also is very vigilant and helpful on escort. Hold the cab," said Eleanor to the driver "I'm just seeing my friend here in."

Arriving at the dimly lit brick building, they made their way through the large lobby with its glass roof only to be confronted by an irate Jo coming in the opposite door from the field.

"You," Jo waggled a finger in Hazel's direction, "have gone too far now."

"What?" Hazel stopped in mid-stride, noticing two other figures rushing through the door behind Jo—none other than Vera and Maxie in hot pursuit.

"I've had it with this 'security' idiocy. How are we supposed to work on our airplanes if we don't have night-time to do it?" Jo stood tall for her slight figure; she positively loomed.

"She tripped over one of the wires—" Breathless, Vera hastened to explain.

"You tripped up?" Eleanor cut in, laughing to ease the tension.

But Jo wasn't laughing. "Yes, your pal here conveniently failed to notify us poor sports that the airplanes were literally booby-trapped." She stood glowering with her hands in her pockets, playing with loose change so that Hazel knew she was trying to contain her fury. Heavy loose change, yes, more like spark plugs.

"Hey, I've been in on it too," Maxie interjected, always one to take blame or credit when due.

"Something very strange is going on here—" Jo began vehemently.

"I'll say," Maxie interrupted.

"I'm not finished," Jo snapped so that Maxie's bushy eyebrows went up and down. "It's as though the tension of racing or your fear of flying is taking a twist, impairing your reason, making you suspicious, even hysterical—"

Hysterical! Hazel wanted to retort but sucked in her breath. Privy rot.

"—as though you are falling into the very trap Mr. Blaine has set up in his verbal tirades against us—that we're not up to it! That we are feeble females."

"Look, Jo, you know you can go to your airplane," Hazel stammered. "It's just a precaution. I had no idea you were coming back here, or I would have warned you."

"Right, and who gets tripped up but your very own contestants?" Then abruptly, Jo held back, but Hazel could tell she wasn't mollified at all. In her fingers Jo held a spent spark-plug which she tossed in the air, then caught. "Tag wanted to meet me here for an engine check. It's been half an hour already. Have you seen him? Should I ask permission now to be given access to my airplane?"

"No, we haven't seen him," said Eleanor smoothly. "If it can wait till morning, why don't you come back to the hotel with me?"

"Maybe I will." Jo seemed to take Eleanor's gentle manner to heart, while the others remained unforgiven—even Maxie.

Hazel threw Maxie and Vera an apologetic though conspiratorial glance before turning to fall in step with Jo. "I'll see you off." Mostly she needed a moment away from Vera, and strangely enough, Jo provided the opportunity. If Vera were putting up trip wires and taking security seriously, was it also somehow to protect herself, give herself cover on the airfield so she could carry out her gambling business? Now there was only Maxie to rely on. Maxie with those brown eyes that could look right into her and see her heart.

The three women walked back out, leaving Maxie and Vera to shrug off the episode and return to their watch on the field. Just as the trio exited the building, Eleanor swore under her breath and pointed to the cab, its rear passenger door slamming shut. Quite clearly someone had grabbed their ride. "Of all the nerve! I told the driver to wait for me, didn't I, H.P.?"

Hailing an oncoming cab, Jo said, "Well, I suppose he's not too worried, look, here comes another, all paid for thanks to the National Air Exchange."

"And my paper, don't forget," grumbled Eleanor. "I told him to wait. "

"Must've been someone coming from the terrace." Hazel looked with mild curiosity, remembering her photo session earlier in the day, but was careful not to mention it since there was no telling what would touch Jo off.

"Are you staying then, Haze?" Jo asked coolly as the new cab pulled up.

"Yes." Hazel could feel herself planting her feet apart, not wanting to read anything into Jo's tone.

"Well, if you see Tag, tell him I'll talk to him in the morning. I've had enough."

"I will." She waved them off, grateful for Eleanor's consistent poise, always keeping squabbles to a minimum. Hazel was also grateful that she wasn't left to confront Jo alone, because she knew she hadn't heard a fraction of Jo's wrath.

It was not Taggart whom she met back in the lobby, but Gregory Fox coming out of the men's room.

"There's a card game at eleven behind the cargo plane in the maintenance hangar. Bets will be taken then," he said in passing, adding as he walked on, "...She'll be there. Meet me on the terrace just before eleven if you want to come."

Hazel's heart stopped in her throat, but she walked on too, and out the opposite door. Well, had Fox's agent, old stooping Harry, dropped a quarter somewhere, or what? In the men's room? She laughed to herself, but more out of nervousness than amusement.

"Well, if you two didn't look so forlorn, I'd think I had arrived on a Valentino set," said Hazel to her fellow campers, upon finding that Maxie had stolen cushions from the pilot's lounge to make their lean-to more cozy at the Zephyr.

"She *laughed,*" said Maxie sulkily, leaning back with an elbow on a cushion. All she lacked was a wine goblet. "Jo laughed and said that as Queen of Safety, she should appreciate being tripped up in front of her own airplane, if it just weren't so annoying. It was you she lambasted, Preston. 'Impairing our reason,' for Christ's sake.... Totally uncalled for—and then to throw all blame to Verie—"

"Oh, it doesn't matter. I'm still glad I put those wires up," Vera cut in.

Maxie went on, "Personally, I think what she was really mad about was not finding Taggart here. I told her that when I went to get cushions from the lounge, he was in there smoking, waiting for her. He said he couldn't wait much longer and that *he* had waited half an hour."

Hazel let herself fall onto a cushion next to Maxie, checking her watch in the dim lantern-light. Fifteen after ten. "Oh, don't worry about them. Let them sort out their own problems. I don't want any part of it. I'm too tired and I have an airplane to fly in the morning."

"I'll take first watch if you two want to catch some shut-eye," volunteered Vera, unfolding a blanket which she tucked around Hazel. Her hands lingered around Hazel's waist, reminding Hazel all too keenly that this night would not be theirs for love-making. Without words the message came clearly from Vera—yes, she *wanted,* but Maxie was there and what could they do? Was the unspoken message honest disappointment for their missed moment out in the field, or just to put her off so that Vera could go to her gambling rendezvous? Hazel lay back, but reminded herself she wasn't going to sleep. She pulled Vera closer, feeling along her body under the blanket. When she gets up, I will feel her leave, she thought, as she let drowsiness take hold, felt Vera's lips gently against her cheek.

Her mind was a jumble of broken thoughts about what Sheldon had said. She remembered Vera's remark about 'cold cash.' What was so bitter or hard about Vera's survival that she had to lend her hand to such a low scheme. The initial conversation with Al still kept replaying, haunting her enough to keep her from total sleep—maybe she had that to be thankful for. More ominous was the thought that Vera would actually go and take bets in the crew hangar. How could Vera, a woman, go into rough company like that time after time *at night?* Hazel was used to crew during the day, and if she had ever worked in the shop during long evening hours, it had been with men like Dewey or Gus around. But Vera was crossing the line of safety that Hazel had always kept at least mentally. Wasn't it ever dangerous, threatening? Was Vera really so cool-headed, so sure of herself?

After what seemed like an eternity and yet, a short moment, Hazel felt Vera move away, rise up, and walk quietly off, first standing near the tail of the Zephyr, before walking up the line of airplanes as if checking on things, or maybe going to relieve herself. Hazel would not have thought anything of it before. She realized in hindsight, that Vera had often moved about, and Hazel had never questioned her motives.

This time Hazel sat up slowly, carefully moved aside the blanket, then crept along the propeller end of the line, angling off towards the terrace. Gregory was there at the corner; he gave a short, low whistle of acknowledgement, then motioned her to follow. Quickly they ran along the face of the building to the opposite corner, from there about fifty feet under cover of the darkness, to the rear of runway equipment—some gravel trucks and a steamroller. This last, massive object was where they crouched to watch.

"See," he said in a low voice, "she has picked Harry to collect the bets at the card table, then bring them to her."

Ah, so she didn't actually sit at the table with the men, but one she could deal with, just one. Hazel saw the stooping figure of a man as he talked jovially with Vera at the wide opening of one of the hangars. From her camera case, Vera pulled out something and handed it to him, then asked him for a drink from the bucket of water nearby. He handed her a ladle full which she sipped while he left her and went into another hangar. Vera lingered, her back to Hazel, still drinking. When she was done she hung the ladle back next to the bucket, and sat down on a crate. She took out her camera and opened the back, removing something—film? It would be a logical time to switch film in the semi-darkness, the only light coming from a distant light bulb hanging above an airplane in for repairs.

The wait was endless. Hazel felt her calf muscles cramping where she crouched behind Greg. Vera finished whatever she was doing and replaced the camera back in its case. Lighting a cigarette, she began to pace back and forth in front of the hangar. At last Harry came back, full front this time. He waved something in his hand, and Hazel could see him grin. The wave had to be for Greg's benefit, because at that motion, Gregory Fox pushed her back a bit. Hazel barely had time to see Vera take whatever Harry handed her.

Once they had made it to the last truck in the line, Greg hissed, "That's it. You'd better be off."

"Wait—" Hazel wanted to ask him what Harry had handed Vera, but Greg had moved off fast, disappearing into shadows, and Hazel was on her

142

own. Silently, she made her way back to the main building, searching out the Ladies' room. Running the cold water in the sink, she splashed her face, gasping. She could feel the tears burning her eyes, a mixture of rage and grief. Who was that ugly, haggard woman in the large mirror with one poor excuse for a nose, even straight on? Backing against the nearest wall for support, she slumped down all the way to the floor, hid her head between her knees.

So much for truth. So much for not being spared it.

There was no way she could make her way back to the lean-to and pretend to be fast asleep, so why pretend? She decided to let herself stagger back, half-asleep, and let the chips fall as they may.

Vera had returned and seemed anxious as she came forward to meet Hazel next to the airplanes, but accepted Hazel's excuse. "I was sick and tired of relieving myself on the runway under the stars. I thought that's where you had gone."

Hazel didn't miss Vera's quick, sharp intake of breath. "Where?"

"To the Ladies' room indoors, but you weren't there." Then more heatedly, "I suppose you're going to tell me you went out picking flowers in the dark."

Vera said playfully, beckoning Hazel to lie down, "a side of you I haven't seen. Go back to sleep, you must be more than exhausted."

"No," said Hazel, pacing up and down to the extent of the lamplight. "I want to tell you something. Look at me—what you see is what you get, a committed pilot, wanting a fair place for women in the field of flying, a chance for any woman pilot to prove herself. That's why I organized this race—no, no, don't try and say anything yet. Hear me through. How do I keep this race safe? How do I protect the pilots? You've seen what I do, yes? You've even seen where I come from. I've opened my heart and body to you. On the other hand, what do I know about you? Do you care about this race, really? Tell me a true story about yourself, Vera. Tell me—"

"What?" Vera had been kneeling, unfolding the blanket and smoothing it out. Maxie slept heavily nearby.

"Vera, I want to keep the basic integrity of this race intact. Do you think that's still possible?"

"Of course it is," Vera said, sitting with her knees drawn up. "Why are you so vexed?"

"Don't you ever feel afraid? Aren't you afraid each time you fly? You lost a camera in all this, but even that doesn't seem to bother you—doesn't that change things for you?"

Vera reached out to Hazel, "Come on, sit down with me. Of course I get afraid. I suppose I learned how not to show my feelings—every time I had to go out on a wing hundreds of feet up in the air. I'm not a top flier trying to keep a reputation, make a career. My point of view is different on this race.

Yes, I want it to succeed, very much. It matters very much to me."

"Why did you really want to come along, Vera? It had to be more than photographing it? Why really?" Hazel sat down in exasperation. She doubted now that her passion had ever reached this woman.

"What if I said it was to pursue you?" Vera smiled. "I don't suppose you let yourself believe anything that simple?"

"I think we plunged in together too fast, too deep—"

Vera drew back. "Oh dear. Is that what this is, quitting time? Second thoughts? I thought so. If you want to know what I dread—it's that."

"It's just that I realize I don't know you at all."

"We have all the world and all the time, don't we?"

How could Vera lie so coolly? If Hazel had hoped for Vera to open up, offer some sign of honesty or need for help, she now despaired at Vera's betrayal. "You say so, but how do I know really? How do I know you'll be there when the race is over? Why do I have the distinct feeling you will melt away, and what we have shared won't matter to you?"

"Oh Hazel, why would I want to melt away?"

"You tell me."

Vera took Hazel's hand, crooning sweetly, "I don't intend to melt away when we get to Cleveland. I don't want to."

Hazel groaned in answer because she knew that once she would have believed it.

"What's wrong? What has happened? Is it Jo? You are all tied up...."

"Never mind." Hazel flung herself down on the blanket and cushions, biting her tongue, grateful for the dark. Go, she wanted to say, leave tonight. Do your dirty work somewhere else. Get away from me. I can't stand this. Get away while you can, because I love you too much. I don't want to be around when it all catches up with you.

Maxie stirred, shifted as Hazel attempted to settle, and in that movement, Hazel had a strong feeling that Maxie was not asleep, and had not been for some time, all the while keeping her back to them. Feeling that back against her own, Hazel took the reassurance it offered. With Max as her witness, sleeping or not, she hadn't demanded the truth from Vera point blank, no, not because of the agreement with Gregory Fox, but from a deeper, demanded loyalty to Max. Yes, Maxie tripping her up and saying that nothing, but nothing must stop them from finding out what was really going on.

The pain of her knowledge, the pain of her silence, rang in her ears. When she felt Vera's fingers gently stroking her hair, she pushed the hand away. "We'd better wake Max. I need to sleep."

Hazel shook Maxie but the woman rolled over with a deep groan, and Vera said, "I'll wake her in a bit. I'm not tired yet. Go to sleep, Hazel."

"Sure." And she lay down to slip into a ragged, broken-hearted sleep.

*I just read that the Texas Oilman, Mr. Blaine who tried to bar our way across Texas, didn't want to see women get the vote either. The warm welcome and the support that all the other Texans offered us on our route, luckily proves him to be outmoded. But I know I'm glad to be safely across the border!*

Hannah Meyer                    *—from a Journalist's Notebook, E.W.*

# 9.

## St. Louis to Terre Haute

There was the question of a publicity photograph now that the pilots faced their last, real working lap to Cincinnati with a stop-over in Terre Haute. On this lap they would face their last crucial test of mechanics and will power, and as the pilots met on the field in the early morning, Eleanor called for them to gather. Not everyone came, not the likes of Stevie with her disgruntled head peering into the guts of her airplane. What did she care for photographs?

Then there was Hazel, hastily roused and groomed by a disconcerted Maxie who didn't know that Hazel had woken to the unbearable thought of wanting Vera to disappear. Had Vera had the sense to flee? Of course not: Hazel could see her approaching with mugs of hot coffee as though it were like any other morning, any other lap.

"Come on, pull yourself together, Preston. They want a photograph—come on, for Eleanor," Maxie barked, fussing with a comb around her head, straightening out the sleep-rumpled collar. "You have a race to get on with." Then that exasperated look, no, the despairing look from those brown eyes at Hazel's sleepiness. "Here, look, Vera has brought coffee."

"What's the matter with our Hazel?" Vera asked too innocently, but wasn't her face pale, haggard too? Maybe fear did lie behind the pretense. At any rate, what had once flattered Hazel, now left her cold.

"It's just the smell of fuel, of engines, that's beginning to get to me," Hazel mumbled with a shake. "One of these days I'm going to have to get off the airfield. The smell is in my skin, my nose."

Maybe the coffee did help, because Hazel found that her legs did work and that she could walk out and join the group, smiling with detachment, nodding her greetings.

The photographer with tripod was none other than the young man who had photographed her the day before. Irked by his presence, perhaps she woke up a bit more. Woke up enough to take a look at the nine other pilots who grouped with her, facing a thinly-veiled sun, Lila's Monocoupe as their backdrop. The tall ones stood at the back—Eleanor, Hazel and Sarah while

145

the others formed a semi-circle in front of them, Pamela on one end in her bathing-suit pose: hand on hip, chin resting against her right shoulder coquettishly. Nor did Hazel fail to notice Jo joking with Nancy to her right. To the sudden glare of a bright sun coming from behind the eastern mist, Madelyn put her arm up, casting a shadow across Jo's face. Standing on tip-toe, Hazel was about to call attention to this, when the photographer thanked them all, and would they hold for another pose?

The pilots heard only the 'thank-you' and began to break away into con-versation or to find their crews, uninterested in his frustration. Eleanor came by with a hat for everyone to draw positions. She met up with Hazel in mid-stride, holding out the hat as she spoke matter-of factly, "H.P., are you fit to race today? Seriously, you look quite ill."

Hazel dipped her hand into the hat for a neatly folded piece of paper. "All I am fit for is flying now."

"I don't want to have to worry about you—"

"You do not have to worry about my ability to fly, El, only my ability to love—which at the moment, is...come on, we have a lap to do."

Eleanor slapped her on the back at that, but without her usual grin. "Mr. Fox has briefed me on the developments of last night. I wish you hadn't gone with him."

"I had to," said Hazel flatly.

"Seeing is believing, yes.... In any case they will arrest her in Cincinnati, whether she has made a connection with anyone else or not. We can't do much more. Mr. Fox said the worst she'll get is a fine, and an order not to return to the state—if it turns out to be small time. Harry seems to think it's not much more than friendly betting—"

"Did he tell you how it works?"

"Well, it's definitely with local ground crews, through informal talk. She approaches someone, asks if they're interested in a round of bets, that it's not associated in anyway with the circuit, though crews all along are participat-ing. Then she asks for a 'local manager.' Well, Harry volunteered rather quickly, said he'd take the bets. Two categories match the weight-class differ-ences. Everyone gets a chart of recorded times. Small money is bet on a given lap, bigger for the whole race. You can bet for a showing or a win. So...where does that leave us? Obviously, she isn't including pilots or anyone officially connected. He maintains she can't be doing it alone—there's too big a pot and there has to be somebody involved who can guarantee payment that the guys trust. And Al was right—the letters F.I.D.O. are printed on the stub with a number that matches the part the bettor keeps."

"You can place on a showing or a win? Where does that leave Jo and myself? What about Al's friend who said Vera remarked that Alli was a long shot?"

"We didn't have time...specifics—I don't know. I had to go meet with reporters. That's all I got, so far. Oh, he did say that the National Air Exchange could exclude Vera from any participation on the circuits—a year or two at the most."

"And the wrath of anyone she hasn't paid up."

"True enough. Anyway, there is a scheme. Maybe she is passing the betting money to Sweeney while they fly."

"Come on—right behind Gus's back?"

Eleanor shrugged. "It wouldn't be hard. She leaves it on the back seat as they get out; Sweeney takes it."

"Why wouldn't Sweeney simply do the betting himself then? Why would Vera be involved at all?" Hazel asked, wishing Sweeney was the only one involved.

"We know she has been taking bets; all we need is how she drops the money off and to whom. Mr. Fox hasn't witnessed any drop-off, nor has she mailed anything that he knows of. Yet. They will be watching for that. Mr. Fox is going along as navigator with Gus. Like that?"

"Mr. Fox in the chicken coop," said Hazel sourly.

"Let it be for now, H.P. We've done what we could. I'll look you up in Terre Haute, but you'll push on. I'm in eighth position, after Hannah."

"Do you know Jo's position?"

"Pamela picked out last, but she's had that. I left them in discussion, but I think Jo's going to switch with her. Goodspeed." Eleanor gave her a brisk hug, then departed with a slight nod, a pointed look, until Hazel smiled slightly.

"Goodspeed." Hazel then turned to her own task, opening up the folded paper to see that she had drawn fourth position.

Gus met her at the Zephyr, having done pre-flight checks. He was prepared to head off himself, but was obviously waiting for her.

"I think you'd better come and see Mrs. Morris-Newton's little discovery this morning," was all he said.

She accompanied him hurriedly over to the Waco-Taperwing where the Morris-Newtons were conferring with officials and crew. Sam was pointing to the large pool of oil underneath the fuselage, directing crew to roll the airplane out of the way so the area could be covered with sawdust.

Hazel choked at the sight, a reflex to any oil slick ever since Dewey's accident. Within a second she had recovered herself, but the chill clung to her skin.

"Do you want to call a delay to your take-off?" The official was saying."

"No, no," Sarah returned. "We're putting oil in right now. I'd just as soon get going."

"Didn't I tell you? Didn't I say—?" said Hazel under her breath to Gus.

147

Then found Maxie, goggles in place for flight, on her other side.

"We'll have to talk later." Gus excused himself to go check the C-175.

"What do you think?" Maxie bellowed over to Sarah without hesitation.

Sarah seemed composed. "We changed the oil last night. Looks like I didn't tighten the drain bolt tight enough."

"You sure?" Hazel pressed with a voice much less confident.

Sarah tucked her long brown hair up into her helmet, shrugged. "Sam and I have no reason to think otherwise, if that's what you want to know. It's not like Louise. The bolt was in place but loose. I might have gotten distracted—there were a lot of spectators around asking questions. I can't remember, but I might not have tightened it with the wrench. Isn't that why we do checks? Besides, Vera and Maxie were on the field when we left, crowds gone and we had already dismissed ground crew." Sarah smiled reassuringly then, but Hazel wasn't convinced though she nodded thoughtfully.

As she walked away with Maxie, she said, "I want Greg Fox to know. It could have been a regular slip up, and if the oil dripped slowly, they may not have noticed in the dusk. But then again..." She paused, "Oh Max, Vera could have easily done it any time while setting up trip wires, or any time in the night. Another independent affected! The point is, I predicted it."

"Wait a minute," Maxie put a hand on Hazel's shoulder, "An oil leak is not a problem. She hasn't even asked for a delay and the five minute penalty that goes with it. That's all that might have happened."

"Five minutes is important at this point! Any delay, any penalty—she's in the top margin!" Hazel threw back hotly.

"Yes, but it didn't happen."

"It was an attempt—"

"Hey, rag, I ain't fighting with ya! We have the fact of it. Now I gotta get going." Maxie gave her a peck on the cheek.

And Hazel was left to mutter to herself; five minutes lost against Jo right now means it's nearly impossible to close the gap. A big difference between ten minutes and fifteen, Max.

By now Gus was already firing up the C-175 which meant both Vera and Sweeney had already boarded with Greg Fox, and would be on their way. What an escort!—and all of them knowing full well about the oil spill by now. And there was Maxie's Spartan out on the runway with clearance to go. How much had her delay meant, considering that Taggart had taken off even before pilots began arriving?

She began to look the Zephyr over, one item at a time. It was like looking at her face in a mirror—something so familiar, yet so easily invisible because of her preconception. How could she really see a new line etched along her eyes, or at the corner of her mouth? How could she really see her airplane, any more than she cared to see her nose? The plane felt sound to her, the way

148

a habit feels—wouldn't she know immediately if something were different, amiss? Just as she used to know, almost instinctively, when a cow or a pig was ailing during routine farm chores? While she might have a broken heart, she didn't doubt for a minute that she had her senses about her, her reflexes. Her nerve was there in spite of herself, keeping her alive. That was why she knew she could fly.

All she found wrong were all the wilted flowers that Vera had left on her seat and along the wing. Hey, I've been dazzled by a dame, but now I race, she thought as she swung into the cockpit. Wasn't that what Dewey had always said after one of his flings? They never seem to rattle him. But she really wasn't acting like her brother, was she? Hadn't she been willing to take Vera seriously? It was Vera who had been deceitful. Maybe Dewey had been right though. She hadn't liked his attitude, and yet, he never made pretenses. Why couldn't she accept her time with Vera as a casual fling? Why was she so attached, so emotional, so undone by it? Had Dewey ever cared about trust, about whether his lovers were honest or not? That was the difference.

The gas fumes from the other planes were bothering her more than usual this morning. She shook her head to clear it of all the residue of feelings that fogged up her mind along with the fumes.

She finished up her cockpit checks and was ready to go. But there was the slight error; Nancy in her Eagle Wright had been pushed by ground crew for take-off ahead of her. She had to unstrap herself, stand up and wave to the official, signalling four with her fingers up. Since she hadn't opened the engine yet, the official waved for Nancy to go on, and Hazel took fifth. The distraction helped clear her head, put her into gear. It was time to pay attention to the business of flying.

Soon great squares of farmland passed below her as Hazel flew northeast towards the Kaskaskia River; then along the same angle, she searched out the Wabash. The winds were favorable to push her speed, but she didn't. She flew the way she might on some regular run, when she had no reason to prove anything, except to keep pace.

Besides, she was disconcerted by the fumes again. Was it her imagination—or what? Up here she should be feeling clear-headed, but the smell of gas was persistent. She had been smelling fumes all morning—why hadn't she taken it seriously? It wasn't something hanging about the airfield; this was something hanging about her airplane. Glancing quickly at the fuel gauge, convincing herself that the needle was right where it should be and no less, the cockpit was still becoming more and more oppressive with the smell of fuel—going right to her head.

Damn it. You're right Maxie, we've got to be able to swear. Damn it. I have a fuel leak somewhere. Banking to port, she looked along her lower port wing, as visibility allowed her. Wasn't the fuel-cap seal holding? Where was the problem? She had checked it, and after Gus, at that. It held during two checks, seemed tight—the manual lock at any rate. But as she glanced at her well-slanted wing, she could see liquid sluicing along the wing surface, evaporating almost immediately. Catching a strong whiff of it, she thought it would send her over into a flip, but gritting her teeth, she steadied her position, found her equilibrium, fumbling in her pockets, then along her seat for a cloth, a rag. There was always one around; she pulled an old, stained rag which had been jammed along side her seat, held it to her nose and mouth. Dog-gonnit, the fuel cap was loose, or the seal wasn't holding, or *something*. And it was...just...beyond...*reach*.

Or something. Why did Vera come to mind so quickly now? Was this it then, the quick jobby, oh wing-walker? Where are you now when I need you to go out there and stuff a rag in? Whatever it was, the fuel cap had been played with. How simple! How effective! She might as well be flying with her fuel tank wide open. Oh good joke, the specialty fuel expert gets hers. How brutal.

Due to the shock, she found she had dropped speed to 140mph, and was losing altitude rapidly. Hell, she was in a dive, down a thousand feet, the winds beginning to play with her. Rallying, she nosed up again to find her smooth ride, keeping the greasy rag to her face—stale grease had to be better than fresh fumes—and began to consult her map for a place to land before she passed out. Thank goodness she had an open cockpit.

Think. Think clearly. How is it possible to think when my head is spinning? Begin descent, *now*. Before the Zephyr takes you down by itself.

She cursed: what a clever tactic! If someone wanted to delay me, that had to be it! Would that I had had the oil spill this morning instead.

No time to worry about who had done it or when. She had to get down. Not too fast. Easy. Watch the altimeter. Take it slow. Where am I?

Only one thing propelled her forward, downward. She had to make it. She was sitting in the middle of fuel tanks, amid the possibility of explosion. Her head was dizzy and sick. She had to make it.

Getting down to a few thousand feet she began to circle, watching for her options. A field, a road. If I landed quickly and took care of it, I wouldn't lose much time. Only a filthy penalty point or two. Lose much time! Dammit, if I fix it, then where is the proof upon landing? No, I'm going to fly sick as a dog, but I'm going to land with proof!

How tired she was, dizzy.

Holding the rag tightly against her face she nosed up again with ferocity. What was her time? Her eyes ached as she looked at her coordinates and wondered whether they were right. The compass looked fuzzy.

If she didn't know better she would have thought she was Marsha coming down with typhoid fever. Marsha had flown a whole day with that coming upon her. I'll be damned—if she could do it, I'll do it. Had it been like this for Alli? Had Alli been inundated by fumes? Damnation—stuck in a closed cockpit, she would be asphyxiated. No wonder she couldn't jump. It was like being drunk. Hazel panted, digging her back against her parachute.

No, I won't jump. I won't have to jump.

A sensation washed over her, beyond the nausea, a sensation which was almost cleansing. She couldn't fathom it at first, too busy keeping to her course at five thousand feet, but it crept up her back, rattled her teeth, ached in her groin. It left a bitter taste in her mouth, a thickness in her throat. It even had a smell of its own beyond the gas fumes. Only when it licked the edges of her mind and pierced her heart, did she realize what it was.

What she felt was fear.

It clawed at her steadfastness, coldly challenging her reason, so that she began to wonder at her decisions. It defied her belief in herself, reminding her constantly that she was nothing but a piece of fluff up there in the ether. And all alone.

Alli had felt this. Alli had felt this.

Perhaps that is what saved Hazel now, gave her the strength to press on. Alli had felt this, and by God, Hazel was going to make it, to bring the proof that was needed. She wasn't going to let it kill her too.

Checking her watch, she calculated that she'd reach the airfield in half an hour. Half an hour. That's all. She had to make it. Open throttle, go all out. Too low, but go. The more fuel used up, the better. How slowly she rumbled through the sky like a big, sluggish bumblebee at the end of summer. Biting on the rag stuck in her mouth, her head reeled, but she kept her hands clenched on the stick. The already gaping seam on her left glove split even further. Knees weak, she kept her feet firm on the rudder. Let the fear drive her on, become the very strength she needed.

And wasn't this exactly what she had been waiting for, waiting to defy?

Terre Haute waited for her not far beyond the border of Indiana. Hazel knew this particular airfield, and moaned with relief when she began to see signs of approach. Then came the joy of that homing beep on the receiver. At last she could even see the few hangars in the distance, the newly built barn-like commercial structure, the welcoming stretches of clear earth making for a choice of approaches depending on the wind; how it danced in her vision so that it was hard to calculate a true bearing. She had to be off—coming in too low. If ground officials had any sense, they'd see she was in trouble. Clear the runway. Please, clear the runway. Please, either have Nancy in already or else not circling about. If she hit anything it was all over. Could she even bear to make the requisite circle? She couldn't see any interference, no sign of another circling airplane. Hanging in a wide, slow wobbly circle—more like the tail-end of a spiral, she announced herself. Ah, the signalman was waving the red and black emergency flag. Hands trembling on the controls, she felt as though she had no more strength to play against the wind with her legs. She'd be lucky if she could keep the plane upright.

Rocking dangerously, she cut the engine to glide in. Surely, she couldn't do any worse than the first time she ever landed, anticipating everything too soon. Bump. Bounce. Bump. That was it. Only when the wheels finally had full contact with the ground, and she was rolling to a stop, flaps braced, did she let herself acknowledge the acute pain in her head.

There's one thing you didn't count on, Vera—too bad the winds were so good, in my favor, or you might really have got me.

Good thing she was in the first half of the draw, so Gus and the lot would still be there. Coasting to the end of the runway, she let herself be carried to a stop by her momentum. Already ground crew were running out to assist. Having shut down her engine early, she'd have to rely on crew to get her off the runway, push her to her allotted spot.

Gus was there all right, first person up on the wing to her, his face like stone. As she spat the rag out over the side of the cockpit, she could see him fanning the air.

"Good God, Preston," was all he said as he helped her unstrap herself. Willingly, she let him help pull her out. Hand to her mouth, she virtually dropped to the ground, heaving. The medic was beside her, helping her out of the parachute. Gus shouted, "Get her away from here."

Heaving, rasping, she fought for gulps of fresh air, too fast, thirsting for air. How dizzy, as she felt arms lifting her body up by her armpits and thighs, running with her to grass. Someone was fanning in front of her face. "Easy, not too deep. Slow easy breathing. With me—in...out...in—"

"Gus—" she tried, "Gus."

"I'm right here. Don't talk. Breathe."

"Don't touch...the Zephyr. No, I must tell you—" she waved urgently, feebly, "get an official. Check the fuel-cap seal. See...." Did she pass out or was she heaving? Or both? Everything was a blur. All she knew was that when she came to a bit, she was propped up, the doctor at her side, taking her pulse. She wondered when she had ever felt so utterly sick. Was that her groaning?

Then who was that kneeling beside her, holding a tin mug to her lips, but Vera? Clumsily, ferociously, Hazel sat up enough to knock away the cup with a swipe of her arm, falling forward at the same time. On her hands and knees she threw up like a dog. And when she was done, she rolled away onto her back, panting. And yet her eyes were riveted to Vera, crying hoarsely, "Security, Vera? Get away from me. Get...away...from me."

"What? Hazel," Vera came closer to touch her, but Hazel pushed away.

152

"Hazel! Oh my God—she's white as a sheet!"

"Leave her be," said the calm voice of the doctor. "She's still very sick. We need to move her. Clear out folks. We don't need a crowd."

"Is she out of the race, Doc?" Came some excited male voice from beyond him.

Hazel clawed her way to kneeling position, blood pounding in her brain. "Out? No way. I'll be damned if I am out! Get that? Keep the swearing off the record—I didn't swear. No swearing on the dang ladies' circuit, eh?" She waggled a finger in the blurry direction of the speaker. One leg forward, she braced herself to stand up. A medic helped her to her feet. Reeling around, but with his support, she saw Vera looking at her dumbfounded, lost. "Vera. You tell me, Vera, how did it happen?"

"I honestly don't know. You must believe me, Hazel. I only went to sleep after Maxie was up. Nothing could have been done at night—"

Gus walked up at that moment with a race official, Gregory Fox beside him, and some other men, one in what looked like a policeman's uniform. In Gus' hand, held there in a clean rag, sat the fuel cap. Obviously missing was the rubber seal. He said, "The cap fell into my hand when I touched the clasp."

"As I thought," Hazel managed through her clenched jaw, "but stuck with something that sustained two checks. Resin that softened with the fuel? What's that?" She pointed to a tiny suggestion of a substance stuck to the rim. The inside of the cap was a squared-off circle where the manual lock clicked into place. "Bonded to the clasp, looks to me. I think the police should have a look at that, eh?"

"Maybe canvas glue, something soluble in petroleum. Adheres to metal too with a tight, if not temporary bond."

A circle of people gathered around to inspect the item, as Gus handed it to the official.

Hazel sighed deeply. The relief of knowing, of having some proof, was an exquisite anti-dote to her persistent head-ache. She thanked the race official.

"Are you sure this was deliberate?" The official pressed. "Uh…you know things can happen during maintenance, uh, Mrs. Morris-Newton experienced an oil spill this morning because the drain plug hadn't been tightened up enough—"

Before Hazel could explode indignantly, suddenly wondering why she risked her life to fly in with proof, Gus cut in smoothly, "One could lose the seal in routine refueling though I've never experienced that because it fits in there snugly. You have to pry it out, don't you see? And then there is the fact of this bit of substance stuck here. That's highly irregular."

"Well, we'll make a report on this then," the official retracted his doubt, "but we'll need the cap. You must also fill out a report, Miss Preston. Delib-

erate tampering, you think? Against you in particular? This is most distress-
ing. Who will you press charges against?"

She sensed masses of people crowding, exclaiming, cameras clicking
around her. Uh oh, and press in on it already. Well fine, let it be known.
Glancing up, she caught Gregory Fox's gaze. No, he said with the thrust of
his lower lip, the wrinkles in his forehead. Not yet, his eyes commanded.
Hazel's shoulders sagged; she looked away as Gus wrapped the cap up carefully and handed it to the official.

"I have no charges to press at this time. I have no idea what happened,"
she said in a detached voice.

Turning to Gus, she took his elbow and began to pace away from the
people. "We'll keep an eye on her, thanks doctor." Gus nodded to one side,
let her lean on his other to lead her away.

She gave him a level look and growled in a low voice, "I'd stake my life
on the fact that the same stunt was pulled on Alexis. Simple, isn't it? I don't
think she had an exhaust problem on that lap at all. Fumes overcame her in
that closed cock-pit, I don't wonder that her crash was fatal. It was bad
enough in my open one. I'll bet she jumped late because she was out of her
mind from the fumes. Her Arctic burned up because there was an explosion
when it hit the ground. We need to cable Gladys Jenney and Al. Perhaps they
can have the clothes she was wearing at the time examined. An autopsy may
be in order. I wonder if Al can remember any smell of gas on her?"

She felt the presence of another person keeping tight behind her. Wasn't
it possible to shake Vera off? When she looked at Vera, what did she see? Was
there no hint of guilt? Fear, yes, that was obvious in those beautifully slanted
eyes.

"Vera," Hazel put a conciliatory hand on her shoulder; for the time being
it would have to do, "rack your brains. If there is *anything....*"

Vera protested urgently. "It couldn't have happened at night, nor while
you were at dinner, both Maxie and I were with the airplanes."

"We need some private conference," a voice commanded them. It was
Gregory Fox, waving people away, steering Gus towards an empty hangar.
He turned to Vera. "Miss Davis, any information you can come up with is
most important."

Damn, thought Hazel, he's giving her permission to confess anything she
knows. Will she?

Vera hunched her shoulders helplessly.

"Who was working on airplanes during dinner?" Greg Fox pressed.

Gus answered that one. "The Morris-Newtons. Frank Wilczynski was
doing a tune-up on the Monocoupe. Sweeney Crawford was changing the
spark plugs on the Rearwyn. Otherwise, routine inspections were already
completed. Oh yes, and Stevie Lamb had her Eagle in for a good bit. Then

154

she was off to dinner too." As he talked, he brought a crate for Hazel to sit on. She accepted gratefully, leaning against the riveted, sheet-metal wall of the hangar at its opening. Resting her heavy head, still in helmet, against the laminated wooden lip of the opening, she looked out to see who was circling, who was in. She could see Louise across the way checking her Moth. Sarah's Taperwing was on the field, but she was off somewhere with Sam who had apparently switched escort places with Sweeney since Jo was last in the draw. Her own Zephyr was in the process of getting scrubbed and washed down, Beech mechanics and extra security all around it. Security—a bit belatedly, but there it was—men in uniform shooing curious people away.

Stevie, having started off in third position had not shown up, had returned to St. Louis in great frustration due to her unsolvable engine troubles—Gus was saying—there was doubt as to whether she could finish the race. Nancy was just now cutting the Eagle Wright's engine to come in.

"I can't believe it," Hazel protested wearily, "how could I have kept my time? And well ahead, at that. I know she's in CW, but still she must have miscalculated her course not to get here before me—"

Gus let out a long whistle. "'Cause you flew instinctively, Preston, or you must have done your navigational homework."

She grinned up at him foolishly then. "No kidding? True—I flew that stretch before, in June, west...into the wind."

"Then you come in like some rookie. Never saw you do such a clumsy landing. You came in too fast, and had flown much too fast for your altitude, I might add. At true altitude you might have broken a record. Too bad."

"Yeah, well I made it. I'm still a contender—let our saboteurs put that in their tobacco and chew on it," she said more triumphantly than she felt, Jo weighing on the back of her mind. Too much hung in the balance, too much was linked. Jo was likely to catch up on this lap, and Taggart would certainly be flavoring *his* tobacco with that. Too convenient.

"Taggart? That's it," Vera said snapping her fingers. "Remember when Jo was supposed to meet up with him for an engine check, but tripped up instead? Remember when we all came running into the lobby with her and left our watch? That's the only time we weren't near the airplanes."

Standing in the shadow of the hangar's interior, Greg Fox scratched his chin in contemplation. "That's right. Taggart was in the lounge..." He stopped abruptly, because of course, he had been lurking too.

Hazel turned to him quickly, realizing his slip-up, said hurriedly, "He wasn't there when we arrived." Then she remembered the rear door of Eleanor's cab shutting, the driver commandeered, perhaps with the flash of a few greenbacks. Someone had come from the terrace in a hurry—the shortest route from the airfield to the street. She stopped herself short of exclamation. "Vera, please, find me a drink of water."

155

"You'll take one from me now?" Vera's tone might have been playful once, this time it was softened with relief.

"Oh yes, please," Hazel beamed, watching her hurry off. "...What now, Mr. Fox? I think Taggart may well have had the time and the opportunity for both Sarah's and my airplane. I can't be sure, but we saw someone take Eleanor Wilson's taxi."

Greg spoke most coolly, "We were both in the lounge. Ostensibly, I was waiting to consult with Miss Wilson though I had quarters with escort crew in the bunkhouse. We were reading old newspapers. He made two comments, one in disgust about stocks in general, another, a derisive comment about all the cushions being taken by 'dames' who wanted to sleep on the ground. Then he went into the men's room shortly before you arrived, and did not come back to the lounge where I was still smoking.... Hm, there was an exit door down the hall, and immediately to the right of the men's room. He may well have gone out that way. I know that when I went into the men's room, he had already left. If he went out to the airplanes to meet Miss Russell when the other incident happened, he could have had just enough time, what with the distraction. How much time, would you say, Gus?"

Gus cleared his throat, thinking. "Ten minutes for Hazel's—if he had resin with him and knew exactly what he wanted to do ahead of time. It used to be common to have some handy for small repairs—for wood and canvas airplanes, that is. It comes in a can, but you can roll some into a ball—it's like a putty. Pry the seal out, one or two dabs to hold the cap on. And of course, the refueling was already complete...."

"I smelled gas in the morning when I woke up. I remember telling Maxie how I was sick of sleeping around smelly machines." Hazel leaned forward over her lap, fighting the urge to heave up. Thinking, oh yeah, he's unreadable all right, one simple plan on his mind.

Greg Fox turned to the sunshine, spying Vera coming back. He tapped his chest. "Well, that's all I need for now. We still have to establish whatever connections there are in all this. Please, be careful what you say to her, Miss Preston. Discretion at this point is essential."

"Yes, well, don't all of you need to get moving ? The first half is in."

"If you are going to be well enough—" Gus began.

"Yes, I'll be fine. I want to put a cable through to Gladys Jenney, and hope I feel well enough not to call a five minute penalty delay for myself, eh? But please, get to Cincinnati. Maxie will be most relieved to have you there, I'm sure. News will be travelling ahead of us."

He gave her a 'thumbs-up' and his wide optimistic grin. "Not going till I check up on the Zephyr."

Vera arrived with the cup of water. Hazel took it gratefully, holding it to her lips, then stopped. Did she dare? She had already taken her life in her hands once that day.

Not asking, nor saying anything, Vera took the cup and drank large gulps, draining a good half of it, then handed it back. The look of pain and dismay around those green eyes made Hazel flush with shame. Hazel took it and drank some. Then without a word Vera turned away, following the men's steps toward the C-175, where Sam Morris-Newton waited. Sarah was being pushed out for take-off before the next in the draw, Madelyn, came in. All Hazel could think about was how Vera's coveralls sagged on her, no longer crisp and white, but well advanced towards the rag-bag.

Was there really a connection between her, the betting scheme and the sabotaging? Hazel brooded—those green eyes seemed to be trying to tell me she isn't connected. She is telling me that. Lordy, I wish she'd just come clean. If she knows I distrust her, she has to be smart enough to know that I'm on to her. So why the pretense? She obviously doesn't trust me enough to tell me what she's up to. So why am I the one feeling ashamed? *Why can't she tell me?*

*Terre Haute to Cincinnati*

The Zephyr sparkled after its wash reminding Hazel that she had better change out of her smelly shirt, at least. Pulling off her helmet, she went in search of a bucket of water from polite, if not subdued, ground crew. They had seen a bit of pluck, and respected that. Dunking her head in the cold water helped dull the headache, and washing up, she went to her airplane locker to find a clean shirt—one that she had been saving for the last lap so she wouldn't arrive in Cleveland too dishevelled.

Then as she ate a sandwich, it was a matter of waiting for El, watching as Louise left and Hannah came in without ado. Hannah was especially pleased because her flight had, at last, been smooth. Whatever fuel-line problems there had been, seemed to have worked themselves out. She felt as though she were making competitive time; indeed she was—her time matched Hazel's on the last lap. Well, she wasn't in the running, too late for that. Had some-one made sure of it?

This thought was on Hazel's mind as Eleanor came gently in. How beautiful, the Vega, lightened up on the fuel now, swooping in to settle neatly. May she land like that in France someday soon for us, Hazel wished as she strode, tucking in her shirt, to find her friend.

"I think we should cable Gladys to have those reinforcements in place by Cincinnati," she said after reporting everything.

"Yes, but we still have nothing but conjecture," said Eleanor, her face visibly wincing with concern. "We can't arrest anyone without proof. Vera? Tag?—If it's Taggart, he can sit and smirk on his laurels all he wants. His airplane and pilot have winged the winds for him beautifully, I'm afraid."

157

"Will you wash a dirty rag for me again, El? Tell Jo about what happened. I'd like to move on now. If I try and talk to her it'll be too much for both of us. I don't feel like coming off as a poor sport. I can't bear it anymore that she keeps blinders on about Taggart. Even if she suspects something, her own ambitions keep her from considering anything we tell her. Hard evidence would be difficult for her to see, at this point, even if we had any."

"It's not dirty work, H.P. I'll wait as long as I can, but I may have to move on before she gets in. She may just have to wait. I'll put a cable through to both Gladys and Al. Perhaps we can talk to them directly this evening again. Investigations go at a much slower pace, you know, than air races. You can only catch villains long after the deed is done, by then it's always too late for the victim."

"That may be so, but we're a fighting victim saving herself for the future of the Derby, for the future of women pilots. Alli has paid the price for our gullibility. Do you realize that even if Jo wins on her own merit, but we get evidence against her sponsor, she will be implicated too. Sarah has done well this last lap. She has only about ten minutes to close on me. You know I feel even now that if I could cause a penalty for Jo, I would. I just might put a tack by her tire so when she rolls out for take-off—"  .

"H.P!" Eleanor looked at her in horror.

"I'm a fighting victim, remember. If this is a rigged race, I'll rig it so Sarah can win. She, at least, will bring integrity and fair play. I could live with that."

Eleanor grabbed her by the forearm. "Yeah, and what if it isn't Taggart but somebody like the Morris-Newtons behind all this!"

"Mr. and Mrs. Rescue Squad? Hardly. Not with what I know."

"For God's sake, please don't do anything rash. Let's see what the times are by Cincinnati."

Hazel smiled. "But I do detect complicity, don't I? If need be. For the sake of future Derbies?"

Eleanor's glance fell away. "If it were to save future Derbies—if we had evidence—oh, Haze, but to take matters into our own hands, well, I don't suppose I have to worry, do I, living with underhanded deeds? If I'm to take on crossing the Atlantic, I'll simply take such secrets with me when I have to ditch into twenty-foot waves."

"Elli!" It was Hazel's turn to gulp. "Don't you dare talk that way."

Eleanor's eyes twinkled then. "I can't be anything but fatalistic. How else will I be lucky? Off with you now."

"Lordy, you know how to put me in my place, don't you? Goodspeed then, El—until Cincinnati. You'll fly the Atlantic with a free conscience, dammit."

Hazel shook her head as she made her way back to the Zephyr, wishing she hadn't been so frank, wishing she had saved such talk for the likes of Maxie. Yes, Maxie…she remembered how Max tripped her up, tackled her, how it wasn't only Vera who had a strength that excited her. But what to make of it all? How befuddled she was; she blamed it on the effects of the gas fumes, slapping her cheeks to alert herself for her next lap.

The Zephyr's flight towards Cincinnati was pleasantly uneventful, sweet relief, in spite of reports before take-off that heavy clouds were moving into the Ohio River Valley from a storm breaking up in the south, and would be providing turbulence.

Keeping at ten thousand, the recommended ceiling to avoid the stronger winds, Hazel peered down between fast moving clouds below to catch a glimpse of the giant "C" for Columbus, Indiana, which would announce itself on a small hillside. Then Hazel was to check her compass and make adjustments to the southeast. This route was considered to offer the best time, but pilots were naturally free to choose whether they wanted to go south, directly into the wind, meet up with the Ohio River, then follow that to Cincinnati. It was true that Columbus would be easy to overshoot what with the north-westerly winds. Cold winds. As it was, she had to compensate heavily and didn't envy those in the lighter weight CW class. But she didn't worry. The farmland below was like a patchwork comforter, something her Gram would make for her to sleep under. She wondered how the Rearwyn would take these winds, even with its alloy reinforcement.

Even with the turbulence, the remains of her headache and the fatigue in her legs as her feet held the rudder, Hazel felt great, using the time to regain her confidence, work away the knot of fear. At last she flew through dense clouds, making her descent towards a brown and choppy Ohio River. Even as she found the runway, she thought she could smell rain in the air. Yes, the unmistakable smell of water, but without the salt in it of the west coast. Her landing was exceptionally smooth. Only the steam-roller at the end of the runaway could make the surface so pleasantly level. Here she was at another modern facility.

As she coasted to an easy stop, ground crew hurried out to sheathe the airplane against possible evening showers. Glancing at her watch, she hoped the rest of the draw would make it in before the rain.

The first pilots in were already being wowed by a cheering crowd of spectators that police had roped off and seemed to be keeping at bay. She could see the swells of enthusiasm as people pushed forward. Didn't she distinctly hear her name: "Preston! Preston!" The mood was terrific. No, it didn't annoy her; it was music to her ears. Jumping out of her cockpit, deftly touching the ground, she whipped off her helmet and waved back, rewarded by happy whistles and shouts.

Gus came up then as she combed her hair with her fingers, and she said,

"I don't suppose you've had a radio bulletin in on Jo's time?"

His sour expression told her everything. "She sailed, Preston. That darn-fool engine just may hold out till Cleveland. You're a well-placed second due to your last lap because she keeps the pace up. It's enough to up any ante. Sarah Morris-Newton ain't far behind."

In irritation Hazel hit the fuselage with her gloves as she stowed them away. "Damned fixed race. I'm sure I'll make a lot of people happy when I come in second—"

"Hold on there now. You can still come in a tidy first," said Gus, his hands slapping down the air in front of him for emphasis.

Chewing her lower lip, Hazel was thinking melodramatically of that well-placed tack in front of Jo's tire, but was distracted by a familiar, robust form.

"Who are these people?" She asked in amazement as she welcomed Maxie's bear hug in greeting, followed by the loud smack of a kiss. "Oh Lordy Max, kisses too?"

"You bet, Preston. I'm a happy fool to see ya safe and sound!" Maxie kissed her again most demonstratively, then with a wave of her hand, "And those are all the people to whom I told the story of your near fatal flight to Terre Haute. They're very impressed."

Hazel almost believed her for a second, then, "Oh, come on, Max."

Maxie's dark eyes grew a touch more sober then. "It's nearly the end of the race, and the newspapers are pretty wild with reports. It's your turn to provide a touch of the dramatic. They want to see that you are really here, in the flesh. A real woman. Go on, go show them. I think they deserve it."

Hazel began to protest, but Maxie escorted her closer to the crowd, waving with her. Then, leading Hazel into the small pilot's clubhouse, she faced Hazel with a bitter twitch to her lips. "I have to tell ya something. Vera has disappeared."

"What?" Hazel braced herself against the door jam into the lounge. "Are you sure? I mean, how can she do that now?—it makes her look real bad—"

"Shh." Maxie tapped her on the shoulder. "Come and get something to drink. I think you'd better sit down for this one. Gus doesn't even know yet—well, he knows that Vera split."

"I don't want a drink or to sit down, Max! Come on, there must be somewhere to talk—they have a Ladies Room, I gotta go."

"Not private enough."

"Then outside somewhere. Aren't airplane wings and hangars the place?"

"Okay, okay. This way. I just don't want to run into press right now. Where's a bit of mesquite when we need it, now that ya have celebrity status?"

They made their way out of the building again, hurrying away from the activity towards the inevitable, open hangar. Maxie looked about her, deciding that a wide range of visibility was the best cover. "I got a cable from my Grandaddy, see, when I came in—to call him immediately. I thought it had something to do with Miss Mack, of course. So, as soon as I got in, before the bulletin about you came through, I put a call through to him. It goes like this—oh hell, Preston—I can't tell you how embarrassed I am to have to tell you this. My grandfather, the dirty scoundrel, was the one who backed the betting scam."

"What?" Hazel sputtered.

Maxie began to pace with hands deep in the pockets of her black britches. "He hired Vera to take the bets. He's the one behind it."

"Why? How did—?"

Maxie put a hand up to stop Hazel. "Hold your helmet, kid. I got to get it out piece by piece. He met her at an air show, friendly like. She was taking photos and he had seen some of her work on display in the airfield clubhouse. He was impressed. He likes to support the arts, don't ya know. They talked about flying, one thing, then another. He mentioned this upcoming Derby that I was going to be in, and you—she specifically knew and had an interest in your career, knew Eleanor by then, too. Anyway, he said if she could get on the circuit, he wondered if he could get her interested in a little side scheme of his, a little scheme he wanted his cronies to get in on, a way, in fact, to support the purse—"

"Betting," Hazel interrupted.

Maxie waved an index finger. "That's it... F. I. D. O. stands for Financially Independent Donors' Organization. A joke! As simple as that. He set it up, thinking to have an extra purse for the winner, since I had carried on about the discrepancy between our purse and the men's races. Now, he couldn't exactly come out and get the boys to donate, but—but, if it was in the guise of a tidy sporting bet, who could say no? He sees she's plucky and maybe game to make some good money herself, so he proposes his idea—philanthropy in disguise! Good, Huh? And she turns out to think it's a keen plan. Then Vera tried to get on the circuit through Eleanor. Finally, she does through you, thanks to yours truly here who fires Sweeney.

"Now, she wasn't supposed to communicate directly with him, but after Pecos she starts sending him sporadic, desperate cables, that she needs to talk to him. She's over her head. But she can't get through because she's out there doing security, and, get this, she begins to understand that she is being suspected by us, even catches on to the fact that we might have someone watching her. He wants us to take Gregory Fox off the case immediately."

"That's it? Just drop it? I mean, how can we?—Eleanor is in on this investigation too—she got him through Lockheed. And Gladys Jenney is willing to help foot the detective's bill."

"Grandaddy'll pay the bill. The thing is, Hazel, Vera has gone. Gone with the betting money. When she came in, she looked in a bad way. Even before what happened today, she had put a cable through to my grandfather saying that the deal had gotten out of hand. He's hoping she'll contact him, now that she has slipped off. The way I see it is she doesn't want to be linked with anyone trying to fix the race. That you almost went down had to be the last straw. She must have had a feeling she was in for big trouble—and she was. Over her head, to put it more bluntly and taking the money to boot."

Hazel fumed, exasperated. "But why couldn't she tell me that? It would have made everything so simple. We could have dealt with your grandfather."

"Because I don't think she was sure herself who was responsible for this mess she was involved in or if it was connected to the sabotage. You can't say betting is an innocent occupation. As it is, she must know that she gave herself away—that Greg Fox is onto her. She was, after all, taking bets."

"But by splitting now, she's going to have a lot of angry guys after her, wanting their money. Or after your grandfather. That sounds like a worse problem."

"Not if the whole thing is blown open, threatened with investigation. Then all bets are off and everyone will skitter like cockroaches. As it is she could square things away with my grandfather. He'd pay up. He's worried enough because my Mackie got it; he understands now the seriousness of the race being rigged."

"And what about Sweeney? She wasn't connected to him?"

"No, Sweeney's still a mystery. My grandfather now wonders whether someone is betting through crew, and that running me out of the race was intentional. I still wonder whether that Mr. Oily-Blaine there has any part in any of this, maybe reacting to my grandfather's article. Or did I just become a convenient target—maybe because I'm so pushy. Maybe someone just thought it would be good to have me out of the race for other reasons."

"But if she knows something, why can't she turn witness? Immune and all that?"

Maxie slapped her thighs and rolled her big brown eyes. "Preston! Where's your head? If she turns witness, then my grandfather is implicated, and he's on the Board of Sponsors!"

Hazel's face fell. "Oh Max, what a mess. No wonder she skipped out."

"Yes, to save face—for all of us—and we, I'm afraid are the ones who have to clean it up. What are we going to do? Alli was killed, and you nearly went down, not to mention my relatively minor mishap. It's all right there, and we still have no evidence to point at anybody. All we have are some betting stubs, my grandfather's explanation, and now Vera's disappearance. I can live with personal scandal, I think ya know I could stand that. But we're talking about the future of women racing. Every single pilot is affected. Gladys Jenney!—all the work she and other sponsors put in to make this race take wing. All Hannah's fund-raising efforts—all Eleanor's work to get people to believe in us. We'll all be finished if this comes to light. That's why I can't help wondering if Mr. Oily is pulling some strings in all this—out to prove we are indeed weak, defenseless females."

Hazel wondered if a whole tank of fuel fumes could be as bad as Maxie spewing the truth. She could feel her body trembling. Holding out her hand to grasp Maxie's, she knew her friend was as shaken as she.

To give herself a moment of respite, she turned to watch another airplane sweep down through the broken clouds; it looked like Madelyn. At length she said, "There's nothing to do but press on. Vera has gone into hiding. She's not stupid. If she's any sense she'll leave the country for awhile."

"Apparently she has enough loot to do that," said Maxie ruefully. "If she does go to him, I'm sure my grandad will tell her to go. Damn it, he'd better, if I have any say in it. He got her into this."

Hazel winced. "Max, I feel used, but smitten too. I do so want to think it's just her free spirit that got her into it. But I remember her telling me that real money, not baubles or hand-outs, was the only thing that made sense to her...; maybe she meant to skip out with the money all along."

Maxie threw an arm around Hazel's shoulders as they turned together to walk back to the hubbub disconsolately. "I know how you feel. I liked her too. I hope she doesn't turn out to be a really bad sort. As for my grandad, well, I haven't really paid attention before to his money-making schemes, except to receive all the benefits, right? Good schooling, travel, an easy life. But this is nothing to him financially anyway—win some, lose some is his motto. He plays the stock market the same way. If it all comes crashing down, he'd be sure to keep clear of the rubble. This time he involved his grand-daughter. Ah, but even family can be sacrificed, if you're a serious player, though I hope this has sobered him."

"So what do we do now? Speak to Fox? Can't we keep him on? He still might be able to find out who's behind the tampering. I'd like Vera cleared too, if at all possible."

"Speaking of the devil—" Maxie tossed her head in the direction of a swiftly approaching Greg Fox who puffed madly on a cigarette before throwing it down under his feet. "Hello, Greg. I just told her Vera—"

"Miss Davis gave me the slip," he said. "I've just been checking down at the railway station. The ticket clerks don't recall anyone of her description."

Hazel thought aloud. "If she took her small valise with her, she would have changed into a dress and hid her camera. I think you'd better fill him in, Max—"

Max told him that her grandfather backed the betting.

"Well," he said, upon reflection as they waited, his hand scratching the back of his neck, "we're still dealing with someone who tampered with the race, betting or no betting. Dog-fighters—these guys never *intend* bodily harm, from what I understand. They think they are only attacking airplanes. They think that's fair game and pilots take risks anyway. Except usually all the players or pilots know it's the game. So, this unsuspecting Laraway pilot who went down, yes, maybe she did succumb to fumes—could have been from a blockage in the exhaust—whatever; she was supposed to out-think it, out-run it, like Miss Preston here. Except she didn't know that. I know fellas that have gone down—and there's always wide open speculation. That kind of racing is a mean sport and part of the daring. Got to have an honest crew. I'll continue to do surveillance on Crawford and Taggart. See if something comes up. And keep looking for real evidence. Somebody is bound to slip up again. Now that Miss Davis is gone though, we don't have any more leads. Could be someone told her to get lost, you know. Now with her testimony we might have something."

"Damn," Hazel sighed. "Why didn't she trust me enough to talk? We could have helped her through this, cleaned up this mess with her evidence. All the talk about trust, trust, but then she doesn't confide in me. It's my fault too for not levelling with her. I almost did one night while you were asleep, Max. I thought if I beat around the bush, maybe she'd get the idea. I could kick myself...."

"Yeah, well we're all loners or we wouldn't be on this junket," Maxie sighed in turn too.

They started back for the main building, Gregory Fox cutting off towards the airplane, promising to contact them if anything came up.

"I'd just as soon hold off on telling Eleanor, if you don't mind, Max. She's going to have her hands full enough as it is," said Hazel as soon as he was out of earshot .

"I hear ya.... Come on, the airplanes are coming in, and I think you need to be visible. It's gonna be a crazy evening of press and dignitaries. And don't go fretting about Verie—I think we'd better leave it be for now. Chin up."

With her head against Maxie's shoulder, Hazel whispered, "I didn't get to say good bye."

"No, dear old Preston. We didn't get to say good bye to Alli either."

That evening there was a deluge of people off the field, and a deluge of rain on the field. Hazel had to let Maxie help ground crew secure extra tarpaulins over the aircraft, while she went to talk to reporters and supporters.

Hazel kept looking for Vera in momentary glances beyond the people in front of her, or else over her shoulder. For once the admiration and interest of the crowd didn't really help. Meanwhile, across the room Jo Russell, talk of the town, and Taggart smiling at her side, were giving optimistic interviews. But Jo seemed as distracted as Hazel felt—was it that Jo was looking for *her* over the heads of people?

Finally, Jo pushed through the crowded lobby of the grand hotel where the gala dinner was held and stood near her, concerned yet stiff, on guard. "Haze, what the hell happened to you in Terre Haute?—Is it true that you think your airplane was tampered with?"

"Hello, hon," Hazel put a tired arm around Jo's shoulders. "I ran into a bad case of fumes almost immediately upon take-off. I had a hunch that if I could make it all the way, I'd have some proof and back up all the misgivings I've been having."

"Well, I must admit that it's most unsettling. Tag is very concerned—I mean, if anyone in the top margin is affected by this, it's pretty scary. Lopsided wins aren't going to help anyone's sales or careers—"

"Typical," said Hazel glumly, taking her arm away. "All he can think about is how it might look for him."

"Oh Haze, sometimes you really tick me off. You won't even let me finish my sentence. I was going to say it makes the whole race lose credibility. He has information that there's some betting scheme going on. He thinks I'm not the one the gamblers expect to be in the lead. Frankly, I find that quite worrisome." Jo looked at her pointedly, "I have some questions of my own—like why Vera Davis wanted to come on this circuit so badly. And why she suddenly disappeared. Sweeney says she takes bets from crew."

Hazel contained her anger. "Does he then? Well, I'll let you know anything I find out. Meanwhile why don't you just be very careful."

Jo moved closer to her as Hazel was about to slip away. "You already know something, don't you? Why don't you tell me?"

"I have my pet theories, but no proof, no leads. A few pieces that tell me something's out of whack. Anything you want to look into, be my guest—"

Jo said quietly, sadly, "You suspect Tag of some sort of interference, don't you? But you see, I think he has been uneasy all along that someone wants to eliminate him from the race too."

Hazel shrugged. "I don't know what to think." More jauntily, "And I hardly want to come off as a poor sport, eh?"

"Damn it, Haze," Jo's tone was more conciliatory than peeved, "you know perfectly well that I want a showing I can be proud of, not something at your expense, or Sarah's, certainly not at Alli's. I don't want a career in aviation if that's what it means."

"Jo, don't you see? Even if nobody cheats, somebody still has to win. You know that. We all push, push, and a few get the glory, the eternal flame. Who will it be? And who will remember Alli? She'll be mentioned in an article along with Sunny Cooke and the rest. Who will think of Eleanor if she ditches in the Atlantic, or *even* if she makes it? Who will remember this Derby, or who *wins* it?

"But, still, each of us has to reach, we have to show what women can

165

achieve—for women in the future—so they will no longer be excluded. One or two names will carry us all. So go do what you can do. Help make the step. Even if there is betting. Even if someone is tampering—toying with us—we don't have to give up." Hazel stopped then, because her rallying cry was just as much for herself in a desperate moment. It seemed suddenly fitting that Jo was there beside her; she could feel that the fondness they had for each other endured. And she was confused again about Jo. She did love her and didn't know what to make of it anymore.

Jo had no time to respond as a clutch of reporters rushed up, along with convivial hosts, calling, "Miss Russell!"

It was too wet to camp under the airplane. Besides, Hazel's problem on the last leg had stirred up enough interest that police were brought in to guard the Derby fleet. Oddly enough, both Maxie and Hazel found themselves giving in to the comfort of a warm room and a decent bed each, since the hosts in Cincinnati had given the fliers a warm welcome and splendid hotel accommodations. Hazel was able to bathe in the luxury of a bath-tub, and decided to wear the cinnamon, silk top of her elegant pajamas, not to bed, but for the last lap.

Derby news was that Stevie still hoped to catch up, having compression problems. And unfortunately, after her fine showing at Terre Haute, Hannah had made a navigational mistake and flown to Columbus, Ohio. Rather than taking the short hop to join everybody else in Cincinnati, she decided to stay put until they all caught up, and swallow the penalty.

Eleanor caught up with her in the hallway, looking gaunt with dark circles under her eyes, but remaining businesslike as if she could still go for hours. "Been looking for you, H.P. Gladys put a call through for me, but I couldn't find you. Al wasn't with her but gave her the go ahead to report to us. Nothing conclusive has been found on the Arctic. No tampering. It's being ruled as an accident."

"An accident!" Hazel exploded. "Are you sure?"

Eleanor sighed. "Beech experts did the investigation. Don't you think they would have found something if it had been there?"

"I will get them to reopen the case. I have to know for sure; I can't let it go. I'll ask Greg Fox. There must be something."

"Fire," said Eleanor. "Fire was there. What can they find. Fuel tanks exploded upon impact. That can happen whether there's a fuel leak prior to impact as well as not. Everything that didn't burn was fused together, melted."

"What about her body?" Hazel felt her own panic rising. "The presence of fumes in her lung tissue or something?"

Eleanor looked at her sadly. "Don't we all have evidence of some fuel poi-

166

soning in our lungs just because of what we do? Al can ask for an autopsy. Maybe he already has. You know, in a way I'd be relieved if it was an accident. I think I can live with that easier."

Hazel thought about that. Maybe Eleanor was right. Accidents did happen. "So there is nothing left to do now, but be careful. And maybe anyone wishing us harm has been scared off, hm?"

Eleanor could only answer by taking hold of Hazel, laying a weary head on her shoulder for a moment. "Oh God, H.P. Oh God."

By midnight when the rain stopped and Hazel had fallen into bed exhausted, she wondered how there was still room left for the raw pain that kept her from sleeping. And for all the bodily comfort and relief of a real mattress, she missed the physical closeness of her companions out under the Zephyr's wing. How strange that a handful of hard-driving days could feel like a way of life. Tossing and turning, drifting in and out of sleep, shivering from nerves not cold, she might as well have been sleeping on rocks. Finally she could bear it no longer. Crawling from her bed, she fell on her knees at Maxie's bedside.

"Max, Max, are you asleep?"

A muffled groan issued from deep in the pillow.

"Please, Max, can I climb in with you? I feel so...terribly alone."

Without a word or sound, without warning that she had absolutely no clothes on, Maxie lifted up a blanketed arm like a wing, opening up her bed. Before Hazel knew it, she had her face comfortably cushioned between Maxie's large, spilling breasts.

Recovering from her surprise, Hazel propped herself up on an elbow, peering at Maxie's face in the dark. Wherever Hazel was bony, Max was round, and where Hazel was round, Max was extra round. "Are you seducing me, Max?"

"Aren't you the one who asked to get in my bed?"

"Well yes...."

"And now you're not alone any more so quit complaining."

"I'm not complaining. Oh Max...," Hazel's head flopped down as Maxie's arm came round her and pulled her close, "I can't believe what this race has become. I expected hard work, but to find it corrupted, full of rot— it's unbearable. And Vera cutting out—oh such a mess with Jo. Vera wanting me anywhere we could, stealing our moments, always teasing me how she wanted me in a proper bed. Jo pushing me away out of her fear of being my lover...and here I am, comfortably snug in your bed...."

Even in the semi-dark, Hazel didn't miss Maxie's wide grin. "Ha-ha, well don't strain yourself wondering why. Anyway, I always did think you fell for women who distressed you. Love as torment. That's you, babe, not me."

167

"No, you always like fun. Do you think we could have fun, Max?"

"You and me? Why I'm so hefty and you're so skinny we'd look like the Laurel and Hardy of aviation."

In spite of her misery, Hazel laughed into Maxie's chest.

"Ha-ha, made you laugh, didn't I? We're coming along." Maxie jabbed Hazel in the back with a finger, then the hand flattened out into a few good pats. "Come on, snuggle down, would ya, and get some shut-eye. You're safe with me, kid."

# 10.

*Cincinnati to Cleveland via Columbus, Ohio*

In the morning Hazel arrived on the airfield under the benign scrutiny of race officials and a cluster of reporters, all men, earnest and eager for so early in the morning, who peppered her with questions:

"How do you think the seal was removed from the cap, Miss Preston?"

"You'd have to use a screwdriver or a pocket knife."

"Why do you think someone would tamper with your airplane?"

"I have no idea."

"Is it because you are neck and neck with Mrs. Morris-Newton and Miss Russell?"

"I don't know."

"What about Mrs. Morris-Newton; do you think the oil spill was deliberate?"

"Both incidents happened on the same lap, that's all I can explain."

"But yours, Miss Preston, was far more lethal, wouldn't you say, life-threatening?"

Hazel laughed in resignation. "Not if I'd caught the problem before I took off."

"Is it true that some of you gals have provided your own security guard?"

"A few of us have, yes."

"So you thought there might be cause for such precautions then?"

"I'd say so. We wanted to be sure for ourselves."

"Because of Miss Laraway's accident?"

"After that, yes."

"But Miss Preston, hasn't that been ruled an accident?"

"Perhaps keeping guard was our way of grieving."

"And what about Miss Schulz's accident?"

"Listen, boys, I can't take any more questions. I have a race to finish. I've got a lot on my mind."

The weather, for one thing, Vera's looming absence, and of course, the sabotage. She wondered whether the tamperer would dare continue now that there was evidence exposing it for what it was. Not to mention the presence

169

of police. In any case, the tamperer's tactics had caused no penalties for either herself or Sarah, they remained intact and very much in the running.

Hazel didn't like the weather. Wind gusted up to 20 mph. from the southeast. Chilly. Whole trees were swaying. Her only consolation was the reports that the wind would subside. Now she wanted the last lap to be done with; even a delay of a few hours would be too much.

Then there was Vera who had walked into Hazel's life quite simply. Her exit had been just as abrupt, just as shocking. She had brought tantalizing joy. With her gone there was nothing but anger and, yes, suspicion instead of longing and mystery. Now there was only disappointment and loss.

*If we could be giddy.* Hazel snorted. Well I did say I'd find her in stolen moments. And I did too. How confident, how brazen I was. Giddy isn't the word. Foolish is more to the point, reckless as any stunt pilot. What was it Louise Gibeau had said, 'defying death, defying gravity'?—With only quick reflexes to count on...and a bit of luck. Privy rot, I've been had.

With a cup of coffee from the race officials who were serving crew and pilots, she stood in the sunshine, waiting and watching the cold front move out. Did it surprise her to see Sweeney working under the open cowling of the Rearwyn's engine? Last minute checks, last minute tuning. Spark plugs again? A change of oil for the final run?

He wasn't the only one at work. Since there was a weather delay, almost every airplane was getting attention. Her own Zephyr was getting a going over from Gus.

Looked like Taggart was waiting out the wind too; his silver airplane sat empty, separate from the contestants.

A little later as she sat in her cockpit firing up the engine for Gus as he checked its idle, she spied Taggart coming out onto the field, followed shortly by Jo striding toward her Rearwyn with what looked like fierce determination. Had they had an argument? Had he put on the pressure? Jo looked positively distraught. Hazel could see her check the wind-sock, and took a look herself. Mm, the wind had flattened out. Looked like the weather front was gone. The heavier airplanes could certainly take off.

As she climbed out of her cockpit, she saw the flash of whirling propeller from Tag's airplane. He was heading out; the argument must be settled then.

Glancing towards Jo, she frowned. Now it looked like a confrontation with Sweeney. Jo was closing up the cowling on the engine, pulling her helmet on. Looked like more than a cockpit check was on. One final test run? Taggart must have thought he needed to to keep the pressure on.

Maxie arrived beside Hazel at that point, watching too, not saying anything, tin mug of coffee in her hand. Hazel nudged her with an elbow, nodding towards Jo who was climbing into her cockpit while waving for brake blocks to be removed. At the same time, Taggart's silver airplane tore down the runway until it caught the air; Jo waited, playing with the throttle, then signalled for contact.

Hazel could see the tail elevators flex, the rudder shift as Jo gauged the ground speed, grumbled, "Why the hell take a test run now? She doesn't need to. I wonder what they were arguing about?"

Maxie cocked her head, "Well, maybe it has something to do with what Taggart said in this morning's newspaper article—"

"What article?"

"This one that I'm gonna have to keep for my scrap book." She pulled a folded paper out of her pocket and handed it to Hazel, pointing to the part she had underlined: '....shown up Beech quite successfully. I think I have succeeded in what I set out to prove, that I have built an airplane so reliable and simple that even a girl can pilot it. When my cargo fleet is ready within the year, you should be able to send even your most precious bundles and be assured of a safe delivery, especially since we will have well-trained male pilots in place to handle the heavier airplanes.....'

"What a bushel of horse apples," Hazel spat in disgust. "And after all the hoopla over her last night. I don't get it. No wonder she looked so upset just now. The nerve!—he can't even appreciate a winner when he's got one."

Maxie took a sip of her coffee, rolled it around in her mouth as she took the article back, shaking her head. "She has to win now. Preston. She of all of us has to make the victory statement on behalf of womankind. Not the likes of you or me—we're the tomboys, she's the real girl, eh?"

They watched first as Jo was pushed out, then as she taxied into position. The wind had conveniently slowed, enough so that Maxie looked at her watch and thought seriously about the possibility of getting under way too.

With throttle wide, the Rearwyn tore down the smooth runway, leaving tracks on the damp surface as she rose to rock on the wind. At last the wings grabbed the air. Hazel marvelled as it climbed the sky until it was a distant spot. Damn, it looked like Taggart did have a fine airplane after all. Reliable, certainly, but *simple?*—hell no. What a line he talked.

"Well, rag," Maxie slapped Hazel on the back gently, "I hate to leave, but I suppose I should go on to Columbus. It's going to be pandemonium, ya know—the crowds. Better see what I can do to pave the way. Maybe there will be word from my grandaddy."

A slight gust of wind made Hazel look up, discouragement creeping over her limbs. There was a shade of autumn to this late summer air. How different from the desert. She had a chill, and seeing Maxie off didn't help. She was missing her already, feeling vulnerable and lonely.

"Goodspeed, Max."

"Ya bet ya. Now don't go looking so hang-doggy." Maxie cuffed Hazel under the chin affectionately. "We did what we set out to do, don't forget.

The race is still on, still a success. We've won; we're still in the game—and the wiser for it. Had to test the waters somehow, hm? And with any luck, my grandaddy will keep his grimy fingers out of our pie in the future, mark my words. And don't give up about Vera, yet." She tossed her head, then more softly said, "If I reckon right, it's Alli's funeral today...I still want to do something somehow, don't ya know, find out what's been going on. I keep wondering if someone wanted Al out of the way because he was on to something, and Alli was a victim of that...makes it even harder to bear. If Al wants to press charges, or investigate more, I'm going to stand by him on that. He's not the duelling sort, but there are other ways...."

"Dewey was," Hazel reflected, "when sorely vexed. He took things very personally. I do too, Max. I take it very personally." Squinting, she watched Maxie climb aboard and settle in her tight seat. "You know what, Max—we *are* taken seriously though, aren't we? The very fact that we've been deliberately meddled with means we must be threatening enough to be taken seriously."

Maxie was pulling on her helmet and goggles, probably with her earplugs in because she said, "What?" Hazel smiled and waved her on.

Maxie had just taken to the air when Eleanor stopped to talk on her way to her Vega. How tired her eyes looked, the sparkle gone out of them.

"I guess the draw is about on. Since we're simply switching halves for this next run, that puts me in second position behind Madelyn, so I had better get with it here," said Eleanor, looking more like a mechanic than a flyer now in her greasy, shapeless coveralls. "Looks like the air has calmed down."

"Oh yeah," Hazel answered more jauntily than she felt, with her hands tucked into her armpits and her feet apart. "Let's just finish the damn race without any hitches. And don't worry, I'm a good sport...I'm not going to put a tack in Jo's way!"

"Glad to hear it. I did talk to her about your gas-cap seal, you know. She was going to talk to you—did she?"

"Briefly, yes...."

"Ah—" Eleanor began. "You know her engine overheated yesterday? She was very upset when she arrived in Terre Haute."

Hazel flinched. "No!—well, we don't talk about much, you know—Jo and I. She has taken a solid edge over me."

"Yes, and I'm surprised she didn't blow a major gasket in the process."

"Oh, so that explains the test run then...."

"Who's that coming in?" Eleanor gave a sharp nod.

Hazel gestured with arms wide open. "None other than Jo, back from her test run—"

"Hm, that's not the wind coming up at the same time, is it?"

They stopped talking abruptly as Jo approached the runway. Something didn't sound right in her engine; she was cutting back power too soon as if the idle wouldn't catch. Eleanor grimaced. Hazel understood in the same instant—the steamroller! Didn't Jo see the steamroller, solid, unmoving, near the end of the runway? Why the hell was she coming in so late?—she had not left herself enough room. Quick, somebody, move the filthy steamroller!

Jo's wheels bounced a bit as they touched the ground, almost as if they were surprised too. The wind was scooping her up.

"Come on, Jo, ground loop, ground loop!" Yelled Hazel, running. "No, the other way, the other way. Jam your rudder, dammit!"

Jo was trying. Oh yes, she had to have seen the steamroller. Too late, too late. The tail of the Rearwyn spun forward as the wheels skidded, the one to port crumpling.

Eleanor ran abreast of Hazel, her hands out as if to brace the airplane from the inevitable. There were others running. The sound of their foot falls resounded in Hazel's head. The dull thud of many feet covering ground was not fast enough, nor would the breathless shouts be any good. A glance to her side, and she hardly had time to take in the fact that Sweeney ran out as frantically as she did. The plane slid sideways slowly, even gently. Jo couldn't complete the ground loop in time. Hazel gritted her teeth as the tail hit the front of the steamroller, splintering. And then the Rearwyn stopped like a silly puppy in the middle of a game, port wing foolishly jabbing the ground.

"Why in hell was the steamroller left there?" Hazel shouted in helpless fury. She wanted to throw something. If she hadn't seen it there herself the night before, she would have sworn it had been moved there out of spite. It had simply and stupidly been left at the end of the runway, having rolled the surface smooth after all the rain, presumably to roll the surface smooth again before Derby take-off. Hadn't everyone exclaimed over their sweet landings? Like landing on a cloud, they had said over dinner. Isn't Cincinnati wonderful? Of course Jo had seen it last night, they all had. The thing was, they had come in from the opposite angle then. And sure, she should have ground-looped the other way. The wind might have taken her a bit, but considering the odds—? She would have spun beyond it, clear. What went wrong? Had she panicked? Jo, panic? Or had she been distracted by other things, her engine, for instance?

The two women reached the cockpit as an emergency crewman commanded them aside, jumping onto the wing to examine Jo's condition.

"Is she all right?" Hazel cried. Medics ran up with a stretcher and blankets; others threw dry ice around the engine to neutralize the fumes. But the ignition was off. Dead. There was no risk of fire.

"Shock," the medic yelled down. "She's conscious. Get the blankets. I'm going to help her out."

The pilot stood up with jerky movements. No smile, no waves. "I can do it myself," She barked back at him. "I'm not hurt at all."

Hazel sighed, felt Eleanor's arm entwined with her own as they huddled against each other. The medic stood aside, ready with his arm to help, but Jo clambered out stiffly, avoiding him as she began unbuckling the chin strap of her helmet. Her hands shook and the medic intervened, pulling the strap loose. Dropping to her knees, she slid off the wing towards Hazel who brought forward a blanket.

How can things change so quickly, thought Hazel, Joe's airplane was supposed to beat her. Her mind churned on a myriad of questions, fumbled to make sense of the senseless in that long moment while she waited for Jo to slide off the wing and touch her.

Hazel held Jo, covering her shoulders with the blanket. Never one for sentimental exhibition, Jo trembled but did not break down, even though her face was drawn and pale. Arm around her waist, Hazel led her in the direction of a hangar across the field. Eleanor brushed people aside, using a gentle but firm command, "Give them room. Move aside, please."

A megaphone howled. "All hands. All hands. Clear the runway. Move the steamroller."

Suddenly Eleanor turned, clasping them for a brief second. "I'll go make a statement."

"No, wait," Jo stopped her, voice rasping as she threw off the blanket, but did not let go of either Eleanor or Hazel.

Eleanor stopped, but her feet kept dancing, treading while she determined the distance between them and the gathering crowd. "Jo?"

"Better tell the truth, El."

"What do you mean?" Eleanor obviously thought it better to move them along as they spoke. Hazel looked on, taut, not wanting to breathe. She could feel Jo shifting away, not leaning anymore.

"You know perfectly well I could have avoided the steamroller. Taggart also knows I wouldn't make that kind of mistake."

"Please?"

"I did it on purpose," said Jo grimly. "Time had run out...I had to act quickly and effectively to stop him. I thought at first I'd just take the last lap real slow. But then he'd still have his airplane, wouldn't he? He could make excuses for himself. No, he had to end up with nothing."

"What?" choked Hazel. "Not revenge? Not because of the damned stuff he said in the paper—!?"

"Oh, that his airplane is so simple that even a girl can crash it? No." A look of scorn flashed across Jo's face, in contrast to her trembling lower lip. "It's more serious than that. El, I want you to say I have put Tag out of business completely. He won't dare touch us again." Jo held something out in her gloved hand. "It slid out of his pocket last night when he was checking the spark plugs. He was obsessed with the plugs. He said, 'Never know with these guys, thieving double-crossers at every turn.' And I said, 'What guys? I'm the one who put those plugs in.' He didn't answer, but just went on with the check, acting nervous, afraid. And my mind was going in circles. I realized he suspected someone of foul play, because of the weakness in the engine he was facing. And I knew what had happened to Hazel. Then—as he was pulling out his ring of gappers from his pocket, this was stuck on one. It fell off and landed behind him without a sound. I caught myself—only in the nick of time—from pointing it out to him. He was too absorbed to notice. I knew as soon as I saw it, what it was. I stepped on it. We *don't use* T-seals."

"He kept it in his pocket?—a trophy?" Hazel fingered the seal in Jo's hand: the distinctive flat ring of compressed felt on red rubber was definitely squared off on one side. A familiar serial number from Beech supplies stared up at her, stamped along that cross-bar. How like Jo, she thought, how like Jo to just go and do that, slam her airplane into a steamroller without explanation or apology, planning to do it even before she took off. I should have known by that look she had. The Queen of Safety in her ultimately protective rage.

Jo went on, "I didn't move, Haze. I was paralyzed. All the stuff you've been saying to me hit me over the head like a stone. I was so afraid, I didn't move. I talked calmly, listened to his instructions. When he left, I picked this up." She gave it to Eleanor who flipped it over, studying it.

Tossing it to Hazel, Eleanor snorted, "And you wanted evidence. It will have to do. I think you'll have to present it to Tag in front of witnesses for it to mean anything. The authorities can't do anything with it."

Pocketing the seal, Hazel choked. "Jo, you could have died destroying the Rearwyn like that."

"No," Jo answered fiercely, an odd triumphant smile spreading across her face, "the wind did it for me. It wasn't hard. In fact it was wonderful. I made a home run when I thwacked that steamroller. I can still hear it, how it cracked like a bat against a fast ball. And I hope he hears it all the way to Columbus."

Eleanor gave a low whistle, a warning that they needed to move somewhere. All the commotion was following them at a quickening pace. "Look, uh, I'd better make a statement. Fast. There's going to be a delay as it is, until things get cleaned up. Get her out of here, H.P."

"Affirmative."

Eleanor darted off towards a male photographer who was already running out to the wreck, his boy assistant lugging his tripod. There was confusion back at the airplane; security crew were saying that nothing could be moved until the picture was taken. Hazel gave one quick glance over her shoulder as she led Jo away, seeing only the double starboard wings poking up at the sky, cables sagging. Curious onlookers screened the rest. She was glad of that and knew she wouldn't look again. Jo clung so tightly that Hazel wondered if she'd have to be pried loose. They reached a nearby hangar which contained only a fuselage in the works. Anyone there had gone off to the excitement. Noticing a camp cot against one wall, Hazel coaxed Jo to lie down a bit, taking off her gloves and helmet, loosening her clothes and unbuckling her boots.

Then sitting on the cot, she took Jo's head on her lap, slowly moved under Jo's body to cradle her; stroked the blond hair gently, brushing strands from the damp forehead; said at length, "You aren't hurt anywhere, are you?"

"Only my heart," mumbled Jo, "but it wasn't our race—not for me to win or lose to you."

"Maybe it is now, Jo. Maybe you just won it back for us. By now, Taggart has to know he lost the seal. I don't know if we can use it in a court of law—in some ways I think this is all beyond that. Well, it's complicated...You know Vera skipped last night?"

Jo almost sat up, then sank back heavily. "No, I didn't—she's involved then?"

"In betting, yes. We think—well Max and I, that is—think she had to run away because once there was an investigation, people involved in the betting would be suspect. We don't know where she went."

Jo sighed. "Even if I had won the race for Tag fair and square, he wasn't going to keep me on, you know. I just dreamed he would. He would have taken the Rearwyn away, having won the race, having used us all, exactly like shop rags to dispose of. His *girl* pilot ignorant and inconsequential. Oh God, what a dupe I've been. So he's finished now. I knew he was pretty desperate, impatient, but he could have been quite a legitimate success with me and his plane, and had his investment come through."

"I know that," Hazel said quietly. "Vera could have been a legitimate success as a photographer on the circuit too."

"Ah well—" Jo struggled to sit up, holding her head. "where does that leave us? I drove you away—right into another woman's arms. What a mess. I can't say I'm very proud of myself. I was caught up in my own kind of desperation too. Well, I don't need it."

Hazel sat in ponderous silence. What could she say? Except that it was different now. They had moved to some ambiguous separateness. She managed to say "All I know is we still have a race on. The majority of fliers have been able to fly with integrity. I don't know how we can vindicate Alli any further for the moment. It's all too circumstantial...Eleanor had a call from Gladys last night—the reports back on the Arctic rule the crash an accident."

"What? I don't believe that now!" Jo bellowed. "They can rule her crash as an accident all they want, but it was deliberately caused—by Tag...A lot of it all has been very deliberate."

"I've asked to get another opinion. I'm not going to be easily convinced either even though Beech did the work. But which state was the crime committed in? At least two or three. We can report our suspicions to government agents, but will there be enough proof to arrest him? Will the seal hold up as proof? He'll no doubt have an alibi for the fifteen minutes we think he used on my plane." Hazel tossed the ring from one hand to the other. "This may be Exhibition A, but we still need more evidence, damn it."

"I don't think you're going to get it," Jo said soberly. "Any more than anyone will suspect that I deliberately crashed up this morning. You can say you know the real story. But it all comes down to the fact of flying being a risky and fickle undertaking. That's what Tag's relying on. We hang on for dear life every time we go up. Fear can cloud judgment. That's why I thought all along that you were so suspicious. You needed to have someone to blame for Alli's death.

"But then last night I got such a shock, such a blow. I trusted Tag, saw him as someone struggling like I was. I mistakenly assumed we had a bond because of that, an understanding. But with each lap he's gotten more furtive, more tense, always going ahead, meeting with people I didn't know, and was never introduced to; I thought, how strange. I saw how other sponsors came openly, the ease with which other fliers socialized. Everything was so cloaked around me and the Rearwyn. Isolated. Isolated for success I kept on thinking. At first I welcomed it. But when Alli went down...and then Maxie getting hit...and then you, everything started to crack—" Jo clasped Hazel's hand. "If I've kept options open for future races, good. I don't know, personally, whether I want to stay in this business. Right now I need a long rest to think things over. I'll follow through about this 'accident'—I'm sure I'll have to go through quite a bit of grilling—then I want to go home—east. I think that would be best...for both of us."

"Jo—" Hazel protested.

Jo held up a hand to stay her. "Haze, I need some time. I've been doing some hard thinking over night. It has all taken too much out of me. And about us, well, you've been feeling it for some time. I haven't been fair to you with my ambivalence. Through all this...well, I probably realized it even before the race...and I did use the race as a barrier—I know that I'm not ready to follow the same course as you—"

"The same course?" Hazel looked at her blankly.

"You know...I thought I'd left romance with girls behind at finishing school, not something more. I can't do it, I can't live like you and Maxie. I don't know whether the looks I get, the whispers I hear are because of...of that or just because I'm a pilot. I can't tell the difference any more." Jo rose to pace then, walking towards a table at the rear of the hangar. It had obviously been the scene of a card game the night before, empty bottles of bootleg scattered about.

Her words came out so bitterly, so charged that Hazel grasped for some quick answer, speaking gently, "You did say we were aberrations of society."

"Did I? Sounds like me. You, on the other hand, go around saying we're a wave of the future." Jo picked up one of the unlabeled, glass bottles, seemed to be contemplating on the last few drops of golden liquid. For a moment Hazel thought Jo would drink it, but Jo set the bottle down with firm disgust, her hands trembling. "I've lost my nerve for it all, Haze. I am just afraid and embarrassed." She shuddered. "All those articles—all tainted, all false. All my flying time—for what? All to prove I can wreck a plane simple and reliable enough for a girl to fly? I feel cheapened, used in more ways than one."

Jaw tightening in agreement, Hazel whispered, "Ah...I've been having that same feeling too."

"Yes, and I drove you right smack into another woman's arms, but of course—Vera. I'm sorry she didn't work out for you either...How can I say this—?"

Dismayed, Hazel jumped up. "No. Don't say anything. I don't think it's necessary. It isn't the right time. You are my friend—what you did just now takes all the previous sting out. What I really care about is that we not fly this race in vain, that Alli didn't die in vain. You know I love you, but yes, yes, it has changed. I do know that."

Jo looked at her then with a half-smile of resolve, of clarity. "Of course, darling, but what I wanted to say is that she isn't the woman I would have wanted to drive you to—"

Hazel dashed towards her to stop her from speaking; somehow she knew just the woman Jo meant, someone whose bed she could climb into without reserve. But it was too close, still too new because she had hardly, until this moment, admitted the truth in her heart even to herself. And she wasn't ready.

Instead, with a quick, defiant sweep of her hand, Hazel knocked over the empty bottles on the table. "Who do you suppose they bet on here last night? God, I hope they all lose. How can I go on? Besides, if Sarah wins, she can provide all the ice cream."

"If you let Sarah beat you," Jo responded matter of factly, "I'll kick your behind so hard you'll wish you'd never become a pilot. Come on—we made a promise back in Phoenix, remember? Press on." And she held out her arm to take Hazel's, fingers curling under the silk sleeve cuff.

I'm going to miss that, thought Hazel.

"May I ask, why on earth you are wearing pajama tops?" Jo looked at her reproachfully.

Hazel blanched. "It's the only clean thing I had left. I thought it was kind of dressy myself."

"Oh Haze, and you wonder why I think you're simple. It's all in the cut, darling. C'mon, I think I have something I can loan you. I left my suitcase in the pilot's area."

"I really don't think anyone will know the difference—"

"Nonsense. You can't arrive gloriously in Cleveland in pajama tops. I won't have it." As they walked out onto the field, Jo swept up her gloves and helmet from the cot. "Here Haze, want your glove back?"

"No, no please—keep it."

By the time Jo had been subjected to a rash of interviews and questions from race officials with Hazel at her side, the wind had stilled, and the wreckage removed—off to one side of the runway. And the draw was on. Since Hannah was already in Columbus, Hazel took that spot behind Eleanor so she could follow her and help with the intensifying press conferences.

Did it surprise Hazel to find that Sweeney had slipped away too? "If he has any sense, Taggart's going to skip out too, unless he is so arrogant, or can't figure what Jo was up to with that crash." Hazel mumbled as the two headed out for their airplanes.

"Goodspeed." Eleanor answered tersely.

All business now, the last minute preparations seemed like a balm. Watching Gus leave in the C-175 with only Frank Wilczynski and two empty seats, Hazel realized why she liked to think mechanically, one step after another. She liked pieces that fit together and in a unified whole, functioned or didn't function depending on the balance. One was able to make that balance happen. The Zephyr sung of that balance as she headed out into the sky. She felt pleasure in the control, in making it fly. The control was what she appreciated.

Finding the aerial landmarks for Columbus wasn't difficult. Hazel had often noted that markings east of the Missouri were much clearer than those in the west, more established. But as far as railroads went, forget it, they were too numerous and erratic a web to be useful. Not to worry, rivers were predictable—the Scioto loomed at her as she descended towards it. Had to be the Scioto. All she needed to do was follow it north for a bit, then locate the airfield to the east. The flight had taken less than an hour.

It would have been easy to mistake the Columbus air field for a state fairground. She was tempted for a moment to pass on, except for the homing beep coming over her receiver. Then it all made sense as she circled—the windsocks, the obvious hangars and neat row of parked airplanes. She could point out the signalmen with their yellow and black checkered flags. What was different from any of the other places, even those with crowds like Phoenix and Terre Haute, was the number of automobiles parked row upon row. As she circled she was overwhelmed that so many people would come to a flying event. Then as she dropped to the last few hundred feet, she could see the throngs, handkerchiefs and hats waving as they seemed to spill from the grandstand. Land Amighty—all this, for the Derby? She kept on expecting to see some baseball diamond below, some game in progress, but no, what she saw most clearly was the long, paved runway waiting for her.

This crowd here in Columbus had to be due to Eleanor's persistent articles that had appeared in daily newspapers, fueled by headlines that had swept along with them. Hadn't there been Jo's sensational crash just this morning in Cincinnati to fuel the fire? Down below was the culmination, an exuberant and receptive crowd. As she taxied to a stop, and ground crew came over to roll her into the contestant line-up, she stood up in her cockpit waving her helmet. She was startled to find that there was a majority of women come to see the pilots; women in their summer hats and pale colors of an early morning sky. Now this was totally novel; this almost made all the pain worth it—to find such support, such recognition. Her eyes stung with tears which she wiped away with her gloves. Where did they all come from, these beautiful women?

The contestants' area was festooned with Stars and Stripes, and streamers of colored ribbon to match. Not to be outdone by any grand finale up Cleveland way, the mayor was coming out to meet each flier as she came in, presenting her with a key to the city. Hazel found out later that Eleanor had had to argue hard against a parade that the City very much wanted to take the pilots on, winning her case mostly on the factor of time. The pilots were, after all, en route, and their Cleveland hosts expected them all in before evening.

The diversion was pleasant, and yet as soon as Hazel's feet had touched the ground, she was looking through and over the crowd of well-wishers for Maxie. For a split second she thought she saw another face among the people jostling around her, and her heart skipped. Those slightly slanted green eyes—Vera? Vera in the funny bowl of a hat like way back in Santa Monica. When she tried to see again, cards and booklets were thrust before her for autographs. Through the blur of eager smiles, she was haunted by the face. Was Vera really here? She dreaded to think so, and yet, wanted it.

Luckily, Lila followed her in not too long afterward, and the exuberant crowd swayed away from her to greet the next pilot. It was Eleanor who came up to grab her for press conferences.

Only after all the remaining contestants had come in were the airplanes cordoned off allowing the pilots to emerge from their private lounge and return to the relative peace of their aircraft checks.

There, a jaunty Maxie met Hazel with a wide, if tired grin, and they sat together on a crate next to the Zephyr's tail end, drinking cola while Hazel explained about Jo's accident in full detail. Gus took in the story too as he went over his own checks, then left for a short break.

"My news is much less dramatic—my sponsors sent a cable," said Maxie with a dour smile, draining her soda bottle. "They reminded me about the banner I'm supposed to trail. So I guess I'm going to bring up the rear, and fly into Cleveland like some last hurrah. Just hope the filthy banner doesn't tangle. What'm I gonna do, Preston?—Marsha isn't out of the hospital yet, and they want me to start their tour, day after tomorrow."

Hazel offered, "Maybe Stevie would like to do it."

Maxie shrugged. "She's too small. All the clothes were tailored for Marsha, and they have someone waiting in Cleveland to make final adjustments on me tomorrow."

"Oh dear."

"I suppose I should look on the bright side and see it as an easy way to get back to California, though it means a bit of a detour east—Pittsburgh, New York, Philadelphia…." She stopped, elbowing Hazel at the approach of Taggart. His perfect, sculpted face was worn with strain, his eyes red from fatigue. Hazel stood up.

He leaned too close. His voice shook with rage as he demanded, "What happened to my plane?"

Hazel eyed him coolly. "Didn't you read the bulletins?" For the first time in what seemed like a life-time, she no longer felt afraid. She knew that whatever power he had had over their lives was destroyed. "I'm surprised that Sweeney hasn't been in touch with you."

"You know the bulletins aren't going to tell me what caused that stupid woman to crash up my plane. If I find that you or any of your boys from Beech messed with my airplane," He poked the air with his forefinger, "I'll make it damn hard for you…."

She tucked her hands up under her armpits standing her ground. "Don't threaten me. It's you that's been tampering."

His eyes narrowed. "I don't know what you're talking about. It's obvious that you've wanted Jo to lose all along."

Hazel said coldly, "It's you who've underestimated Jo from the start, not giving her the respect, believing she could win on her own as a very competent woman pilot—without underhanded help from you. Obviously you didn't know she could think for herself, that the success of the airplane depended on her skill and will to win."

His face twisted. "What the hell are you talking about?"

She reached into her trousers pocket and pulled out the T-seal, dangled it from her outstretched hand. "Recognize this? With compliments from Jo."

He didn't visibly flinch, but his hand slipped into his pocket.

"Don't bother checking your pockets. It fell out last night when you were gapping plugs. Jo picked it up. The thing is…is it mine or Alexis Laraway's?"

"I can carry all the engine parts around I want," He snapped.

"A T-seal? That's a Beech part. You don't use Beech parts. You don't have anything to do with Beech, unless it's tampering." Hazel insisted.

"It's a plant." There was fear in his eyes now. "You can't prove anything."

"We know when you did it. We know exactly when—"

"Lies!" He interrupted. Then he smiled tightly, held his hands out wide. "Speculate all you want. That's all you can do. I'm not a rash man, or stupid—"

"Oh?" Hazel knew she had to push further and quickly. "Too bad you couldn't do everything yourself then. It gets trickier when you get others to help you out, like the ground crewman in Yuma, for instance, not to mention the drunk whose car smashed into Maxie's plane."

He paused, for a split second too long in Hazel's estimation, then recovered. "You're bluffing. You don't know a thing. He can't afford to talk."

"Ah, you've got too much on him then?—Blackmail? Which one, the man in Yuma or the drunk? Or both?"

As if realizing he had slipped up, he resorted to a stony silence.

From her seat on the crate Maxie said, "Didn't you realize that if you messed around with the machines somebody could get hurt? Or was that your intention?"

He growled defensively, "You can't say I didn't warn you."

Hazel held up her right hand so that the long red mark was visible. "The friendly hand shake? Maybe that was your first rash move. The second was when you fixed my gas seal, the way you had Alexis' fixed."

He shook his head. His tone becoming cocky, lips in a sneer "Too bad she didn't bail out soon enough. You girls ought to know better than to play a man's game. You should've thought about that before you started the race. We play rough to win."

A loud, "Damn you," came from behind him and he turned quickly to find that they had plenty of company. It was Eleanor standing with Gregory Fox and Gus.

"Why does that sound like an admission to me?" Hazel pressed. "Aren't we talking about repeated tampering? All to make your investors happy, all those men you go ahead of us to meet so we won't know what you're up to."

"I don't know what you're talking about," said Taggart curtly, but his eyes shifted nervously.

Gregory Fox cut in. "Sure you do; we all know. You've been damaging other aircraft to guarantee yourself of a win."

Taggart spun on his heel. "This isn't a court of law. You're wasting my time."

Maxie yelled after him in her deep rolling voice. "We are witnesses to the fact that you have confessed to Alli's murder."

He swung back for a moment, gave a sharp look in their direction as if about to say something, then thought better of it.

Maxie kept yelling. "And you're going to wish you were in protective custody. You may well want to 'fess up. We aren't the ones you have to worry about; it's those other fellas—the ones who are looking for ya to pay up...all your investors and their shady deals with you! They're not going to be at all happy about Jo's crash, are they?"

He retreated to the temporary shelter of the people milling about the hangars. With a snap of his fingers, Gregory Fox gave a signal to a man in a business suit standing nearby who took off after Taggart.

"Whew," Hazel whistled. "I hadn't thought of that."

"It's only because I'm a chip off the old block," Maxie said into Hazel's ear. "I don't think his particular kind of investors take their losses lightly."

"*That's it?*" Gus' shoulders drooped. "He just gets to walk away?"

"He won't get far," said Greg Fox, "and we'll follow up on his two accomplices. I think if they know he's been arrested, they'll talk. Let's hope so because that seal won't do by itself, nor will our testimony to his verbal confession. It's not enough."

A gloomy silence followed.

"But I was coming to tell you," he added, "that I've had his own plane confiscated, along with Miss Russell's. It's under guard now—"

"What?" Everyone chorused in different pitches.

He shrugged. "On inspecting the engine of Miss Russell's airplane, we do have evidence that it as well as the one in his plane are constructed from two stolen Curtiss, patent pending, engine designs."

The others let out a unified groan, recalling their own conjectures.

"I wanted to tell you that I'm not charging you for my services," he went on, "because I was investigating for the Curtiss Company to track down proof of these design thefts. When Miss Wilson here put out a call for an investigator, I took the opportunity to come aboard since we had suspected Taggart. Sweeney was our original informer—he owed us a favor, you might say. He swore up and down that they looked like Curtiss engines to him, but with some alterations. Each engine was tuned to take a much higher oil-gas ratio, but less fuel over-all. Trouble was, at higher speeds Miss Russell's engine overheated due to the out-take, or exhaust system. For regular cargo travel that would have been fine, but obviously he wanted to impress investors. And there was nothing wrong with him adapting a Curtiss if he wanted to buy it legitimately.

"Sweeney delivered a letter to some fella back in Pecos for Taggart, before moving on. We hope he can help us identify this man—may turn out to be that drunk driver. He swears up and down he doesn't know about the betting, except that he thought some was going on. Taggart didn't let him in on much, but Sweeney says he would meet at every stop with men not associated with the circuit in any way—maybe his backers. Miss Davis could be helpful on clearing that matter, if you come across her. So, our man will be taken into custody, thanks to Miss Russell. Due to her crash, I could get near enough the engine to make the investigation I needed. He'll cooperate with questioning once in custody, I think, because he'll feel safe there from his gang related investors. Miss Schulz, since you flew ahead and saw some of those associates, we may need your help to identify them."

"Certainly." Maxie nodded.

Gus didn't say anything, he just grinned and nodded, almost as if he had a tick. Hazel had only seen him do that when he was totally stumped over an engine problem.

"So we have a place to start. Maybe we will find more evidence from Al Laraway on this guy." Hand tapping a cigarette on his case, Greg Fox seemed to wait for someone to offer a light. He smiled, remembering that he couldn't smoke next to the airplanes. Pocketing his cigarettes, he went on, "I think Miss Preston is right that we need to reinvestigate the Arctic debris. I have an expert who can probably determine how long after impact the plane caught fire. Depending on that factor, we can then calculate whether there was volatile fuel or whether the fuel was well-contained in the tank—that is, whether there was a fuel leak or not. He will also be able to detect traces of burned seal material if the seal was in place in the cap, even if it is fused together. We have a file on Mr. Taggart from other circuits. Maybe we can find something conclusive this time. So, I guess that's all I can say for now. Thank you for your cooperation." Mr. Fox shook hands all around, and took his leave.

"His name probably isn't Mr. Fox, either," said Maxie. And they all laughed, relief edging the fatigue from their faces.

Hazel sat back down on the crate, picking up her nearly empty cola bottle from the ground. Swirling the last dregs around, she took a final swallow. "I thought he was going to say Vera was their undercover man. Why couldn't Vera have been that? No, she still comes up short somehow—"

"Oh, that's why I'm here." Eleanor handed Hazel a letter, reverse side up. "The postal clerk was paging you for this. I said I'd give it to you."

Hazel took the letter, glancing at the handwriting on the back flap of the envelope. *Vera Davis*, the liquid blue writing said, followed by a San Francisco address. "Oh dear. I don't think I want this."

"Oh, go on." Maxie, poked Hazel in the ribs. "Do yourself the favor. El and I need to go start checks, anyway. The last hop, rag!"

Hazel smiled reluctantly at their departing figures, felt in her pocket for her small jack-knife, opened the blade and made a neat slice in the fold of the envelope. She pulled out two items, one she recognized. Even though it was folded in half, it was still sealed: the letter she had given Vera for safe-keeping. Reluctantly she opened the second item, a folded sheet of paper:

*Dear Hazel,*
*You give a woman the sweetest of dreams. But now there is no time. I wish*
*there was some way to let you down easy, but our time has run out sooner than I*
*hoped. For a while there I almost believed that somehow, after settling this betting*
*scheme, I could find you on the west coast, and stick to a career in photography.*
*But it turns out I'm still a wing-walker at heart and have other plans.*
*You must realize that things would always have been extremely complicated*
*for us. We are such different people. I did warn you that we found each other*
*under strained and unusual circumstances. Now I realize my wanting you was*
*purely selfish, though from the heart. I knew when I saw where you came from,*
*your farm and family, that I was being unfair to you. Yes, I took you in stolen*
*moments because they were ours alone. I hope that in time you will see they were a*
*pleasant distraction and see it in your heart to forgive me.*
*I know you were trying to get me to level with you the other night. If I had*
*been acting alone, I would have come clean, but I have associates who may be*
*known to you by now. At that time, I still thought there might be a way of pulling*
*the betting scheme off. Now that the scheme has been exposed, I have to move on,*
*and quickly.*
*I want to make one thing clear. As far as I know the betting was not related*
*to Taggart in any way. Nor did it have any bearing on Alli's terrible accident.*
*That's why I could help you. When I realized you thought the betting had*
*something to do with the accidents and got the cops involved, I had to get out.*
*Luckily I can go abroad to an old friend who also happens to owe me a favor or*
*two, especially since I won't be able to show my face on the women's circuits for*
*some years. I think this is best for us too.*
*Yours, —V. Cincinnati.*
*P.S. I will mail what photographs I do have to Gladys Jenney as they may*
*prove useful sometime. Also enclosed, your sealed letter. If it spoke of love, I don't*
*think it should be for me to keep.*

Why had she hoped it would say 'Meet me behind the third hangar' or
something? How final. *Our time has run out!* Crumpling the letter in her
hand, Hazel didn't really know if the burning tears she felt were out of anger
or sadness. Anger over the fact that Vera kept on collecting bets even when
she knew that something else was happening. Sadness, because how could she
ever really understand what it was to have lived Vera's life?

No more stolen moments. And yet, Hazel could have sworn that Vera
was right there on the Columbus airfield, teasing her with a fleeting presence—or come around for a last glimpse? Hazel threw the crumpled letter
into the Zephyr's open fuselage locker. Rot, I've been had; serves me right.

And Jo was right too, Vera did have designs on me. Oh, what a fool. *Pleasant distraction*—indeed. Oh, Maxie, wait till you hear this.

The airfield had taken on a mood of serious preparation, and the crowds were congregating again to watch take-off. Hazel scuffed the dirt at her feet, wondering if Vera would go to Paris. Maxie always said France was the place to go. An enthusiastic man wearing official trappings came hurrying up to Hazel. "Fifteen minutes, Miss Preston. As the winner, you lead the draw!"

Hazel did a double-take, shocked out of her introspection. "That's official then?"

"Yes, ma'am. You ahead, leading off. The rest of the DW class follows you, then—"

"In what order?"

He looked at his chart. "Yourself: official winning time of 19:35:04, then Sarah Morris-Newton, Eleanor Wilson, Pamela Christy and Hannah Meyer. Followed by CW: Lila Wilczynski with 22:14:32, Madelyn Burnett-Eades, Louise Gibeau, Nancy Saunders—and Stevie Lamb is on her way."

Hazel bowed slightly, "Thank you."

"Oh, Miss Preston, before you climb aboard there will be a moment of silence on the field for Miss Laraway whose burial is today."

"Yes. Yes, of course."

# 11.

*Victory Lap, Columbus to Cleveland, Ohio*

Cheers from the sightseers diminished to a murmur and then a hush for the long minute accompanying the pilots' recognition of Alli, almost as if the crowd held its breath.

An eternal moment, a brief flicker. With her eyes closed, Hazel remembered what Alli described seeing when she flew over the vast stretches of Alaskan tundra, when summer melted the snows, and when caribou began migrating.

And then there came the explosion of sound, shocking her to her present place, as the people waved to the pilots who, all geared up in helmets, goggles and parachutes, broke the circle and made for their airplanes. The spectators were throwing out red roses—a shower of cheers and petals. Hazel wondered if all the women of Columbus had turned out, never having confronted anything like it. There was even a red carpet rolled out towards the *Zephyr*, and she was supposed to walk on it. As she pulled her goggles into place, she stooped to pick a rose out of the dust. Placing it between her teeth, she yanked on her gloves, flexed the left one until she could feel more stitches pop, as though that would help her gain enough confidence to take the applause, and walk the honorary carpet.

Gus waited for her next to the Zephyr, grinning as he pointed to a new emblem on the fuselage, a neat white tracing of a T-seal. She could bet the paint was still wet. Saluting him with 'thumbs-up,' she accepted the quick thump on her back, before he sprinted off to take up advance escort.

Waving, she climbed into her cockpit, a final sign towards the crewman to remove the brake blocks, running through her last checks as diligently as she could. While the C-175 took off, she fired up. The racket from her airfoil cut through the cheers.

As she flew at eight thousand feet toward Cleveland, she felt the race fall away behind her. She only had to finish it physically. It had become too simple without Jo on her tail, too 'humdrum' as Pamela would say. No, it was only bearable to bring it to a conclusion if she knew they could all fly again together; in that last gathering of her fellow pilots, she had seen a glow of triumph. If she found herself swept along, it also had to be due to the crowds in Columbus. The giddiness she felt was as good as being in love...almost. She flew on, over the slate blue of Lake Erie, a rose clenched between her teeth the whole way.

Her stomach knotted up on her last descent and circle, this time to a huge crowd gathered at what looked like a converted horse-track. How fitting, she thought, bring the old nag in. Banking to port, she circled, then nosed down. Land Amighty, if she overshot, she'd land right in the lake.

The grandstands were full of people again, and she could see many airplanes parked in mid-field. A view of the windsocks told her the wind was coming off the lake a bit, so she adjusted her approach. Seeing the clear signal for landing, she came in, wheels making a slight bounce.

All the way home—for you, Alli, for us all.

More than crew rushed forward to meet her, but Gus was in the lead, ready to give her a hand down from the wing; he looked happy as a little kid. Steadying herself, she sat up on the fuselage and waved. The crew pushed her forward in the Zephyr towards the Winner's Circle so that Gus had to grab for a hold and get his feet up on the wing. She reached out to ruffle his hair, rubbing his bald spot instead. Not having time to recoil in embarrassment at her familiarity, she let a big toothy smile spread across her face.

Spying the press corp and all the bigwigs, she could also see a huge wreath of red roses waiting on a special stand.

"Not for around my neck, I hope," she quipped to Gus as they began to shake hands all around.

He helped her place the thorny wreath on the Zephyr, and then she was given the ornate silver cup which proclaimed the National Women's Derby, 1929 with a little dash afterwards where—a race official pointed out—her name would be engraved next to the DW. A large white envelope was also presented to her. She held it up for the photographers.

"What will you do with the prize?" voices clamored.

Rallying, she said, "In memory of Alli Laraway, this will start a fund to support independent contestants in future Derbies."

Why not? That's what her win was about—the future of women fliers.

"We know Miss Wilson is going to take on the Atlantic in September. What are your plans Miss Preston?" Someone shouted.

Hazel shrugged, and then she had it. "I plan to race for the Mason Trophy in the spring." She could feel the collective gasp.

"But it isn't open to women," another voice exclaimed, as cameras clicked.

Holding up the trophy above her head, she grinned. "It will be now. I think the performance of the women pilots in this Derby is sufficient proof of our readiness. The field triumphed over all kinds of mechanical obstacles including sabotage. I think we have had more than our share of training."

"So you think you're ready for a real race now?" someone snapped.

"You can bet your bottom dollar," she said firmly.

"What airplane will you use?"

"Whirlwind double-seater."

"And who'll be the co-pilot?" Yet another challenged.

Like a flash of lightning, an instant in which Hazel finally understood something, the answer came without pause. "Maxie Schulz."

Maxie. She is strong and dependable.

Hazel decided that the pleasure about coming in first was watching everyone else arrive, each one to fanfare, maybe more so for Eleanor—though it was hard to tell because Pamela Christy made quite a splash, so to speak. And Lila, well, it was her home town. Apparently, the steel-mill workers had taken an afternoon vacation just to turn out and see her. Her name would be on the trophy too, under CW.

But if Hazel lingered in the afterglow, it wasn't to sign the autographs or make light conversation. At last she saw what she was waiting for. Shielding her eyes like many others, she watched the Spartan make a loop-the-loop before its final descent, a long ribbon of words trailing after it: *Mortons Apparel Salutes Derby.*

Oh Maxeee, how you do it! Wait till you hear you're going to fly in the Mason with me. Hope you like the idea.

When Maxie finally came to a rolling stop, Hazel loped out to greet her.

"Ah, for once," cried Maxie, wriggling out of her parachute, "you come out to greet *me*."

"Yes, well, I have something I ought to explain—"

Maxie climbed down and caught her up in an enthusiastic hug. "You were saying?"

Hazel caught her breath, but held on tightly. "Max, Max—please be Ollie to my Stan—"

"What? You proposing or something?"

"Yes, even better—I want you to enter the Mason with me!"

"We've been invited?"

"Not yet. But I'll bet Sarah and Sam would be keen too."

"Hm." Maxie pulled off her helmet and gloves, fluffing up her hair with her fingers. "Now why did I think you would be going off romantically questing for old Verie?"

Hazel's face fell. "I don't see how, Max. She deceived me, never took me into her confidence, used me. And in her letter she tells me she's going abroad, that she had other plans anyway! She said she wished there was a way to let me down easy. I knew she was tough...and I liked that—her strength.

And then—"

"Ah, the femme fatale. Broke that little heart of yours—has to be true love then, huh? Sure you don't want to go chase after her?"

"No, no I can't," Hazel said firmly, steadily. "Surely *you* should know that I can't. There would decks and dining rooms between us just like there was for you on your ship that time."

A flick of light flashed in those brown eyes. "Oh…and do you think you'd end up in your cabin with a widow who takes you for sea-sick?"

Letting go, Hazel braved a smile. "Mm, more like a co-pilot in the Mason who knows it's not airsickness that's ailing me?"

Maxie looked at her askance, hands digging deep into the pockets of her black britches as she swung back and forth on her heels. "Yeah, well, I'll have ya know, this 'widow' likes sex, likes to have a good time—mostly fun. But I don't know about you…Because that's what I'd ask you for. Don't ya know?"

Hazel laughed, "Yes, I remember, something about 'ooh, ahh and all.'"

"Hm, you think you're heart-broken when what happened was that old Verie there simply showed you a good time. And you damn well liked it. And because ya climbed into bed with me last night, you want to make an honest woman out of me now. You'll get over it."

"Max, the way you put things! Maybe I don't want to get over it."

"Well, I dunno, Preston. I learned my lesson on that thar ship. I don't pursue unless I think I'm gonna get somewhere, see, not just—"

"Me too, Max." Maybe Hazel said it over-eagerly because Maxie cuffed her gently on the chin, then the hand stayed there. "And we already have a few confidences, like a bag of dirty rags, in common! Seriously, I want to be with *you*, Max—"

"I did kinda think you were blind as a bat, not to see me right in front of you all this time. I was wondering how I could shake you up a bit since you like that sort of thing, maybe wear a bit of perfume too…look, if it's strength you want, feel my muscle!" And with chin jutting out, Maxie flexed her arm muscles.

Hazel had to laugh then. "I know, I know!"

"Just what I like, a woman who can laugh. Look, I thought I was really civil about Vera…and Jo too, when it wasn't for her that I invited you down to my ranch for the barnstorming that time."

"Oh," Hazel said too slowly.

"But if you want to fly instead, we can just, ya know, fly—in tandem!" Maxie took Hazel's arm to stride towards the grandstand, a slight nod from her head. "Sure cure."

Hazel turned Maxie's face towards her own and planted a moist kiss on those full lips, lingering.

Maxie shut her eyes, savored the kiss. "Mmm, that's my girl."

"Do you really have to tour for the Mortons?" Hazel asked softly.

Maxie opened her eyes wide, rallying. "Don't you go breaking *my* heart now. I'm no fool. I'm gonna wait until you really mean what those lips can give out."

"I do mean it, Max. I know I've been blind and stupid."

"I'm sure you do. But wouldn't I make the third lover in a week?—Not likely, kid, not until you've had time to sort yourself out a bit." Max laughed her rolling laugh. "That reminds me—I was talking to 'for the sport of it' Nancy. Turns out she'd be more than happy to do the Morton tour. Leaves me a free woman, now don't it? I think you and I need a bit of a vacation, don't you think? Mend that heart of yours. I think we should go see Eleanor off in New York. Then we gotta go West and see Al, make sure we get all the evidence we can to convict Taggart. We have a lot to take care of, Preston. First I gotta get hold of those Mortons."

"Max, I have to have some sales conferences, and then I'm scheduled to test Hannah's *Whirlwind*—in four days...."

"So? Nothing we can't sort out, rag, c'mon—"

"I just want to know one thing, uh, when..if...we're lovers—who gets to be on top?"

"Trust you to think of that, ha-ha! I'm the grease britches...."

"Like hell...."

191

## P.S

Eleanor Wilson's September Atlantic attempt was scratched due to bad weather after waiting three days. Uncertainty about autumn storms over the Atlantic caused a postponement till spring of 1930. In October of '29 the stock market crashed, and sponsors and speculators backed out. She was not able to make another attempt until 1932.

Jo Russell kept on friendly terms with Hazel Preston but did not pursue a career in flying. She eventually married a lawyer and settled in New York.

Nothing conclusive was ever found in Alli Laraway's accident.

Maxie Schulz and Hazel Preston placed second out of a field of fifty, the first female team placement, in the Mason race, 1930. With Maxie's ranch as a base, they pursued separate interests in aviation.

R.Q. Taggart served three years in prison for theft of aircraft engines designs, with time off for good behaviour. He was banned from all race circuits for five years. No hard evidence could be found to implicate him in any tampering. His projects, like many others in aviation at the time, collapsed after the stock market crash of October, 1929.

Vera Davis never returned to the United States but pursued a career as a photographer and foreign correspondent in Europe, covering Eleanor's triumphant arrival in Paris after that successful flight of '32. She died in France in '44, after being captured as a member of the Resistance.

ReBecca Béguin works with New Victoria, and farms the rest of the time up a dirt road in the Vermont backhills where the winters are extra long and the summers exquisite. She aims to finish a pre-school curriculum book, incorporating early childhood literature.
Other titles: *In Unlikely Places, Runway at Eland Springs* and *Her Voice in the Drum*